Jane Austen was bor near Basingstoke, the seventh child of the rector of the parish. She lived with her family at Steventon until they moved to Bath when her father retired in 1801. After his death in 1805, she moved around with her mother; in 1809 they settled in Chawton, near Alton, Hampshire. Here she remained, except for a few visits to London, until May 1817, when she moved to Winchester to be near her doctor. There she died on 18 July 1817. Jane Austen was extremely modest about her own genius, describing her work to her nephew, Edward, as 'the little bit (two Inches wide) of Ivory, on which I work with so fine a Brush, as produces little effect after much labour'. As a girl she wrote stories, including burlesques of popular romances. Her works were published only after much revision, four novels being published in her lifetime. These are *Sense and Sensibility* (1811), *Pride and Prejudice* (1813), *Mansfield Park* (1814) and *Emma* (1815). Two other novels, *Northanger Abbey* and *Persuasion*, were published posthumously in 1818 with a biographical notice by her brother, Henry Austen, the first formal announcement of her authorship. *Persuasion* was written in a race against failing health in 1815–16. She also left two earlier compositions, a short epistolary novel, *Lady Susan*, and an unfinished novel, *The Watsons*. At the time of her death she was working on a new novel, *Sanditon*, a fragmentary draft of which survives.

JANE AUSTEN

Northanger Abbey

PENGUIN BOOKS

PENGUIN BOOKS

Published by the Penguin Group
Penguin Books Ltd, 80 Strand, London WC2R ORL, England
Penguin Group (USA), Inc., 375 Hudson Street, New York, New York 10014, USA
Penguin Group (Canada), 90 Eglinton Avenue East, Suite 700, Toronto, Ontario, Canada M4P 2Y3
(a division of Pearson Penguin Canada Inc.)
Penguin Ireland, 25 St Stephen's Green, Dublin 2, Ireland (a division of Penguin Books Ltd)
Penguin Group (Australia), 250 Camberwell Road, Camberwell, Victoria 3124, Australia
(a division of Pearson Australia Group Pty Ltd)
Penguin Books India Pvt Ltd, 11 Community Centre, Panchsheel Park, New Delhi – 110 017, India
Penguin Group (NZ), 67 Apollo Drive, Rosedale, North Shore 0632, New Zealand
(a division of Pearson New Zealand Ltd)
Penguin Books (South Africa) (Pty) Ltd, 24 Sturdee Avenue, Rosebank,
Johannesburg 2196, South Africa

Penguin Books Ltd, Registered Offices: 80 Strand, London WC2R ORL, England

www.penguin.com

First published 1818
Published as a Pocket Penguin Classic 2006
9

All spelling and punctuation follow the first edition.

Set in 11/13 pt PostScript Monotype Dante
Printed in England by Clays Ltd, St Ives plc

ISBN 13: 978-0-141-02813-2

www.greenpenguin.co.uk

Penguin Books is committed to a sustainable future
for our business, our readers and our planet.
The book in your hands is made from paper
certified by the Forest Stewardship Council.

Volume I

ADVERTISEMENT,

BY THE AUTHORESS,

to

NORTHANGER ABBEY

This little work was finished in the year 1803, and intended for immediate publication. It was disposed of to a bookseller, it was even advertised, and why the business proceeded no farther, the author has never been able to learn. That any bookseller should think it worth while to purchase what he did not think it worth while to publish seems extraordinary. But with this, neither the author nor the public have any other concern than as some observation is necessary upon those parts of the work which thirteen years have made comparatively obsolete. The public are entreated to bear in mind that thirteen years have passed since it was finished, many more since it was begun, and that during that period, places, manners, books, and opinions have undergone considerable changes.

Chapter 1

No one who had ever seen Catherine Morland in her infancy, would have supposed her born to be an heroine. Her situation in life, the character of her father and mother; her own person and disposition, were all equally against her. Her father was a clergyman, without being neglected, or poor, and a very respectable man, though his name was Richard – and he had never been handsome. He had a considerable independence, besides two good livings – and he was not in the least addicted to locking up his daughters. Her mother was a woman of useful plain sense, with a good temper, and, what is more remarkable, with a good constitution. She had three sons before Catherine was born; and instead of dying in bringing the latter into the world, as any body might expect, she still lived on – lived to have six children more – to see them growing up around her, and to enjoy excellent health herself. A family of ten children will be always called a fine family, where there are heads and arms and legs enough for the number; but the Morlands had little other right to the word, for they were in general very plain, and Catherine, for many years of her life, as plain as any. She had a thin awkward figure, a sallow skin without colour, dark lank hair, and strong features; – so much for her person; – and not less unpropitious for heroism seemed her mind. She was fond of all boys' plays, and greatly preferred cricket not merely to dolls, but to the more

heroic enjoyments of infancy, nursing a dormouse, feed-
ing a canary-bird, or watering a rose-bush. Indeed she
had no taste for a garden; and if she gathered flowers at
all, it was chiefly for the pleasure of mischief – at least
so it was conjectured from her always preferring those
which she was forbidden to take. – Such were her propensities – her abilities were quite as extraordinary. She
never could learn or understand any thing before she was
taught; and sometimes not even then, for she was often
inattentive, and occasionally stupid. Her mother was
three months in teaching her only to repeat the 'Beggar's
Petition;' and after all, her next sister, Sally, could say
it better than she did. Not that Catherine was always
stupid, – by no means; she learnt the fable of 'The Hare
and many Friends,' as quickly as any girl in England. Her
mother wished her to learn music; and Catherine was
sure she should like it, for she was very fond of tinkling
the keys of the old forlorn spinnet; so, at eight years old
she began. She learnt a year, and could not bear it; – and
Mrs Morland, who did not insist on her daughters being
accomplished in spite of incapacity or distaste, allowed
her to leave off. The day which dismissed the music-
master was one of the happiest of Catherine's life. Her
taste for drawing was not superior; though whenever
she could obtain the outside of a letter from her mother,
or seize upon any other odd piece of paper, she did what
she could in that way, by drawing houses and trees, hens
and chickens, all very much like one another. – Writing
and accounts she was taught by her father; French by her
mother: her proficiency in either was not remarkable, and
she shirked her lessons in both whenever she could. What
a strange, unaccountable character! – for with all these

symptoms of profligacy at ten years old, she had neither a bad heart nor a bad temper; was seldom stubborn, scarcely ever quarrelsome, and very kind to the little ones, with few interruptions of tyranny; she was moreover noisy and wild, hated confinement and cleanliness, and loved nothing so well in the world as rolling down the green slope at the back of the house.

Such was Catherine Morland at ten. At fifteen, appearances were mending; she began to curl her hair and long for balls; her complexion improved, her features were softened by plumpness and colour, her eyes gained more animation, and her figure more consequence. Her love of dirt gave way to an inclination for finery; and she grew clean as she grew smart; she had now the pleasure of sometimes hearing her father and mother remark on her personal improvement. 'Catherine grows quite a good-looking girl, – she is almost pretty to day,' were words which caught her ears now and then; and how welcome were the sounds! To look *almost* pretty, is an acquisition of higher delight to a girl who has been looking plain the first fifteen years of her life, than a beauty from her cradle can ever receive.

Mrs Morland was a very good woman, and wished to see her children every thing they ought to be; but her time was so much occupied in lying-in and teaching the little ones, that her elder daughters were inevitably left to shift for themselves; and it was not very wonderful that Catherine, who had by nature nothing heroic about her, should prefer cricket, base ball, riding on horseback, and running about the country at the age of fourteen, to books – or at least books of information – for, provided that nothing like useful knowledge could be gained from them, provided they were all story and no reflection, she had never any objection to books at all. But from fifteen to seventeen she was in training for a heroine; she read all such works as heroines must read to supply their memories with those quotations which are so serviceable and so soothing in the vicissitudes of their eventful lives.

From Pope, she learnt to censure those who

'bear about the mockery of woe.'

From Gray, that

'Many a flower is born to blush unseen,

'And waste its fragrance on the desert air.'

From Thompson, that

————'It is a delightful task

'To teach the young idea how to shoot.'

And from Shakespeare she gained a great store of information – amongst the rest, that

————'Trifles light as air,

'Are, to the jealous, confirmation strong,

'As proofs of Holy Writ.'

That

'The poor beetle, which we tread upon,

'In corporal sufferance feels a pang as great

'As when a giant dies.'

And that a young woman in love always looks

——'like Patience on a monument

'Smiling at Grief.'

So far her improvement was sufficient – and in many other points she came on exceedingly well; for though she could not write sonnets, she brought herself to read them; and though there seemed no chance of her throwing a whole party into raptures by a prelude on the pianoforte, of her own composition, she could listen to other people's performance with very little fatigue. Her greatest deficiency was in the pencil – she had no notion of drawing – not enough even to attempt a sketch of her lover's profile, that she might be detected in the design. There she fell miserably short of the true heroic height. At present she did not know her own poverty, for she had no lover to pourtray. She had reached the age of seventeen, without having seen one amiable youth who could call forth her sensibility; without having inspired one real passion, and without having excited even any admiration but what was very moderate and very transient. This was strange indeed! But strange things may be generally accounted for if their cause be fairly searched out. There was not one lord in the neighbourhood; no – not even a baronet. There was not one family among their acquaintance who had reared and supported a boy accidentally found at their door – not one young man whose origin was unknown. Her father had no ward, and the squire of the parish no children.

But when a young lady is to be a heroine, the perverseness of forty surrounding families cannot prevent her. Something must and will happen to throw a hero in her way.

Mr Allen, who owned the chief of the property about Fullerton, the village in Wiltshire where the Morlands lived, was ordered to Bath for the benefit of a gouty constitution; – and his lady, a good-humoured woman, fond of Miss Morland, and probably aware that if adventures will not befal a young lady in her own village, she must seek them abroad, invited her to go with them. Mr and Mrs Morland were all compliance, and Catherine all happiness.

Chapter 2

In addition to what has been already said of Catherine Morland's personal and mental endowments, when about to be launched into all the difficulties and dangers of a six weeks' residence in Bath, it may be stated, for the reader's more certain information, lest the following pages should otherwise fail of giving any idea of what her character is meant to be; that her heart was affectionate, her disposition cheerful and open, without conceit or affectation of any kind – her manners just removed from the awkwardness and shyness of a girl; her person pleasing, and, when in good looks, pretty – and her mind about as ignorant and uninformed as the female mind at seventeen usually is.

When the hour of departure drew near, the maternal anxiety of Mrs Morland will be naturally supposed to be most severe. A thousand alarming presentiments of evil to her beloved Catherine from this terrific separation must oppress her heart with sadness, and drown her in tears for the last day or two of their being together; and advice of the most important and applicable nature must of course flow from her wise lips in their parting conference in her closet. Cautions against the violence of such noblemen and baronets as delight in forcing young ladies away to some remote farm-house, must, at such a moment, relieve the fulness of her heart. Who would not think so? But Mrs Morland knew so little of lords and baronets, that she entertained no notion of their general mischievousness, and was wholly unsuspicious of danger to her daughter from their machinations. Her cautions were confined to the following points. 'I beg, Catherine, you will always wrap yourself up very warm about the throat, when you come from the Rooms at night; and I wish you would try to keep some account of the money you spend; – I will give you this little book on purpose.'

Sally, or rather Sarah, (for what young lady of common gentility will reach the age of sixteen without altering her name as far as she can?) must from situation be at this time the intimate friend and confidante of her sister. It is remarkable, however, that she neither insisted on Catherine's writing by every post, nor exacted her promise of transmitting the character of every new acquaintance, nor a detail of every interesting conversation that Bath might produce. Every thing indeed relative to this important journey was done, on the part of the Morlands, with a degree of moderation and composure, which seemed rather consistent with the common feelings of common life, than with the refined susceptibilities, the tender emotions which the first separation of a heroine from her family ought always to excite. Her father, instead of giving her an unlimited order on his banker, or even putting an hundred pounds bank-bill into her hands, gave her only ten guineas, and promised her more when she wanted it.

Under these unpromising auspices, the parting took place, and the journey began. It was performed with suitable quietness and uneventful safety. Neither robbers nor tempests befriended them, nor one lucky overturn to introduce them to the hero. Nothing more alarming occurred than a fear on Mrs Allen's side, of having once left her clogs behind her at an inn, and that fortunately proved to be groundless.

They arrived at Bath. Catherine was all eager delight; – her eyes were here, there, every where, as they approached its fine and striking environs, and afterwards drove through those streets which conducted them to the hotel. She was come to be happy, and she felt happy already.

They were soon settled in comfortable lodgings in Pulteney-street.

It is now expedient to give some description of Mrs Allen, that the reader may be able to judge, in what manner her actions will hereafter tend to promote the general distress of the work, and how she will, probably, contribute to reduce poor Catherine to all the desperate wretchedness of which a last volume is capable – whether by her imprudence, vulgarity, or jealousy – whether by intercepting her letters, ruining her character, or turning her out of doors.

Mrs Allen was one of that numerous class of females, whose society can raise no other emotion than surprise at there being any men in the world who could like them well enough, to marry them. She had neither beauty, genius, accomplishment, nor manner. The air of a gentlewoman, a great deal of quiet, inactive good temper, and a trifling turn of mind, were all that could account for her being the choice of a sensible, intelligent man, like Mr Allen. In one respect she was admirably fitted to introduce a young lady into public, being as fond of going every where and seeing every thing herself as any young lady could be. Dress was her passion. She had a most harmless delight in being fine; and our heroine's entrée into life could not take place till after three or four days had been spent in learning what was mostly worn, and her chaperon was provided with a dress of the newest fashion. Catherine too made some purchases herself, and when all these matters were arranged, the important evening came which was to usher her into the Upper Rooms. Her hair was cut and dressed by the best hand, her clothes put on with care, and both Mrs Allen and her maid declared she looked quite as she should do. With such encouragement, Catherine hoped at least to pass uncensured through the crowd. As for admiration, it was always very welcome when it came, but she did not depend on it.

Mrs Allen was so long in dressing, that they did not enter the ball-room till late. The season was full, the room crowded; and the two ladies squeezed in as well as they could. As for Mr Allen, he repaired directly to the card-room, and left them to enjoy a mob by themselves. With more care for the safety of her new gown than for the comfort of her protegée, Mrs Allen made her way through the throng of men by the door, as swiftly as the necessary caution would allow; Catherine, however, kept close at her side, and linked her arm too firmly within her friend's to be torn asunder by any common effort of a struggling assembly. But to her utter amazement she found that to proceed along the room was by no means the way to disengage themselves from the crowd; it seemed rather to increase as they went on, whereas she had imagined that when once fairly within the door, they should easily find seats and be able to watch the dances with perfect convenience. But this was far from being the case, and though by unwearied diligence they gained even the top of the room, their situation was just the same; they saw nothing of the dancers but the high feathers of some of the ladies. Still they moved on – something better was yet in view; and by a continued exertion of strength and ingenuity they found themselves at last in the passage behind the highest bench. Here there was something less of crowd than below; and hence Miss Morland had a comprehensive view of all the company beneath her, and of all the dangers of her late passage through them. It was a splendid sight, and she began, for the first time that evening, to feel herself at a ball: she longed to dance, but she had not an acquaintance in the room. Mrs Allen did all that she could do in such a case by saying very placidly, every now and then, 'I wish you could dance, my dear, – I wish you could get a partner.' For some time her young friend felt obliged to her for these wishes; but they were repeated so often, and proved so totally ineffectual, that Catherine grew tired at last, and would thank her no more.

They were not long able, however, to enjoy the repose of the eminence they had so laboriously gained. – Every body was shortly in motion for tea, and they must squeeze out like the rest. Catherine began to feel something of disappointment – she was tired of being continually pressed against by people, the generality of whose faces possessed nothing to interest, and with all of whom she was so wholly unacquainted, that she could not relieve the irksomeness of imprisonment by the exchange of a syllable with any of her fellow captives; and when at last arrived in the tea-room, she felt yet more the awkwardness of having no party to join, no acquaintance to claim, no gentleman to assist them. – They saw nothing of Mr Allen; and after looking about them in vain for a more eligible situation, were obliged to sit down at the end of a table, at which a large party were already placed, without having any thing to do there, or any body to speak to, except each other.

Mrs Allen congratulated herself, as soon as they were seated, on having preserved her gown from injury. 'It would have been very shocking to have it torn,' said she, 'would not it? – It is such a delicate muslin. – For my part I have not seen any thing I like so well in the whole room, I assure you.'

'How uncomfortable it is,' whispered Catherine, 'not to have a single acquaintance here!'

'Yes, my dear,' replied Mrs Allen, with perfect serenity, 'it is very uncomfortable indeed.'

'What shall we do? – The gentlemen and ladies at this table look as if they wondered why we came here – we seem forcing ourselves into their party.'

'Aye, so we do. – That is very disagreeable. I wish we had a large acquaintance here.'

'I wish we had *any*; – it would be somebody to go to.'

'Very true, my dear; and if we knew anybody we would join them directly. The Skinners were here last year – I wish they were here now.'

'Had not we better go away as it is? – Here are no tea things for us, you see.'

'No more there are, indeed. – How very provoking! But I think we had better sit still, for one gets so tumbled in such a crowd! How is my head, my dear? – Somebody gave me a push that has hurt it I am afraid.'

'No, indeed, it looks very nice. – But, dear Mrs Allen, are you sure there is nobody you know in all this multitude of people? I think you *must* know somebody.'

'I don't upon my word – I wish I did. I wish I had a large acquaintance here with all my heart, and then I should get you a partner. – I should be so glad to have you dance. There goes a strange-looking woman! What an odd gown she has got on! – How old fashioned it is! Look at the back.'

After some time they received an offer of tea from one of their neighbours; it was thankfully accepted, and this introduced a light conversation with the gentleman who offered it, which was the only time that any body spoke to them during the evening, till they were discovered and joined by Mr Allen when the dance was over.

'Well, Miss Morland,' said he, directly, 'I hope you have had an agreeable ball.'

'Very agreeable indeed,' she replied, vainly endeavouring to hide a great yawn.

'I wish she had been able to dance,' said his wife, 'I wish we could have got a partner for her. – I have been saying how glad I should be if the Skinners were here this winter instead of last; or if the Parrys had come, as they talked of once, she might have danced with George Parry. I am so sorry she has not had a partner!'

'We shall do better another evening I hope,' was Mr Allen's consolation.

The company began to disperse when the dancing was over – enough to leave space for the remainder to walk about in some comfort; and now was the time for a heroine, who had not yet played a very distinguished part in the events of the evening, to be noticed and admired. Every five minutes, by removing some of the crowd, gave greater openings for her charms. She was now seen by many young men who had not been near her before. Not one, however, started with rapturous wonder on beholding her, no whisper of eager inquiry ran round the room, nor was she once called a divinity by any body. Yet Catherine was in very good looks, and had the company only seen her three years before, they would *now* have thought her exceedingly handsome.

She *was* looked at however, and with some admiration; for, in her own hearing, two gentlemen pronounced her to be a pretty girl. Such words had their due effect; she immediately thought the evening pleasanter than she had found it before – her humble vanity was contented – she felt more obliged to the two young men for this simple praise than a true quality heroine would have been for fifteen sonnets in celebration of her charms, and went to her chair in good humour with every body, and perfectly satisfied with her share of public attention.

Chapter 3

Every morning now brought its regular duties; – shops were to be visited; some new part of the town to be looked at; and the Pump-room to be attended, where they paraded up and down for an hour, looking at every body and speaking to no one. The wish of a numerous acquaintance in Bath was still uppermost with Mrs Allen, and she repeated it after every fresh proof, which every morning brought, of her knowing nobody at all.

They made their appearance in the Lower Rooms; and here fortune was more favourable to our heroine. The master of the ceremonies introduced to her a very gentlemanlike young man as a partner; – his name was Tilney. He seemed to be about four or five and twenty, was rather tall, had a pleasing countenance, a very intelligent and lively eye, and, if not quite handsome, was very near it. His address was good, and Catherine felt herself in high luck. There was little leisure for speaking while they danced; but when they were seated at tea, she found him as agreeable as she had already given him credit for being. He talked with fluency and spirit – and there was an archness and pleasantry in his manner which interested, though it was hardly understood by her. After chatting some time on such matters as naturally arose from the objects around them, he suddenly addressed her with – 'I have hitherto been very remiss, madam, in the proper attentions of a partner here; I have not yet asked you how long you have been in Bath; whether you were ever here before; whether you have been at the Upper Rooms, the theatre, and the concert; and how you like the place altogether. I have been very negligent – but are you now at leisure to satisfy me in these particulars? If you are I will begin directly.'

'You need not give yourself that trouble, sir.'

'No trouble I assure you, madam.' Then forming his features into a set smile, and affectedly softening his voice, he added, with a simpering air, 'Have you been long in Bath, madam?'

'About a week, sir,' replied Catherine, trying not to laugh.

'Really!' with affected astonishment.

'Why should you be surprized, sir?'

'Why, indeed!' said he, in his natural tone – 'but some emotion must appear to be raised by your reply, and surprize is more easily assumed, and not less reasonable than any other. – Now let us go on. Were you never here before, madam?'

'Never, sir.'

'Indeed! Have you yet honoured the Upper Rooms?'

'Yes, sir, I was there last Monday.'

'Have you been to the theatre?'

'Yes, sir, I was at the play on Tuesday.'

'To the concert?'

'Yes, sir, on Wednesday.'

'And are you altogether pleased with Bath?'

'Yes – I like it very well.'

'Now I must give one smirk, and then we may be rational again.'

Catherine turned away her head, not knowing whether she might venture to laugh.

'I see what you think of me,' said he gravely – 'I shall make but a poor figure in your journal to-morrow.'

'My journal!'

'Yes, I know exactly what you will say: Friday, went to the Lower Rooms; wore my sprigged muslin robe with blue trimmings – plain black shoes – appeared to much advantage; but was strangely harassed by a queer, half-witted man, who would make me dance with him, and distressed me by his nonsense.'

'Indeed I shall say no such thing.'

'Shall I tell you what you ought to say?'

'If you please.'

'I danced with a very agreeable young man, introduced by Mr King; had a great deal of conversation with him – seems a most extraordinary genius – hope I may know more of him. *That*, madam, is what I *wish* you to say.'

'But, perhaps, I keep no journal.'

'Perhaps you are not sitting in this room, and I am not sitting by you. These are points in which a doubt is equally possible. Not keep a journal! How are your absent cousins to understand the tenour of your life in Bath without one? How are the civilities and compliments of every day to be related as they ought to be, unless noted down every evening in a journal? How are your various dresses to be remembered, and the particular state of your complexion, and curl of your hair to be described in all their diversities, without having constant recourse to a journal? – My dear madam, I am not so ignorant of young ladies' ways as you wish to believe me; it is this delightful habit of journalizing which largely contributes to form the easy style of writing for which ladies are so generally celebrated. Every body allows that the talent of writing agreeable letters is peculiarly female. Nature may have done something, but I am sure it must be essentially assisted by the practice of keeping a journal.'

'I have sometimes thought,' said Catherine, doubtingly, 'whether ladies do write so much better letters than gentlemen! That is – I should not think the superiority was always on our side.'

'As far as I have had opportunity of judging, it appears to me that the usual style of letter-writing among women is faultless, except in three particulars.'

'And what are they?'

'A general deficiency of subject, a total inattention to stops, and a very frequent ignorance of grammar.'

'Upon my word! I need not have been afraid of disclaiming the compliment. You do not think too highly of us in that way.'

'I should no more lay it down as a general rule that women write better letters than men, than that they sing better duets, or draw better landscapes. In every power, of which taste is the foundation, excellence is pretty fairly divided between the sexes.'

They were interrupted by Mrs Allen: – 'My dear Catherine,' said she, 'do take this pin out of my sleeve; I am afraid it has torn a hole already; I shall be quite sorry if it has, for this is a favourite gown, though it cost but nine shillings a yard.'

'That is exactly what I should have guessed it, madam,' said Mr Tilney, looking at the muslin.

'Do you understand muslins, sir?'

'Particularly well; I always buy my own cravats, and am allowed to be an excellent judge; and my sister has often trusted me in the choice of a gown. I bought one for her the other day, and it was pronounced to be a prodigious bargain by every lady who saw it. I gave but five shillings a yard for it, and a true Indian muslin.'

Mrs Allen was quite struck by his genius. 'Men commonly take so little notice of those things,' said she: 'I can never get Mr Allen to know one of my gowns from another. You must be a great comfort to your sister, sir.'

'I hope I am, madam.'

'And pray, sir, what do you think of Miss Morland's gown?'

'It is very pretty, madam,' said he, gravely examining it; 'but I do not think it will wash well; I am afraid it will fray.'

'How can you,' said Catherine, laughing, 'be so–' she had almost said, strange.

'I am quite of your opinion, sir,' replied Mrs Allen; 'and so I told Miss Morland when she bought it.'

'But then you know, madam, muslin always turns to some account or other; Miss Morland will get enough out of it for a handkerchief, or a cap, or a cloak. – Muslin can never be said to be wasted. I have heard my sister say so forty times, when she has been extravagant in buying more than she wanted, or careless in cutting it to pieces.'

'Bath is a charming place, sir; there are so many good shops here. – We are sadly off in the country; not but what we have very good shops in Salisbury, but it is so far to go; – eight miles is a long way; Mr Allen says it is nine, measured nine; but I am sure it cannot be more than eight; and it is such a fag – I come back tired to death. Now here one can step out of doors and get a thing in five minutes.'

Mr Tilney was polite enough to seem interested in what she said; and she kept him on the subject of muslins till the dancing recommenced. Catherine feared, as she listened to their discourse, that he indulged himself a little too much with the foibles of others. – 'What are you thinking of so earnestly?' said he, as they walked back to the ball-room; – 'not of your partner, I hope, for, by that shake of the head, your meditations are not satisfactory.'

Catherine coloured, and said, 'I was not thinking of any thing.'

'That is artful and deep, to be sure; but I had rather be told at once that you will not tell me.'

'Well then, I will not.'

'Thank you; for now we shall soon be acquainted, as I am authorized to tease you on this subject whenever we meet, and nothing in the world advances intimacy so much.'

They danced again; and, when the assembly closed, parted, on the lady's side at least, with a strong inclination for continuing the acquaintance. Whether she thought of him so much, while she drank her warm wine and water, and prepared herself for bed, as to dream of him when there, cannot be ascertained; but I hope it was no more than in a slight slumber, or a morning doze at most; for if it be true, as a celebrated writer has maintained, that no young lady can be justified in falling in love before the gentleman's love is declared, it must be very improper that a young lady should dream of a gentleman before the gentleman is first known to have dreamt of her. How proper Mr Tilney might be as a dreamer or a lover, had not yet perhaps entered Mr Allen's head, but that he was not objectionable as a common acquaintance for his young charge he was on inquiry satisfied; for he had early in the evening taken pains to know who her partner was, and had been assured of Mr Tilney's being a clergyman, and of a very respectable family in Gloucestershire.

Chapter 4

With more than usual eagerness did Catherine hasten to the Pump-room the next day, secure within herself of seeing Mr Tilney there before the morning were over, and ready to meet him with a smile: – but no smile was demanded – Mr Tilney did not appear. Every creature in Bath, except himself, was to be seen in the room at different periods of the fashionable hours; crowds of people were every moment passing in and out, up the steps and down; people whom nobody cared about, and nobody wanted to see; and he only was absent. 'What a delightful place Bath is,' said Mrs Allen, as they sat down near the great clock, after parading the room till they were tired; 'and how pleasant it would be if we had any acquaintance here.'

This sentiment had been uttered so often in vain, that Mrs Allen had no particular reason to hope it would be followed with more advantage now; but we are told to 'despair of nothing we would attain,' as 'unwearied diligence our point would gain;' and the unwearied diligence with which she had every day wished for the same thing was at length to have its just reward, for hardly had she been seated ten minutes before a lady of about her own age, who was sitting by her, and had been looking at her attentively for several minutes, addressed her with great complaisance in these words: – 'I think, madam, I cannot be mistaken; it is a long time since I had the pleasure of seeing you, but is not your name Allen?' This question answered, as it readily was, the stranger pronounced her's to be Thorpe; and Mrs Allen immediately recognized the features of a former schoolfellow and intimate, whom she had seen only once since their respective marriages, and that many years ago. Their joy on this meeting was very great, as well it might, since they had been contented to know nothing of each other for the last fifteen years. Compliments on good looks now passed; and, after observing how time had slipped away since they were last together, how little they had thought of meeting in Bath, and what a pleasure it was to see an old friend, they proceeded to make inquiries and give intelligence as to their families, sisters and cousins, talking both together, far more ready to give than to receive information, and each hearing very little of what the other said. Mrs Thorpe, however, had one great advantage as a talker, over Mrs Allen, in a family of children; and when she expatiated on the talents of her sons, and the beauty of her daughters, – when she related their different situations and views – that John was at Oxford, Edward at Merchant-Taylors', and William at sea, – and all of them more beloved and respected in their different station than any other three beings ever were, Mrs Allen had no similar information to give, no similar triumphs to press on the unwilling and unbelieving ear of her friend, and was forced to sit and appear to listen to all these maternal effusions, consoling herself, however, with the discovery, which her keen eye soon made, that the lace on Mrs Thorpe's pelisse was not half so handsome as that on her own.

'Here come my dear girls,' cried Mrs Thorpe, pointing

at three smart looking females, who, arm in arm, were then moving towards her. 'My dear Mrs Allen, I long to introduce them; they will be so delighted to see you: the tallest is Isabella, my eldest; is not she a fine young woman? The others are very much admired too, but I believe Isabella is the handsomest.'

The Miss Thorpes were introduced; and Miss Morland, who had been for a short time forgotten, was introduced likewise. The name seemed to strike them all; and, after speaking to her with great civility, the eldest young lady observed aloud to the rest, 'How excessively like her brother Miss Morland is!'

'The very picture of him indeed!' cried the mother – and 'I should have known her any where for his sister!' was repeated by them all, two or three times over. For a moment Catherine was surprized; but Mrs Thorpe and her daughters had scarcely begun the history of their acquaintance with Mr James Morland, before she remembered that her eldest brother had lately formed an intimacy with a young man of his own college, of the name of Thorpe; and that he had spent the last week of the Christmas vacation with his family, near London.

The whole being explained, many obliging things were said by the Miss Thorpes of their wish of being better acquainted with her; of being considered as already friends, through the friendship of their brothers, &c. which Catherine heard with pleasure, and answered with all the pretty expressions she could command; and, as the first proof of amity, she was soon invited to accept an arm of the eldest Miss Thorpe, and take a turn with her about the room. Catherine was delighted with this extension of her Bath acquaintance, and almost forgot

Mr Tilney while she talked to Miss Thorpe. Friendship is certainly the finest balm for the pangs of disappointed love.

Their conversation turned upon those subjects, of which the free discussion has generally much to do in perfecting a sudden intimacy between two young ladies; such as dress, balls, flirtations, and quizzes. Miss Thorpe, however, being four years older than Miss Morland, and at least four years better informed, had a very decided advantage in discussing such points; she could compare the balls of Bath with those of Tunbridge; its fashions with the fashions of London; could rectify the opinions of her new friend in many articles of tasteful attire; could discover a flirtation between any gentleman and lady who only smiled on each other; and point out a quiz through the thickness of a crowd. These powers received due admiration from Catherine, to whom they were entirely new; and the respect which they naturally inspired might have been too great for familiarity, had not the easy gaiety of Miss Thorpe's manners, and her frequent expressions of delight on this acquaintance with her, softened down every feeling of awe, and left nothing but tender affection. Their increasing attachment was not to be satisfied with half a dozen turns in the Pump-room, but required, when they all quitted it together, that Miss Thorpe should accompany Miss Morland to the very door of Mr Allen's house; and that they should there part with a most affectionate and lengthened shake of hands, after learning, to their mutual relief, that they should see each other across the theatre at night, and say their prayers in the same chapel the next morning. Catherine then ran directly up stairs, and watched Miss

Thorpe's progress down the street from the drawing-room window; admired the graceful spirit of her walk, the fashionable air of her figure and dress, and felt grateful, as well she might, for the chance which had procured her such a friend.

Mrs Thorpe was a widow, and not a very rich one; she was a good-humoured, well-meaning woman, and a very indulgent mother. Her eldest daughter had great personal beauty, and the younger ones, by pretending to be as handsome as their sister, imitating her air, and dressing in the same style, did very well.

This brief account of the family is intended to supersede the necessity of a long and minute detail from Mrs Thorpe herself, of her past adventures and sufferings, which might otherwise be expected to occupy the three or four following chapters; in which the worthlessness of lords and attornies might be set forth, and conversations, which had passed twenty years before, be minutely repeated.

Chapter 5

Catherine was not so much engaged at the theatre that evening, in returning the nods and smiles of Miss Thorpe, though they certainly claimed much of her leisure, as to forget to look with an inquiring eye for Mr Tilney in every box which her eye could reach; but she looked in vain. Mr Tilney was no fonder of the play than the Pump-room. She hoped to be more fortunate the next day; and when her wishes for fine weather were answered by seeing a beautiful morning, she hardly felt a doubt of it; for a fine Sunday in Bath empties every house of its inhabitants, and all the world appears on such an occasion to walk about and tell their acquaintance what a charming day it is.

As soon as divine service was over, the Thorpes and Allens eagerly joined each other; and after staying long enough in the Pump-room to discover that the crowd was insupportable, and that there was not a genteel face to be seen, which every body discovers every Sunday throughout the season, they hastened away to the Crescent, to breathe the fresh air of better company. Here Catherine and Isabella, arm in arm, again tasted the sweets of friendship in an unreserved conversation; – they talked much, and with much enjoyment; but again was Catherine disappointed in her hope of reseeing her partner. He was no where to be met with; every search for him was equally unsuccessful, in morning lounges or evening assemblies; neither at the upper nor lower rooms, at dressed or undressed balls, was he perceivable; nor among the walkers, the horsemen, or the curricle-drivers of the morning. His name was not in the Pump-room book, and curiosity could do no more. He must be gone from Bath. Yet he had not mentioned that his stay would be so short! This sort of mysteriousness, which is always so becoming in a hero, threw a fresh grace in Catherine's imagination around his person and manners, and increased her anxiety to know more of him. From the Thorpes she could learn nothing, for they had been only two days in Bath before they met with Mrs Allen. It was a subject, however, in which she often indulged with her fair friend; from whom she received every possible encouragement to continue to think of him; and his impression on her fancy was not suffered therefore to weaken. Isabella was very sure that he must be a charming young man; and was equally sure that he must have been delighted with her dear Catherine, and would therefore shortly return. She liked him the better for being a clergyman, 'for she must confess herself very partial to the profession;' and something like a sigh escaped her as she said it. Perhaps Catherine was wrong in not demanding the cause of that gentle emotion – but she was not experienced enough in the finesse of love, or the duties of friendship, to know when delicate raillery was properly called for, or when a confidence should be forced.

Mrs Allen was now quite happy – quite satisfied with Bath. She had found some acquaintance, had been so lucky too as to find in them the family of a most worthy old friend; and, as the completion of good fortune, had found these friends by no means so expensively dressed as herself. Her daily expressions were no longer, 'I wish we had some acquaintance in Bath!' They were changed into – 'How glad I am we have met with Mrs Thorpe!' – and she was as eager in promoting the intercourse of the two families, as her young charge and Isabella themselves could be; never satisfied with the day unless she spent the chief of it by the side of Mrs Thorpe, in what they called conversation, but in which there was scarcely ever any exchange of opinion, and not often any resemblance of subject, for Mrs Thorpe talked chiefly of her children, and Mrs Allen of her gowns.

The progress of the friendship between Catherine and Isabella was quick as its beginning had been warm, and they passed so rapidly through every gradation of increasing tenderness, that there was shortly no fresh proof of it, to be given to their friends or themselves. They called each other by their Christian name, were always arm in arm when they walked, pinned up each other's train for the dance, and were not to be divided in the set; and if a rainy morning deprived them of other enjoyments, they were still resolute in meeting in defiance of wet and dirt, and shut themselves up, to read novels together. Yes, novels; – for I will not adopt that ungenerous and impolitic custom so common with novel writers, of degrading by their contemptuous censure the very performances, to the number of which they are themselves adding – joining with their greatest enemies in bestowing the harshest epithets on such works, and scarcely ever permitting them to be read by their own heroine, who, if she accidentally take up a novel, is sure to turn over its insipid pages with disgust. Alas! if the heroine of one novel be not patronized by the heroine of another, from whom can she expect protection and regard? I cannot approve of it. Let us leave it to the Reviewers to abuse such effusions of fancy at their leisure, and over every new novel to talk in threadbare strains of the trash with which the press now groans. Let us not desert one another; we are an injured body. Although our productions have afforded more extensive and unaffected pleasure than those of any other literary corporation in the world, no species of composition has been so much decried. From pride, ignorance, or fashion, our foes are almost as many as our readers. And while the abilities of the nine-hundredth abridger of the History of England, or of the man who collects and publishes in a volume some dozen lines of Milton, Pope, and Prior, with a paper from the Spectator, and a chapter from Sterne, are eulogized by a thousand pens, – there seems almost a general wish of decrying the capacity and undervaluing the labour of the novelist, and of slighting the performances which have only genius, wit, and taste to recommend them. 'I am no novel reader – I seldom look into novels – Do not imagine that I often read novels – It is really very well for a novel.' – Such is the common cant. – 'And what are you reading, Miss –?' 'Oh! it is only a novel!' replies the young lady; while she lays down her book with affected indifference, or momentary shame. – 'It is only Cecilia, or Camilla, or Belinda;' or, in short, only some work in which the greatest powers of the mind are displayed, in which the most thorough knowledge of human nature, the happiest delineation of its varieties, the liveliest effusions of wit and humour are conveyed to the world in the best chosen language. Now, had the same young lady been engaged with a volume of the Spectator, instead of such a work, how proudly would she have produced the book, and told its name; though the chances must be against her being occupied by any part of that voluminous publication, of which either the matter or manner would not disgust a young person of taste; the substance of its papers so often consisting in the statement of improbable circumstances, unnatural characters, and topics of conversation, which no longer concern any one living; and their language, too, frequently so coarse as to give no very favourable idea of the age that could endure it.

Chapter 6

The following conversation, which took place between the two friends in the Pump-room one morning, after an acquaintance of eight or nine days, is given as a specimen of their very warm attachment, and of the delicacy, discretion, originality of thought, and literary taste which marked the reasonableness of that attachment.

They met by appointment; and as Isabella had arrived nearly five minutes before her friend, her first address naturally was – 'My dearest creature, what can have made you so late? I have been waiting for you at least this age!'

'Have you, indeed! – I am very sorry for it; but really I thought I was in very good time. It is but just one. I hope you have not been here long?'

'Oh! these ten ages at least. I am sure I have been here this half hour. But now, let us go and sit down at the other end of the room, and enjoy ourselves. I have an hundred things to say to you. In the first place, I was so afraid it would rain this morning, just as I wanted to set off; it looked very showery, and that would have thrown me into agonies! Do you know, I saw the prettiest hat you can imagine, in a shop window in Milsom-street just now – very like yours, only with coquelicot ribbons instead of green; I quite longed for it. But, my dearest Catherine, what have you been doing with yourself all this morning? – Have you gone on with Udolpho?'

'Yes, I have been reading it ever since I woke; and I am got to the black veil.'

'Are you, indeed? How delightful! Oh! I would not tell you what is behind the black veil for the world! Are not you wild to know?'

'Oh! yes, quite; what can it be? – But do not tell me – I would not be told upon any account. I know it must be a skeleton, I am sure it is Laurentina's skeleton. Oh! I am delighted with the book! I should like to spend my whole life in reading it. I assure you, if it had not been to meet you, I would not have come away from it for all the world.'

'Dear creature! how much I am obliged to you; and when you have finished Udolpho, we will read the Italian together; and I have made out a list of ten or twelve more of the same kind for you.'

'Have you, indeed! How glad I am! – What are they all?'

'I will read you their names directly; here they are, in my pocketbook. Castle of Wolfenbach, Clermont, Mysterious Warnings, Necromancer of the Black Forest, Midnight Bell, Orphan of the Rhine, and Horrid Mysteries. Those will last us some time.'

'Yes, pretty well; but are they all horrid, are you sure they are all horrid?'

'Yes, quite sure; for a particular friend of mine, a Miss Andrews, a sweet girl, one of the sweetest creatures in the world, has read every one of them. I wish you knew Miss Andrews, you would be delighted with her. She is netting herself the sweetest cloak you can conceive. I think her as beautiful as an angel, and I am so vexed with the men for not admiring her! – I scold them all amazingly about it.'

'Scold them! Do you scold them for not admiring her?'

'Yes, that I do. There is nothing I would not do for those who are really my friends. I have no notion of loving people by halves, it is not my nature. My attachments are always excessively strong. I told Capt. Hunt at one of our assemblies this winter, that if he was to tease me all night, I would not dance with him, unless he would allow Miss Andrews to be as beautiful as an angel. The men think us incapable of real friendship you know, and I am determined to shew them the difference. Now, if I were to hear any body speak slightingly of you, I should fire up in a moment: – but that is not at all likely, for *you* are just the kind of girl to be a great favourite with the men.'

'Oh! dear,' cried Catherine, colouring, 'how can you say so?'

'I know you very well; you have so much animation, which is exactly what Miss Andrews wants, for I must confess there is something amazingly insipid about her. Oh! I must tell you, that just after we parted yesterday, I saw a young man looking at you so earnestly – I am sure he is in love with you.' Catherine coloured, and disclaimed again. Isabella laughed. 'It is very true, upon my honour, but I see how it is; you are indifferent to every body's admiration, except that of one gentleman, who shall be nameless. Nay, I cannot blame you – (speaking more seriously) – your feelings are easily understood. Where the heart is really attached, I know very well how little one can be pleased with the attention

of any body else. Every thing is so insipid, so uninteresting, that does not relate to the beloved object! I can
perfectly comprehend your feelings.'

'But you should not persuade me that I think so very
much about Mr Tilney, for perhaps I may never see
him again.'

'Not see him again! My dearest creature, do not
talk of it. I am sure you would be miserable if you
thought so.'

'No, indeed, I should not. I do not pretend to say that
I was not very much pleased with him; but while I have
Udolpho to read, I feel as if nobody could make me
miserable. Oh! the dreadful black veil! My dear Isabella,
I am sure there must be Laurentina's skeleton behind it.'

'It is so odd to me, that you should never have read
Udolpho before; but I suppose Mrs Morland objects to
novels.'

'No, she does not. She very often reads Sir Charles
Grandison herself; but new books do not fall in our way.'

'Sir Charles Grandison! That is an amazing horrid
book, is it not? – I remember Miss Andrews could not
get through the first volume.'

'It is not like Udolpho at all; but yet I think it is very
entertaining.'

'Do you indeed! – you surprize me; I thought it had
not been readable. But, my dearest Catherine, have
you settled what to wear on your head tonight? I am
determined at all events to be dressed exactly like you.
The men take notice of *that* sometimes you know.'

'But it does not signify if they do;' said Catherine, very
innocently.

'Signify! Oh, heavens! I make it a rule never to mind

what they say. They are very often amazingly imperti-nent if you do not treat them with spirit, and make them keep their distance.'

'Are they? – Well, I never observed *that*. They always behave very well to me.'

'Oh! they give themselves such airs. They are the most conceited creatures in the world, and think themselves of so much importance! – By the bye, though I have thought of it a hundred times, I have always forgot to ask you what is your favourite complexion in a man. Do you like them best dark or fair?'

'I hardly know. I never much thought about it. Some-thing between both, I think. Brown – not fair, and and not very dark.'

'Very well, Catherine. That is exactly he. I have not forgot your description of Mr Tilney; – "a brown skin, with dark eyes, and rather dark hair." – Well, my taste is different. I prefer light eyes, and as to complexion – do you know – I like a sallow better than any other. You must not betray me, if you should ever meet with one of your acquaintance answering that description.'

'Betray you! – What do you mean?'

'Nay, do not distress me. I believe I have said too much. Let us drop the subject.'

Catherine, in some amazement, complied; and after remaining a few moments silent, was on the point of reverting to what interested her at that time rather more than any thing else in the world, Laurentina's skeleton; when her friend prevented her, by saying, – 'For Heaven's sake! let us move away from this end of the room. Do you know, there are two odious young men who have been staring at me this half hour. They really put me quite out of countenance. Let us go and look at the arrivals. They will hardly follow us there.'

Away they walked to the book; and while Isabella examined the names, it was Catherine's employment to watch the proceedings of these alarming young men.

'They are not coming this way, are they? I hope they are not so impertinent as to follow us. Pray let me know if they are coming. I am determined I will not look up.'

In a few moments Catherine, with unaffected pleasure, assured her that she need not be longer uneasy, as the gentlemen had just left the Pump-room.

'And which way are they gone?' said Isabella, turning hastily round. 'One was a very good-looking young man.'

'They went towards the church-yard.'

'Well, I am amazingly glad I have got rid of them! And now, what say you to going to Edgar's Buildings with me, and looking at my new hat? You said you should like to see it.'

Catherine readily agreed. 'Only,' she added, 'perhaps we may overtake the two young men.'

'Oh! never mind that. If we make haste, we shall pass by them presently, and I am dying to shew you my hat.'

'But if we only wait a few minutes, there will be no danger of our seeing them at all.'

'I shall not pay them any such compliment, I assure you. I have no notion of treating men with such respect. *That* is the way to spoil them.'

Catherine had nothing to oppose against such reasoning; and therefore, to shew the independence of Miss Thorpe, and her resolution of humbling the sex, they set off immediately as fast as they could walk, in pursuit of the two young men.

Chapter 7

Half a minute conducted them through the Pump-yard to the archway, opposite Union-passage; but here they were stopped. Every body acquainted with Bath may remember the difficulties of crossing Cheap-street at this point; it is indeed a street of so impertinent a nature, so unfortunately connected with the great London and Oxford roads, and the principal inn of the city, that a day never passes in which parties of ladies, however important their business, whether in quest of pastry, millinery, or even (as in the present case) of young men, are not detained on one side or other by carriages, horsemen, or carts. This evil had been felt and lamented, at least three times a day, by Isabella since her residence in Bath; and she was now fated to feel and lament it once more, for at the very moment of coming opposite to Union-passage, and within view of the two gentlemen who were proceeding through the crowds, and threading the gutters of that interesting alley, they were prevented crossing by the approach of a gig, driven along on bad pavement by a most knowing-looking coachman with all the vehemence that could most fitly endanger the lives of himself, his companion, and his horse.

'Oh, these odious gigs!' said Isabella, looking up, 'how I detest them.' But this detestation, though so just, was of short duration, for she looked again and exclaimed, 'Delightful! Mr Morland and my brother!'

'Good heaven! 'tis James!' was uttered at the same moment by Catherine; and, on catching the young men's eyes, the horse was immediately checked with a violence which almost threw him on his haunches, and the servant having now scampered up, the gentlemen jumped out, and the equipage was delivered to his care.

Catherine, by whom this meeting was wholly unexpected, received her brother with the liveliest pleasure; and he, being of a very amiable disposition, and sincerely attached to her, gave every proof on his side of equal satisfaction, which he could have leisure to do, while the bright eyes of Miss Thorpe were incessantly challenging his notice; and to her his devoirs were speedily paid, with a mixture of joy and embarrassment which might have informed Catherine, had she been more expert in the development of other people's feelings, and less simply engrossed by her own, that her brother thought her friend quite as pretty as she could do herself.

John Thorpe, who in the mean time had been giving orders about the horses, soon joined them, and from him she directly received the amends which were her due; for while he slightly and carelessly touched the hand of Isabella, on her he bestowed a whole scrape and half a short bow. He was a stout young man of middling height, who, with a plain face and ungraceful form, seemed fearful of being too handsome unless he wore the dress of a groom, and too much like a gentleman unless he were easy where he ought to be civil, and impudent where he might be allowed to be easy. He took out his watch: 'How long do you think we have been running it from Tetbury, Miss Morland?'

'I do not know the distance.' Her brother told her that it was twenty-three miles.

'*Three*-and-twenty!' cried Thorpe; 'five-and-twenty if it is an inch.' Morland remonstrated, pleaded the authority of road-books, innkeepers, and milestones; but his friend disregarded them all; he had a surer test of distance. 'I know it must be five-and-twenty,' said he, 'by the time we have been doing it. It is now half after one; we drove out of the inn-yard at Tetbury as the town-clock struck eleven; and I defy any man in England to make my horse go less than ten miles an hour in harness; that makes it exactly twenty-five.'

'You have lost an hour,' said Morland; 'it was only ten o'clock when we came from Tetbury.'

'Ten o'clock! it was eleven, upon my soul! I counted every stroke. This brother of yours would persuade me out of my senses, Miss Morland; do but look at my horse; did you ever see an animal so made for speed in your life?' (The servant had just mounted the carriage and was driving off.) 'Such true blood! Three hours and a half indeed coming only three-and-twenty miles! look at that creature, and suppose it possible if you can.'

'He *does* look very hot to be sure.'

'Hot! he had not turned a hair till we came to Walcot Church: but look at his forehand; look at his loins; only see how he moves; that horse *cannot* go less than ten miles an hour: tie his legs and he will get on. What do you think of my gig, Miss Morland? a neat one, is not it? Well hung; town built; I have not had it a month. It was built for a Christchurch man, a friend of mine, a very good sort of fellow; he ran it a few weeks, till, I believe, it was convenient to have done with it. I happened just then to be looking out for some light thing of the kind, though I had pretty well determined on a curricle too; but I chanced to meet him on Magdalen Bridge, as he was driving into Oxford, last term: "Ah! Thorpe," said he, "do you happen to want such a little thing as this? it is a capital one of the kind, but I am cursed tired of it." "Oh! d – ," said I, "I am your man; what do you ask?" And how much do you think he did, Miss Morland?'

'I am sure I cannot guess at all.'

'Curricle-hung you see; seat, trunk, sword-case, splashing-board, lamps, silver moulding, all you see complete; the iron-work as good as new, or better. He asked fifty guineas; I closed with him directly, threw down the money, and the carriage was mine.'

'And I am sure,' said Catherine. 'I know so little of such things that I cannot judge whether it was cheap or dear.'

'Neither one nor t'other; I might have got it for less I dare say; but I hate haggling, and poor Freeman wanted cash.'

'That was very good-natured of you,' said Catherine, quite pleased.

'Oh! d – it, when one has the means of doing a kind thing by a friend, I hate to be pitiful.'

An inquiry now took place into the intended movements of the young ladies; and, on finding whither they were going, it was decided that the gentlemen should accompany them to Edgar's Buildings, and pay their respects to Mrs Thorpe. James and Isabella led the way; and so well satisfied was the latter with her lot, so contentedly was she endeavouring to ensure a pleasant walk to him who brought the double recommendation of being her brother's friend, and her friend's brother, so pure and uncoquettish were her feelings, that, though they overtook and passed the two offending young men in Milsom-street, she was so far from seeking to attract their notice, that she looked back at them only three times.

John Thorpe kept of course with Catherine, and, after a few minutes' silence, renewed the conversation about his gig – 'You will find, however, Miss Morland, it would be reckoned a cheap thing by some people, for I might have sold it for ten guineas more the next day; Jackson, of Oriel, bid me sixty at once; Morland was with me at the time.'

'Yes,' said Morland, who overheard this; 'but you forget that your horse was included.'

'My horse! oh, d – it! I would not sell my horse for a hundred. Are you fond of an open carriage, Miss Morland?'

'Yes, very; I have hardly ever an opportunity of being in one; but I am particularly fond of it.'

'I am glad of it; I will drive you out in mine every day.'

'Thank you,' said Catherine, in some distress, from a doubt of the propriety of accepting such an offer.

'I will drive you up Lansdown Hill to-morrow.'

'Thank you; but will not your horse want rest?'

'Rest! he has only come three-and-twenty miles to-day; all nonsense; nothing ruins horses so much as rest; nothing knocks them up so soon. No, no; I shall exercise mine at the average of four hours every day while I am here.'

'Shall you indeed!' said Catherine very seriously, 'that will be forty miles a day.'

'Forty! aye fifty, for what I care. Well, I will drive you up Lansdown to-morrow; mind, I am engaged.'

'How delightful that will be!' cried Isabella, turning round; 'my dearest Catherine, I quite envy you; but I am afraid, brother, you will not have room for a third.'

'A third indeed! no, no; I did not come to Bath to drive my sisters about; that would be a good joke, faith! Morland must take care of you.'

This brought on a dialogue of civilities between the other two; but Catherine heard neither the particulars nor the result. Her companion's discourse now sunk from its hitherto animated pitch, to nothing more than a short decisive sentence of praise or condemnation on the face of every woman they met; and Catherine, after listening and agreeing as long as she could, with all the civility and deference of the youthful female mind, fearful of hazarding an opinion of its own in opposition to that of a self-assured man, especially where the beauty of her own sex is concerned, ventured at length to vary the subject by a question which had been long uppermost in her thoughts; it was, 'Have you ever read Udolpho, Mr Thorpe?'

'Udolpho! Oh, Lord! not I; I never read novels; I have something else to do.'

Catherine, humbled and ashamed, was going to apologize for her question, but he prevented her by saying, 'Novels are all so full of nonsense and stuff; there has not been a tolerably decent one come out since Tom Jones, except the Monk; I read that t'other day; but as for all the others, they are the stupidest things in creation.'

'I think you must like Udolpho, if you were to read it; it is so very interesting.'

'Not I, faith! No, if I read any it shall be Mrs Radcliff's; her novels are amusing enough; they are worth reading; some fun and nature in *them*.'

'Udolpho was written by Mrs Radcliff,' said Catherine, with some hesitation, from the fear of mortifying him.

'No sure; was it? Aye, I remember, so it was; I was thinking of that other stupid book, written by that woman they make such a fuss about, she who married the French emigrant.'

'I suppose you mean Camilla?'

'Yes, that's the book; such unnatural stuff! – An old man playing at see-saw! I took up the first volume once and looked it over, but I soon found it would not do; indeed I guessed what sort of stuff it must be before I saw it: as soon as I heard she had married an emigrant, I was sure I should never be able to get through it.'

'I have never read it.'

'You had no loss I assure you; it is the horridest nonsense you can imagine; there is nothing in the world in it but an old man's playing at see-saw and learning Latin; upon my soul there is not.'

This critique, the justness of which was unfortunately lost on poor Catherine, brought them to the door of Mrs Thorpe's lodgings, and the feelings of the discerning and unprejudiced reader of Camilla gave way to the feelings of the dutiful and affectionate son, as they met Mrs Thorpe, who had descried them from above, in the passage. 'Ah, mother! how do you do?' said he, giving her a hearty shake of the hand: 'where did you get that quiz of a hat, it makes you look like an old witch? Here is Morland and I come to stay a few days with you, so you must look out for a couple of good beds some where near.' And this address seemed to satisfy all the fondest wishes of the mother's heart, for she received him with the most delighted and exulting affection. On his two younger sisters he then bestowed an equal portion of his fraternal tenderness, for he asked each of them how they did, and observed that they both looked very ugly.

These manners did not please Catherine; but he was James's friend and Isabella's brother; and her judgment was further bought off by Isabella's assuring her, when they withdrew to see the new hat, that John thought her the most charming girl in the world, and by John's engaging her before they parted to dance with him that evening. Had she been older or vainer, such attacks might have done little; but, where youth and diffidence are united, it requires uncommon steadiness of reason to resist the attraction of being called the most charming girl in the world, and of being so very early engaged as a partner; and the consequence was, that, when the two Morlands, after sitting an hour with the Thorpes, set off to walk together to Mr Allen's, and James, as the door was closed on them, said, 'Well, Catherine, how do you like my friend Thorpe?' instead of answering, as she probably would have done, had there been no friendship and no flattery in the case, 'I do not like him at all;' she directly replied, 'I like him very much; he seems very agreeable.'

'He is as good-natured a fellow as ever lived; a little

of a rattle; but that will recommend him to your sex I believe: and how do you like the rest of the family?'

'Very, very much indeed: Isabella particularly.'

'I am very glad to hear you say so; she is just the kind of young woman I could wish to see you attached to; she has so much good sense, and is so thoroughly unaffected and amiable; I always wanted you to know her; and she seems very fond of you. She said the highest things in your praise that could possibly be; and the praise of such a girl as Miss Thorpe even you, Catherine,' taking her hand with affection, 'may be proud of.'

'Indeed I am,' she replied; 'I love her exceedingly, and am delighted to find that you like her too. You hardly mentioned any thing of her, when you wrote to me after your visit there.'

'Because I thought I should soon see you myself. I hope you will be a great deal together while you are in Bath. She is a most amiable girl; such a superior understanding! How fond all the family are of her; she is evidently the general favourite; and how much she must be admired in such a place as this – is not she?'

'Yes, very much indeed, I fancy; Mr Allen thinks her the prettiest girl in Bath.'

'I dare say he does; and I do not know any man who is a better judge of beauty than Mr Allen. I need not ask you whether you are happy here, my dear Catherine; with such a companion and friend as Isabella Thorpe, it would be impossible for you to be otherwise; and the Allens I am sure are very kind to you?'

'Yes, very kind; I never was so happy before; and now you are come it will be more delightful than ever; how good it is of you to come so far on purpose to see *me*.'

James accepted this tribute of gratitude, and qualified his conscience for accepting it too, by saying with perfect sincerity, 'Indeed, Catherine, I love you dearly.'

Inquiries and communications concerning brothers and sisters, the situation of some, the growth of the rest, and other family matters, now passed between them, and continued, with only one small digression on James's part, in praise of Miss Thorpe, till they reached Pulteney-street, where he was welcomed with great kindness by Mr and Mrs Allen, invited by the former to dine with them, and summoned by the latter to guess the price and weigh the merits of a new muff and tippet. A pre-engagement in Edgar's Buildings prevented his accepting the invitation of one friend, and obliged him to hurry away as soon as he had satisfied the demands of the other. The time of the two parties uniting in the Octagon Room being correctly adjusted, Catherine was then left to the luxury of a raised, restless, and frightened imagination over the pages of Udolpho, lost from all worldly concerns of dressing and dinner, incapable of soothing Mrs Allen's fears on the delay of an expected dress-maker, and having only one minute in sixty to bestow even on the reflection of her own felicity, in being already engaged for the evening.

Chapter 8

In spite of Udolpho and the dress-maker, however, the party from Pulteney-street reached the Upper-rooms in very good time. The Thorpes and James Morland were there only two minutes before them; and Isabella having gone through the usual ceremonial of meeting her friend with the most smiling and affectionate haste, of admiring the set of her gown, and envying the curl of her hair, they followed their chaperons, arm in arm, into the ball-room, whispering to each other whenever a thought occurred, and supplying the place of many ideas by a squeeze of the hand or a smile of affection.

The dancing began within a few minutes after they were seated; and James, who had been engaged quite as long as his sister, was very importunate with Isabella to stand up; but John was gone into the card-room to speak to a friend, and nothing, she declared, should induce her to join the set before her dear Catherine could join it too: 'I assure you,' said she, 'I would not stand up without your dear sister for all the world; for if I did we should certainly be separated the whole evening.' Catherine accepted this kindness with gratitude, and they continued as they were for three minutes longer, when Isabella, who had been talking to James on the other side of her, turned again to his sister and whispered, 'My dear creature, I am afraid I must leave you, your brother is so amazingly impatient to begin; I know you will not

51

mind my going away, and I dare say John will be back in a moment, and then you may easily find me out.' Catherine, though a little disappointed, had too much good-nature to make any opposition, and the others rising up, Isabella had only time to press her friend's hand and say, 'Good bye, my dear love,' before they hurried off. The younger Miss Thorpes being also dancing, Catherine was left to the mercy of Mrs Thorpe and Mrs Allen, between whom she now remained. She could not help being vexed at the non-appearance of Mr Thorpe, for she not only longed to be dancing, but was likewise aware that, as the real dignity of her situation could not be known, she was sharing with the scores of other young ladies still sitting down all the discredit of wanting a partner. To be disgraced in the eye of the world, to wear the appearance of infamy while her heart is all purity, her actions all innocence, and the misconduct of another the true source of her debasement, is one of those circumstances which peculiarly belong to the heroine's life, and her fortitude under it what particularly dignifies her character. Catherine had fortitude too; she suffered, but no murmur passed her lips.

From this state of humiliation, she was roused, at the end of ten minutes, to a pleasanter feeling, by seeing, not Mr Thorpe, but Mr Tilney, within three yards of the place where they sat; he seemed to be moving that way, but he did not see her, and therefore the smile and the blush, which his sudden reappearance raised in Catherine, passed away without sullying her heroic importance. He looked as handsome and as lively as ever, and was talking with interest to a fashionable and pleasing-looking young woman, who leant on his arm, and whom

Catherine immediately guessed to be his sister; thus unthinkingly throwing away a fair opportunity of considering him lost to her for ever, by being married already. But guided only by what was simple and probable, it had never entered her head that Mr Tilney could be married; he had not behaved, he had not talked, like the married men to whom she had been used; he had never mentioned a wife, and he had acknowledged a sister. From these circumstances sprang the instant conclusion of his sister's now being by his side; and therefore, instead of turning of a deathlike paleness, and falling in a fit on Mrs Allen's bosom, Catherine sat erect, in the perfect use of her senses, and with cheeks only a little redder than usual.

Mr Tilney and his companion, who continued, though slowly, to approach, were immediately preceded by a lady, an acquaintance of Mrs Thorpe; and this lady stopping to speak to her, they, as belonging to her, stopped likewise, and Catherine, catching Mr Tilney's eye, instantly received from him the smiling tribute of recognition. She returned it with pleasure, and then advancing still nearer, he spoke both to her and Mrs Allen, by whom he was very civilly acknowledged. 'I am very happy to see you again, sir, indeed; I was afraid you had left Bath.' He thanked her for her fears, and said that he had quitted it for a week, on the very morning after his having had the pleasure of seeing her.

'Well, sir, and I dare say you are not sorry to be back again, for it is just the place for young people – and indeed for every body else too. I tell Mr Allen, when he talks of being sick of it, that I am sure he should not complain, for it is so very agreeable a place, that it is much better to be here than at home at this dull time of year. I tell him he is quite in luck to be sent here for his health.'

'And I hope, madam, that Mr Allen will be obliged to like the place, from finding it of service to him.'

'Thank you, sir. I have no doubt that he will. – A neighbour of ours, Dr Skinner, was here for his health last winter, and came away quite stout.'

'That circumstance must give great encouragement.'

'Yes, sir – and Dr Skinner and his family were here three months; so I tell Mr Allen he must not be in a hurry to get away.'

Here they were interrupted by a request from Mrs Thorpe to Mrs Allen, that she would move a little to accommodate Mrs Hughes and Miss Tilney with seats, as they had agreed to join their party. This was accordingly done, Mr Tilney still continuing standing before them; and after a few minutes consideration, he asked Catherine to dance with him. This compliment, delightful as it was, produced severe mortification to the lady; and in giving her denial, she expressed her sorrow on the occasion so very much as if she really felt it, that had Thorpe, who joined her just afterwards, been half a minute earlier, he might have thought her sufferings rather too acute. The very easy manner in which he then told her that he had kept her waiting, did not by any means reconcile her more to her lot; nor did the particulars which he entered into while they were standing up, of the horses and dogs of the friend whom he had just left, and of a proposed exchange of terriers between them, interest her so much as to prevent her looking very often towards that part of the room where she had left Mr Tilney. Of her dear Isabella, to whom she particularly longed to point out that gentleman, she could see nothing. They were in different sets. She was separated from all her party, and away from all her acquaintance; – one mortification succeeded another, and from the whole she deduced this useful lesson, that to go previously engaged to a ball, does not necessarily increase either the dignity or enjoyment of a young lady. From such a moralizing strain as this, she was suddenly roused by a touch on the shoulder, and turning round, perceived Mrs Hughes directly behind her, attended by Miss Tilney and a gentleman. 'I beg your pardon, Miss Morland,' said she, 'for this liberty, – but I cannot any how get to Miss Thorpe, and Mrs Thorpe said she was sure you would not have the least objection to letting in this young lady by you.' Mrs Hughes could not have applied to any creature in the room more happy to oblige her than Catherine. The young ladies were introduced to each other, Miss Tilney expressing a proper sense of such goodness, Miss Morland with the real delicacy of a generous mind making light of the obligation; and Mrs Hughes, satisfied with having so respectably settled her young charge, returned to her party.

Miss Tilney had a good figure, a pretty face, and a very agreeable countenance; and her air, though it had not all the decided pretension, the resolute stilishness of Miss Thorpe's, had more real elegance. Her manners shewed good sense and good breeding; they were neither shy, nor affectedly open; and she seemed capable of being young, attractive, and at a ball, without wanting to fix the attention of every man near her, and without exaggerated feelings of extatic delight or inconceivable vexation on every little trifling occurrence. Catherine, interested at once by her appearance and her relationship to Mr Tilney, was desirous of being acquainted with her, and readily talked therefore whenever she could think of any thing to say, and had courage and leisure for saying it. But the hindrance thrown in the way of a very speedy intimacy, by the frequent want of one or more of these requisites, prevented their doing more than going through the first rudiments of an acquaintance, by informing themselves how well the other liked Bath, how much she admired its buildings and surrounding country, whether she drew, or played or sang, and whether she was fond of riding on horseback.

The two dances were scarcely concluded before Catherine found her arm gently seized by her faithful Isabella, who in great spirits exclaimed – 'At last I have got you. My dearest creature, I have been looking for you this hour. What could induce you to come into this set, when you knew I was in the other? I have been quite wretched without you.'

'My dear Isabella, how was it possible for me to get at you? I could not even see where you were.'

'So I told your brother all the time – but he would not believe me. Do go and see for her, Mr Morland, said I – but all in vain – he would not stir an inch. Was not it so, Mr Morland? But you men are all so immoderately lazy! I have been scolding him to such a degree, my dear Catherine, you would be quite amazed. – You know I never stand upon ceremony with such people.'

'Look at that young lady with the white beads round her head,' whispered Catherine, detaching her friend from James – 'It is Mr Tilney's sister.'

'Oh! heavens! You don't say so! Let me look at her this moment. What a delightful girl! I never saw any thing half so beautiful! But where is her all-conquering brother? Is he in the room? Point him out to me this instant, if he is. I die to see him. Mr Morland, you are not to listen. We are not talking about you.'

'But what is all this whispering about? What is going on?'

'There now, I knew how it would be. You men have such restless curiosity! Talk of the curiosity of women, indeed! – 'tis nothing. But be satisfied, for you are not to know any thing at all of the matter.'

'And is that likely to satisfy me, do you think?'

'Well, I declare I never knew any thing like you. What can it signify to you, what we are talking of? Perhaps we are talking about you, therefore I would advise you not to listen, or you may happen to hear something not very agreeable.'

In this common-place chatter, which lasted some time, the original subject seemed entirely forgotten; and though Catherine was very well pleased to have it dropped for a while, she could not avoid a little suspicion at the total suspension of all Isabella's impatient desire to see Mr Tilney. When the orchestra struck up a fresh dance, James would have led his fair partner away, but she resisted. 'I tell you, Mr Morland,' she cried, 'I would not do such a thing for all the world. How can you be so teasing; only conceive, my dear Catherine, what your brother wants me to do. He wants me to dance with him again, though I tell him that it is a most improper thing, and entirely against the rules. It would make us the talk of the place, if we were not to change partners.'

'Upon my honour,' said James, 'in these public assemblies, it is as often done as not.'

'Nonsense, how can you say so? But when you men have a point to carry, you never stick at any thing. My sweet Catherine, do support me, persuade your brother how impossible it is. Tell him, that it would quite shock you to see me do such a thing; now would not it?'

'No, not at all; but if you think it wrong, you had much better change.'

'There,' cried Isabella, 'you hear what your sister says, and yet you will not mind her. Well, remember that it is not my fault, if we set all the old ladies in Bath in a bustle. Come along, my dearest Catherine, for heaven's sake, and stand by me.' And off they went, to regain their former place. John Thorpe, in the meanwhile, had walked away; and Catherine, ever willing to give Mr Tilney an opportunity of repeating the agreeable request which had already flattered her once, made her way to Mrs Allen and Mrs Thorpe as fast as she could, in the hope of finding him still with them – a hope which, when it proved to be fruitless, she felt to have been highly unreasonable. 'Well, my dear,' said Mrs Thorpe, impatient for praise of her son, 'I hope you have had an agreeable partner.'

'Very agreeable, madam.'

'I am glad of it. John has charming spirits, has not he?'

'Did you meet Mr Tilney, my dear?' said Mrs Allen.

'No, where is he?'

'He was with us just now, and said he was so tired of lounging about, that he was resolved to go and dance; so I thought perhaps he would ask you, if he met with you.'

'Where can he be?' said Catherine, looking round; but she had not looked round long before she saw him leading a young lady to the dance.

'Ah! he has got a partner, I wish he had asked *you*,' said Mrs Allen; and after a short silence, she added, 'he is a very agreeable young man.'

'Indeed he is, Mrs Allen,' said Mrs Thorpe, smiling complacently; 'I must say it, though I *am* his mother, that there is not a more agreeable young man in the world.'

This inapplicable answer might have been too much for the comprehension of many; but it did not puzzle Mrs Allen, for after only a moment's consideration, she said, in a whisper to Catherine, 'I dare say she thought I was speaking of her son.'

Catherine was disappointed and vexed. She seemed to have missed by so little the very object she had had in view; and this persuasion did not incline her to a very gracious reply, when John Thorpe came up to her soon afterwards, and said, 'Well, Miss Morland, I suppose you and I are to stand up and jig it together again.'

'Oh, no; I am much obliged to you, our two dances are over; and, besides, I am tired, and do not mean to dance any more.'

'Do not you? – then let us walk about and quiz people. Come along with me, and I will shew you the four greatest quizzes in the room; my two younger sisters and their partners. I have been laughing at them this half hour.'

Again Catherine excused herself; and at last he walked off to quiz his sisters by himself. The rest of the evening she found very dull; Mr Tilney was drawn away from their party at tea, to attend that of his partner; Miss Tilney, though belonging to it, did not sit near her, and James and Isabella were so much engaged in conversing together, that the latter had no leisure to bestow more on her friend than one smile, one squeeze, and one 'dearest Catherine.'

Chapter 9

The progress of Catherine's unhappiness from the events of the evening, was as follows. It appeared first in a general dissatisfaction with every body about her, while she remained in the rooms, which speedily brought on considerable weariness and a violent desire to go home. This, on arriving in Pulteney-street, took the direction of extraordinary hunger, and when that was appeased, changed into an earnest longing to be in bed; such was the extreme point of her distress; for when there she immediately fell into a sound sleep which lasted nine hours, and from which she awoke perfectly revived, in excellent spirits, with fresh hopes and fresh schemes. The first wish of her heart was to improve her acquaintance with Miss Tilney, and almost her first resolution, to seek her for that purpose, in the Pump-room at noon. In the Pump-room, one so newly arrived in Bath must be met with, and that building she had already found so favourable for the discovery of female excellence, and the completion of female intimacy, so admirably adapted for secret discourses and unlimited confidence, that she was most reasonably encouraged to expect another friend from within its walls. Her plan for the morning thus settled, she sat quietly down to her book after breakfast, resolving to remain in the same place and the same employment till the clock struck one; and from habitude very little incommoded by the remarks and ejaculations of Mrs Allen, whose vacancy of mind and incapacity for thinking were such, that as she never talked a great deal, so she could never be entirely silent; and, therefore, while she sat at her work, if she lost her needle or broke her thread, if she heard a carriage in the street, or saw a speck upon her gown, she must observe it aloud, whether there were any one at leisure to answer her or not. At about half past twelve, a remarkably loud rap drew her in haste to the window, and scarcely had she time to inform Catherine of there being two open carriages at the door, in the first only a servant, her brother driving Miss Thorpe in the second, before John Thorpe came running up stairs, calling out, 'Well, Miss Morland, here I am. Have you been waiting long? We could not come before; the old devil of a coachmaker was such an eternity finding out a thing fit to be got into, and now it is ten thousand to one, but they break down before we are out of the street. How do you do, Mrs Allen? a famous ball last night, was not it? Come, Miss Morland, be quick, for the others are in a confounded hurry to be off. They want to get their tumble over.'

'What do you mean?' said Catherine, 'where are you all going to?'

'Going to? Why, you have not forgot our engagement! Did not we agree together to take a drive this morning? What a head you have! We are going up Claverton Down.'

'Something was said about it, I remember,' said Catherine, looking at Mrs Allen for her opinion; 'but really I did not expect you.'

'Not expect me! that's a good one! And what a dust you would have made, if I had not come.'

Catherine's silent appeal to her friend, meanwhile, was entirely thrown away, for Mrs Allen, not being at all in the habit of conveying any expression herself by a look, was not aware of its being ever intended by any body else; and Catherine, whose desire of seeing Miss Tilney again could at that moment bear a short delay in favour of a drive, and who thought there could be no impropriety in her going with Mr Thorpe, as Isabella was going at the same time with James, was therefore obliged to speak plainer. 'Well, ma'am, what do you say to it? Can you spare me for an hour or two? shall I go?'

'Do just as you please, my dear,' replied Mrs Allen, with the most placid indifference. Catherine took the advice, and ran off to get ready. In a very few minutes she re-appeared, having scarcely allowed the two others time enough to get through a few short sentences in her praise, after Thorpe had procured Mrs Allen's admiration of his gig; and then receiving her friend's parting good wishes, they both hurried down stairs. 'My dearest creature,' cried Isabella, to whom the duty of friendship immediately called her before she could get into the carriage, 'you have been at least three hours getting ready. I was afraid you were ill. What a delightful ball we had last night. I have a thousand things to say to you; but make haste and get in, for I long to be off.'

Catherine followed her orders and turned away, but not too soon to hear her friend exclaim aloud to James, 'What a sweet girl she is! I quite doat on her.'

'You will not be frightened, Miss Morland,' said Thorpe, as he handed her in, 'if my horse should dance about a little at first setting off. He will, most likely, give a plunge or two, and perhaps take the rest for a minute;

63

but he will soon know his master. He is full of spirits, playful as can be, but there is no vice in him.'

Catherine did not think the portrait a very inviting one, but it was too late to retreat, and she was too young to own herself frightened; so, resigning herself to her fate, and trusting to the animal's boasted knowledge of its owner, she sat peaceably down, and saw Thorpe sit down by her. Every thing being then arranged, the servant who stood at the horse's head was bid in an important voice 'to let him go,' and off they went in the quietest manner imaginable, without a plunge or a caper, or any thing like one. Catherine, delighted at so happy an escape, spoke her pleasure aloud with grateful surprize; and her companion immediately made the matter perfectly simple by assuring her that it was entirely owing to the peculiarly judicious manner in which he had then held the reins, and the singular discernment and dexterity with which he had directed his whip. Catherine, though she could not help wondering that with such perfect command of his horse, he should think it necessary to alarm her with a relation of its tricks, congratulated herself sincerely on being under the care of so excellent a coachman; and perceiving that the animal continued to go on in the same quiet manner, without shewing the smallest propensity towards any unpleasant vivacity, and (considering its inevitable pace was ten miles an hour) by no means alarmingly fast, gave herself up to all the enjoyment of air and exercise of the most invigorating kind, in a fine mild day of February, with the consciousness of safety. A silence of several minutes succeeded their first short dialogue; – it was broken by Thorpe's saying very abruptly, 'Old

Allen is as rich as a Jew – is not he?' Catherine did not understand him – and he repeated his question, adding in explanation, 'Old Allen, the man you are with.'

'Oh! Mr Allen, you mean. Yes, I believe, he is very rich.'

'And no children at all?'

'No – not any.'

'A famous thing for his next heirs. He is *your* godfather, is not he?'

'My godfather! – no.'

'But you are always very much with them.'

'Yes, very much.'

'Aye, that is what I meant. He seems a good kind of old fellow enough, and has lived very well in his time, I dare say; he is not gouty for nothing. Does he drink his bottle a-day now?'

'His bottle a-day! – no. Why should you think of such a thing? He is a very temperate man, and you could not fancy him in liquor last night?'

'Lord help you! – You women are always thinking of men's being in liquor. Why you do not suppose a man is overset by a bottle? I am sure of *this* – that if every body was to drink their bottle a-day, there would not be half the disorders in the world there are now. It would be a famous good thing for us all.'

'I cannot believe it.'

'Oh! lord, it would be the saving of thousands. There is not the hundredth part of the wine consumed in this kingdom, that there ought to be. Our foggy climate wants help.'

'And yet I have heard that there is a great deal of wine drank in Oxford.'

'Oxford! There is no drinking at Oxford now, I assure you. Nobody drinks there. You would hardly meet with a man who goes beyond his four pints at the utmost. Now, for instance, it was reckoned a remarkable thing at the last party in my rooms, that upon an average we cleared about five pints a head. It was looked upon as something out of the common way. *Mine* is famous good stuff to be sure. You would not often meet with any thing like it in Oxford – and that may account for it. But this will just give you a notion of the general rate of drinking there.'

'Yes, it does give a notion,' said Catherine, warmly, 'and that is, that you all drink a great deal more wine than I thought you did. However, I am sure James does not drink so much.'

This declaration brought on a loud and overpowering reply, of which no part was very distinct, except the frequent exclamations, amounting almost to oaths, which adorned it, and Catherine was left, when it ended, with rather a strengthened belief of there being a great deal of wine drank in Oxford, and the same happy conviction of her brother's comparative sobriety.

Thorpe's ideas then all reverted to the merits of his own equipage, and she was called on to admire the spirit and freedom with which his horse moved along, and the ease which his paces, as well as the excellence of the springs, gave the motion of the carriage. She followed him in all his admiration as well as she could. To go before, or beyond him was impossible. His knowledge and her ignorance of the subject, his rapidity of expression, and her diffidence of herself put that out of her power; she could strike out nothing new in commendation, but she readily echoed whatever he chose to assert, and it was finally settled between them without any difficulty, that his equipage was altogether the most complete of its kind in England, his carriage the neatest, his horse the best goer, and himself the best coachman. – 'You do not really think, Mr Thorpe,' said Catherine, venturing after some time to consider the matter as entirely decided, and to offer some little variation on the subject, 'that James's gig will break down?'

'Break down! Oh! lord! Did you ever see such a little tittuppy thing in your life? There is not a sound piece of iron about it. The wheels have been fairly worn out these ten years at least – and as for the body! Upon my soul, you might shake it to pieces yourself with a touch. It is the most devilish little ricketty business I ever beheld! – Thank God! we have got a better. I would not be bound to go two miles in it for fifty thousand pounds.'

'Good heavens!' cried Catherine, quite frightened, 'then pray let us turn back; they will certainly meet with an accident if we go on. Do let us turn back, Mr Thorpe; stop and speak to my brother, and tell him how very unsafe it is.'

'Unsafe! Oh, lord! what is there in that? they will only get a roll if it does break down; and there is plenty of dirt, it will be excellent falling. Oh, curse it! the carriage is safe enough, if a man knows how to drive it; a thing of that sort in good hands will last above twenty years after it is fairly worn out. Lord bless you! I would undertake for five pounds to drive it to York and back again, without losing a nail.'

Catherine listened with astonishment; she knew not how to reconcile two such very different accounts of the same thing; for she had not been brought up to understand the propensities of a rattle, nor to know to how many idle assertions and impudent falsehoods the excess of vanity will lead. Her own family were plain matter-of-fact people, who seldom aimed at wit of any kind; her father, at the utmost, being contented with a pun, and her mother with a proverb; they were not in the habit therefore of telling lies to increase their importance, or of asserting at one moment what they would contradict the next. She reflected on the affair for some time in much perplexity, and was more than once on the point of requesting from Mr Thorpe a clearer insight into his real opinion on the subject; but she checked herself, because it appeared to her that he did not excel in giving those clearer insights, in making those things plain which he had before made ambiguous; and, joining to this, the consideration, that he would not really suffer his sister and his friend to be exposed to a danger from which he might easily preserve them, she concluded at last, that he must know the carriage to be in fact perfectly safe, and therefore would alarm herself no longer. By him the whole matter seemed entirely forgotten; and all the rest of his conversation, or rather talk, began and ended with himself and his own concerns. He told her of horses which he had bought for a trifle and sold for incredible sums; of racing matches, in which his judgment had infallibly foretold the winner; of shooting parties, in which he had killed more birds (though without having one good shot) than all his companions together; and described to her some famous day's sport, with the fox-hounds, in which his foresight and skill in directing the dogs had repaired the mistakes of the most experienced huntsman, and in which the boldness of his riding, though it had never endangered his own life for a moment, had been constantly leading others into difficulties, which he calmly concluded had broken the necks of many.

Little as Catherine was in the habit of judging for herself, and unfixed as were her general notions of what men ought to be, she could not entirely repress a doubt, while she bore with the effusions of his endless conceit, of his being altogether completely agreeable. It was a bold surmise, for he was Isabella's brother; and she had been assured by James, that his manners would recommend him to all her sex; but in spite of this, the extreme weariness of his company, which crept over her before they had been out an hour, and which continued unceasingly to increase till they stopped in Pulteney-street again, induced her, in some small degree, to resist such high authority, and to distrust his powers of giving universal pleasure.

When they arrived at Mrs Allen's door, the astonishment of Isabella was hardly to be expressed, on finding that it was too late in the day for them to attend her friend into the house: – 'Past three o'clock!' it was inconceivable, incredible, impossible! and she would neither believe her own watch, nor her brother's, nor the servant's; she would believe no assurance of it founded on reason or reality, till Morland produced his watch, and ascertained the fact; to have doubted a moment longer *then*, would have been equally inconceivable, incredible, and impossible; and she could only protest, over and over again, that no two hours and a half had ever gone off so swiftly before, as Catherine was called on to confirm; Catherine could not tell a falsehood even to please Isabella; but the latter was spared the misery of her friend's dissenting voice, by not waiting for her answer. Her own feelings entirely engrossed her; her wretchedness was most acute on finding herself obliged to go directly home. – It was ages since she had had a moment's conversation with her dearest Catherine; and, though she had such thousands of things to say to her, it appeared as if they were never to be together again; so, with smiles of most exquisite misery, and the laughing eye of utter despondency, she bade her friend adieu and went on.

Catherine found Mrs Allen just returned from all the busy idleness of the morning, and was immediately greeted with, 'Well, my dear, here you are;' a truth which she had no greater inclination than power to dispute; 'and I hope you have had a pleasant airing?'

'Yes, ma'am, I thank you; we could not have had a nicer day.'

'So Mrs Thorpe said; she was vastly pleased at your all going.'

'You have seen Mrs Thorpe then?'

'Yes, I went to the Pump-room as soon as you were gone, and there I met her, and we had a great deal of talk together. She says there was hardly any veal to be got at market this morning, it is so uncommonly scarce.'

'Did you see any body else of our acquaintance?'

'Yes; we agreed to take a turn in the Crescent, and there we met Mrs Hughes, and Mr and Miss Tilney walking with her.'

'Did you indeed? and did they speak to you?'

'Yes, we walked along the Crescent together for half

an hour. They seem very agreeable people. Miss Tilney was in a very pretty spotted muslin, and I fancy, by what I can learn, that she always dresses very handsomely. Mrs Hughes talked to me a great deal about the family.'

'And what did she tell you of them?'

'Oh! a vast deal indeed; she hardly talked of any thing else.'

'Did she tell you what part of Gloucestershire they come from?'

'Yes, she did; but I cannot recollect now. But they are very good kind of people, and very rich. Mrs Tilney was a Miss Drummond, and she and Mrs Hughes were school-fellows; and Miss Drummond had a very large fortune; and, when she married, her father gave her twenty thousand pounds, and five hundred to buy wedding-clothes. Mrs Hughes saw all the clothes after they came from the warehouse.'

'And are Mr and Mrs Tilney in Bath?'

'Yes, I fancy they are, but I am not quite certain. Upon recollection, however, I have a notion they are both dead; at least the mother is; yes, I am sure Mrs Tilney is dead, because Mrs Hughes told me there was a very beautiful set of pearls that Mr Drummond gave his daughter on her wedding-day and that Miss Tilney has got now, for they were put by for her when her mother died.'

'And is Mr Tilney, my partner, the only son?'

'I cannot be quite positive about that, my dear; I have some idea he is; but, however, he is a very fine young man Mrs Hughes says, and likely to do very well.'

Catherine inquired no further; she had heard enough to feel that Mrs Allen had no real intelligence to give, and that she was most particularly unfortunate herself in having missed such a meeting with both brother and sister. Could she have foreseen such a circumstance, nothing should have persuaded her to go out with the others; and, as it was, she could only lament her ill-luck, and think over what she had lost, till it was clear to her, that the drive had by no means been very pleasant and that John Thorpe himself was quite disagreeable.

Chapter 10

The Allens, Thorpes, and Morlands, all met in the evening at the theatre; and, as Catherine and Isabella sat together, there was then an opportunity for the latter to utter some few of the many thousand things which had been collecting within her for communication, in the immeasurable length of time which had divided them. – 'Oh, heavens! my beloved Catherine, have I got you at last?' was her address on Catherine's entering the box and sitting by her. 'Now, Mr Morland,' for he was close to her on the other side, 'I shall not speak another word to you all the rest of the evening; so I charge you not to expect it. My sweetest Catherine, how have you been this long age? but I need not ask you, for you look delightfully. You really have done your hair in a more heavenly style than ever: you mischievous creature, do you want to attract every body? I assure you, my brother is quite in love with you already; and as for Mr Tilney – but *that* is a settled thing – even *your* modesty cannot doubt his attachment now; his coming back to Bath makes it too plain. Oh! what would not I give to see him! I really am quite wild with impatience. My mother says he is the most delightful young man in the world; she saw him this morning you know: you must introduce him to me. Is he in the house now? – Look about for heaven's sake! I assure you, I can hardly exist till I see him.'

'No,' said Catherine, 'he is not here; I cannot see him any where.'

'Oh, horrid! am I never to be acquainted with him? How do you like my gown? I think it does not look amiss; the sleeves were entirely my own thought. Do you know I get so immoderately sick of Bath; your brother and I were agreeing this morning that, though it is vastly well to be here for a few weeks, we would not live here for millions. We soon found out that our tastes were exactly alike in preferring the country to every other place; really, our opinions were so exactly the same, it was quite ridiculous! There was not a single point in which we differed; I would not have had you by for the world; you are such a sly thing, I am sure you would have made some droll remark or other about it.'

'No, indeed I should not.'

'Oh, yes you would indeed; I know you better than you know yourself. You would have told us that we seemed born for each other, or some nonsense of that kind, which would have distressed me beyond concep-tion; my cheeks would have been as red as your roses; I would not have had you by for the world.'

'Indeed you do me injustice; I would not have made so improper a remark upon any account; and besides, I am sure it would never have entered my head.'

Isabella smiled incredulously, and talked the rest of the evening to James.

Catherine's resolution of endeavouring to meet Miss Tilney again continued in full force the next morning; and till the usual moment of going to the Pump-room, she felt some alarm from the dread of a second pre-vention. But nothing of that kind occurred, no visitors appeared to delay them, and they all three set off in good time for the Pump-room, where the ordinary course of events and conversation took place; Mr Allen, after drinking his glass of water, joined some gentlemen to talk over the politics of the day and compare the accounts of their newspapers; and the ladies walked about together, noticing every new face, and almost every new bonnet in the room. The female part of the Thorpe family, attended by James Morland, appeared among the crowd in less than a quarter of an hour, and Catherine immediately took her usual place by the side of her friend. James, who was now in constant attendance, maintained a similar position, and separating themselves from the rest of their party, they walked in that manner for some time, till Catherine began to doubt the happiness of a situation which confining her entirely to her friend and brother, gave her very little share in the notice of either. They were always engaged in some sentimental discussion or lively dispute, but their sentiment was conveyed in such whispering voices, and their vivacity attended with so much laughter, that though Catherine's supporting opinion was not unfrequently called for by one or the other, she was never able to give any, from not having heard a word of the subject. At length however she was empowered to disengage herself from her friend, by the avowed necessity of speaking to Miss Tilney, whom she most joyfully saw just entering the room with Mrs Hughes, and whom she instantly joined, with a firmer determination to be acquainted, than she might have had courage to command, had she not been urged by the disappointment of the day before. Miss Tilney met her with great civility, returned her advances with equal good will, and they continued talking together as long as both parties remained in the room; and though in all probability not an observation was made, nor an expression used by either which had not been made and used some thousands of times before, under that roof, in every Bath season, yet the merit of their being spoken with simplicity and truth, and without personal conceit, might be something uncommon. –

'How well your brother dances!' was an artless exclamation of Catherine's towards the close of their conversation, which at once surprized and amused her companion.

'Henry!' she replied with a smile. 'Yes, he does dance very well.'

'He must have thought it very odd to hear me say I was engaged the other evening, when he saw me sitting down. But I really had been engaged the whole day to Mr Thorpe.' Miss Tilney could only bow. 'You cannot think,' added Catherine after a moment's silence, 'how surprized I was to see him again. I felt so sure of his being quite gone away.'

'When Henry had the pleasure of seeing you before, he was in Bath but for a couple of days. He came only to engage lodgings for us.'

'*That* never occurred to me; and of course, not seeing him any where, I thought he must be gone. Was not the young lady he danced with on Monday a Miss Smith?'

'Yes, an acquaintance of Mrs Hughes.'

'I dare say she was very glad to dance. Do you think her pretty?'

'Not very.'

'He never comes to the Pump-room, I suppose?'

'Yes, sometimes; but he has rid out this morning with my father.'

Mrs Hughes now joined them, and asked Miss Tilney if she was ready to go. 'I hope I shall have the pleasure of seeing you again soon,' said Catherine. 'Shall you be at the cotillion ball to-morrow?'

'Perhaps we – yes, I think we certainly shall.'

'I am glad of it, for we shall all be there.' – This civility was duly returned; and they parted – on Miss Tilney's side with some knowledge of her new acquaintance's feelings, and on Catherine's, without the smallest consciousness of having explained them.

She went home very happy. The morning had answered all her hopes, and the evening of the following day was now the object of expectation, the future good. What gown and what head-dress she should wear on the occasion became her chief concern. She cannot be justified in it. Dress is at all times a frivolous distinction, and excessive solicitude about it often destroys its own aim. Catherine knew all this very well; her great aunt had read her a lecture on the subject only the Christmas before; and yet she lay awake ten minutes on Wednesday night debating between her spotted and her tamboured muslin, and nothing but the shortness of the time prevented her buying a new one for the evening. This would have been an error in judgment, great though not uncommon, from which one of the other sex rather than her own, a brother rather than a great aunt might have warned her, for man only can be aware of the insensibility of man towards a new gown. It would be mortifying to the feelings of many ladies, could they be made to understand how little the heart of man is affected by what is costly or new in their attire; how little it is biassed by the texture of their muslin, and how unsusceptible of peculiar tenderness towards the spotted, the sprigged, the mull or the jackonet. Woman is fine for her own satisfaction alone. No man will admire her the more, no woman will like her the better for it. Neatness and fashion are enough for the former, and a something of shabbiness or impropriety will be most endearing to the latter. – But not one of these grave reflections troubled the tranquillity of Catherine.

She entered the rooms on Thursday evening with feelings very different from what had attended her thither the Monday before. She had then been exulting in her engagement to Thorpe, and was now chiefly anxious to avoid his sight, lest he should engage her again; for though she could not, dared not expect that Mr Tilney should ask her a third time to dance, her wishes, hopes and plans all centered in nothing less. Every young lady may feel for my heroine in this critical moment, for every young lady has at some time or other known the same agitation. All have been, or at least all have believed themselves to be, in danger from the pursuit of some one whom they wished to avoid; and all have been anxious for the attentions of some one whom they wished to please. As soon as they were joined by the Thorpes, Catherine's agony began; she fidgetted about if John Thorpe came towards her, hid herself as much as possible from his view, and when he spoke to her pretended not to hear him. The cotillions were over, the country-dancing beginning, and she saw nothing of the Tilneys. 'Do not be frightened, my dear Catherine,' whispered Isabella, 'but I am really going to dance with your brother again. I declare positively it is quite shocking. I tell him he ought to be ashamed of himself, but you and John must keep us in countenance. Make haste, my dear creature, and come to us. John is just walked off, but he will be back in a moment.'

Catherine had neither time nor inclination to answer. The others walked away, John Thorpe was still in view, and she gave herself up for lost. That she might not appear, however, to observe or expect him, she kept her eyes intently fixed on her fan; and a self-condemnation for her folly, in supposing that among such a crowd they should even meet with the Tilneys in any reasonable time, had just passed through her mind, when she suddenly found herself addressed and again solicited to dance, by Mr Tilney himself. With what sparkling eyes and ready motion she granted his request, and with how pleasing a flutter of heart she went with him to the set, may be easily imagined. To escape, and, as she believed, so narrowly escape John Thorpe, and to be asked, so immediately on his joining her, asked by Mr Tilney, as if he had sought her on purpose! – it did not appear to her that life could supply any greater felicity.

Scarcely had they worked themselves into the quiet possession of a place, however, when her attention was claimed by John Thorpe, who stood behind her. 'Heyday, Miss Morland!' said he, 'what is the meaning of this? – I thought you and I were to dance together.'

'I wonder you should think so, for you never asked me.' 'That is a good one, by Jove! – I asked you as soon as I came into the room, and I was just going to ask you again, but when I turned round, you were gone! – this is a cursed shabby trick! I only came for the sake of dancing with *you*, and I firmly believe you were engaged to me ever since Monday. Yes; I remember, I asked you while you were waiting in the lobby for your cloak. And here have I been telling all my acquaintance that I was going to dance with the prettiest girl in the room; and when they see you standing up with somebody else, they will quiz me famously.'

'Oh, no; they will never think of *me*, after such a description as that.'

'By heavens, if they do not, I will kick them out of the room for blockheads. What chap have you there?' Catherine satisfied his curiosity. 'Tilney,' he repeated, 'Hum – I do not know him. A good figure of a man; well put together. – Does he want a horse? – Here is a friend of mine, Sam Fletcher, has got one to sell that would suit any body. A famous clever animal for the road – only forty guineas. I had fifty minds to buy it myself, for it is one of my maxims always to buy a good horse when I meet with one; but it would not answer my purpose, it would not do for the field. I would give any money for a real good hunter. I have three now, the best that ever were back'd. I would not take eight hundred guineas for them. Fletcher and I mean to get a house in Leicestershire, against the next season. It is so d – uncomfortable, living at an inn.'

This was the last sentence by which he could weary Catherine's attention, for he was just then born off by the resistless pressure of a long string of passing ladies. Her partner now drew near, and said, 'That gentleman would have put me out of patience, had he staid with you half a minute longer. He has no business to withdraw the attention of my partner from me. We have entered into a contract of mutual agreeableness for the space of an evening, and all our agreeableness belongs solely to each other for that time. Nobody can fasten themselves on the notice of one, without injuring the rights of the other. I consider a country-dance as an emblem of marriage. Fidelity and complaisance are the principal duties of both; and those men who do not chuse to dance or marry themselves, have no business with the partners or wives of their neighbours.'

'But they are such very different things! –'

' – That you think they cannot be compared together.'

'To be sure not. People that marry can never part, but must go and keep house together. People that dance, only stand opposite each other in a long room for half an hour.'

'And such is your definition of matrimony and dancing. Taken in that light certainly, their resemblance is not striking; but I think I could place them in such a view. – You will allow, that in both, man has the advantage of choice, woman only the power of refusal; that in both, it is an engagement between man and woman, formed for the advantage of each; and that when once entered into, they belong exclusively to each other till the moment of its dissolution; that it is their duty, each to endeavour to give the other no cause for wishing that he or she had bestowed themselves elsewhere, and their best interest to keep their own imaginations from wandering towards the perfections of their neighbours, or fancying that they should have been better off with any one else. You will allow all this?'

'Yes, to be sure, as you state it, all this sounds very well; but still they are so very different. – I cannot look upon them at all in the same light, nor think the same duties belong to them.'

'In one respect, there certainly is a difference. In marriage, the man is supposed to provide for the support of the woman; the woman to make the home agreeable to the man; he is to purvey, and she is to smile. But in dancing, their duties are exactly changed; the agreeableness, the compliance are expected from him, while she furnishes the fan and the lavender water. *That*, I suppose, was the difference of duties which struck you, as rendering the conditions incapable of comparison.'

'No, indeed, I never thought of that.'

'Then I am quite at a loss. One thing, however, I must observe. This disposition on your side is rather alarming. You totally disallow any similarity in the obligations; and may I not thence infer, that your notions of the duties of the dancing state are not so strict as your partner might wish? Have I not reason to fear, that if the gentleman who spoke to you just now were to return, or if any other gentleman were to address you, there would be nothing to restrain you from conversing with him as long as you chose?'

'Mr Thorpe is such a very particular friend of my brother's, that if he talks to me, I must talk to him again; but there are hardly three young men in the room besides him, that I have any acquaintance with.'

'And is that to be my only security? alas, alas!'

'Nay, I am sure you cannot have a better; for if I do not know any body, it is impossible for me to talk to them; and, besides, I do not *want* to talk to any body.'

'Now you have given me a security worth having; and I shall proceed with courage. Do you find Bath as agreeable as when I had the honour of making the inquiry before?'

'Yes, quite – more so, indeed.'

'More so! – Take care, or you will forget to be tired of it at the proper time. – You ought to be tired at the end of six weeks.'

'I do not think I should be tired, if I were to stay here six months.'

'Bath, compared with London, has little variety, and so every body finds out every year. "For six weeks, I allow Bath is pleasant enough; but beyond *that*, it is the most tiresome place in the world." You would be told so by people of all descriptions, who come regularly every winter, lengthen their six weeks into ten or twelve, and go away at last because they can afford to stay no longer.'

'Well, other people must judge for themselves, and those who go to London may think nothing of Bath. But I, who live in a small retired village in the country, can never find greater sameness in such a place as this, than in my own home; for here are a variety of amusements, a variety of things to be seen and done all day long, which I can know nothing of there.'

'You are not fond of the country.'

'Yes, I am. I have always lived there, and always been very happy. But certainly there is much more sameness in a country life than in a Bath life. One day in the country is exactly like another.'

'But then you spend your time so much more rationally in the country.'

'Do I?'

'Do you not?'

'I do not believe there is much difference.'

'Here you are in pursuit only of amusement all day long.'

'And so I am at home – only I do not find so much of it. I walk about here, and so I do there; – but here I see a variety of people in every street, and there I can only go and call on Mrs Allen.'

Mr Tilney was very much amused. 'Only go and call on Mrs Allen!' he repeated. 'What a picture of intellectual poverty! However, when you sink into this abyss again, you will have more to say. You will be able to talk of Bath, and of all that you did here.'

'Oh! yes. I shall never be in want of something to talk of again to Mrs Allen, or any body else. I really believe I shall always be talking of Bath, when I am at home again – I *do* like it so very much. If I could but have papa and mamma, and the rest of them here, I suppose I should be too happy! James's coming (my eldest brother) is quite delightful – and especially as it turns out, that the very family we are just got so intimate with, are his intimate friends already. Oh! who can ever be tired of Bath?'

'Not those who bring such fresh feelings of every sort to it, as you do. But papas and mammas, and brothers and intimate friends are a good deal gone by, to most of the frequenters of Bath – and the honest relish of balls and plays, and every-day sights, is past with them.'

Here their conversation closed; the demands of the dance becoming now too importunate for a divided attention.

Soon after their reaching the bottom of the set, Catherine perceived herself to be earnestly regarded by a gentleman who stood among the lookers-on, immediately behind her partner. He was a very handsome man, of a commanding aspect, past the bloom, but not past the vigour of life; and with his eye still directed towards her, she saw him presently address Mr Tilney in a familiar whisper. Confused by his notice, and blushing from the fear of its being excited by something wrong in her appearance, she turned away her head. But while she did so, the gentleman retreated, and her partner coming nearer, said, 'I see that you guess what I have just been asked. That gentleman knows your name, and you have a right to know his. It is General Tilney, my father.'

Catherine's answer was only 'Oh!' – but it was an 'Oh!' expressing every thing needful; attention to his words, and perfect reliance on their truth. With real interest and strong admiration did her eye now follow the General, as he moved through the crowd, and 'How handsome a family they are!' was her secret remark.

In chatting with Miss Tilney before the evening concluded, a new source of felicity arose to her. She had never taken a country walk since her arrival in Bath. Miss Tilney, to whom all the commonly-frequented environs were familiar, spoke of them in terms which made her all eagerness to know them too; and on her openly fearing that she might find nobody to go with her, it was proposed by the brother and sister that they should join in a walk, some morning or other. 'I shall like it,' she cried, 'beyond any thing in the world; and do not let us put it off – let us go to-morrow.' This was readily agreed to, with only a proviso of Miss Tilney's, that it did not rain, which Catherine was sure it would not. At twelve o'clock, they were to call for her in Pulteney-street – and 'remember – twelve o'clock,' was her parting speech to her new friend. Of her other, her older, her more established friend, Isabella, of whose fidelity and worth she had enjoyed a fortnight's experience, she scarcely saw any thing during the evening. Yet, though longing to make her acquainted with her happiness, she cheerfully submitted to the wish of Mr Allen, which took them rather early away, and her spirits danced within her, as she danced in her chair all the way home.

Chapter 11

The morrow brought a very sober looking morning; the sun making only a few efforts to appear; and Catherine augured from it, every thing most favourable to her wishes. A bright morning so early in the year, she allowed would generally turn to rain, but a cloudy one foretold improvement as the day advanced. She applied to Mr Allen for confirmation of her hopes, but Mr Allen not having his own skies and barometer about him, declined giving any absolute promise of sunshine. She applied to Mrs Allen, and Mrs Allen's opinion was more positive. 'She had no doubt in the world of its being a very fine day, if the clouds would only go off, and the sun keep out.'

At about eleven o'clock however, a few specks of small rain upon the windows caught Catherine's watchful eye, and 'Oh! dear, I do believe it will be wet,' broke from her in a most desponding tone.

'I thought how it would be,' said Mrs Allen.

'No walk for me to-day,' sighed Catherine; – 'but perhaps it may come to nothing, or it may hold up before twelve.'

'Perhaps it may, but then, my dear, it will be so dirty.'

'Oh! that will not signify; I never mind dirt.'

'No,' replied her friend very placidly, 'I know you never mind dirt.'

After a short pause, 'It comes on faster and faster!' said Catherine, as she stood watching at a window.

'So it does indeed. If it keeps raining, the streets will be very wet.'

'There are four umbrellas up already. How I hate the sight of an umbrella!'

'They are disagreeable things to carry. I would much rather take a chair at any time.'

'It was such a nice looking morning! I felt so convinced it would be dry!'

'Any body would have thought so indeed. There will be very few people in the Pump-room, if it rains all the morning. I hope Mr Allen will put on his great coat when he goes, but I dare say he will not, for he had rather do any thing in the world than walk out in a great coat; I wonder he should dislike it, it must be so comfortable.'

The rain continued – fast, though not heavy. Catherine went every five minuets to the clock, threatening on each return that, if it still kept on raining another five minutes, she would give up the matter as hopeless. The clock struck twelve, and it still rained. – 'You will not be able to go, my dear.'

'I do not quite despair yet. I shall not give it up till a quarter after twelve. This is just the time of day for it to clear up, and I do think it looks a little lighter. There, it is twenty minutes after twelve, and now I *shall* give it up entirely. Oh! that we had such weather here as they had at Udolpho, or at least in Tuscany and the South of France! – the night that poor St Aubin died! – such beautiful weather!'

At half past twelve, when Catherine's anxious attention to the weather was over, and she could no longer claim any merit from its amendment, the sky began voluntarily to clear. A gleam of sunshine took her quite by surprize; she looked round; the clouds were parting, and she instantly returned to the window to watch over and encourage the happy appearance. Ten minutes more made it certain that a bright afternoon would succeed, and justified the opinion of Mrs Allen, who had 'always thought it would clear up.' But whether Catherine might still expect her friends, whether there had not been too much rain for Miss Tilney to venture, must yet be a question.

It was too dirty for Mrs Allen to accompany her husband to the Pump-room; he accordingly set off by himself, and Catherine had barely watched him down the street, when her notice was claimed by the approach of the same two open carriages, containing the same three people that had surprized her so much a few mornings back.

'Isabella, my brother, and Mr Thorpe, I declare! They are coming for me perhaps – but I shall not go – I cannot go indeed, for you know Miss Tilney may still call.' Mrs Allen agreed to it. John Thorpe was soon with them, and his voice was with them yet sooner, for on the stairs he was calling out to Miss Morland to be quick. 'Make haste! make haste!' as he threw open the door – 'put on your hat this moment – there is no time to be lost – we are going to Bristol. – How d'ye do, Mrs Allen?'

'To Bristol! Is not that a great way off? – But, however, I cannot go with you to-day, because I am engaged; I expect some friends every moment.' This was of course vehemently talked down as no reason at all; Mrs Allen was called on to second him, and the two others walked in, to give their assistance. 'My sweetest Catherine, is not this delightful? We shall have a most heavenly drive. You are to thank your brother and me for the scheme; it darted into our heads at breakfast-time, I verily believe at the same instant; and we should have been off two hours ago if it had not been for this detestable rain. But it does not signify, the nights are moonlight, and we shall do delightfully. Oh! I am in such extasies at the thoughts of a little country air and quiet! – so much better than going to the Lower Rooms. We shall drive directly to Clifton and dine there; and, as soon as dinner is over, if there is time for it, go on to Kingsweston.'

'I doubt our being able to do so much,' said Morland.

'You croaking fellow!' cried Thorpe, 'we shall be able to do ten times more. Kingsweston! aye, and Blaize Castle too, and any thing else we can hear of; but here is your sister says she will not go.'

'Blaize Castle!' cried Catherine; 'what is that?'

'The finest place in England – worth going fifty miles at any time to see.'

'What, is it really a castle, an old castle?'

'The oldest in the kingdom.'

'But is it like what one reads of?'

'Exactly – the very same.'

'But now really – are there towers and long galleries?'

'By dozens.'

'Then I should like to see it; but I cannot – I cannot go.'

'Not go! – my beloved creature, what do you mean?'

'I cannot go, because' – (looking down as she spoke, fearful of Isabella's smile) 'I expect Miss Tilney and her brother to call on me to take a country walk. They promised to come at twelve, only it rained; but now, as it is so fine, I dare say they will be here soon.'

'Not they indeed,' cried Thorpe; 'for, as we turned into Broad-street, I saw them – does he not drive a phaeton with bright chesnuts?'

'I do not know indeed.'

'Yes, I know he does; I saw him. You are talking of the man you danced with last night, are not you?'

'Yes.'

'Well, I saw him at that moment turn up the Lans-down Road, – driving a smart-looking girl.'

'Did you indeed?'

'Did upon my soul; knew him again directly, and he seemed to have got some very pretty cattle too.'

'It is very odd! but I suppose they thought it would be too dirty for a walk.'

'And well they might, for I never saw so much dirt in my life. Walk! you could no more walk than you could fly! it has not been so dirty the whole winter; it is ancle-deep every where.'

Isabella corroborated it: – 'My dearest Catherine, you cannot form an idea of the dirt; come, you must go; you cannot refuse going now.'

'I should like to see the castle; but may we go all over it? may we go up every staircase, and into every suite of rooms?'

'Yes, yes, every hole and corner.'

'But then, – if they should only be gone out for an hour till it is drier, and call by and bye?'

'Make yourself easy, there is no danger of that, for

I heard Tilney hallooing to a man who was just passing by on horseback, that they were going as far as Wick Rocks.'

'Then I will. Shall I go, Mrs Allen?'

'Just as you please, my dear.'

'Mrs Allen, you must persuade her to go,' was the general cry. Mrs Allen was not inattentive to it: – 'Well, my dear,' said she, 'suppose you go.' – And in two minutes they were off.

Catherine's feelings, as she got into the carriage, were in a very unsettled state; divided between regret for the loss of one great pleasure, and the hope of soon enjoying another, almost its equal in degree, however unlike in kind. She could not think the Tilneys had acted quite well by her, in so readily giving up their engagement, without sending her any message of excuse. It was now but an hour later than the time fixed on for the beginning of their walk; and, in spite of what she had heard of the prodigious accumulation of dirt in the course of that hour, she could not from her own observation help thinking, that they might have gone with very little inconvenience. To feel herself slighted by them was very painful. On the other hand, the delight of exploring an edifice like Udolpho, as her fancy represented Blaize Castle to be, was such a counterpoise of good, as might console her for almost any thing.

They passed briskly down Pulteney-street, and through Laura-place, without the exchange of many words. Thorpe talked to his horse, and she meditated, by turns, on broken promises and broken arches, phae-tons and false hangings, Tilneys and trap-doors. As they entered Argyle-buildings, however, she was roused by this address from her companion, 'Who is that girl who looked at you so hard as she went by?'

'Who? – where?'

'On the right-hand pavement – she must be almost out of sight now.' Catherine looked round and saw Miss Tilney leaning on her brother's arm, walking slowly down the street. She saw them both looking back at her. 'Stop, stop, Mr Thorpe,' she impatiently cried, 'it is Miss Tilney; it is indeed. – How could you tell me they were gone? – Stop, stop, I will get out this moment and go to them.' But to what purpose did she speak? – Thorpe only lashed his horse into a brisker trot; the Tilneys, who had soon ceased to look after her, were in a moment out of sight round the corner of Laura-place, and in another moment she was herself whisked into the Market-place. Still, however, and during the length of another street, she intreated him to stop. 'Pray, pray stop, Mr Thorpe. – I cannot go on. – I will not go on. – I must go back to Miss Tilney.' But Mr Thorpe only laughed, smacked his whip, encouraged his horse, made odd noises, and drove on; and Catherine, angry and vexed as she was, having no power of getting away, was obliged to give up the point and submit. Her reproaches, however, were not spared. 'How could you deceive me so, Mr Thorpe? – How could you say, that you saw them driving up the Lansdown-road? – I would not have had it happen so for the world. – They must think it so strange; so rude of me! to go by them, too, without saying a word! You do not know how vexed I am – I shall have no pleasure at Clifton, nor in any thing else. I had rather, ten thousand times rather get out now, and walk back to them. How could you say, you saw them driving out in a phaeton?'

Thorpe defended himself very stoutly, declared he had never seen two men so much alike in his life, and would hardly give up the point of its having been Tilney himself.

Their drive, even when this subject was over, was not likely to be very agreeable. Catherine's complaisance was no longer what it had been in their former airing. She listened reluctantly, and her replies were short. Blaize Castle remained her only comfort; towards *that*, she still looked at intervals with pleasure; though rather than be disappointed of the promised walk, and especially rather than be thought ill of by the Tilneys, she would willingly have given up all the happiness which its walls could supply – the happiness of a progress through a long suite of lofty rooms, exhibiting the remains of magnificent furniture, though now for many years deserted – the happiness of being stopped in their way along narrow, winding vaults, by a low, grated door; or even of having their lamp, their only lamp, extinguished by a sudden gust of wind, and of being left in total darkness. In the meanwhile, they proceeded on their journey without any mischance; and were within view of the town of Keynsham, when a halloo from Morland, who was behind them, made his friend pull up, to know what was the matter. The others then came close enough for conversation, and Morland said, 'We had better go back, Thorpe; it is too late to go on to-day; your sister thinks so as well as I. We have been exactly an hour coming from Pulteney-street, very little more than seven miles; and, I suppose, we have at least eight more to go. It will never do. We set out a great deal too late. We had much better put it off till another day, and turn round.'

'It is all one to me,' replied Thorpe rather angrily; and instantly turning his horse, they were on their way back to Bath.

'If your brother had not got such a d—— beast to drive,' said he soon afterwards, 'we might have done it very well. My horse would have trotted to Clifton within the hour, if left to himself, and I have almost broke my arm with pulling him in to that cursed broken-winded jade's pace. Morland is a fool for not keeping a horse and gig of his own.'

'No, he is not,' said Catherine warmly, 'for I am sure he could not afford it.'

'And why cannot he afford it?'

'Because he has not money enough.'

'And whose fault is that?'

'Nobody's, that I know of.' Thorpe then said something in the loud, incoherent way to which he had often recourse, about its being a d—— thing to be miserly; and that if people who rolled in money could not afford things, he did not know who could; which Catherine did not even endeavour to understand. Disappointed of what was to have been the consolation for her first disappointment, she was less and less disposed either to be agreeable herself, or to find her companion so; and they returned to Pulteney-street without her speaking twenty words.

As she entered the house, the footman told her, that a gentleman and lady had called and inquired for her a few minutes after her setting off; that, when he told them she was gone out with Mr Thorpe, the lady had asked whether any message had been left for her; and on his saying no, had felt for a card, but said she had none about her, and went away. Pondering over these heart-rending tidings, Catherine walked slowly up stairs. At the head of them she was met by Mr Allen, who, on hearing the reason of their speedy return, said, 'I am glad your brother had so much sense; I am glad you are come back. It was a strange, wild scheme.'

They all spent the evening together at Thorpe's. Catherine was disturbed and out of spirits; but Isabella seemed to find a pool of commerce, in the fate of which she shared, by private partnership with Morland, a very good equivalent for the quiet and country air of an inn at Clifton. Her satisfaction, too, in not being at the Lower Rooms, was spoken more than once. 'How I pity the poor creatures that are going there! How glad I am that I am not amongst them! I wonder whether it will be a full ball or not! They have not begun dancing yet. I would not be there for all the world: It is so delightful to have an evening now and then to oneself. I dare say it will not be a very good ball. I know the Mitchells will not be there. I am sure I pity every body that is. But I dare say, Mr Morland, you long to be at it, do not you? I am sure you do. Well, pray do not let any body here be a restraint on you. I dare say we could do very well without you; but you men think yourselves of such consequence.'

Catherine could almost have accused Isabella of being wanting in tenderness towards herself and her sorrows; so very little did they appear to dwell on her mind, and so very inadequate was the comfort she offered. 'Do not be so dull, my dearest creature,' she whispered. 'You will quite break my heart. It was amazingly shocking to be sure; but the Tilneys were entirely to blame. Why were not they more punctual? It was dirty, indeed, but what did that signify? I am sure John and I should not have minded it. I never mind going through anything, where a friend is concerned; that is my disposition, and John is just the same; he has amazing strong feelings. Good heavens! what a delightful hand you have got! Kings, I vow! I never was so happy in my life! I would fifty times rather you should have them than myself.'

And now I may dismiss my heroine to the sleepless couch, which is the true heroine's portion; to a pillow strewed with thorns and wet with tears. And lucky may she think herself, if she get another good night's rest in the course of the next three months.

Chapter 12

'Mrs Allen,' said Catherine the next morning, 'will there be any harm in my calling on Miss Tilney today? I shall not be easy till I have explained every thing.'

'Go by all means, my dear; only put on a white gown; Miss Tilney always wears white.'

Catherine cheerfully complied; and being properly equipped, was more impatient than ever to be at the Pump-room, that she might inform herself of General Tilney's lodgings, for though she believed they were in Milsom-street, she was not certain of the house, and Mrs Allen's wavering convictions only made it more doubtful. To Milsom-street she was directed; and having made herself perfect in the number, hastened away with eager steps and a beating heart to pay her visit, explain her conduct, and be forgiven; tripping lightly through the church-yard, and resolutely turning away her eyes, that she might not be obliged to see her beloved Isabella and her dear family, who, she had reason to believe, were in a shop hard by. She reached the house without any impediment, looked at the number, knocked at the door, and inquired for Miss Tilney. The man believed Miss Tilney to be at home, but was not quite certain. Would she be pleased to send up her name? She gave her card. In a few minutes the servant returned, and with a look which did not quite confirm his words, said he had been mistaken, for that Miss Tilney was walked out. Catherine, with a blush of mortification, left the house. She felt almost persuaded that Miss Tilney *was* at home, and too much offended to admit her; and as she retired down the street, could not withhold one glance at the drawing-room windows, in expectation of seeing her there, but no one appeared at them. At the bottom of the street, however, she looked back again, and then, not at a window, but issuing from the door, she saw Miss Tilney herself. She was followed by a gentleman, whom Catherine believed to be her father, and they turned up towards Edgar's-buildings. Catherine, in deep mortification, proceeded on her way. She could almost be angry herself at such angry incivility; but she checked the resentful sensation; she remembered her own ignorance. She knew not how such an offence as her's might be classed by the laws of worldly politeness, to what a degree of unforgivingness it might with property lead, nor to what rigours of rudeness in return it might justly make her amenable.

Dejected and humbled, she had even some thoughts of not going with the others to the theatre that night; but it must be confessed that they were not of long continuance: for she soon recollected, in the first place, that she was without any excuse for staying at home; and, in the second, that it was a play she wanted very much to see. To the theatre accordingly they all went; no Tilneys appeared to plague or please her; she feared that, amongst the many perfections of the family, a fondness for plays was not to be ranked; but perhaps it was because they were habituated to the finer perform-ances of the London stage, which she knew, on Isabella's authority, rendered every thing else of the kind 'quite horrid.' She was not deceived in her own expectation of pleasure; the comedy so well suspended her care, that no one, observing her during the first four acts, would have supposed she had any wretchedness about her. On the beginning of the fifth, however, the sudden view of Mr Henry Tilney and his father, joining a party in the opposite box, recalled her to anxiety and distress. The stage could no longer excite genuine merriment – no longer keep her whole attention. Every other look upon an average was directed towards the opposite box; and, for the space of two entire scenes, did she thus watch Henry Tilney, without being once able to catch his eye. No longer could he be suspected of indifference for a play; his notice was never withdrawn from the stage during two whole scenes. At length, however, he did look towards her, and he bowed – but such a bow! no smile, no continued observance attended it; his eyes were immediately returned to their former direction. Catherine was restlessly miserable; she could almost have run round to the box in which he sat, and forced him to hear her explanation. Feelings rather natural than heroic possessed her; instead of considering her own dignity injured by this ready condemnation – instead of proudly resolving, in conscious innocence, to shew her resentment towards him who could harbour a doubt of it, to leave to him all the trouble of seeking an explanation, and to enlighten him on the past only by avoiding his sight, or flirting with somebody else, she took to herself all the shame of misconduct, or at least of its appearance, and was only eager for an opportunity of explaining its cause.

The play concluded – the curtain fell – Henry Tilney

was no longer to be seen where he had hitherto sat, but his father remained, and perhaps he might be now coming round to their box. She was right; in a few minutes he appeared, and, making his way through the then thinning rows, spoke with like calm politeness to Mrs Allen and her friend. – Not with such calmness was he answered by the latter: 'Oh! Mr Tilney, I have been quite wild to speak to you, and make my apologies. You must have thought me so rude; but indeed it was not my own fault, – was it, Mrs Allen? Did not they tell me that Mr Tilney and his sister were gone out in a phaeton together? and then what could I do? But I had ten thousand times rather have been with you; now had not I, Mrs Allen?'

'My dear, you tumble my gown,' was Mrs Allen's reply.

Her assurance, however, standing sole as it did, was not thrown away; it brought a more cordial, more natural smile into his countenance, and he replied in a tone which retained only a little affected reserve: – 'We were much obliged to you at any rate for wishing us a pleasant walk after our passing you in Argyle-street: you were so kind as to look back on purpose.'

'But indeed I did not wish you a pleasant walk; I never thought of such a thing; but I begged Mr Thorpe so earnestly to stop; I called out to him as soon as ever I saw you; now, Mrs Allen, did not – Oh! you were not there; but indeed I did; and, if Mr Thorpe would only have stopped, I would have jumped out and run after you.'

Is there a Henry in the world who could be insensible to such a declaration? Henry Tilney at least was not.

With a yet sweeter smile, he said every thing that need be said of his sister's concern, regret, and dependence on Catherine's honour. – 'Oh! do not say Miss Tilney was not angry,' cried Catherine, 'because I know she was; for she would not see me this morning when I called; I saw her walk out of the house the next minute after my leaving it; I was hurt, but I was not affronted. Perhaps you did not know I had been there.'

'I was not within at the time; but I heard of it from Eleanor, and she has been wishing ever since to see you, to explain the reason of such incivility; but perhaps I can do it as well. It was nothing more than that my father – they were just preparing to walk out, and he being hurried for time, and not caring to have it put off, made a point of her being denied. That was all, I do assure you. She was very much vexed, and meant to make her apology as soon as possible.'

Catherine's mind was greatly eased by this information, yet a something of solicitude remained, from which sprang the following question, thoroughly artless in itself, though rather distressing to the gentleman: – 'But, Mr Tilney, why were *you* less generous than your sister? If she felt such confidence in my good intentions, and could suppose it to be only a mistake, why should *you* be so ready to take offence?'

'Me! – I take offence!'

'Nay, I am sure by your look, when you came into the box, you were angry.'

'I angry! I could have no right.'

'Well, nobody would have thought you had no right who saw your face.' He replied by asking her to make room for him, and talking of the play.

He remained with them some time, and was only too agreeable for Catherine to be contented when he went away. Before they parted, however, it was agreed that the projected walk should be taken as soon as possible; and, setting aside the misery of his quitting their box, she was, upon the whole, left one of the happiest creatures in the world.

While talking to each other, she had observed with some surprize, that John Thorpe, who was never in the same part of the house for ten minutes together, was engaged in conversation with General Tilney; and she felt something more than surprize, when she thought she could perceive herself the object of their attention and discourse. What could they have to say of her? She feared General Tilney did not like her appearance: she found it was implied in his preventing her admittance to his daughter, rather than postpone his own walk a few minutes. 'How came Mr Thorpe to know your father?' was her anxious inquiry, as she pointed them out to her companion. He knew nothing about it; but his father, like every military man, had a very large acquaintance.

When the entertainment was over, Thorpe came to assist them in getting out. Catherine was the immediate object of his gallantry; and, while they waited in the lobby for a chair, he prevented the inquiry which had travelled from her heart almost to the tip of her tongue, by asking, in a consequential manner, whether she had seen him talking with General Tilney: – 'He is a fine old fellow, upon my soul! – stout, active – looks as young as his son. I have a great regard for him, I assure you: a gentleman-like, good sort of fellow as ever lived.'

'But how came you to know him?'

'Know him! – There are few people much about town that I do not know. I have met him for ever at the Bedford; and I knew his face again to-day the moment he came into the billiard-room. One of the best players we have, by the bye; and we had a little touch together, though I was almost afraid of him at first: the odds were five to four against me; and, if I had not made one of the cleanest strokes that perhaps ever was made in this world – I took his ball exactly – but I could not make you understand it without a table; – however I *did* beat him. A very fine fellow; as rich as a Jew. I should like to dine with him; I dare say he gives famous dinners. But what do you think we have been talking of? – You. Yes, by heavens! – and the General thinks you the finest girl in Bath.'

'Oh! nonsense! how can you say so?'

'And what do you think I said?' (lowering his voice) 'Well done, General, said I, I am quite of your mind.'

Here Catherine, who was much less gratified by his admiration than by General Tilney's, was not sorry to be called away by Mr Allen. Thorpe, however, would see her to her chair, and, till she entered it, continued the same kind of delicate flattery, in spite of her entreating him to have done.

That General Tilney, instead of disliking, should admire her, was very delightful; and she joyfully thought, that there was not one of the family whom she need now fear to meet. – The evening had done more, much more, for her, than could have been expected.

Chapter 13

Monday, Tuesday, Wednesday, Thursday, Friday and Saturday have now passed in review before the reader; the events of each day, its hopes and fears, mortifications and pleasures have been separately stated, and the pangs of Sunday only now remain to be described, and close the week. The Clifton scheme had been deferred, not relinquished, and on the afternoon's Crescent of this day, it was brought forward again. In a private consultation between Isabella and James, the former of whom had particularly set her heart upon going, and the latter no less anxiously placed his upon pleasing her, it was agreed that, provided the weather were fair, the party should take place on the following morning; and they were to set off very early, in order to be at home in good time. The affair thus determined, and Thorpe's approbation secured, Catherine only remained to be apprized of it. She had left them for a few minutes to speak to Miss Tilney. In that interval the plan was completed, and as soon as she came again, her agreement was demanded; but instead of the gay acquiescence expected by Isabella, Catherine looked grave, was very sorry, but could not go. The engagement which ought to have kept her from joining in the former attempt, would make it impossible for her to accompany them now. She had that moment settled with Miss Tilney to take their promised walk to-morrow; it was quite determined, and she would not, upon any account, retract. But that she *must* and *should* retract, was instantly the eager cry of both the Thorpes; they must go to Clifton to-morrow, they would not go without her, it would be nothing to put off a mere walk for one day longer, and they would not hear of a refusal. Catherine was distressed, but not subdued. 'Do not urge me, Isabella. I am engaged to Miss Tilney. I cannot go.' This availed nothing. The same arguments assailed her again; she must go, she should go, and they would not hear of a refusal. 'It would be so easy to tell Miss Tilney that you had just been reminded of a prior engagement, and must only beg to put off the walk till Tuesday.'

'No, it would not be easy. I could not do it. There has been no prior engagement.' But Isabella became only more and more urgent; calling on her in the most affectionate manner; addressing her by the most endearing names. She was sure her dearest, sweetest Catherine would not seriously refuse such a trifling request to a friend who loved her so dearly. She knew her beloved Catherine to have so feeling a heart, so sweet a temper, to be so easily persuaded by those she loved. But all in vain; Catherine felt herself to be in the right, and though pained by such tender, such flattering supplication, could not allow it to influence her. Isabella then tried another method. She reproached her with having more affection for Miss Tilney, though she had known her so little a while, than for her best and oldest friends; with being grown cold and indifferent, in short, towards herself. 'I cannot help being jealous, Catherine, when I see myself slighted for strangers, I, who love you so excessively! When once my affections are placed, it is not in the power of any thing to change them. But I believe my feelings are stronger than any body's; I am sure they are too strong for my own peace; and to see myself supplanted in your friendship by strangers, does cut me to the quick, I own. These Tilneys seem to swallow up every thing else.'

Catherine thought this reproach equally strange and unkind. Was it the part of a friend thus to expose her feelings to the notice of others? Isabella appeared to her ungenerous and selfish, regardless of every thing but her own gratification. These painful ideas crossed her mind, though she said nothing. Isabella, in the mean-while, had applied her handkerchief to her eyes; and Morland, miserable at such a sight, could not help saying, 'Nay, Catherine. I think you cannot stand out any longer now. The sacrifice is not much; and to oblige such a friend – I shall think you quite unkind, if you still refuse.'

This was the first time of her brother's openly siding against her, and anxious to avoid his displeasure, she proposed a compromise. If they would only put off their scheme till Tuesday, which they might easily do, as it depended only on themselves, she could go with them, and every body might then be satisfied. But 'No, no, no!' was the immediate answer; 'that could not be, for Thorpe did not know that he might not go to town on Tuesday.' Catherine was sorry, but could do no more; and a short silence ensued, which was broken by Isabella; who in a voice of cold resentment said, 'Very well, then there is an end of the party. If Catherine does not go, I cannot. I cannot be the only woman. I would not, upon any account in the world, do so improper a thing.'

'Catherine, you must go,' said James.

'But why cannot Mr Thorpe drive one of his other sisters? I dare say either of them would like to go.'

'Thank ye,' cried Thorpe, 'but I did not come to Bath to drive my sisters about, and look like a fool. No, if you do not go, d—— me if I do. I only go for the sake of driving you.'

'That is a compliment which gives me no pleasure.' But her words were lost on Thorpe, who had turned abruptly away.

The three others still continued together, walking in a most uncomfortable manner to poor Catherine; sometimes not a word was said, sometimes she was again attacked with supplications or reproaches, and her arm was still linked within Isabella's, though their hearts were at war. At one moment she was softened, at another irritated; always distressed, but always steady.

'I did not think you had been so obstinate, Catherine,' said James; 'you were not used to be so hard to persuade; you once were the kindest, best-tempered of my sisters.'

'I hope I am not less so now,' she replied, very feelingly; 'but indeed I cannot go. If I am wrong, I am doing what I believe to be right.'

'I suspect,' said Isabella, in a low voice, 'there is no great struggle.'

Catherine's heart swelled; she drew away her arm, and Isabella made no opposition. Thus passed a long ten minutes, till they were again joined by Thorpe, who coming to them with a gayer look, said, 'Well, I have settled the matter, and now we may all go to-morrow with a safe conscience. I have been to Miss Tilney, and made your excuses.'

'You have not!' cried Catherine.

'I have, upon my soul. Left her this moment. Told her you had sent me to say, that having just recollected a prior engagement of going to Clifton with us to-morrow, you could not have the pleasure of walking with her till Tuesday. She said very well, Tuesday was just as convenient to her; so there is an end of all our difficulties. – A pretty good thought of mine – hey?'

Isabella's countenance was once more all smiles and good-humour, and James too looked happy again.

'A most heavenly thought indeed! Now, my sweet Catherine, all our distresses are over; you are honourably acquitted, and we shall have a most delightful party.'

'This will not do,' said Catherine; 'I cannot submit to this. I must run after Miss Tilney directly and set her right.'

Isabella, however, caught hold of one hand; Thorpe of the other; and remonstrances poured in from all three. Even James was quite angry. When every thing was settled, when Miss Tilney herself said that Tuesday would suit her as well, it was quite ridiculous, quite absurd to make any further objection.

'I do not care. Mr Thorpe had no business to invent any such message. If I had thought it right to put it off, I could have spoken to Miss Tilney myself. This is only doing it in a ruder way; and how do I know that Mr Thorpe has——he may be mistaken again perhaps; he led me into one act of rudeness by his mistake on Friday. Let me go, Mr Thorpe; Isabella, do not hold me.'

Thorpe told her it would be in vain to go after the Tilneys; they were turning the corner into Brock-street, when he had overtaken them, and were at home by this time.

'Then I will go after them,' said Catherine; 'wherever they are I will go after them. It does not signify talking. If I could not be persuaded into doing what I thought wrong, I never will be tricked into it.' And with these words she broke away and hurried off. Thorpe would have darted after her, but Morland withheld him. 'Let her go, let her go, if she will go.'

'She is as obstinate as———'

Thorpe never finished the simile, for it could hardly have been a proper one.

Away walked Catherine in great agitation, as fast as the crowd would permit her, fearful of being pursued, yet determined to persevere. As she walked, she reflected on what had passed. It was painful to her to disappoint and displease them, particularly to displease her brother; but she could not repent her resistance. Setting her own inclination apart, to have failed a second time in her engagement to Miss Tilney, to have retracted a promise voluntarily made only five minutes before, and on a false pretence too, must have been wrong. She had not been withstanding them on selfish principles alone, she had not consulted merely her own gratification; *that* might have been ensured in some degree by the excursion itself, by seeing Blaize Castle; no, she had attended to what was due to others, and to her own character in their opinion. Her conviction of being right however was not enough to restore her composure, till she had spoken to Miss Tilney she could not be at ease; and quickening her pace when she got clear of the Crescent, she almost ran over the remaining ground till she gained the top of Milsom-street. So rapid had been her movements, that in spite of the Tilneys' advantage in the outset, they were but just turning into their lodgings as she came within view of them; and the servant still remaining at the open door, she used only the ceremony of saying that she must speak with Miss Tilney that moment, and hurrying by him proceeded up stairs. Then, opening the first door before her, which happened to be the right, she immediately found herself in the drawing-room with General Tilney, his son and daughter. Her explanation, defective only in being – from her irritation of nerves and shortness of breath – no explanation at all, was instantly given. 'I am come in a great hurry – It was all a mistake – I never promised to go – I told them from the first I could not go. – I ran away in a great hurry to explain it. – I did not care what you thought of me. – I would not stay for the servant.'

The business however, though not perfectly eluci-dated by this speech, soon ceased to be a puzzle. Cath-erine found that John Thorpe *had* given the message; and Miss Tilney had no scruple in owning herself greatly surprized by it. But whether her brother had still exceeded her in resentment, Catherine, though she instinctively addressed herself as much to one as to the other in her vindication, had no means of knowing. Whatever might have been felt before her arrival, her eager declarations immediately made every look and sentence as friendly as she could desire.

The affair thus happily settled, she was introduced by Miss Tilney to her father, and received by him with such ready, such solicitous politeness as recalled Thorpe's information to her mind, and made her think with plea-sure that he might be sometimes depended on. To such anxious attention was the general's civility carried, that not aware of her extraordinary swiftness in entering the house, he was quite angry with the servant whose neglect had reduced her to open the door of the apartment herself. 'What did William mean by it? He should make a point of inquiring into the matter.' And if Catherine had not most warmly asserted his innocence, it seemed likely that William would lose the favour of his master for ever, if not his place, by her rapidity.

After sitting with them a quarter of an hour, she rose to take leave, and was then most agreeably surprized by General Tilney's asking her if she would do his daughter the honour of dining and spending the rest of the day with her. Miss Tilney added her own wishes. Catherine was greatly obliged; but it was quite out of her power. Mr and Mrs Allen would expect her back every moment. The general declared he could say no more; the claims of Mr and Mrs Allen were not to be superseded; but on some other day he trusted, when longer notice could be given, they would not refuse to spare her to her friend. 'Oh, no; Catherine was sure they would not have the least objection, and she should have great pleasure in coming.' The general attended her himself to the street-door, saying every thing gallant as they went down stairs, admiring the elasticity of her walk, which corresponded exactly with the spirit of her dancing, and making her one of the most graceful bows she had ever beheld, when they parted.

Catherine, delighted by all that had passed, proceeded gaily to Pulteney-street; walking, as she concluded, with great elasticity, though she had never thought of it before. She reached home without seeing any thing more of the offended party; and now that she had been triumphant throughout, had carried her point and was secure of her walk, she began (as the flutter of her spirits subsided) to doubt whether she had been perfectly right. A sacrifice was always noble; and if she had given way to their entreaties, she should have been spared the distressing idea of a friend displeased, a brother angry, and a scheme of great happiness to both destroyed, perhaps through her means. To ease her mind, and ascertain by the opinion of an unprejudiced person what her own conduct had really been, she took occasion to mention before Mr Allen the half-settled scheme of her brother and the Thorpes for the following day. Mr Allen caught at it directly. 'Well,' said he, 'and do you think of going too?'

'No; I had just engaged myself to walk with Miss Tilney before they told me of it; and therefore you know I could not go with them, could I?'

'No, certainly not; and I am glad you do not think of it. These schemes are not at all the thing. Young men and women driving about the country in open carriages! Now and then it is very well; but going to inns and public places together! It is not right; and I wonder Mrs Thorpe should allow it. I am glad you do not think of going; I am sure Mrs Morland would not be pleased. Mrs Allen, are not you of my way of thinking? Do not you think these kind of projects objectionable?'

'Yes, very much so indeed. Open carriages are nasty things. A clean gown is not five minutes wear in them. You are splashed getting in and getting out; and the wind takes your hair and your bonnet in every direction. I hate an open carriage myself.'

'I know you do; but that is not the question. Do not

you think it has an odd appearance, if young ladies are frequently driven about in them by young men, to whom they are not even related?'

'Yes, my dear, a very odd appearance indeed. I cannot bear to see it.'

'Dear madam,' cried Catherine, 'then why did not you tell me so before? I am sure if I had known it to be improper, I would not have gone with Mr Thorpe at all; but I always hoped you would tell me, if you thought I was doing wrong.'

'And so I should, my dear, you may depend on it; for as I told Mrs Morland at parting, I would always do the best for you in my power. But one must not be over particular. Young people *will* be young people, as your good mother says herself. You know I wanted you, when we first came, not to buy that sprigged muslin, but you would. Young people do not like to be always thwarted.'

'But this was something of real consequence; and I do not think you would have found me hard to persuade.'

'As far as it has gone hitherto, there is no harm done,' said Mr Allen; 'and I would only advise you, my dear, not to go out with Mr Thorpe any more.'

'That is just what I was going to say,' added his wife.

Catherine, relieved for herself, felt uneasy for Isabella; and after a moment's thought, asked Mr Allen whether it would not be both proper and kind in her to write to Miss Thorpe, and explain the indecorum of which she must be as insensible as herself; for she considered that Isabella might otherwise perhaps be going to Clifton the next day, in spite of what had passed. Mr Allen however discouraged her from doing any such thing. 'You had better leave her alone, my dear, she is old enough to know what she is about; and if not, has a mother to advise her. Mrs Thorpe is too indulgent beyond a doubt; but however you had better not interfere. She and your brother chuse to go, and you will be only getting ill-will.'

Catherine submitted; and though sorry to think that Isabella should be doing wrong, felt greatly relieved by Mr Allen's approbation of her own conduct, and truly rejoiced to be preserved by his advice from the danger of falling into such an error herself. Her escape from being one of the party to Clifton was now an escape indeed; for what would the Tilneys have thought of her, if she had broken her promise to them in order to do what was wrong in itself? if she had been guilty of one breach of propriety, only to enable her to be guilty of another?

Chapter 14

The next morning was fair, and Catherine almost expected another attack from the assembled party. With Mr Allen to support her, she felt no dread of the event: but she would gladly be spared a contest, where victory itself was painful; and was heartily rejoiced therefore at neither seeing nor hearing any thing of them. The Tilneys called for her at the appointed time; and no new difficulty arising, no sudden recollection, no unexpected summons, no impertinent intrusion to disconcert their measures, my heroine was most unnaturally able to fulfil her engagement, though it was made with the hero himself. They determined on walking round Beechen Cliff, that noble hill, whose beautiful verdure and hanging coppice render it so striking an object from almost every opening in Bath.

'I never look at it,' said Catherine, as they walked along the side of the river, 'without thinking of the south of France.'

'You have been abroad then?' said Henry, a little surprized.

'Oh! no, I only mean what I have read about. It always puts me in mind of the country that Emily and her father travelled through, in the "Mysteries of Udolpho." But you never read novels, I dare say?'

'Why not?'

'Because they are not clever enough for you – gentlemen read better books.'

'The person, be it gentleman or lady, who has not pleasure in a good novel, must be intolerably stupid. I have read all Mrs Radcliffe's works, and most of them with great pleasure. The Mysteries of Udolpho, when I had once begun it, I could not lay down again; – I remember finishing it in two days – my hair standing on end the whole time.'

'Yes,' added Miss Tilney, 'and I remember that you undertook to read it aloud to me, and that when I was called away for only five minutes to answer a note, instead of waiting for me, you took the volume into the Hermitage-walk, and I was obliged to stay till you had finished it.'

'Thank you, Eleanor; – a most honourable testimony. You see, Miss Morland, the injustice of your suspicions. Here was I, in my eagerness to get on, refusing to wait only five minutes for my sister; breaking the promise I had made of reading it aloud, and keeping her in suspense at a most interesting part, by running away with the volume, which, you are to observe, was her own, particularly her own. I am proud when I reflect on it, and I think it must establish me in your good opinion.'

'I am very glad to hear it indeed, and now I shall never be ashamed of liking Udolpho myself. But I really thought before, young men despised novels amazingly.'

'It is *amazingly*; it may well suggest *amazement* if they do – for they read nearly as many as women. I myself have read hundreds and hundreds. Do not imagine that you can cope with me in a knowledge of Julias and Louisas. If we proceed to particulars, and engage in the never-ceasing inquiry of "Have you read this?" and "Have you read that?" I shall soon leave you as far behind me as – what shall I say? – I want an appropriate simile; – as far as your friend Emily herself left poor Valancourt when she went with her aunt into Italy. Consider how many years I have had the start of you. I had entered on my studies at Oxford, while you were a good little girl working your sampler at home!'

'Not very good I am afraid. But now really, do not you think Udolpho the nicest book in the world?'

'The nicest; – by which I suppose you mean the neatest. That must depend upon the binding.'

'Henry,' said Miss Tilney, 'you are very impertinent. Miss Morland, he is treating you exactly as he does his sister. He is for ever finding fault with me, for some incorrectness of language, and now he is taking the same liberty with you. The word "nicest," as you used it, did not suit him; and you had better change it as soon as you can, or we shall be overpowered with Johnson and Blair all the rest of the way.'

'I am sure,' cried Catherine, 'I did not mean to say any thing wrong; but it *is* a nice book, and why should not I call it so?'

'Very true,' said Henry, 'and this is a very nice day, and we are taking a very nice walk, and you are two very nice young ladies. Oh! it is a very nice word indeed! – it does for every thing. Originally perhaps it was applied only to express neatness, propriety, delicacy, or refinement; – people were nice in their dress, in their sentiments, or their choice. But now every commendation on every subject is comprised in that one word.'

'While, in fact,' cried his sister, 'it ought only to be applied to you, without any commendation at all. You are more nice than wise. Come, Miss Morland, let us leave him to meditate over our faults in the utmost propriety of diction, while we praise Udolpho in whatever terms we like best. It is a most interesting work. You are fond of that kind of reading?'

'To say the truth, I do not much like any other.'

'Indeed!'

'That is, I can read poetry and plays, and things of that sort, and do not dislike travels. But history, real solemn history, I cannot be interested in. Can you?'

'Yes, I am fond of history.'

'I wish I were too. I read it a little as a duty, but it tells me nothing that does not either vex or weary me. The quarrels of popes and kings, with wars or pestilences, in every page; the men all so good for nothing, and hardly any women at all – it is very tiresome: and yet I often think it odd that it should be so dull, for a great deal of it must be invention. The speeches that are put into the heroes' mouths, their thoughts and designs – the chief of all this must be invention, and invention is what delights me in other books.'

'Historians, you think,' said Miss Tilney, 'are not happy in their flights of fancy. They display imagination without raising interest. I am fond of history – and am very well contented to take the false with the true. In the principal facts they have sources of intelligence in former histories and records, which may be as much depended on, I conclude, as any thing that does not actually pass under one's own observation; and as for the little embellishments you speak of, they are embellishments, and I like them as such. If a speech be well drawn up, I read it with pleasure, by whomsoever it may be made – and probably with much greater, if the production of Mr Hume or Mr Robertson, than if the genuine words of Caractacus, Agricola, or Alfred the Great.'

'You are fond of history! – and so are Mr Allen and my father; and I have two brothers who do not dislike it. So many instances within my small circle of friends is remarkable! At this rate, I shall not pity the writers of history any longer. If people like to read their books, it is all very well, but to be at so much trouble in filling great volumes, which, as I used to think, nobody would willingly ever look into, to be labouring only for the torment of little boys and girls, always struck me as a hard fate; and though I know it is all very right and necessary, I have often wondered at the person's courage that could sit down on purpose to do it.'

'That little boys and girls should be tormented,' said Henry, 'is what no one at all acquainted with human nature in a civilized state can deny; but in behalf of our most distinguished historians, I must observe, that they might well be offended at being supposed to have no higher aim; and that by their method and style, they are perfectly well qualified to torment readers of the most advanced reason and mature time of life. I use the verb "to torment," as I observed to be your own method, instead of "to instruct," supposing them to be now admitted as synonimous.'

'You think me foolish to call instruction a torment, but if you had been as much used as myself to hear poor little children first learning their letters and then learning to spell, if you had ever seen how stupid they can be for a whole morning together, and how tired my poor mother is at the end of it, as I am in the habit of seeing almost every day of my life at home, you would allow that to *torment* and to *instruct* might sometimes be used as synonimous words.'

'Very probably. But historians are not accountable for the difficulty of learning to read; and even you yourself, who do not altogether seem particularly friendly to very severe, very intense application, may perhaps be brought to acknowledge that it is very well worth while to be tormented for two or three years of one's life, for the sake of being able to read all the rest of it. Consider – if reading had not been taught, Mrs Radcliffe would have written in vain – or perhaps might not have written at all.'

Catherine assented – and a very warm panegyric from her on that lady's merits, closed the subject. – The Tilneys were soon engaged in another on which she had nothing to say. They were viewing the country with the eyes of persons accustomed to drawing, and decided on its capability of being formed into pictures, with all the eagerness of real taste. Here Catherine was quite lost. She knew nothing of drawing – nothing of taste: – and she listened to them with an attention which brought her little profit, for they talked in phrases which conveyed scarcely any idea to her. The little which she could understand however appeared to contradict the very few notions she had entertained on the matter before. It seemed as if a good view were no longer to be taken from the top of an high hill, and that a clear blue sky was no longer a proof of a fine day. She was heartily ashamed of her ignorance. A misplaced shame. Where people wish to attach, they should always be ignorant. To come with a well-informed mind, is to come with an inability of administering to the vanity of others, which a sensible person would always wish to avoid. A woman especially, if she have the misfortune of knowing any thing, should conceal it as well as she can.

The advantages of natural folly in a beautiful girl have been already set forth by the capital pen of a sister author; – and to her treatment of the subject I will only add in justice to men, that though to the larger and more trifling part of the sex, imbecility in females is a great enhancement of their personal charms, there is a portion of them too reasonable and too well informed themselves to desire any thing more in woman than ignorance. But Catherine did not know her own advantages – did not know that a good-looking girl, with an affectionate heart and a very ignorant mind, cannot fail of attracting a clever young man, unless circumstances are particularly untoward. In the present instance, she confessed and lamented her want of knowledge; declared that she would give any thing in the world to be able to draw; and a lecture on the picturesque immediately followed, in which his instructions were so clear that she soon began to see beauty in every thing admired by him, and her attention was so earnest, that he became perfectly satisfied of her having a great deal of natural taste. He talked of fore-grounds, distances, and second distances – side-screens and perspectives – lights and shades; – and Catherine was so hopeful a scholar, that when they gained the top of Beechen Cliff, she voluntarily rejected the whole city of Bath, as unworthy to make part of a landscape. Delighted with her progress, and fearful of wearying her with too much wisdom at once, Henry suffered the subject to decline, and by an easy transition from a piece of rocky fragment and the withered oak which he had placed near its summit, to oaks in general, to forests, the inclosure of them, waste lands, crown lands and government, he shortly found himself arrived at politics; and from politics, it was an easy step to silence. The general pause which succeeded his short disquisition on the state of the nation, was put an end to by Catherine, who, in rather a solemn tone of voice, uttered these words, 'I have heard that something very shocking indeed, will soon come out in London.'

Miss Tilney, to whom this was chiefly addressed, was startled, and hastily replied, 'Indeed! – and of what nature?'

'That I do not know, nor who is the author. I have only heard that it is to be more horrible than any thing we have met with yet.'

'Good heaven! – Where could you hear of such a thing?'

'A particular friend of mine had an account of it in a letter from London yesterday. It is to be uncommonly dreadful. I shall expect murder and every thing of the kind.'

'You speak with astonishing composure! But I hope your friend's accounts have been exaggerated; – and if such a design is known beforehand, proper measures will undoubtedly be taken by government to prevent its coming to effect.'

'Government,' said Henry, endeavouring not to smile, 'neither desires nor dares to interfere in such matters. There must be murder; and government cares not how much.'

The ladies stared. He laughed, and added, 'Come,

shall I make you understand each other, or leave you to puzzle out an explanation as you can? No – I will be noble. I will prove myself a man, no less by the generosity of my soul than the clearness of my head. I have no patience with such of my sex as disdain to let themselves sometimes down to the comprehension of yours. Perhaps the abilities of women are neither sound nor acute – neither vigorous nor keen. Perhaps they may want observation, discernment, judgment, fire, genius, and wit.'

'Miss Morland, do not mind what he says; – but have the goodness to satisfy me as to this dreadful riot.'

'Riot! – what riot?'

'My dear Eleanor, the riot is only in your own brain. The confusion there is scandalous. Miss Morland has been talking of nothing more dreadful than a new publication which is shortly to come out, in three duodecimo volumes, two hundred and seventy-six pages in each, with a frontispiece to the first, of two tombstones and a lantern – do you understand? – And you, Miss Morland – my stupid sister has mistaken all your clearest expressions. You talked of expected horrors in London – and instead of instantly conceiving, as any rational creature would have done, that such words could relate only to a circulating library, she immediately pictured to herself a mob of three thousand men assembling in St George's Fields; the Bank attacked, the Tower threatened, the streets of London flowing with blood, a detachment of the 12th Light Dragoons, (the hopes of the nation,) called up from Northampton to quell the insurgents, and the gallant Capt. Frederick Tilney, in the moment of charging at the head of his troop, knocked off his horse by a brickbat from an upper window. Forgive her stupidity. The fears of the sister have added to the weakness of the woman; but she is by no means a simpleton in general.'

Catherine looked grave. 'And now, Henry,' said Miss Tilney, 'that you have made us understand each other, you may as well make Miss Morland understand yourself – unless you mean to have her think you intolerably rude to your sister, and a great brute in your opinion of women in general. Miss Morland is not used to your odd ways.'

'I shall be most happy to make her better acquainted with them.'

'No doubt; – but that is no explanation of the present.'

'What am I to do?'

'You know what you ought to do. Clear your character handsomely before her. Tell her that you think very highly of the understanding of women.'

'Miss Morland, I think very highly of the understanding of all the women in the world – especially of those – whoever they may be – with whom I happen to be in company.'

'That is not enough. Be more serious.'

'Miss Morland, no one can think more highly of the understanding of women than I do. In my opinion, nature has given them so much, that they never find it necessary to use more than half.'

'We shall get nothing more serious from him now, Miss Morland. He is not in a sober mood. But I do assure you that he must be entirely misunderstood, if he can ever appear to say an unjust thing of any woman at all, or an unkind one of me.'

It was no effort to Catherine to believe that Henry Tilney could never be wrong. His manner might some-times surprize, but his meaning must always be just: – and what she did not understand, she was almost as ready to admire, as what she did. The whole walk was delightful, and though it ended too soon, its conclusion was delightful too; – her friends attended her into the house, and Miss Tilney, before they parted, addressing herself with respectful form, as much to Mrs Allen as to Catherine, petitioned for the pleasure of her company to dinner on the day after the next. No difficulty was made on Mrs Allen's side – and the only difficulty on Catherine's was in concealing the excess of her pleasure.

The morning had passed away so charmingly as to banish all her friendship and natural affection; for no thought of Isabella or James had crossed her during their walk. When the Tilneys were gone, she became amiable again, but she was amiable for some time to little effect; Mrs Allen had no intelligence to give that could relieve her anxiety, she had heard nothing of any of them. Towards the end of the morning however, Catherine having occasion for some indispensable yard of ribbon which must be bought without a moment's delay, walked out into the town, and in Bond-street overtook the second Miss Thorpe, as she was loitering towards Edgar's Buildings between two of the sweetest girls in the world, who had been her dear friends all the morning. From her, she soon learned that the party to Clifton had taken place. 'They set off at eight this morn-ing,' said Miss Anne, 'and I am sure I do not envy them their drive. I think you and I are very well off to be out of the scrape. – It must be the dullest thing in the world, for there is not a soul at Clifton at this time of year. Belle went with your brother, and John drove Maria.'

Catherine spoke the pleasure she really felt on hearing this part of the arrangement.

'Oh! yes,' rejoined the other, 'Maria is gone. She was quite wild to go. She thought it would be something very fine. I cannot say I admire her taste; and for my part I was determined from the first not to go, if they pressed me ever so much.'

Catherine, a little doubtful of this, could not help answering, 'I wish you could have gone too. It is a pity you could not all go.'

'Thank you; but it is quite a matter of indifference to me. Indeed, I would not have gone on any account. I was saying so to Emily and Sophia when you overtook us.'

Catherine was still unconvinced; but glad that Anne should have the friendship of an Emily and a Sophia to console her, she bade her adieu without much uneasiness, and returned home, pleased that the party had not been prevented by her refusing to join it, and very heartily wishing that it might be too pleasant to allow either James or Isabella to resent her resistance any longer.

Chapter 15

Early the next day, a note from Isabella, speaking peace and tenderness in every line, and entreating the immediate presence of her friend on a matter of the utmost importance, hastened Catherine, in the happiest state of confidence and curiosity, to Edgar's Buildings. – The two youngest Miss Thorpes were by themselves in the parlour; and, on Anne's quitting it to call her sister, Catherine took the opportunity of asking the other for some particulars of their yesterday's party. Maria desired no greater pleasure than to speak of it; and Catherine immediately learnt that it had been altogether the most delightful scheme in the world; that nobody could imagine how charming it had been, and that it had been more delightful than any body could conceive. Such was the information of the first five minutes; the second unfolded thus much in detail, – that they had driven directly to the York Hotel, ate some soup, and bespoke an early dinner, walked down to the Pump-room, tasted the water, and laid out some shillings in purses and spars; thence adjourned to eat ice at a pastry-cook's, and hurrying back to the Hotel, swallowed their dinner in haste, to prevent being in the dark; and then had a delightful drive back, only the moon was not up, and it rained a little, and Mr Morland's horse was so tired he could hardly get it along.

Catherine listened with heartfelt satisfaction. It

appeared that Blaize Castle had never been thought of; and, as for all the rest, there was nothing to regret for half an instant. – Maria's intelligence concluded with a tender effusion of pity for her sister Anne, whom she represented as insupportably cross, from being excluded the party.

'She will never forgive me, I am sure; but, you know, how could I help it? John would have me go, for he vowed he would not drive her, because she had such thick ancles. I dare say she will not be in good humour again this month; but I am determined I will not be cross; it is not a little matter that puts me out of temper.'

Isabella now entered the room with so eager a step, and a look of such happy importance, as engaged all her friend's notice. Maria was without ceremony sent away, and Isabella, embracing Catherine, thus began: – 'Yes, my dear Catherine, it is so indeed; your penetration has not deceived you. – Oh! that arch eye of yours! – It sees through every thing.'

Catherine replied only by a look of wondering ignorance.

'Nay, my beloved, sweetest friend,' continued the other, 'compose yourself. – I am amazingly agitated, as you perceive. Let us sit down and talk in comfort. Well, and so you guessed it the moment you had my note? – Sly creature! – Oh! my dear Catherine, you alone who know my heart can judge of my present happiness. Your brother is the most charming of men. I only wish I were more worthy of him. – But what will your excellent father and mother say? – Oh! heavens! when I think of them I am so agitated!'

Catherine's understanding began to awake: an idea of the truth suddenly darted into her mind; and, with the natural blush of so new an emotion, she cried out, 'Good heaven! – my dear Isabella, what do you mean? Can you – can you really be in love with James?'

This bold surmise, however, she soon learnt comprehended but half the fact. The anxious affection, which she was accused of having continually watched in Isabella's every look and action, had, in the course of their yesterday's party, received the delightful confession of an equal love. Her heart and faith were alike engaged to James. – Never had Catherine listened to any thing so full of interest, wonder, and joy. Her brother and her friend engaged! – New to such circumstances, the importance of it appeared unspeakably great, and she contemplated it as one of those grand events, of which the ordinary course of life can hardly afford a return. The strength of her feelings she could not express; the nature of them, however, contented her friend. The happiness of having such a sister was their first effusion, and the fair ladies mingled in embraces and tears of joy.

Delighting, however, as Catherine sincerely did in the prospect of the connexion, it must be acknowledged that Isabella far surpassed her in tender anticipations. – 'You will be so infinitely dearer to me, my Catherine, than either Anne or Maria: I feel that I shall be so much more attached to my dear Morland's family than to my own.'

This was a pitch of friendship beyond Catherine.

'You are so like your dear brother,' continued Isabella, 'that I quite doated on you the first moment I saw you. But so it always is with me; the first moment settles every thing. The very first day that Morland came to us last Christmas – the very first moment I beheld him – my heart was irrecoverably gone. I remember I wore my yellow gown, with my hair done up in braids; and when I came into the drawing-room, and John introduced him, I thought I never saw any body so handsome before.'

Here Catherine secretly acknowledged the power of love; for, though exceedingly fond of her brother, and partial to all his endowments, she had never in her life thought him handsome.

'I remember too, Miss Andrews drank tea with us that evening, and wore her puce-coloured sarsenet; and she looked so heavenly, that I thought your brother must certainly fall in love with her; I could not sleep a wink all night for thinking of it. Oh! Catherine, the many sleepless nights I have had on your brother's account! – I would not have you suffer half what I have done! I am grown wretchedly thin I know; but I will not pain you by describing my anxiety; you have seen enough of it. I feel that I have betrayed myself perpetually; – so unguarded in speaking of my partiality for the church! – But my secret I was always sure would be safe with *you*.'

Catherine felt that nothing could have been safer; but ashamed of an ignorance little expected, she dared no longer contest the point, nor refuse to have been as full of arch penetration and affectionate sympathy as Isabella chose to consider her. Her brother she found was preparing to set off with all speed to Fullerton, to make known his situation and ask consent; and here was a source of some real agitation to the mind of Isabella. Catherine endeavoured to persuade her, as she was herself persuaded, that her father and mother would never oppose their son's wishes. – 'It is impossible,' said she, 'for parents to be more kind, or more desirous of their children's happiness; I have no doubt of their consenting immediately.'

'Morland says exactly the same,' replied Isabella; 'and yet I dare not expect it; my fortune will be so small; they never can consent to it. Your brother, who might marry any body!'

Here Catherine again discerned the force of love.

'Indeed, Isabella, you are too humble. – The difference of fortune can be nothing to signify.'

'Oh! my sweet Catherine, in *your* generous heart I know it would signify nothing; but we must not expect such disinterestedness in many. As for myself, I am sure I only wish our situations were reversed. Had I the command of millions, were I mistress of the whole world, your brother would be my only choice.'

This charming sentiment, recommended as much by sense as novelty, gave Catherine a most pleasing remembrance of all the heroines of her acquaintance; and she thought her friend never looked more lovely than in uttering the grand idea. – 'I am sure they will consent,' was her frequent declaration; 'I am sure they will be delighted with you.'

'For my own part,' said Isabella, 'my wishes are so moderate, that the smallest income in nature would be enough for me. Where people are really attached, poverty itself is wealth: grandeur I detest: I would not settle in London for the universe. A cottage in some retired village would be extasy. There are some charming little villas about Richmond.'

'Richmond!' cried Catherine – 'You must settle near Fullerton. You must be near us.'

'I am sure I shall be miserable if we do not. If I can but be near *you*, I shall be satisfied. But this is idle talking! I will not allow myself to think of such things, till we have your father's answer. Morland says that by sending it to-night to Salisbury, we may have it to-morrow. – To-morrow? – I know I shall never have courage to open the letter. I know it will be the death of me.'

A reverie succeeded this conviction – and when Isabella spoke again, it was to resolve on the quality of her wedding-gown.

Their conference was put an end to by the anxious young lover himself, who came to breathe his parting sigh before he set off for Wiltshire. Catherine wished to congratulate him, but knew not what to say, and her eloquence was only in her eyes. From them however the eight parts of speech shone out most expressively, and James could combine them with ease. Impatient for the realization of all that he hoped at home, his adieus were not long; and they would have been yet shorter, had he not been frequently detained by the urgent entreaties of his fair one that he would go. Twice was he called almost from the door by her eagerness to have him gone. 'Indeed, Morland, I must drive you away. Consider how far you have to ride. I cannot bear to see you linger so. For Heaven's sake, waste no more time. There, go, go – I insisted on it.'

The two friends, with hearts now more united than ever, were inseparable for the day; and in schemes of sisterly happiness the hours flew along. Mrs Thorpe and her son, who were acquainted with every thing, and who seemed only to want Mr Morland's consent, to consider Isabella's engagement as the most fortunate circumstance imaginable for their family, were allowed to join their counsels, and add their quota of significant looks and mysterious expressions to fill up the measure of curiosity to be raised in the unprivileged younger sisters. To Catherine's simple feelings, this odd sort of reserve seemed neither kindly meant, nor consistently supported; and its unkindness she would hardly have forborn pointing out, had its inconsistency been less their friend; – but Anne and Maria soon set her heart at ease by the sagacity of their 'I know what;' and the evening was spent in a sort of war of wit, a display of family ingenuity; on one side in the mystery of an affected secret, on the other of undefined discovery, all equally acute.

Catherine was with her friend again the next day, endeavouring to support her spirits, and while away the many tedious hours before the delivery of the letters; a needful exertion, for as the time of reasonable expectation drew near, Isabella became more and more desponding, and before the letter arrived, had worked herself into a state of real distress. But when it did come, where could distress be found? 'I have had no difficulty in gaining the consent of my kind parents, and am promised that every thing in their power shall be done to forward my happiness,' were the first three lines, and in one moment all was joyful security. The brightest glow was instantly spread over Isabella's features, all care and anxiety seemed removed, her spirits became almost too high for control, and she called herself without scruple the happiest of mortals.

Mrs Thorpe, with tears of joy, embraced her daughter, her son, her visitor, and could have embraced half the inhabitants of Bath with satisfaction. Her heart was overflowing with tenderness. It was 'dear John,' and 'dear Catherine' at every word; – 'dear Anne and dear Maria' must immediately be made sharers in their felicity; and two 'dears' at once before the name of Isabella were not more than that beloved child had now well earned. John himself was no skulker in joy. He not only bestowed on Mr Morland the high commendation of being one of the finest fellows in the world, but swore off many sentences in his praise.

The letter, whence sprang all this felicity, was short, containing little more than this assurance of success; and every particular was deferred till James could write again. But for particulars Isabella could well afford to wait. The needful was comprised in Mr Morland's promise; his honour was pledged to make every thing easy; and by what means their income was to be formed, whether landed property were to be resigned, or funded money made over, was a matter in which her disinterested spirit took no concern. She knew enough to feel secure of an honourable and speedy establishment, and her imagination took a rapid flight over its attendant felicities. She saw herself at the end of a few weeks, the gaze and admiration of every new acquaintance at Fullerton, the envy of every valued old friend in Putney, with a carriage at her command, a new name on her tickets, and a brilliant exhibition of hoop rings on her finger.

When the contents of the letter were ascertained, John Thorpe, who had only waited its arrival to begin his journey to London, prepared to set off. 'Well, Miss Morland,' said he, on finding her alone in the parlour, 'I am come to bid you good bye.' Catherine wished him a good journey. Without appearing to hear her, he walked to the window, fidgeted about, hummed a tune, and seemed wholly self-occupied.

'Shall not you be late at Devizes?' said Catherine. He

made no answer; but after a minute's silence burst out with, 'A famous good thing this marrying scheme, upon my soul! A clever fancy of Morland's and Belle's. What do you think of it, Miss Morland? *I* say it is no bad notion.'

'I am sure I think it a very good one.'

'Do you? – that's honest, by heavens! I am glad you are no enemy to matrimony however. Did you ever hear the old song, "Going to one wedding brings on another?" I say, you will come to Belle's wedding, I hope.'

'Yes; I have promised your sister to be with her, if possible.'

'And then you know' – twisting himself about and forcing a foolish laugh – 'I say, then you know, we may try the truth of this same old song.'

'May we? – but I never sing. Well, I wish you a good journey. I dine with Miss Tilney to-day, and must now be going home.'

'Nay, but there is no such confounded hurry. – Who knows when we may be together again? – Not but that I shall be down again by the end of a fortnight, and a devilish long fortnight it will appear to me.'

'Then why do you stay away so long?' replied Catherine – finding that he waited for an answer.

'That is kind of you, however – kind and good-natured. – I shall not forget it in a hurry. – But you have more good-nature and all that, than any body living I believe. A monstrous deal of good-nature, and it is not only good-nature, but you have so much, so much of every thing; and then you have such – upon my soul I do not know any body like you.'

'Oh! dear, there are a great many people like me, I dare say, only a great deal better. Good morning to you.'

'But I say, Miss Morland, I shall come and pay my respects at Fullerton before it is long, if not disagreeable.'

'Pray do. – My father and mother will be very glad to see you.'

'And I hope – I hope, Miss Morland, *you* will not be sorry to see me.'

'Oh! dear, not at all. There are very few people I am sorry to see. Company is always cheerful.'

'That is just my way of thinking. Give me but a little cheerful company, let me only have the company of the people I love, let me only be where I like and with whom I like, and the devil take the rest, say I. – And I am heartily glad to hear you say the same. But I have a notion, Miss Morland, you and I think pretty much alike upon most matters.'

'Perhaps we may; but it is more than I ever thought of. And as to *most matters*, to say the truth, there are not many that I know my own mind about.'

'By Jove, no more do I. It is not my way to bother my brains with what does not concern me. My notion of things is simple enough. Let me only have the girl I like, say I, with a comfortable house over my head, and what care I for all the rest? Fortune is nothing. I am sure of a good income of my own; and if she had not a penny, why so much the better.'

'Very true. I think like you there. If there is a good fortune on one side, there can be no occasion for any on the other. No matter which has it, so that there is enough. I hate the idea of one great fortune looking out for another. And to marry for money I think the wickedest thing in existence. – Good day. – We shall be very glad to see you at Fullerton, whenever it is convenient.' And away she went. It was not in the power of all his gallantry to detain her longer. With such news to communicate, and such a visit to prepare for, her departure was not to be delayed by any thing in his nature to urge; and she hurried away, leaving him to the undivided consciousness of his own happy address, and her explicit encouragement.

The agitation which she had herself experienced on first learning her brother's engagement, made her expect to raise no inconsiderable emotion in Mr and Mrs Allen, by the communication of the wonderful event. How great was her disappointment! The important affair, which many words of preparation ushered in, had been foreseen by them both ever since her brother's arrival; and all that they felt on the occasion was comprehended in a wish for the young people's happiness, with a remark, on the gentleman's side, in favour of Isabella's beauty, and on the lady's, of her great good luck. It was to Catherine the most surprizing insensibility. The disclosure however of the great secret of James's going to Fullerton the day before, did raise some emotion in Mrs Allen. She could not listen to that with perfect calmness; but repeatedly regretted the necessity of its concealment, wished she could have known his intention, wished she could have seen him before he went, as she should certainly have troubled him with her best regards to his father and mother, and her kind compliments to all the Skinners.

END OF VOL. I

Volume II

Chapter 1

Catherine's expectations of pleasure from her visit in Milsom-street were so very high, that disappointment was inevitable; and accordingly, though she was most politely received by General Tilney, and kindly welcomed by his daughter, though Henry was at home, and no one else of the party, she found, on her return, without spending many hours in the examination of her feelings, that she had gone to her appointment preparing for happiness which it had not afforded. Instead of finding herself improved in acquaintance with Miss Tilney, from the intercourse of the day, she seemed hardly so intimate with her as before; instead of seeing Henry Tilney to greater advantage than ever, in the ease of a family party, he had never said so little, nor been so little agreeable; and, in spite of their father's great civilities to her – in spite of his thanks, invitations, and compliments – it had been a release to get away from him. It puzzled her to account for all this. It could not be General Tilney's fault. That he was perfectly agreeable and good-natured, and altogether a very charming man, did not admit of a doubt, for he was tall and handsome, and Henry's father. *He* could not be accountable for his children's want of spirits, or for her want of enjoyment in his company. The former she hoped at last might have been accidental, and the latter she could only attribute to her own stupidity. Isabella, on hearing the particulars of the visit, gave a different explanation: 'It was all pride, pride, insufferable haughtiness and pride! She had long suspected the family to be very high, and this made it certain. Such insolence of behaviour as Miss Tilney's she had never heard of in her life! Not to do the honours of her house with common good-breeding! – To behave to her guest with such superciliousness! – Hardly even to speak to her!'

'But it was not so bad as that, Isabella; there was no superciliousness; she was very civil.'

'Oh! don't defend her! And then the brother, he, who had appeared so attached to you! Good heavens! well, some people's feelings are incomprehensible. And so he hardly looked once at you the whole day?'

'I do not say so; but he did not seem in good spirits.'

'How contemptible! Of all things in the world inconstancy is my aversion. Let me entreat you never to think of him again, my dear Catherine; indeed he is unworthy of you.'

'Unworthy! I do not suppose he ever thinks of me.'

'That is exactly what I say; he never thinks of you. – Such fickleness! Oh! how different to your brother and to mine! I really believe John has the most constant heart.'

'But as for General Tilney, I assure you it would be impossible for any body to behave to me with greater civility and attention; it seemed to be his only care to entertain and make me happy.'

'Oh! I know no harm of him; I do not suspect him of pride. I believe he is a very gentleman-like man. John thinks very well of him, and John's judgment–'

'Well, I shall see how they behave to me this evening; we shall meet them at the rooms.'

'And must I go?'

'Do not you intend it? I thought it was all settled.'

'Nay, since you make such a point of it, I can refuse you nothing. But do not insist upon my being very agreeable, for my heart, you know, will be some forty miles off. And as for dancing, do not mention it I beg; *that* is quite out of the question. Charles Hodges will plague me to death I dare say; but I shall cut him very short. Ten to one but he guesses the reason, and that is exactly what I want to avoid, so I shall insist on his keeping his conjecture to himself.'

Isabella's opinion of the Tilneys did not influence her friend; she was sure there had been no insolence in the manners either of brother or sister; and she did not credit there being any pride in their hearts. The evening rewarded her confidence; she was met by one with the same kindness, and by the other with the same attention as heretofore: Miss Tilney took pains to be near her, and Henry asked her to dance.

Having heard the day before in Milsom-street, that their elder brother, Captain Tilney, was expected almost every hour, she was at no loss for the name of a very fashionable-looking, handsome young man, whom she had never seen before, and who now evidently belonged to their party. She looked at him with great admiration, and even supposed it possible, that some people might think him handsomer than his brother, though, in her eyes, his air was more assuming, and his countenance less prepossessing. His taste and manners were beyond a doubt decidedly inferior; for, within her hearing, he not only protested against every thought of dancing himself, but even laughed openly at Henry for finding it possible. From the latter circumstance it may be presumed, that, whatever might be our heroine's opinion of him, his admiration of her was not of a very dangerous kind; not likely to produce animosities between the brothers, nor persecutions to the lady. *He* cannot be the instigator of the three villains in horsemen's great coats, by whom she will hereafter be forced into a travelling-chaise and four, which will drive off with incredible speed. Catherine, meanwhile, undisturbed by presentiments of such an evil, or of any evil at all, except that of having but a short set to dance down, enjoyed her usual happiness with Henry Tilney, listening with sparkling eyes to every thing he said; and, in finding him irresistible, becoming so herself.

At the end of the first dance, Captain Tilney came towards them again, and, much to Catherine's dissatisfaction, pulled his brother away. They retired whispering together; and, though her delicate sensibility did not take immediate alarm, and lay it down as fact, that Captain Tilney must have heard some malevolent misrepresentation of her, which he now hastened to communicate to his brother, in the hope of separating them for ever, she could not have her partner conveyed from her sight without very uneasy sensations. Her suspense was of full five minutes' duration; and she was beginning to think it a very long quarter of an hour, when they both returned, and an explanation was given, by Henry's requesting to know, if she thought her friend, Miss Thorpe, would have any objection to dancing, as his brother would be most happy to be introduced to her. Catherine, without hesitation, replied, that she was very sure Miss Thorpe did not mean to dance at all. The cruel reply was passed on to the other, and he immediately walked away.

'Your brother will not mind it I know,' said she, 'because I heard him say before, that he hated dancing; but it was very good-natured in him to think of it. I suppose he saw Isabella sitting down, and fancied she might wish for a partner; but he is quite mistaken, for she would not dance upon any account in the world.'

Henry smiled, and said, 'How very little trouble it can give you to understand the motive of other people's actions.'

'Why? – What do you mean?'

'With you, it is not, How is such a one likely to be influenced? What is the inducement most likely to act upon such a person's feelings, age, situation, and probable habits of life considered? – but, how should *I* be influenced, what would be *my* inducement in acting so and so?'

'I do not understand you.'

'Then we are on very unequal terms, for I understand you perfectly well.'

'Me? – yes; I cannot speak well enough to be unintelligible.'

'Bravo! – an excellent satire on modern language.'

'But pray tell me what you mean.'

'Shall I indeed? – Do you really desire it? – But you are not aware of the consequences; it will involve you in a very cruel embarrassment, and certainly bring on a disagreement between us.'

'No, no; it shall not do either; I am not afraid.'

'Well then, I only meant that your attributing my

brother's wish of dancing with Miss Thorpe to good-nature alone, convinced me of your being superior in good-nature yourself to all the rest of the world.'

Catherine blushed and disclaimed, and the gentleman's predictions were verified. There was a something, however, in his words which repaid her for the pain of confusion; and that something occupied her mind so much, that she drew back for some time, forgetting to speak or to listen, and almost forgetting where she was; till, roused by the voice of Isabella, she looked up and saw her with Captain Tilney preparing to give them hands across.

Isabella shrugged her shoulders and smiled, the only explanation of this extraordinary change which could at that time be given; but as it was not quite enough for Catherine's comprehension, she spoke her astonishment in very plain terms to her partner.

'I cannot think how it could happen! Isabella was so determined not to dance.'

'And did Isabella never change her mind before?'

'Oh! but, because – and your brother! – After what you told him from me, how could he think of going to ask her?'

'I cannot take surprize to myself on that head. You bid me be surprized on your friend's account, and therefore I am; but as for my brother, his conduct in the business, I must own, has been no more than I believed him perfectly equal to. The fairness of your friend was an open attraction; her firmness, you know, could only be understood by yourself.'

'You are laughing; but, I assure you, Isabella is very firm in general.'

'It is as much as should be said of any one. To be always firm must be to be often obstinate. When properly to relax is the trial of judgment; and, without reference to my brother, I really think Miss Thorpe has by no means chosen ill in fixing on the present hour.'

The friends were not able to get together for any confidential discourse till all the dancing was over; but then, as they walked about the room arm in arm, Isabella thus explained herself: – 'I do not wonder at your surprize; and I am really fatigued to death. He is such a rattle! – Amusing enough, if my mind had been disengaged; but I would have given the world to sit still.'

'Then why did not you?'

'Oh! my dear! it would have looked so particular; and you know how I abhor doing that. I refused him as long as I possibly could, but he would take no denial. You have no idea how he pressed me. I begged him to excuse me, and get some other partner – but no, not he; after aspiring to my hand, there was nobody else in the room he could bear to think of; and it was not that he wanted merely to dance, he wanted to be with *me*. Oh! such nonsense! – I told him he had taken a very unlikely way to prevail upon me; for, of all things in the world, I hated fine speeches and compliments; – and so – and so then I found there would be no peace if I did not stand up. Besides, I thought Mrs Hughes, who introduced him, might take it ill if I did not: and your dear brother, I am sure he would have been miserable if I had sat down the whole evening. I am so glad it is over! My spirits are quite jaded with listening to his nonsense: and then, – being such a smart young fellow, I saw every eye was upon us.'

'He is very handsome indeed.'

'Handsome! – Yes, I suppose he may, I dare say people would admire him in general; but he is not at all in my style of beauty. I hate a florid complexion and dark eyes in a man. However, he is very well. Amazingly conceited, I am sure. I took him down several times you know in my way.'

When the young ladies next met, they had a far more interesting subject to discuss. James Morland's second letter was then received, and the kind intentions of his father fully explained. A living, of which Mr Morland was himself patron and incumbent, of about four hundred pounds yearly value, was to be resigned to his son as soon as he should be old enough to take it; no trifling deduction from the family income, no niggardly assignment to one of ten children. An estate of at least equal value, moreover, was assured as his future inheritance.

James expressed himself on the occasion with becoming gratitude; and the necessity of waiting between two and three years before they could marry, being, however unwelcome, no more than he had expected, was born by him without discontent. Catherine, whose expectations had been as unfixed as her ideas of her father's income, and whose judgment was now entirely led by her brother, felt equally well satisfied, and heartily congratulated Isabella on having every thing so pleasantly settled.

'It is very charming indeed,' said Isabella, with a grave face. 'Mr Morland has behaved vastly handsome indeed,' said the gentle Mrs Thorpe, looking anxiously at her daughter. 'I only wish I could do as much. One could not expect more from him you know. If he finds he *can* do more by and bye, I dare say he will, for I am sure he must be an excellent good hearted man. Four hundred is but a small income to begin on indeed, but your wishes, my dear Isabella, are so moderate, you do not consider how little you ever want, my dear.'

'It is not on my own account I wish for more; but I cannot bear to be the means of injuring my dear Morland, making him sit down upon an income hardly enough to find one in the common necessaries of life. For myself, it is nothing; I never think of myself.'

'I know you never do, my dear; and you will always find your reward in the affection it makes every body feel for you. There never was a young woman so beloved as you are by every body that knows you; and I dare say when Mr Morland sees you, my dear child – but do not let us distress our dear Catherine by talking of such things. Mr Morland has behaved so very handsome you know. I always heard he was a most excellent man; and you know, my dear, we are not to suppose but what, if you had had a suitable fortune, he would have come down with something more, for I am sure he must be a most liberal-minded man.'

'Nobody can think better of Mr Morland than I do, I am sure. But every body has their failing you know, and every body has a right to do what they like with their own money.' Catherine was hurt by these insinuations. 'I am very sure,' said she, 'that my father has promised to do as much as he can afford.'

Isabella recollected herself. 'As to that, my sweet Catherine, there cannot be a doubt, and you know me well enough to be sure that a much smaller income would satisfy me. It is not the want of more money that makes me just at present a little out of spirits; I hate money; and if our union could take place now upon only fifty pounds a year, I should not have a wish unsatisfied. Ah! my Catherine, you have found me out. There's the sting. The long, long, endless two years and half that are to pass before your brother can hold the living.'

'Yes, yes, my darling Isabella,' said Mrs Thorpe, 'we perfectly see into your heart. You have no disguise. We perfectly understand the present vexation; and every body must love you the better for such a noble honest affection.'

Catherine's uncomfortable feelings began to lessen. She endeavoured to believe that the delay of the marriage was the only source of Isabella's regret; and when she saw her at their next interview as cheerful and amiable as ever, endeavoured to forget that she had for a minute thought otherwise. James soon followed his letter, and was received with the most gratifying kindness.

Chapter 2

The Allens had now entered on the sixth week of their stay in Bath; and whether it should be the last, was for some time a question, to which Catherine listened with a beating heart. To have her acquaintance with the Tilneys end so soon, was an evil which nothing could counterbalance. Her whole happiness seemed at stake, while the affair was in suspense, and every thing secured when it was determined that the lodgings should be taken for another fortnight. What this additional fortnight was to produce to her beyond the pleasure of sometimes seeing Henry Tilney, made but a small part of Catherine's speculation. Once or twice indeed, since James's engagement had taught her what *could* be done, she had got so far as to indulge in a secret 'perhaps,' but in general the felicity of being with him for the present bounded her views: the present was now comprised in another three weeks, and her happiness being certain for that period, the rest of her life was at such a distance as to excite but little interest. In the course of the morning which saw this business arranged, she visited Miss Tilney, and poured forth her joyful feelings. It was doomed to be a day of trial. No sooner had she expressed her delight in Mr Allen's lengthened stay, than Miss Tilney told her of her father's having just determined upon quitting Bath by the end of another week. Here was a blow! The past suspense of the morning had been ease and quiet to the present disappointment. Catherine's countenance fell, and in a voice of most sincere concern she echoed Miss Tilney's concluding words, 'By the end of another week!'

'Yes, my father can seldom be prevailed on to give the waters what I think a fair trial. He has been disappointed of some friends' arrival whom he expected to meet here, and as he is now pretty well, is in a hurry to get home.'

'I am very sorry for it,' said Catherine dejectedly, 'if I had known this before –'

'Perhaps,' said Miss Tilney in an embarrassed manner, 'you would be so good – it would make me very happy if –'

The entrance of her father put a stop to the civility, which Catherine was beginning to hope might introduce a desire of their corresponding. After addressing her with his usual politeness, he turned to his daughter and said, 'Well, Eleanor, may I congratulate you on being successful in your application to your fair friend?'

'I was just beginning to make the request, sir, as you came in.'

'Well, proceed by all means. I know how much your heart is in it. My daughter, Miss Morland,' he continued, without leaving his daughter time to speak, 'has been forming a very bold wish. We leave Bath, as she has perhaps told you, on Saturday se'nnight. A letter from my steward tells me that my presence is wanted at home; and being disappointed in my hope of seeing the Marquis of Longtown and General Courteney here, some of my very old friends, there is nothing to detain me longer in Bath. And could we carry our selfish point with you, we should leave it without a single regret. Can you, in short, be prevailed on to quit this scene of public triumph and oblige your friend Eleanor with your company in Gloucestershire? I am almost ashamed to make the request, though its presumption would certainly appear greater to every creature in Bath than yourself. Modesty such as your's – but not for the world would I pain it by open praise. If you can be induced to honour us with a visit, you will make us happy beyond expression. 'Tis true, we can offer you nothing like the gaieties of this lively place; we can tempt you neither by amusement nor splendour, for our mode of living, as you see, is plain and unpretending; yet no endeavours shall be wanting on our side to make Northanger Abbey not wholly disagreeable.'

Northanger Abbey! – These were thrilling words, and wound up Catherine's feelings to the highest point of extasy. Her grateful and gratified heart could hardly restrain its expressions within the language of tolerable calmness. To receive so flattering an invitation! To have her company so warmly solicited! Every thing honourable and soothing, every present enjoyment, and every future hope was contained in it; and her acceptance, with only the saving clause of papa and mamma's approbation was eagerly given. – 'I will write home directly,' said she, 'and if they do not object, as I dare say they will not' –

General Tilney was not less sanguine, having already waited on her excellent friends in Pulteney-street, and obtained their sanction of his wishes. 'Since they can consent to part with you,' said he, 'we may expect philosophy from all the world.'

Miss Tilney was earnest, though gentle, in her secondary civilities, and the affair became in a few minutes as nearly settled, as this necessary reference to Fullerton would allow.

The circumstances of the morning had led Catherine's feelings through the varieties of suspense, security, and disappointment; but they were now safely lodged in perfect bliss; and with spirits elated to rapture, with Henry at her heart, and Northanger Abbey on her lips, she hurried home to write her letter. Mr and Mrs Morland, relying on the discretion of the friends to whom they had already entrusted their daughter, felt no doubt of the propriety of an acquaintance which had been formed under their eye, and sent therefore by return of post their ready consent to her visit in Gloucestershire. This indulgence, though not more than Catherine had hoped for, completed her conviction of being favoured beyond every other human creature, in friends and fortune, circumstance and chance. Every thing seemed to co-operate for her advantage. By the kindness of her first friends the Allens, she had been introduced into scenes, where pleasures of every kind had met her. Her feelings, her preferences had each known the happiness of a return. Wherever she felt attachment, she had been able to create it. The affection of Isabella was to be secured to her in a sister. The Tilneys, they, by whom above all, she desired to be favourably thought of, outstripped even her wishes in the flattering measures by which their intimacy was to be continued. She was to be their chosen visitor, she was to be for weeks under the same roof with the person whose society she mostly prized – and, in addition to all the rest, this roof was to be the roof of an abbey! – Her passion for ancient edifices was next in degree to her passion for Henry Tilney – and castles and abbies made usually the charm of those reveries which his image did not fill. To see and explore either the ramparts and keep of the one, or the cloisters of the other, had been for many weeks a darling wish, though to be more than the visitor of an hour, had seemed too nearly impossible for desire. And yet, this was to happen. With all the chances against her of house, hall, place, park, court, and cottage, Northanger turned up an abbey, and she was to be its inhabitant. Its long, damp passages, its narrow cells and ruined chapel, were to be within her daily reach, and she could not entirely subdue the hope of some traditional legends, some awful memorials of an injured and ill-fated nun.

It was wonderful that her friends should seem so little elated by the possession of such a home; that the consciousness of it should be so meekly born. The power of early habit only could account for it. A distinction to which they had been born gave no pride. Their superiority of abode was no more to them than their superiority of person.

Many were the inquiries she was eager to make of Miss Tilney; but so active were her thoughts, that when these inquiries were answered, she was hardly more assured than before, of Northanger Abbey having been a richly-endowed convent at the time of the Reformation, of its having fallen into the hands of an ancestor of the Tilneys on its dissolution, of a large portion of the ancient building still making a part of the present dwelling although the rest was decayed, or of its standing low in a valley, sheltered from the north and east by rising woods of oak.

Chapter 3

With a mind thus full of happiness, Catherine was hardly aware that two or three days had passed away, without her seeing Isabella for more than a few minutes together. She began first to be sensible of this, and to sigh for her conversation, as she walked along the Pump-room one morning, by Mrs Allen's side, without any thing to say or to hear; and scarcely had she felt a five minutes' longing of friendship, before the object of it appeared, and inviting her to a secret conference, led the way to a seat. 'This is my favourite place,' said she, as they sat down on a bench between the doors, which commanded a tolerable view of every body entering at either, 'it is so out of the way.'

Catherine, observing that Isabella's eyes were continually bent towards one door or the other, as in eager expectation, and remembering how often she had been falsely accused of being arch, thought the present a fine opportunity for being really so; and therefore gaily said, 'Do not be uneasy, Isabella. James will soon be here.'

'Psha! my dear creature,' she replied, 'do not think me such a simpleton as to be always wanting to confine him to my elbow. It would be hideous to be always together; we should be the jest of the place. And so you are going to Northanger! – I am amazingly glad of it. It is one of the finest old places in England, I understand. I shall depend upon a most particular description of it.'

'You shall certainly have the best in my power to give. But who are you looking for? Are your sisters coming?'

'I am not looking for any body. One's eyes must be somewhere, and you know what a foolish trick I have of fixing mine, when my thoughts are an hundred miles off. I am amazingly absent; I believe I am the most absent creature in the world. Tilney says it is always the case with minds of a certain stamp.'

'But I thought, Isabella, you had something in particular to tell me?'

'Oh! yes, and so I have. But here is a proof of what I was saying. My poor head! I had quite forgot it. Well, the thing is this, I have just had a letter from John; – you can guess the contents.'

'No, indeed, I cannot.'

'My sweet love, do not be so abominably affected. What can he write about, but yourself? You know he is over head and ears in love with you.'

'With *me*, dear Isabella!'

'Nay, my sweetest Catherine, this is being quite absurd! Modesty, and all that, is very well in its way, but really a little common honesty is sometimes quite as becoming. I have no idea of being so overstrained! It is fishing for compliments. His attentions were such as a child must have noticed. And it was but half an hour before he left Bath, that you gave him the most positive encouragement. He says so in this letter, says that he as good as made you an offer, and that you received his advances in the kindest way; and now he wants me to urge his suit, and say all manner of pretty things to you. So it is in vain to affect ignorance.'

Catherine, with all the earnestness of truth, expressed

her astonishment at such a charge, protesting her innocence of every thought of Mr Thorpe's being in love with her, and the consequent impossibility of her having ever intended to encourage him. 'As to any attentions on his side, I do declare, upon my honour, I never was sensible of them for a moment – except just his asking me to dance the first day of his coming. And as to making me an offer, or any thing like it, there must be some unaccountable mistake. I could not have misunderstood a thing of that kind, you know! – and, as I ever wish to be believed, I solemnly protest that no syllable of such a nature ever passed between us. The last half hour before he went away! – It must be all and completely a mistake – for I did not see him once that whole morning.'

'But *that* you certainly did, for you spent the whole morning in Edgar's Buildings – it was the day your father's consent came – and I am pretty sure that you and John were alone in the parlour, some time before you left the house.'

'Are you? – Well, if you say it, it was so, I dare say – but for the life of me, I cannot recollect it. – I *do* remember now being with you, and seeing him as well as the rest – but that we were ever alone for five minutes – However, it is not worth arguing about, for whatever might pass on his side, you must be convinced, by my having no recollection of it, that I never thought, nor expected, nor wished for any thing of the kind from him. I am excessively concerned that he should have any regard for me – but indeed it has been quite unintentional on my side, I never had the smallest idea of it. Pray undeceive him as soon as you can, and tell him I beg his pardon – that is – I do not know what I ought to say –

but make him understand what I mean, in the properest way. I would not speak disrespectfully of a brother of your's, Isabella, I am sure; but you know very well that if I could think of one man more than another – *he* is not the person.' Isabella was silent. 'My dear friend, you must not be angry with me. I cannot suppose your brother cares so very much about me. And, you know, we shall still be sisters.'

'Yes, yes,' (with a blush) 'there are more ways than one of our being sisters. – But where am I wandering to? – Well, my dear Catherine, the case seems to be, that you are determined against poor John – is not it so?'

'I certainly cannot return his affection, and as certainly never meant to encourage it.'

'Since that is the case, I am sure I shall not tease you any further. John desired me to speak to you on the subject, and therefore I have. But I confess, as soon as I read his letter, I thought it a very foolish, imprudent business, and not likely to promote the good of either; for what were you to live upon, supposing you came together? You have both of you something to be sure, but it is not a trifle that will support a family now-a-days; and after all that romancers may say, there is no doing without money. I only wonder John could think of it; he could not have received my last.'

'You *do* acquit me then of any thing wrong? – You are convinced that I never meant to deceive your brother, never suspected him of liking me till this moment?'

'Oh! as to that,' answered Isabella laughingly, 'I do not pretend to determine what your thoughts and designs in time past may have been. All that is best known to yourself. A little harmless flirtation or so will occur, and one is often drawn on to give more encouragement than one wishes to stand by. But you may be assured that I am the last person in the world to judge you severely. All those things should be allowed for in youth and high spirits. What one means one day, you know, one may not mean the next. Circumstances change, opinions alter.'

'But my opinion of your brother never did alter; it was always the same. You are describing what never happened.'

'My dearest Catherine,' continued the other without at all listening to her, 'I would not for all the world be the means of hurrying you into an engagement before you knew what you were about. I do not think any thing would justify me in wishing you to sacrifice all your happiness merely to oblige my brother, because he is my brother, and who perhaps after all, you know, might be just as happy without you, for people seldom know what they would be at, young men especially, they are so amazingly changeable and inconstant. What I say is, why should a brother's happiness be dearer to me than a friend's? You know I carry my notions of friendship pretty high. But, above all things, my dear Catherine, do not be in a hurry. Take my word for it, that if you are in too great a hurry, you will certainly live to repent it. Tilney says, there is nothing people are so often deceived in, as the state of their own affections, and I believe he is very right. Ah! here he comes; never mind, he will not see us, I am sure.'

Catherine, looking up, perceived Captain Tilney; and Isabella, earnestly fixing her eye on him as she spoke, soon caught his notice. He approached immediately, and took the seat to which her movements invited him. His first address made Catherine start. Though spoken low, she could distinguish, 'What! always to be watched, in person or by proxy!'

'Psha, nonsense!' was Isabella's answer in the same half whisper. 'Why do you put such things into my head? If I could believe it – my spirit, you know, is pretty independent.'

'I wish your heart were independent. That would be enough for me.'

'My heart, indeed! What can you have to do with hearts? You men have none of you any hearts.'

'If we have not hearts, we have eyes; and they give us torment enough.'

'Do they? I am sorry for it; I am sorry they find any thing so disagreeable in me. I will look another way. I hope this pleases you, (turning her back on him,) I hope your eyes are not tormented now.'

'Never more so; for the edge of a blooming cheek is still in view – at once too much and too little.'

Catherine heard all this, and quite out of countenance could listen no longer. Amazed that Isabella could endure it, and jealous for her brother, she rose up, and saying she should join Mrs Allen, proposed their walking. But for this Isabella shewed no inclination. She was so amazingly tired, and it was so odious to parade about the Pump-room; and if she moved from her seat she should miss her sisters, she was expecting her sisters every moment; so that her dearest Catherine must excuse her, and must sit quietly down again. But Catherine could be stubborn too; and Mrs Allen just then coming up to propose their returning home, she joined her and walked out of the Pump-room, leaving Isabella still sitting with

Captain Tilney. With much uneasiness did she thus leave them. It seemed to her that Captain Tilney was falling in love with Isabella, and Isabella unconsciously encouraging him; unconsciously it must be, for Isabella's attachment to James was as certain and well acknowledged as her engagement. To doubt her truth or good intentions was impossible; and yet, during the whole of their conversation her manner had been odd. She wished Isabella had talked more like her usual self, and not so much about money; and had not looked so well pleased at the sight of Captain Tilney. How strange that she should not perceive his admiration! Catherine longed to give her a hint of it, to put her on her guard, and prevent all the pain which her too lively behaviour might otherwise create both for him and her brother.

The compliment of John Thorpe's affection did not make amends for this thoughtlessness in his sister. She was almost as far from believing as from wishing it to be sincere; for she had not forgotten that he could mistake, and his assertion of the offer and of her encouragement convinced her that his mistakes could sometimes be very egregious. In vanity therefore she gained but little, her chief profit was in wonder. That he should think it worth his while to fancy himself in love with her, was a matter of lively astonishment. Isabella talked of his attentions; *she* had never been sensible of any; but Isabella had said many things which she hoped had been spoken in haste, and would never be said again; and upon this she was glad to rest altogether for present ease and comfort.

Chapter 4

A few days passed away, and Catherine, though not allowing herself to suspect her friend, could not help watching her closely. The result of her observations was not agreeable. Isabella seemed an altered creature. When she saw her indeed surrounded only by their immediate friends in Edgar's Buildings or Pulteney-street, her change of manners was so trifling that, had it gone no farther, it might have passed unnoticed. A something of languid indifference, or of that boasted absence of mind which Catherine had never heard of before, would occasionally come across her; but had nothing worse appeared, *that* might only have spread a new grace and inspired a warmer interest. But when Catherine saw her in public, admitting Captain Tilney's attentions as readily as they were offered, and allowing him almost an equal share with James in her notice and smiles, the alteration became too positive to be past over. What could be meant by such unsteady conduct, what her friend could be at, was beyond her comprehension. Isabella could not be aware of the pain she was inflicting; but it was a degree of wilful thoughtlessness which Catherine could not but resent. James was the sufferer. She saw him grave and uneasy; and however careless of his present comfort the woman might be who had given him her heart, to *her* it was always an object. For poor Captain Tilney too she was greatly concerned. Though his looks did not please her, his name was a passport to her good will, and she thought with sincere compassion of his approaching disappointment; for, in spite of what she had believed herself to overhear in the Pump-room, his behaviour was so incompatible with a knowledge of Isabella's engagement, that she could not, upon reflection, imagine him aware of it. He might be jealous of her brother as a rival, but if more had seemed implied, the fault must have been in her misapprehension. She wished, by a gentle remonstrance, to remind Isabella of her situation, and make her aware of this double unkindness; but for remonstrance, either opportunity or comprehension was always against her. If able to suggest a hint, Isabella could never understand it. In this distress, the intended departure of the Tilney family became her chief consolation; their journey into Gloucestershire was to take place within a few days, and Captain Tilney's removal would at least restore peace to every heart but his own. But Captain Tilney had at present no intention of removing; he was not to be of the party to Northanger, he was to continue at Bath. When Catherine knew this, her resolution was directly made. She spoke to Henry Tilney on the subject, regretting his brother's evident partiality for Miss Thorpe, and entreating him to make known her prior engagement.

'My brother does know it,' was Henry's answer.

'Does he? – then why does he stay here?'

He made no reply, and was beginning to talk of something else; but she eagerly continued, 'Why do not you persuade him to go away? The longer he stays, the worse it will be for him at last. Pray advise him for his own sake, and for every body's sake, to leave Bath directly. Absence will in time make him comfortable again; but he can have no hope here, and it is only staying to be miserable.' Henry smiled and said, 'I am sure my brother would not wish to do that.'

'Then you will persuade him to go away?'

'Persuasion is not at command; but pardon me, if I cannot even endeavour to persuade him. I have myself told him that Miss Thorpe is engaged. He knows what he is about, and must be his own master.'

'No, he does not know what he is about,' cried Catherine; 'he does not know the pain he is giving my brother. Not that James has ever told me so, but I am sure he is very uncomfortable.'

'And are you sure it is my brother's doing?'

'Yes, very sure.'

'Is it my brother's attentions to Miss Thorpe, or Miss Thorpe's admission of them, that gives the pain?'

'Is not it the same thing?'

'I think Mr Morland would acknowledge a difference. No man is offended by another man's admiration of the woman he loves; it is the woman only who can make it a torment.'

Catherine blushed for her friend, and said, 'Isabella is wrong. But I am sure she cannot mean to torment, for she is very much attached to my brother. She has been in love with him ever since they first met, and while my father's consent was uncertain, she fretted herself almost into a fever. You know she must be attached to him.'

'I understand: she is in love with James, and flirts with Frederick.'

'Oh! no, not flirts. A woman in love with one man cannot flirt with another.'

'It is probable that she will neither love so well, nor flirt so well, as she might do either singly. The gentlemen must each give up a little.'

After a short pause, Catherine resumed with 'Then you do not believe Isabella so very much attached to my brother?'

'I can have no opinion on that subject.'

'But what can your brother mean? If he knows her engagement, what can he mean by his behaviour?'

'You are a very close questioner.'

'Am I? – I only ask what I want to be told.'

'But do you only ask what I can be expected to tell?'

'Yes, I think so; for you must know your brother's heart.'

'My brother's heart, as you term it, on the present occasion, I assure you I can only guess at.'

'Well?'

'Well! – Nay, if it is to be guess-work, let us all guess for ourselves. To be guided by second-hand conjecture is pitiful. The premises are before you. My brother is a lively, and perhaps sometimes a thoughtless young man; he has had about a week's acquaintance with your friend, and he has known her engagement almost as long as he has known her.'

'Well,' said Catherine, after some moments' consideration, '*you* may be able to guess at your brother's intentions from all this; but I am sure I cannot. But is not your father uncomfortable about it? – Does not he want Captain Tilney to go away? – Sure, if your father were to speak to him, he would go.'

'My dear Miss Morland,' said Henry, 'in this amiable solicitude for your brother's comfort, may you not be a little mistaken? Are you not carried a little too far? Would he thank you, either on his own account or Miss Thorpe's, for supposing that her affection, or at least her good-behaviour, is only to be secured by her seeing nothing of Captain Tilney? Is he safe only in solitude? – or, is her heart constant to him only when unsolicited by any one else? – He cannot think this – and you may be sure that he would not have you think it. I will not say, "Do not be uneasy," because I know that you are so, at this moment; but be as little uneasy as you can. You have no doubt of the mutual attachment of your brother and your friend; depend upon it therefore, that real jealousy never can exist between them; depend upon it that no disagreement between them can be of any duration. Their hearts are open to each other, as neither heart can be to you; they know exactly what is required and what can be borne; and you may be certain, that one will never tease the other beyond what is known to be pleasant.'

Perceiving her still to look doubtful and grave, he added, 'Though Frederick does not leave Bath with us, he will probably remain but a very short time, perhaps only a few days behind us. His leave of absence will soon expire, and he must return to his regiment. – And what will then be their acquaintance? – The mess-room will drink Isabella Thorpe for a fortnight, and she will laugh with your brother over poor Tilney's passion for a month.'

Catherine would contend no longer against comfort. She had resisted its approaches during the whole length of a speech, but it now carried her captive. Henry Tilney must know best. She blamed herself for the extent of her fears, and resolved never to think so seriously on the subject again.

Her resolution was supported by Isabella's behaviour in their parting interview. The Thorpes spent the last evening of Catherine's stay in Pulteney-street, and nothing passed between the lovers to excite her uneasiness, or make her quit them in apprehension. James was in excellent spirits, and Isabella most engagingly placid. Her tenderness for her friend seemed rather the first feeling of her heart; but that at such a moment was allowable; and once she gave her lover a flat contradiction, and once she drew back her hand; but Catherine remembered Henry's instructions, and placed it all to judicious affection. The embraces, tears, and promises of the parting fair ones may be fancied.

Chapter 5

Mr and Mrs Allen were sorry to lose their young friend, whose good-humour and cheerfulness had made her a valuable companion, and in the promotion of whose enjoyment their own had been gently increased. Her happiness in going with Miss Tilney, however, prevented their wishing it otherwise; and, as they were to remain only one more week in Bath themselves, her quitting them now would not long be felt. Mr Allen attended her to Milsom-street, where she was to breakfast, and saw her seated with the kindest welcome among her new friends; but so great was her agitation in finding herself as one of the family, and so fearful was she of not doing exactly what was right, and of not being able to preserve their good opinion, that, in the embarrassment of the first five minutes, she could almost have wished to return with him to Pulteney-street.

Miss Tilney's manners and Henry's smile soon did away some of her unpleasant feelings; but still she was far from being at ease; nor could the incessant attentions of the General himself entirely reassure her. Nay, perverse as it seemed, she doubted whether she might not have felt less, had she been less attended to. His anxiety for her comfort – his continual solicitations that she would eat, and his often-expressed fears of her seeing nothing to her taste – though never in her life before had she beheld half such variety on a breakfast-table –

made it impossible for her to forget for a moment that she was a visitor. She felt utterly unworthy of such respect, and knew not how to reply to it. Her tranquillity was not improved by the General's impatience for the appearance of his eldest son, nor by the displeasure he expressed at his laziness when Captain Tilney at last came down. She was quite pained by the severity of his father's reproof, which seemed disproportionate to the offence; and much was her concern increased, when she found herself the principal cause of the lecture; and that his tardiness was chiefly resented from being disrespectful to her. This was placing her in a very uncomfortable situation, and she felt great compassion for Captain Tilney, without being able to hope for his good-will.

He listened to his father in silence, and attempted not any defence, which confirmed her in fearing, that the inquietude of his mind, on Isabella's account, might, by keeping him long sleepless, have been the real cause of his rising late. – It was the first time of her being decidedly in his company, and she had hoped to be now able to form her opinion of him; but she scarcely heard his voice while his father remained in the room; and even afterwards, so much were his spirits affected, she could distinguish nothing but these words, in a whisper to Eleanor, 'How glad I shall be when you are all off.'

The bustle of going was not pleasant. – The clock struck ten while the trunks were carrying down, and the General had fixed to be out of Milsom-street by that hour. His great coat, instead of being brought for him to put on directly, was spread out in the curricle in which he was to accompany his son. The middle seat of the chaise was not drawn out, though there were three people to go in it, and his daughter's maid had so crowded it with parcels, that Miss Morland would not have room to sit; and, so much was he influenced by this apprehension when he handed her in, that she had some difficulty in saving her own new writing-desk from being thrown out into the street. – At last, however, the door was closed upon the three females, and they set off at the sober pace in which the handsome, highly-fed four horses of a gentleman usually perform a journey of thirty miles: such was the distance of Northanger from Bath, to be now divided into two equal stages. Catherine's spirits revived as they drove from the door; for with Miss Tilney she felt no restraint; and, with the interest of a road entirely new to her, of an abbey before, and a curricle behind, she caught the last view of Bath without any regret, and met with every mile-stone before she expected it. The tediousness of a two hours' bait at Petty-France, in which there was nothing to be done but to eat without being hungry, and loiter about without any thing to see, next followed – and her admiration of the style in which they travelled, of the fashionable chaise-and-four – postilions handsomely liveried, rising so regularly in their stirrups, and numerous out-riders properly mounted, sunk a little under this consequent inconvenience. Had their party been perfectly agreeable, the delay would have been nothing; but General Tilney, though so charming a man, seemed always a check upon his children's spirits, and scarcely any thing was said but by himself; the observation of which, with his discontent at whatever the inn afforded, and his angry impatience at the waiters, made Catherine grow every moment more in awe of him, and appeared to lengthen the two hours into four. – At last, however, the order of release was given; and much was Catherine then surprized by the General's proposal of her taking his place in his son's curricle for the rest of the journey: – 'the day was fine, and he was anxious for her seeing as much of the country as possible.'

The remembrance of Mr Allen's opinion, respecting young men's open carriages, made her blush at the mention of such a plan, and her first thought was to decline it; but her second was of greater deference for General Tilney's judgment; he could not propose any thing improper for her; and, in the course of a few minutes, she found herself with Henry in the curricle, as happy a being as ever existed. A very short trial convinced her that a curricle was the prettiest equipage in the world; the chaise-and-four wheeled off with some grandeur, to be sure, but it was a heavy and troublesome business, and she could not easily forget its having stopped two hours at Petty-France. Half the time would have been enough for the curricle, and so nimbly were the light horses disposed to move, that, had not the General chosen to have his own carriage lead the way, they could have passed it with ease in half a minute. But the merit of the curricle did not all belong to the horses; – Henry drove so well, – so quietly – without making any disturbance, without parading to her, or swearing at them; so different from the only gentleman-coachman whom it was in her power to compare him with! – And then his hat sat so well, and the innumerable capes of his great coat looked so becomingly important! – To be driven by him, next to dancing with him, was certainly the greatest happiness in the world. In addition to every other delight, she had now that of listening to her own praise; of being thanked at least, on his sister's account, for her kindness in thus becoming her visitor; of hearing it ranked as real friendship, and described as creating real gratitude. His sister, he said, was uncomfortably circumstanced – she had no female companion – and, in the frequent absence of her father, was sometimes without any companion at all.

'But how can that be?' said Catherine, 'are not you with her?'

'Northanger is not more than half my home; I have an establishment at my own house in Woodston, which is nearly twenty miles from my father's, and some of my time is necessarily spent there.'

'How sorry you must be for that!'

'I am always sorry to leave Eleanor.'

'Yes; but besides your affection for her, you must be so fond of the abbey! – After being used to such a home as the abbey, an ordinary parsonage-house must be very disagreeable.'

He smiled, and said, 'You have formed a very favourable idea of the abbey.'

'To be sure I have. Is not it a fine old place, just like what one reads about?'

'And are you prepared to encounter all the horrors that a building such as "what one reads about" may produce? – Have you a stout heart? – Nerves fit for sliding pannels and tapestry?'

'Oh! yes – I do not think I should be easily frightened, because there would be so many people in the house – and besides, it has never been uninhabited and left deserted for years, and then the family come back to it unawares, without giving any notice, as generally happens.'

'No, certainly. – We shall not have to explore our way into a hall dimly lighted by the expiring embers of a wood fire – nor be obliged to spread our beds on the floor of a room without windows, doors, or furniture. But you must be aware that when a young lady is (by whatever means) introduced into a dwelling of this kind, she is always lodged apart from the rest of the family. While they snugly repair to their own end of the house, she is formally conducted by Dorothy the ancient house-keeper up a different staircase, and along many gloomy passages, into an apartment never used since some cousin or kin died in it about twenty years before. Can you stand such a ceremony as this? Will not your mind misgive you, when you find yourself in this gloomy chamber – too lofty and extensive for you, with only the feeble rays of a single lamp to take in its size – its walls hung with tapestry exhibiting figures as large as life, and the bed, of dark green stuff or purple velvet, presenting even a funereal appearance. Will not your heart sink within you?'

'Oh! but this will not happen to me, I am sure.'

'How fearfully will you examine the furniture of your apartment! – And what will you discern? – Not tables, toilettes, wardrobes, or drawers, but on one side perhaps the remains of a broken lute, on the other a ponderous chest which no efforts can open, and over the fire-place the portrait of some handsome warrior, whose features will so incomprehensibly strike you, that you will not be able to withdraw your eyes from it. Dorothy meanwhile, no less struck by your appearance, gazes on you in great agitation, and drops a few unintelligible hints. To raise your spirits, moreover, she gives you reason to suppose that the part of the abbey you inhabit is undoubtedly haunted, and informs you that you will not have a single domestic within call. With this parting cordial she curtseys off – you listen to the sound of her receding footsteps as long as the last echo can reach you – and when, with fainting spirits, you attempt to fasten your door, you discover, with increased alarm, that it has no lock.'

'Oh! Mr Tilney, how frightful! – This is just like a book! – But it cannot really happen to me. I am sure your housekeeper is not really Dorothy. – Well, what then?'

'Nothing further to alarm perhaps may occur the first night. After surmounting your *unconquerable* horror of the bed, you will retire to rest, and get a few hours' unquiet slumber. But on the second, or at farthest the *third* night after your arrival, you will probably have a violent storm. Peals of thunder so loud as to seem to shake the edifice to its foundation will roll round the neighbouring mountains – and during the frightful gusts of wind which accompany it, you will probably think you discern (for your lamp is not extinguished) one part of the hanging more violently agitated than the rest. Unable of course to repress your curiosity in so favourable a moment for indulging it, you will instantly arise, and throwing your dressing-gown around you, proceed to examine this mystery. After a very short search, you will discover a division in the tapestry so artfully constructed as to defy the minutest inspection, and on opening it, a door will immediately appear – which door being only secured by massy bars and a padlock, you will, after a few efforts, succeed in opening, – and, with your lamp in your hand, will pass through it into a small vaulted room.'

'No, indeed; I should be too much frightened to do any such thing.'

'What! not when Dorothy has given you to understand that there is a secret subterraneous communication between your apartment and the chapel of St Anthony, scarcely two miles off – Could you shrink from so simple an adventure? No, no, you will proceed into this small vaulted room, and through this into several others, without perceiving any thing very remarkable in either. In one perhaps there may be a dagger, in another a few drops of blood, and in a third the remains of some instrument of torture; but there being nothing in all this out of the common way, and your lamp being nearly exhausted, you will return towards your own apartment. In repassing through the small vaulted room, however, your eyes will be attracted towards a large, old-fashioned cabinet of ebony and gold, which, though narrowly examining the furniture before, you had passed unnoticed. Impelled by an irresistible presentiment, you will eagerly advance to it, unlock its folding doors, and search into every drawer; – but for some time without discovering any thing of importance – perhaps nothing but a considerable hoard of diamonds. At last, however, by touching a secret spring, an inner compartment will open – a roll of paper appears: – you seize it – it contains many sheets of manuscript – you hasten with the precious treasure into your own chamber, but scarcely have you been able to decipher "Oh! thou – whomsoever thou mayst be, into whose hands these memoirs of the wretched Matilda may fall" – when your lamp suddenly expires in the socket, and leaves you in total darkness.'

'Oh! no, no – do not say so. Well, go on.'

But Henry was too much amused by the interest he had raised, to be able to carry it farther; he could no longer command solemnity either of subject or voice, and was obliged to entreat her to use her own fancy in the perusal of Matilda's woes. Catherine, recollecting herself, grew ashamed of her eagerness, and began earnestly to assure him that her attention had been fixed without the smallest apprehension of really meeting with what he related. 'Miss Tilney, she was sure, would never put her into such a chamber as he had described! – She was not at all afraid.'

As they drew near the end of their journey, her impatience for a sight of the abbey – for some time suspended by his conversation on subjects very different – returned in full force, and every bend in the road was expected with solemn awe to afford a glimpse of its massy walls of grey stone, rising amidst a grove of ancient oaks, with the last beams of the sun playing in beautiful splendour on its high Gothic windows. But so low did the building stand, that she found herself passing through the great gates of the lodge into the very grounds of Northanger, without having discerned even an antique chimney.

She knew not that she had any right to be surprized, but there was a something in this mode of approach which she certainly had not expected. To pass between lodges of a modern appearance, to find herself with such ease in the very precincts of the abbey, and driven so rapidly along a smooth, level road of fine gravel, without obstacle, alarm or solemnity of any kind, struck her as odd and inconsistent. She was not long at leisure however for such considerations. A sudden scud of rain driving full in her face, made it impossible for her to observe any thing further, and fixed all her thoughts on the welfare of her new straw bonnet: – and she was actually under the Abbey walls, was springing, with Henry's assistance, from the carriage, was beneath the shelter of the old porch, and had even passed on to the hall, where her friend and the General were waiting to welcome her, without feeling one aweful foreboding of future misery to herself, or one moment's suspicion of any past scenes of horror being acted within the solemn edifice. The breeze had not seemed to waft the sighs of the murdered to her; it had wafted nothing worse than a thick mizzling rain; and having given a good shake to her habit, she was ready to be shewn into the common drawing-room, and capable of considering where she was.

An abbey! – yes, it was delightful to be really in an abbey! – but she doubted, as she looked round the room, whether any thing within her observation, would have given her the consciousness. The furniture was in all the profusion and elegance of modern taste. The fire-place, where she had expected the ample width and ponderous carving of former times, was contracted to a Rumford, with slabs of plain though handsome marble, and ornaments over it of the prettiest English china. The windows, to which she looked with peculiar dependence, from having heard the General talk of his preserving them in their Gothic form with reverential care, were yet less what her fancy had portrayed. To be sure, the pointed arch was preserved – the form of them was Gothic – they might be even casements – but every pane was so large, so clear, so light! To an imagination which had hoped for the smallest divisions, and the heaviest stone-work, for painted glass, dirt and cobwebs, the difference was very distressing.

The General, perceiving how her eye was employed, began to talk of the smallness of the room and simplicity of the furniture, where every thing being for daily use, pretended only to comfort, &c.; flattering himself however that there were some apartments in the Abbey not unworthy her notice – and was proceeding to mention the costly gilding of one in particular, when taking out his watch, he stopped short to pronounce it, with surprize within twenty minutes of five! This seemed the word of separation, and Catherine found herself hurried away by Miss Tilney in such a manner as convinced her that the strictest punctuality to the family hours would be expected at Northanger.

Returning through the large and lofty hall, they ascended a broad staircase of shining oak, which, after many flights and many landing-places, brought them upon a long wide gallery. On one side it had a range of doors, and it was lighted on the other by windows which Catherine had only time to discover looked into a quadrangle, before Miss Tilney led the way into a chamber, and scarcely staying to hope she would find it comfortable, left her with an anxious entreaty that she would make as little alteration as possible in her dress.

Chapter 6

A moment's glance was enough to satisfy Catherine that her apartment was very unlike the one which Henry had endeavoured to alarm her by the description of. – It was by no means unreasonably large, and contained neither tapestry nor velvet. – The walls were papered, the floor was carpeted; the windows were neither less perfect, nor more dim than those of the drawing-room below; the furniture, though not of the latest fashion, was handsome and comfortable, and the air of the room altogether far from uncheerful. Her heart instantaneously at ease on this point, she resolved to lose no time in particular examination of anything, as she greatly dreaded disobliging the General by any delay. Her habit therefore was thrown off with all possible haste, and she was preparing to unpin the linen package, which the chaise-seat had conveyed for her immediate accommodation, when her eye suddenly fell on a large high chest, standing back in a deep recess on one side of the fire-place. The sight of it made her start; and, forgetting every thing else, she stood gazing on it in motionless wonder, while, these thoughts crossed her: –

'This is strange indeed! I did not expect such a sight as this! – An immense heavy chest! – What can it hold? – Why should it be placed here? – Pushed back too, as if meant to be out of sight! – I will look into it – cost me what it may, I will look into it – and directly too – by day-light. – If I stay till evening my candle may go out.' She advanced and examined it closely: it was of cedar, curiously inlaid with some darker wood, and raised, about a foot from the ground, on a carved stand of the same. The lock was silver, though tarnished from age; at each end were the imperfect remains of handles also of silver, broken perhaps prematurely by some strange violence; and, on the centre of the lid, was a mysterious cypher, in the same metal. Catherine bent over it intently, but without being able to distinguish any thing with certainty. She could not, in whatever direction she took it, believe the last letter to be a *T*; and yet that it should be any thing else in that house was a circumstance to raise no common degree of astonishment. If not originally their's, by what strange events could it have fallen into the Tilney family?

Her fearful curiosity was every moment growing greater; and seizing, with trembling hands, the hasp of the lock, she resolved at all hazards to satisfy herself at least as to its contents. With difficulty, for something seemed to resist her efforts, she raised the lid a few inches; but at that moment a sudden knocking at the door of the room made her, starting, quit her hold, and the lid closed with alarming violence. This ill-timed intruder was Miss Tilney's maid, sent by her mistress to be of use to Miss Morland; and though Catherine immediately dismissed her, it recalled her to the sense of what she ought to be doing, and forced her, in spite of her anxious desire to penetrate this mystery, to pro-ceed in her dressing without further delay. Her progress was not quick, for her thoughts and her eyes were still bent on the object so well calculated to interest and alarm; and though she dared not waste a moment upon a second attempt, she could not remain many paces from the chest. At length, however, having slipped one arm into her gown, her toilette seemed so nearly finished, that the impatience of her curiosity might safely be indulged. One moment surely might be spared; and, so desperate should be the exertion of her strength, that, unless secured by supernatural means, the lid in one moment should be thrown back. With this spirit she sprang forward, and her confidence did not deceive her. Her resolute effort threw back the lid, and gave to her astonished eyes the view of a white cotton counterpane, properly folded, reposing at one end of the chest in undisputed possession!

She was gazing on it with the first blush of surprize, when Miss Tilney, anxious for her friend's being ready, entered the room, and to the rising shame of having harboured for some minutes an absurd expectation, was then added the shame of being caught in so idle a search. 'That is a curious old chest, is not it?' said Miss Tilney, as Catherine hastily closed it and turned away to the glass. 'It is impossible to say how many generations it has been here. How it came to be first put in this room I know not, but I have not had it moved, because I thought it might sometimes be of use in holding hats and bonnets. The worst of it is that its weight makes it difficult to open. In that corner, however, it is at least out of the way.'

Catherine had no leisure for speech, being at once blushing, tying her gown, and forming wise resolutions with the most violent dispatch. Miss Tilney gently hinted her fear of being late; and in half a minute they ran down stairs together, in an alarm not wholly unfounded, for General Tilney was pacing the drawing-room, his watch in his hand, and having, on the very instant of their entering, pulled the bell with violence, ordered 'Dinner to be on table *directly!*'

Catherine trembled at the emphasis with which he spoke, and sat pale and breathless, in a most humble mood, concerned for his children, and detesting old chests; and the General recovering his politeness as he looked at her, spent the rest of his time in scolding his daughter, for so foolishly hurrying her fair friend, who was absolutely out of breath from haste, when there was not the least occasion for hurry in the world: but Catherine could not at all get over the double distress of having involved her friend in a lecture and been a great simpleton herself, till they were happily seated at the dinner-table, when the General's complacent smiles, and a good appetite of her own, restored her to peace. The dining-parlour was a noble room, suitable in its dimensions to a much larger drawing-room than the one in common use, and fitted up in a style of luxury and expense which was almost lost on the unpractised eye of Catherine, who saw little more than its spaciousness and the number of their attendants. Of the former, she spoke aloud her admiration; and the General, with a very gracious countenance, acknowledged that it was by no means an ill-sized room; and further confessed, that, though as careless on such subjects as most people, he did look upon a tolerably large eating-room as one of the necessaries of life; he supposed, however, 'that she must have been used to much better sized apartments at Mr Allen's?'

'No, indeed,' was Catherine's honest assurance; 'Mr Allen's dining-parlour was not more than half as large:' and she had never seen so large a room as this in her life. The General's good-humour increased. – Why, as he *had* such rooms, he thought it would be simple not to make use of them; but, upon his honour, he believed there might be more comfort in rooms of only half their size. Mr Allen's house, he was sure, must be exactly of the true size for rational happiness.

The evening passed without any further disturbance, and, in the occasional absence of General Tilney, with much positive cheerfulness. It was only in his presence that Catherine felt the smallest fatigue from her journey; and even then, even in moments of languor or restraint, a sense of general happiness preponderated, and she could think of her friends in Bath without one wish of being with them.

The night was stormy; the wind had been rising at intervals the whole afternoon; and by the time the party broke up, it blew and rained violently. Catherine, as she crossed the hall, listened to the tempest with sensations of awe; and, when she heard it rage round a corner of the ancient building and close with sudden fury a distant door, felt for the first time that she was really in an Abbey. – Yes, these were characteristic sounds; – they brought to her recollection a countless variety of dreadful situations and horrid scenes, which such buildings had witnessed, and such storms ushered in; and most heartily did she rejoice in the happier circumstances attending her entrance within walls so solemn! – *She* had nothing to dread from midnight assassins or drunken gallants. Henry had certainly been only in jest in what he had told her that morning. In a house so furnished, and so guarded, she could have nothing to explore or to suffer; and might go to her bedroom as securely as if it had been her own chamber at Fullerton. Thus wisely fortifying her mind, as she proceeded up stairs, she was enabled, especially on perceiving that Miss Tilney slept only two doors from her, to enter her room with a tolerably stout heart; and her spirits were immediately assisted by the cheerful blaze of a wood fire. 'How much better is this,' said she, as she walked to the fender – 'how much better to find a fire ready lit, than to have to wait shivering in the cold till all the family are in bed, as so many poor girls have been obliged to do, and then to have a faithful old servant frightening one by coming in with a faggot! How glad I am that Northanger is what it is! If it had been like some other places, I do not know that, in such a night as this, I could have answered for my courage: – but now, to be sure, there is nothing to alarm one.'

She looked round the room. The window curtains seemed in motion. It could be nothing but the violence of the wind penetrating through the divisions of the shutters; and she stept boldly forward, carelessly humming a tune, to assure herself of its being so, peeped courageously behind each curtain, saw nothing on either low window seat to scare her, and on placing a hand against the shutter, felt the strongest conviction of the wind's force. A glance at the old chest, as she turned away from this examination, was not without its use; she scorned the causeless fears of an idle fancy, and began with a most happy indifference to prepare herself for bed. 'She should take her time; she should not hurry herself; she did not care if she were the last person up in the house. But she would not make up her fire; *that* would seem cowardly, as if she wished for the protection of light after she were in bed.' The fire therefore died away, and Catherine, having spent the best part of an hour in her arrangements, was beginning to think of stepping into bed, when, on giving a parting glance round the room, she was struck by the appearance of a high, old-fashioned black cabinet, which, though in a situation conspicuous enough, had never caught her notice before. Henry's words, his description of the ebony cabinet which was to escape her observation at first, immediately rushed across her; and though there could be nothing really in it, there was something whimsical, it was certainly a very remarkable coincidence! She took her candle and looked closely at the cabinet. It was not absolutely ebony and gold; but it was Japan, black and yellow Japan of the handsomest kind; and as she held her candle, the yellow had very much the effect of gold. The key was in the door, and she had a strange fancy to look into it; not however with the smallest expectation of finding any thing, but it was so very odd, after what Henry had said. In short, she could not sleep till she had examined it. So, placing the candle with great caution on a chair, she seized the key with a very tremulous hand and tried to turn it; but it resisted her utmost strength. Alarmed, but not discouraged, she tried it another way; a bolt flew, and she believed herself successful; but how strangely mysterious! – the door was still immoveable. She paused a moment in breathless wonder. The wind roared down the chimney, the rain beat in torrents against the windows, and every thing seemed to speak the awfulness of her situation. To retire to bed, however, unsatisfied on such a point, would be vain, since sleep must be impossible with the consciousness of a cabinet so mysteriously closed in her immediate vicinity. Again therefore she applied herself to the key, and after moving it in every possible way for some instants with the determined celerity of hope's last effort, the door suddenly yielded to her hand: her heart leaped with exultation at such a victory, and having thrown open each folding door, the second being secured only by bolts of less wonderful construction than the lock, though in that her eye could not discern any thing unusual, a double range of small drawers appeared in view, with some larger drawers above and below them; and in the centre, a small door, closed also with a lock and key, secured in all probability a cavity of importance.

Catherine's heart beat quick, but her courage did not fail her. With a cheek flushed by hope, and an eye straining with curiosity, her fingers grasped the handle of a drawer and drew it forth. It was entirely empty. With less alarm and greater eagerness she seized a second, a third, a fourth; each was equally empty. Not one was left unsearched, and in not one was any thing found. Well read in the art of concealing a treasure, the possibility of false linings to the drawers did not escape her, and she felt round each with anxious acuteness in vain. The place in the middle alone remained now unexplored; and though she had 'never from the first had the smallest idea of finding any thing in any part of the cabinet, and was not in the least disappointed at her ill success thus far, it would be foolish not to examine it thoroughly while she was about it.' It was some time however before she could unfasten the door, the same difficulty occurring in the management of this inner lock as of the outer; but at length it did open; and not vain, as hitherto, was her search; her quick eyes directly fell on a roll of paper pushed back into the further part of the cavity, apparently for concealment, and her feelings at that moment were indescribable. Her heart fluttered, her knees trembled, and her cheeks grew pale. She seized, with an unsteady hand, the precious manuscript, for half a glance sufficed to ascertain written characters; and while she acknowledged with awful sensations this striking exemplification of what Henry had foretold, resolved instantly to peruse every line before she attempted to rest.

The dimness of the light her candle emitted made her turn to it with alarm; but there was no danger of its sudden extinction, it had yet some hours to burn; and that she might not have any greater difficulty in distinguishing the writing than what its ancient date might occasion, she hastily snuffed it. Alas! it was snuffed and extinguished in one. A lamp could not have expired with more awful effect. Catherine, for a few moments, was motionless with horror. It was done completely; not a remnant of light in the wick could give hope to the rekindling breath. Darkness impenetrable and immoveable filled the room. A violent gust of wind, rising with sudden fury, added fresh horror to the moment. Catherine trembled from head to foot. In the pause which succeeded, a sound like receding footsteps and the closing of a distant door struck on her affrighted ear. Human nature could support no more. A cold sweat stood on her forehead, the manuscript fell from her hand, and groping her way to the bed, she jumped hastily in, and sought some suspension of agony by creeping far underneath the clothes. To close her eyes in sleep that night, she felt must be entirely out of the question. With a curiosity so justly awakened, and feelings in every way so agitated, repose must be absolutely impossible. The storm too abroad so dreadful! – She had not been used to feel alarm from wind, but now every blast seemed fraught with awful intelligence. The manuscript so wonderfully found, so wonderfully accomplishing the morning's prediction, how was it to be accounted for? – What could it contain? – to whom could it relate? – by what means could it have been so long concealed? – and how singularly strange that it should fall to her lot to discover it! Till she had made herself mistress of its contents, however, she could have neither response nor comfort; and with the sun's first rays she was determined to peruse it. But many were the tedious hours which must yet intervene. She shuddered, tossed about in her bed, and envied every quiet sleeper. The storm still raged, and various were the noises, more terrific even than the wind, which struck at intervals on her startled ear. The very curtains of her bed seemed at one moment in motion, and at another the lock of her door was agitated, as if by the attempt of somebody to enter. Hollow murmurs seemed to creep along the gallery, and more than once her blood was chilled by the sound of distant moans. Hour after hour passed away, and the wearied Catherine had heard three proclaimed by all the clocks in the house, before the tempest subsided, or she unknowingly fell fast asleep.

Chapter 7

The housemaid's folding back her window-shutters at eight o'clock the next day, was the sound which first roused Catherine; and she opened her eyes, wondering that they could ever have been closed, on objects of cheerfulness; her fire was already burning, and a bright morning had succeeded the tempest of the night. Instantaneously with the consciousness of existence, returned her recollection of the manuscript; and springing from the bed in the very moment of the maid's going away, she eagerly collected every scattered sheet which had burst from the roll on its falling to the ground, and flew back to enjoy the luxury of their perusal on her pillow. She now plainly saw that she must not expect a manuscript of equal length with the generality of what she had shuddered over in books, for the roll, seeming to consist entirely of small disjointed sheets, was altogether but of trifling size, and much less than she had supposed it to be at first.

Her greedy eye glanced rapidly over a page. She started at its import. Could it be possible, or did not her sense play her false? – An inventory of linen, in coarse and modern characters, seemed all that was before her! If the evidence of sight might be trusted, she held a washing-bill in her hand. She seized another sheet, and saw the same articles with little variation; a third, a fourth, and a fifth presented nothing new. Shirts, stockings, cravats and waistcoats faced her in each. Two others, penned by the same hand, marked an expenditure scarcely more interesting, in letters, hair-powder, shoe-string and breeches-ball. And the larger sheet, which had inclosed the rest, seemed by its first cramp line, 'To poultice chesnut mare,' – a farrier's bill! Such was the collection of papers, (left perhaps, as she could then suppose, by the negligence of a servant in the place whence she had taken them,) which had filled her with expectation and alarm, and robbed her of half her night's rest! She felt humbled to the dust. Could not the adventure of the chest have taught her wisdom? A corner of it catching her eye as she lay, seemed to rise up in judgment against her. Nothing could now be clearer than the absurdity of her recent fancies. To suppose that a manuscript of many generations back could have remained undiscovered in a room such as that, so modern, so habitable! – or that she should be the first to possess the skill of unlocking a cabinet, the key of which was open to all!

How could she have so imposed on herself? – Heaven forbid that Henry Tilney should ever know her folly! And it was in a great measure his own doing, for had not the cabinet appeared so exactly to agree with his description of her adventures, she should never have felt the smallest curiosity about it. This was the only comfort that occurred. Impatient to get rid of those hateful evidences of her folly, those detestable papers then scattered over the bed, she rose directly, and folding them up as nearly as possible in the same shape as before, returned them to the same spot within the cabinet, with a very hearty wish that no untoward accident might ever bring them forward again, to disgrace her even with herself.

Why the locks should have been so difficult to open however, was still something remarkable, for she could now manage them with perfect ease. In this there was surely something mysterious, and she indulged in the flattering suggestion for half a minute, till the possibility of the door's having been at first unlocked, and of being herself its fastener, darted into her head, and cost her another blush.

She got away as soon as she could from a room in which her conduct produced such unpleasant reflections, and found her way with all speed to the breakfast-parlour, as it had been pointed out to her by Miss Tilney the evening before. Henry was alone in it; and his immediate hope of her having been undisturbed by the tempest, with an arch reference to the character of the building they inhabited, was rather distressing. For the world would she not have her weakness suspected; and yet, unequal to an absolute falsehood, was constrained to acknowledge that the wind had kept her awake a little. 'But we have a charming morning after it,' she added, desiring to get rid of the subject; 'and storms and sleeplessness are nothing when they are over. What beautiful hyacinths! – I have just learnt to love a hyacinth.'

'And how might you learn? – By accident or argument?'

'Your sister taught me; I cannot tell how. Mrs Allen used to take pains, year after year, to make me like them; but I never could, till I saw them the other day in Milsom-street; I am naturally indifferent about flowers.'

'But now you love a hyacinth. So much the better. You have gained a new source of enjoyment, and it is well to have as many holds upon happiness as possible. Besides, a taste for flowers is always desirable in your sex, as a means of getting you out of doors, and tempting you to more frequent exercise than you would otherwise take. And though the love of a hyacinth may be rather domestic, who can tell, the sentiment once raised, but you may in time come to love a rose?'

'But I do not want any such pursuit to get me out of doors. The pleasure of walking and breathing fresh air is enough for me, and in fine weather I am out more than half my time. – Mamma says, I am never within.'

'At any rate, however, I am pleased that you have learnt to love a hyacinth. The mere habit of learning to love is the thing; and a teachableness of disposition in a young lady is a great blessing. – Has my sister a pleasant mode of instruction?'

Catherine was saved the embarrassment of attempting an answer, by the entrance of the General, whose smiling compliments announced a happy state of mind, but whose gentle hint of sympathetic early rising did not advance her composure.

The elegance of the breakfast set forced itself on Catherine's notice when they were seated at table; and, luckily, it had been the General's choice. He was enchanted by her approbation of his taste, confessed it to be neat and simple, thought it right to encourage the manufacture of his country; and for his part, to his uncritical palate, the tea was as well flavoured from the clay of Staffordshire, as from that of Dresden or Sève. But this was quite an old set, purchased two years ago.

The manufacture was much improved since that time; he had seen some beautiful specimens when last in town, and had he not been perfectly without vanity of that kind, might have been tempted to order a new set. He trusted, however, that an opportunity might ere long occur of selecting one – though not for himself. Catherine was probably the only one of the party who did not understand him.

Shortly after breakfast Henry left them for Woodston, where business required and would keep him two or three days. They all attended in the hall to see him mount his horse, and immediately on re-entering the breakfast room, Catherine walked to a window in the hope of catching another glimpse of his figure. 'This is a somewhat heavy call upon your brother's fortitude,' observed the General to Eleanor. 'Woodston will make but a sombre appearance to-day.'

'Is it a pretty place?' asked Catherine.

'What say you, Eleanor? – speak your opinion, for ladies can best tell the taste of ladies in regard to places as well as men. I think it would be acknowledged by the most impartial eye to have many recommendations. The house stands among fine meadows facing the south-east, with an excellent kitchen-garden in the same aspect; the walls surrounding which I built and stocked myself about ten years ago, for the benefit of my son. It is a family living, Miss Morland; and the property in the place being chiefly my own, you may believe I take care that it shall not be a bad one. Did Henry's income depend solely on this living, he would not be ill provided for. Perhaps it may seem odd, that with only two younger children, I should think any profession necessary for him; and certainly there are moments when we could all wish him disengaged from every tie of business. But though I may not exactly make converts of you young ladies, I am sure your father, Miss Morland, would agree with me in thinking it expedient to give every young man some employment. The money is nothing, it is not an object, but employment is the thing. Even Frederick, my eldest son, you see, who will perhaps inherit as considerable a landed property as any private man in the county, has his profession.'

The imposing effect of this last argument was equal to his wishes. The silence of the lady proved it to be unanswerable.

Something had been said the evening before of her being shewn over the house, and he now offered himself as her conductor; and though Catherine had hoped to explore it accompanied only by his daughter, it was a proposal of too much happiness in itself, under any circumstances, not to be gladly accepted; for she had been already eighteen hours in the Abbey, and had seen only a few of its rooms. The netting-box, just leisurely drawn forth, was closed with joyful haste, and she was ready to attend him in a moment. 'And when they had gone over the house, he promised himself moreover the pleasure of accompanying her into the shrubberies and garden.' She curtsied her acquiescence. 'But perhaps it might be more agreeable to her to make those her first object. The weather was at present favourable, and at this time of year the uncertainty was very great of its continuing so. – Which would she prefer? He was equally at her service. – Which did his daughter think would most accord with her fair friend's wishes? – But he thought he could discern. – Yes, he certainly read in Miss Morland's eyes a judicious desire of making use of the present smiling weather. – But when did she judge amiss? – The Abbey would be always safe and dry. – He yielded implicitly, and would fetch his hat and attend them in a moment.' He left the room, and Catherine, with a disappointed, anxious face, began to speak of her unwillingness that he should be taking them out of doors against his own inclination, under a mistaken idea of pleasing her; but she was stopt by Miss Tilney's saying, with a little confusion, 'I believe it will be wisest to take the morning while it is so fine; and do not be uneasy on my father's account, he always walks out at this time of day.'

Catherine did not exactly know how this was to be understood. Why was Miss Tilney embarrassed? Could there be any unwillingness on the General's side to shew her over the Abbey? The proposal was his own. And was not it odd that he should *always* take his walk so early? Neither her father nor Mr Allen did so. It was certainly very provoking. She was all impatience to see the house, and had scarcely any curiosity about the grounds. If Henry had been with them indeed! – but now she should not know what was picturesque when she saw it. Such were her thoughts, but she kept them to herself, and put on her bonnet in patient discontent.

She was struck however, beyond her expectation, by the grandeur of the Abbey, as she saw it for the first time from the lawn. The whole building enclosed a large court; and two sides of the quadrangle, rich in Gothic ornaments, stood forward for admiration. The remainder was shut off by knolls of old trees, or luxuriant plantations, and the steep woody hills rising behind to give it shelter, were beautiful even in the leafless month of March. Catherine had seen nothing to compare with it; and her feelings of delight were so strong, that without waiting for any better authority, she boldly burst forth in wonder and praise. The General listened with assenting gratitude; and it seemed as if his own estimation of Northanger had waited unfixed till that hour.

The kitchen-garden was to be next admired, and he led the way to it across a small portion of the park.

The number of acres contained in this garden was such as Catherine could not listen to without dismay, being more than double the extent of all Mr Allen's, as well as her father's, including church-yard and orchard. The walls seemed countless in number, endless in length; a village of hot-houses seemed to arise among them, and a whole parish to be at work within the inclosure. The General was flattered by her looks of surprize, which told him almost as plainly, as he soon forced her to tell him in words, that she had never seen any gardens at all equal to them before; – and he then modestly owned that, 'without any ambition of that sort himself – without any solicitude about it, – he did believe them to be unrivalled in the kingdom. If he had a hobby-horse, it was *that*. He loved a garden. Though careless enough in most matters of eating, he loved good fruit – or if he did not, his friends and children did. There were great vexations however attending such a garden as his. The utmost care could not always secure the most valuable fruits. The pinery had yielded only one hundred in the last year. Mr Allen, he supposed, must feel these inconveniences as well as himself.'

'No, not at all. Mr Allen did not care about the garden, and never went into it.'

With a triumphant smile of self-satisfaction, the General wished he could do the same, for he never entered his, without being vexed in some way or other, by its falling short of his plan.

'How were Mr Allen's succession-houses worked?' describing the nature of his own as they entered them.

'Mr Allen had only one small hot-house, which Mrs Allen had the use of for her plants in winter, and there was a fire in it now and then.'

'He is a happy man!' said the General, with a look of very happy contempt.

Having taken her into every division, and led her under every wall, till she was heartily weary of seeing and wondering, he suffered the girls at last to seize the advantage of an outer door, and then expressing his wish to examine the effect of some recent alterations about the tea-house, proposed it as no unpleasant extension of their walk, if Miss Morland were not tired. 'But where are you going, Eleanor? – Why do you chuse that cold, damp path to it? Miss Morland will get wet. Our best way is across the park.'

'This is so favourite a walk of mine,' said Miss Tilney, 'that I always think it the best and nearest way. But perhaps it may be damp.'

It was a narrow winding path through a thick grove of old Scotch firs; and Catherine, struck by its gloomy aspect, and eager to enter it, could not, even by the General's disapprobation, be kept from stepping forward. He perceived her inclination, and having again urged the plea of health in vain, was too polite to make further opposition. He excused himself however from attending them: – 'The rays of the sun were not too cheerful for him, and he would meet them by another course.' He turned away; and Catherine was shocked to find how much her spirits were relieved by the separation. The shock however being less real than the relief, offered it no injury; and she began to talk with easy gaiety of the delightful melancholy which such a grove inspired.

'I am particularly fond of this spot,' said her companion, with a sigh. 'It was my mother's favourite walk.'

Catherine had never heard Mrs Tilney mentioned in the family before, and the interest excited by this tender remembrance, shewed itself directly in her altered countenance, and in the attentive pause with which she waited for something more.

'I used to walk here so often with her!' added Eleanor; 'though I never loved it then, as I have loved it since. At that time indeed I used to wonder at her choice. But her memory endears it now.'

'And ought it not,' reflected Catherine, 'to endear it to her husband? Yet the General would not enter it.' Miss Tilney continuing silent, she ventured to say, 'Her death must have been a great affliction!'

'A great and increasing one,' replied the other, in a low voice. 'I was only thirteen when it happened; and though I felt my loss perhaps as strongly as one so young could feel it, I did not, I could not then know what a loss it was.' She stopped for a moment, and then added, with great firmness, 'I have no sister, you know – and though Henry – though my brothers are very affectionate, and

Henry is a great deal here, which I am most thankful for, it is impossible for me not to be often solitary.'

'To be sure you must miss him very much.'

'A mother would have been always present. A mother would have been a constant friend; her influence would have been beyond all other.'

'Was she a very charming woman? Was she handsome? Was there any picture of her in the Abbey? And why had she been so partial to that grove? Was it from dejection of spirits?' – were questions now eagerly poured forth; – the first three received a ready affirmative, the two others were passed by; and Catherine's interest in the deceased Mrs Tilney augmented with every question, whether answered or not. Of her unhappiness in marriage, she felt persuaded. The General certainly had been an unkind husband. He did not love her walk: – could he therefore have loved her? And besides, handsome as he was, there was a something in the turn of his features which spoke his not having behaved well to her.

'Her picture, I suppose,' blushing at the consummate art of her own question, 'hangs in your father's room?'

'No; – it was intended for the drawing-room; but my father was dissatisfied with the painting, and for some time it had no place. Soon after her death I obtained it for my own, and hung it in my bed-chamber – where I shall be happy to shew it you; – it is very like.' – Here was another proof. A portrait – very like – of a departed wife, not valued by the husband! – He must have been dreadfully cruel to her!

Catherine attempted no longer to hide from herself the nature of the feelings which, in spite of all his attentions, he had previously excited; and what had been terror and dislike before, was now absolute aversion. Yes, aversion! His cruelty to such a charming woman made him odious to her. She had often read of such characters; characters, which Mr Allen had been used to call unnatural and overdrawn; but here was proof positive of the contrary.

She had just settled this point, when the end of the path brought them directly upon the General; and in spite of all her virtuous indignation, she found herself again obliged to walk with him, listen to him, and even to smile when he smiled. Being no longer able however to receive pleasure from the surrounding objects, she soon began to walk with lassitude; the General perceived it, and with a concern for her health, which seemed to reproach her for her opinion of him, was most urgent for returning with his daughter to the house. He would follow them in a quarter of an hour. Again they parted – but Eleanor was called back in half a minute to receive a strict charge against taking her friend round the Abbey till his return. This second instance of his anxiety to delay what she so much wished for, struck Catherine as very remarkable.

Chapter 8

An hour passed away before the General came in, spent, on the part of his young guest, in no very favourable consideration of his character. – 'This lengthened absence, these solitary rambles, did not speak a mind at ease, or a conscience void of reproach.' – At length he appeared; and, whatever might have been the gloom of his meditations, he could still smile with *them*. Miss Tilney, understanding in part her friend's curiosity to see the house, soon revived the subject; and her father being, contrary to Catherine's expectations, unprovided with any pretence for further delay, beyond that of stopping five minutes to order refreshments to be in the room by their return, was at last ready to escort them.

They set forward; and, with a grandeur of air, a dignified step, which caught the eye, but could not shake the doubts of the well-read Catherine, he led the way across the hall, through the common drawing-room and one useless anti-chamber, into a room magnificent both in size and furniture – the real drawing-room, used only with company of consequence. – It was very noble – very grand – very charming! – was all that Catherine had to say, for her indiscriminating eye scarcely discerned the colour of the satin; and all minuteness of praise, all praise that had much meaning, was supplied by the General: the costliness or elegance of any room's fitting-up could be nothing to her; she cared for no furniture of a more modern date than the fifteenth century. When the General had satisfied his own curiosity, in a close examination of every well-known ornament, they proceeded into the library, an apartment, in its way, of equal magnificence, exhibiting a collection of books, on which an humble man might have looked with pride. – Catherine heard, admired, and wondered with more genuine feeling than before – gathered all that she could from this storehouse of knowledge, by running over the titles of half a shelf, and was ready to proceed. But suites of apartments did not spring up with her wishes. – Large as was the building, she had already visited the greatest part; though, on being told that, with the addition of the kitchen, the six or seven rooms she had now seen surrounded three sides of the court, she could scarcely believe it, or overcome the suspicion of there being many chambers secreted. It was some relief, however, that they were to return to the rooms in common use, by passing through a few of less importance, looking into the court, which, with occasional passages, not wholly unintricate, connected the different sides; – and she was further soothed in her progress, by being told, that she was treading what had once been a cloister, having traces of cells pointed out, and observing several doors, that were neither opened nor explained to her; – by finding herself successively in a billiard-room, and in the General's private apartment, without comprehending their connexion, or being able to turn aright when she left them; and lastly, by passing through a dark little room, owning Henry's authority, and strewed with his litter of books, guns, and great coats.

From the dining-room of which, though already seen,

and always to be seen at five o'clock, the General could not forego the pleasure of pacing out the length, for the more certain information of Miss Morland, as to what she neither doubted nor cared for, they proceeded by quick communication to the kitchen – the ancient kitchen of the convent, rich in the massy walls and smoke of former days, and in the stoves and hot closets of the present. The General's improving hand had not loitered here: every modern invention to facilitate the labour of the cooks, had been adopted within this, their spacious theatre; and, when the genius of others had failed, his own had often produced the perfection wanted. His endowments of this spot alone might at any time have placed him high among the benefactors of the convent.

With the walls of the kitchen ended all the antiquity of the Abbey; the fourth side of the quadrangle having, on account of its decaying state, been removed by the General's father, and the present erected in its place. All that was venerable ceased here. The new building was not only new, but declared itself to be so; intended only for offices, and enclosed behind by stable-yards, no uniformity of architecture had been thought necessary. Catherine could have raved at the hand which had swept away what must have been beyond the value of all the rest, for the purposes of mere domestic economy; and would willingly have been spared the mortification of a walk through scenes so fallen, had the General allowed it; but if he had a vanity, it was in the arrangement of his offices; and as he was convinced, that, to a mind like Miss Morland's, a view of the accommodations and comforts, by which the labours of her inferiors were softened, must always be gratifying, he should make no apology for leading her on. They took a slight survey of all; and Catherine was impressed, beyond her expectation, by their multiplicity and their convenience. The purposes for which a few shapeless pantries and a comfortless scullery were deemed sufficient at Fullerton, were here carried on in appropriate divisions, commodious and roomy. The number of servants continually appearing, did not strike her less than the number of their offices. Wherever they went, some pattened girl stopped to curtsey, or some footman in dishabille sneaked off. Yet this was an Abbey! – How inexpressibly different in these domestic arrangements from such as she had read about – from abbeys and castles, in which, though certainly larger than Northanger, all the dirty work of the house was to be done by two pair of female hands at the utmost. How they could get through it all, had often amazed Mrs Allen; and, when Catherine saw what was necessary here, she began to be amazed herself.

They returned to the hall, that the chief staircase might be ascended, and the beauty of its wood, and ornaments of rich carving might be pointed out: having gained the top, they turned in an opposite direction from the gallery in which her room lay, and shortly entered one on the same plan, but superior in length and breadth. She was here shewn successively into three large bedchambers, with their dressing-rooms, most completely and handsomely fitted up; every thing that money and taste could do, to give comfort and elegance to apartments, had been bestowed on these; and, being furnished within the last five years, they were perfect in all that would be generally pleasing, and wanting in all that could give pleasure to Catherine. As they were surveying the last, the General, after slightly naming a few of the distinguished characters, by whom they had at times been honoured, turned with a smiling countenance to Catherine, and ventured to hope, that hence-forward some of their earliest tenants might be 'our friends from Fullerton.' She felt the unexpected compliment, and deeply regretted the impossibility of thinking well of a man so kindly disposed towards herself, and so full of civility to all her family.

The gallery was terminated by folding doors, which Miss Tilney, advancing, had thrown open, and passed through, and seemed on the point of doing the same by the first door to the left, in another long reach of gallery, when the General, coming forwards, called her hastily, and, as Catherine thought, rather angrily back, demanding whither she were going? – And what was there more to be seen? – Had not Miss Morland already seen all that could be worth her notice? – And did she not suppose her friend might be glad of some refresh-ment after so much exercise? Miss Tilney drew back directly, and the heavy doors were closed upon the mortified Catherine, who, having seen, in a momentary glance beyond them, a narrower passage, more numer-ous openings, and symptoms of a winding staircase, believed herself at last within the reach of something worth her notice; and felt, as she unwillingly paced back the gallery, that she would rather be allowed to examine that end of the house, than see all the finery of all the rest. – The General's evident desire of preventing such an examination was an additional stimulant. Something was certainly to be concealed; her fancy, though it had trespassed lately once or twice, could not mislead her here; and what that something was, a short sentence of Miss Tilney's, as they followed the General at some distance down stairs, seemed to point out: – 'I was going to take you into what was my mother's room – the room in which she died–' were all her words; but few as they were, they conveyed pages of intelligence to Catherine. It was no wonder that the General should shrink from the sight of such objects as that room must contain; a room in all probability never entered by him since the dreadful scene had passed, which released his suffering wife, and left him to the stings of conscience.

She ventured, when next alone with Eleanor, to express her wish of being permitted to see it, as well as all the rest of that side of the house; and Eleanor promised to attend her there, whenever they should have a convenient hour. Catherine understood her: – the General must be watched from home, before that room could be entered. 'It remains as it was, I suppose?' said she, in a tone of feeling.

'Yes, entirely.'

'And how long ago may it be that your mother died?'

'She has been dead these nine years.' And nine years, Catherine knew was a trifle of time, compared with what generally elapsed after the death of an injured wife, before her room was put to rights.

'You were with her, I suppose, to the last?'

'No,' said Miss Tilney, sighing; 'I was unfortunately from home. – Her illness was sudden and short; and, before I arrived it was all over.'

Catherine's blood ran cold with the horrid suggestions which naturally sprang from these words. Could it be possible? – Could Henry's father?–And yet how many were the examples to justify even the blackest suspicions! – And, when she saw him in the evening, while she worked with her friend, slowly pacing the drawing-room for an hour together in silent thoughtfulness, with downcast eyes and contracted brow, she felt secure from all possibility of wronging him. It was the air and attitude of a Montoni! – What could more plainly speak the gloomy workings of a mind not wholly dead to every sense of humanity, in its fearful review of past scenes of guilt? Unhappy man! – And the anxiousness of her spirits directed her eyes towards his figure so repeatedly, as to catch Miss Tilney's notice. 'My father,' she whispered, 'often walks about the room in this way; it is nothing unusual.'

'So much the worse!' thought Catherine; such ill-timed exercise was of a piece with the strange unseasonableness of his morning walks, and boded nothing good.

After an evening, the little variety and seeming length of which made her peculiarly sensible of Henry's importance among them, she was heartily glad to be dismissed; though it was a look from the General not designed for her observation which sent his daughter to the bell. When the butler would have lit his master's candle, however, he was forbidden. The latter was not going to retire. 'I have many pamphlets to finish,' said he to Catherine, 'before I can close my eyes; and perhaps may be poring over the affairs of the nation for hours after you are asleep. Can either of us be more meetly employed? *My* eyes will be blinding for the good of others; and *yours* preparing by rest for future mischief.'

But neither the business alleged, nor the magnificent compliment, could win Catherine from thinking, that some very different object must occasion so serious a delay of proper repose. To be kept up for hours, after the family were in bed, by stupid pamphlets, was not very likely. There must be some deeper cause: something was to be done which could be done only while the household slept; and the probability that Mrs Tilney yet lived, shut up for causes unknown, and receiving from the pitiless hands of her husband a nightly supply of coarse food, was the conclusion which necessarily followed. Shocking as was the idea, it was at least better than a death unfairly hastened, as, in the natural course of things, she must ere long be released. The suddenness of her reputed illness; the absence of her daughter, and probably of her other children, at the time – all favoured the supposition of her imprisonment. – Its origin – jealousy perhaps, or wanton cruelty – was yet to be unravelled.

In revolving these matters, while she undressed, it suddenly struck her as not unlikely, that she might that morning have passed near the very spot of this unfortunate woman's confinement – might have been within a few paces of the cell in which she languished out her days; for what part of the Abbey could be more fitted for the purpose than that which yet bore the traces of monastic division? In the high-arched passage, paved with stone, which already she had trodden with peculiar awe, she well remembered the doors of which the General had given no account. To what might not those doors lead? In support of the plausibility of this conjecture, it further occurred to her, that the forbidden gallery, in which lay the apartments of the unfortunate Mrs Tilney, must be, as certainly as her memory could guide her, exactly over this suspected range of cells, and the staircase by the side of those apartments of which she had caught a transient glimpse, communicating by some secret means with those cells, might well have favoured the barbarous proceedings of her husband. Down that stair-case she had perhaps been conveyed in a state of well-prepared insensibility!

Catherine sometimes started at the boldness of her own surmises, and sometimes hoped or feared that she had gone too far; but they were supported by such appearances as made their dismissal impossible.

The side of the quadrangle, in which she supposed the guilty scene to be acting, being, according to her belief, just opposite her own, it struck her that, if judiciously watched, some rays of light from the General's lamp might glimmer through the lower windows, as he passed to the prison of his wife; and, twice before she stepped into bed, she stole gently from her room to the corresponding window in the gallery, to see if it appeared; but all abroad was dark, and it must yet be too early. The various ascending noises convinced her that the servants must still be up. Till midnight, she supposed it would be in vain to watch; but then, when the clock had struck twelve, and all was quiet, she would, if not quite appalled by darkness, steal out and look once more. The clock struck twelve – and Catherine had been half an hour asleep.

Chapter 9

The next day afforded no opportunity for the proposed examination of the mysterious apartments. It was Sunday, and the whole time between morning and afternoon service was required by the General in exercise abroad or eating cold meat at home; and great as was Catherine's curiosity, her courage was not equal to a wish of exploring them after dinner, either by the fading light of the sky between six and seven o'clock, or by the yet more partial though stronger illumination of a treacherous lamp. The day was unmarked therefore by any thing to interest her imagination beyond the sight of a very elegant monument to the memory of Mrs Tilney, which immediately fronted the family pew. By that her eye was instantly caught and long retained; and the perusal of the highly-strained epitaph, in which every virtue was ascribed to her by the inconsolable husband, who must have been in some way or other her destroyer, affected her even to tears.

That the General, having erected such a monument, should be able to face it, was not perhaps very strange, and yet that he could sit so boldly collected within its view, maintain so elevated an air, look so fearlessly around, nay, that he should even enter the church, seemed wonderful to Catherine. Not however that many instances of beings equally hardened in guilt might not be produced. She could remember dozens who had persevered in every possible vice, going on from crime to crime, murdering whomsoever they chose, without any feeling of humanity or remorse; till a violent death or a religious retirement closed their black career. The erection of the monument itself could not in the smallest degree affect her doubts of Mrs Tilney's actual decease. Were she even to descend into the family vault where her ashes were supposed to slumber, were she to behold the coffin in which they were said to be enclosed – what could it avail in such a case? Catherine had read too much not to be perfectly aware of the ease with which a waxen figure might be introduced, and a supposititious funeral carried on.

The succeeding morning promised something better. The General's early walk, ill-timed as it was in every other view, was favourable here; and when she knew him to be out of the house, she directly proposed to Miss Tilney the accomplishment of her promise. Eleanor was ready to oblige her; and Catherine reminding her as they went of another promise, their first visit in consequence was to the portrait in her bed-chamber. It represented a very lovely woman, with a mild and pensive countenance, justifying, so far, the expectations of its new observer; but they were not in every respect answered, for Catherine had depended upon meeting with features, air, complexion that should be the very counterpart, the very image, if not of Henry's, of Eleanor's; – the only portraits of which she had been in the habit of thinking, bearing always an equal resemblance of mother and child. A face once taken was taken for generations. But here she was obliged to look and consider and study for a likeness. She contemplated it, however, in spite of this drawback, with much emotion; and, but for a yet stronger interest, would have left it unwillingly.

Her agitation as they entered the great gallery was too much for any endeavour at discourse; she could only look at her companion. Eleanor's countenance was dejected, yet sedate; and its composure spoke her enured to all the gloomy objects to which they were advancing. Again she passed through the folding-doors, again her hand was upon the important lock, and Catherine, hardly able to breathe, was turning to close the former with fearful caution, when the figure, the dreaded figure of the General himself at the further end of the gallery, stood before her! The name of 'Eleanor' at the same moment, in his loudest tone, resounded through the building, giving to his daughter the first intimation of his presence, and to Catherine terror upon terror. An attempt at concealment had been her first instinctive movement on perceiving him, yet she could scarcely hope to have escaped his eye; and when her friend, who with an apologizing look darted hastily by her, had joined and disappeared with him, she ran for safety to her own room, and, locking herself in, believed that she should never have courage to go down again. She remained there at least an hour, in the greatest agitation, deeply commiserating the state of her poor friend, and expecting a summons herself from the angry General to attend him in his own apartment. No summons however arrived; and at last, on seeing a carriage drive up to the Abbey, she was emboldened to descend and meet him under the protection of visitors. The breakfast-room was gay with company; and she was named to them by the

General, as the friend of his daughter, in a complimentary style, which so well concealed his resentful ire, as to make her feel secure at least of life for the present. And Eleanor, with a command of countenance which did honour to her concern for his character, taking an early occasion of saying to her, 'My father only wanted me to answer a note,' she began to hope that she had either been unseen by the General, or that from some consideration of policy she should be allowed to suppose herself so. Upon this trust she dared still to remain in his presence, after the company left them, and nothing occurred to disturb it.

In the course of this morning's reflections, she came to a resolution of making her next attempt on the forbidden door alone. It would be much better in every respect that Eleanor should know nothing of the matter. To involve her in the danger of a second detection, to court her into an apartment which must wring her heart, could not be the office of a friend. The General's utmost anger could not be to herself what it might be to a daughter; and, besides, she thought the examination itself would be more satisfactory if made without any companion. It would be impossible to explain to Eleanor the suspicions, from which the other had, in all likelihood, been hitherto happily exempt; nor could she therefore, in *her* presence, search for those proofs of the General's cruelty, which however they might yet have escaped discovery, she felt confident of somewhere drawing forth, in the shape of some fragmented journal, continued to the last gasp. Of the way to the apartment she was now perfectly mistress; and as she wished to get it over before Henry's return, who was expected on the morrow, there was no time to be lost. The day was bright, her courage high; at four o'clock, the sun was now two hours above the horizon, and it would be only her retiring to dress half an hour earlier than usual.

It was done; and Catherine found herself alone in the gallery before the clocks had ceased to strike. It was no time for thought; she hurried on, slipped with the least possible noise through the folding doors, and without stopping to look or breathe, rushed forward to the one in question. The lock yielded to her hand, and, luckily, with no sullen sound that could alarm a human being. On tip-toe she entered; the room was before her; but it was some minutes before she could advance another step. She beheld what fixed her to the spot and agitated every feature. – She saw a large, well-proportioned apartment, an handsome dimity bed, arranged as unoccupied with an housemaid's care, a bright Bath stove, mahogany wardrobes and neatly-painted chairs, on which the warm beams of a western sun gaily poured through two sash windows! Catherine had expected to have her feelings worked, and worked they were. Astonishment and doubt first seized them; and a shortly succeeding ray of common sense added some bitter emotions of shame. She could not be mistaken as to the room; but how grossly mistaken in every thing else! – in Miss Tilney's meaning, in her own calculation! This apartment, to which she had given a date so ancient, a position so awful, proved to be one end of what the General's father had built. There were two other doors in the chamber, leading probably into dressing-closets; but she had no inclination to open either. Would the veil in which Mrs Tilney had last walked, or the volume in which she had last read, remain to tell what nothing else was allowed to whisper? No: whatever might have been the General's crimes, he had certainly too much wit to let them sue for detection. She was sick of exploring, and desired but to be safe in her own room, with her own heart only privy to its folly; and she was on the point of retreating as softly as she had entered, when the sound of foot-steps, she could hardly tell where, made her pause and tremble. To be found there, even by a servant, would be unpleasant; but by the General, (and he seemed always at hand when least wanted,) much worse! – She listened – the sound had ceased; and resolving not to lose a moment, she passed through and closed the door. At that instant a door underneath was hastily opened; some one seemed with swift steps to ascend the stairs, by the head of which she had yet to pass before she could gain the gallery. She had no power to move. With a feeling of terror not very definable, she fixed her eyes on the staircase, and in a few moments it gave Henry to her view. 'Mr Tilney!' she exclaimed in a voice of more than common astonishment. He looked astonished too. 'Good God!' she continued, not attending to his address, 'how came you here? – how came you up that staircase?'

'How came I up that staircase!' he replied, greatly surprised. 'Because it is my nearest way from the stable-yard to my own chamber; and why should I not come up it?'

Catherine recollected herself, blushed deeply, and could say no more. He seemed to be looking in her countenance for that explanation which her lips did not afford. She moved on towards the gallery. 'And may I not, in my turn,' said he, as he pushed back the folding doors, 'ask how *you* came here? – This passage is at least as extraordinary a road from the breakfast-parlour to your apartment, as that staircase can be from the stables to mine.'

'I have been,' said Catherine, looking down, 'to see your mother's room.'

'My mother's room! – Is there any thing extraordinary to be seen there?'

'No, nothing at all. – I thought you did not mean to come back till to-morrow.'

'I did not expect to be able to return sooner, when I went away; but three hours ago I had the pleasure of finding nothing to detain me. – You look pale. – I am afraid I alarmed you by running so fast up those stairs. Perhaps you did not know – you were not aware of their leading from the offices in common use?'

'No, I was not. – You have had a very fine day for your ride.'

'Very; – and does Eleanor leave you to find your way into all the rooms in the house by yourself?'

'Oh! no; she shewed me over the greatest part on Saturday – and we were coming here to these rooms – but only – (dropping her voice) – your father was with us.'

'And that prevented you;' said Henry, earnestly regarding her. – 'Have you looked into all the rooms in that passage?'

'No, I only wanted to see – Is not it very late? I must go and dress.'

'It is only a quarter past four, (shewing his watch) and you are not now in Bath. No theatre, no rooms to pre-pare for. Half an hour at Northanger must be enough.'

She could not contradict it, and therefore suffered herself to be detained, though her dread of further questions made her, for the first time in their acquaintance, wish to leave him. They walked slowly up the gallery. 'Have you had any letter from Bath since I saw you?'

'No, and I am very much surprized. Isabella promised so faithfully to write directly.'

'Promised so faithfully! – A faithful promise! – That puzzles me. – I have heard of a faithful performance. But a faithful promise – the fidelity of promising! It is a power little worth knowing however, since it can deceive and pain you. My mother's room is very commodious, is it not? Large and cheerful-looking, and the dressing closets so well disposed! It always strikes me as the most comfortable apartment in the house, and I rather wonder that Eleanor should not take it for her own. She sent you to look at it, I suppose?'

'No.'

'It has been your own doing entirely?' – Catherine said nothing – After a short silence, during which he had closely observed her, he added, 'As there is nothing in the room in itself to raise curiosity, this must have proceeded from a sentiment of respect for my mother's character, as described by Eleanor, which does honour to her memory. The world, I believe, never saw a better woman. But it is not often that virtue can boast an interest such as this. The domestic, unpretending merits of a person never known, do not often create that kind of fervent, venerating tenderness which would prompt a visit like yours. Eleanor, I suppose, has talked of her a great deal?'

'Yes, a great deal. That is – no, not much, but what

she did say, was very interesting. Her dying so suddenly,' (slowly, and with hesitation it was spoken,) 'and you – none of you being at home – and your father, I thought – perhaps had not been very fond of her.'

'And from these circumstances,' he replied, (his quick eye fixed on her's), 'you infer perhaps the probability of some negligence – some – (involuntarily she shook her head) – or it may be – of something still less pardonable.' She raised her eyes towards him more fully than she had ever done before. 'My mother's illness,' he continued, 'the seizure which ended in her death *was* sudden. The malady itself, one from which she had often suffered, a bilious fever – its cause therefore constitutional. On the third day, in short as soon as she could be prevailed on, a physician attended her, a very respectable man, and one in whom she had always placed great confidence. Upon his opinion of her danger, two others were called in the next day, and remained in almost constant attendance for four-and-twenty hours. On the fifth day she died. During the progress of her disorder, Frederick and I (*we* were both at home) saw her repeatedly; and from our own observation can bear witness to her having received every possible attention which could spring from the affection of those about her, or which her situation in life could command. Poor Eleanor *was* absent, and at such a distance as to return only to see her mother in her coffin.'

'But your father,' said Catherine, 'was *he* afflicted?'

'For a time, greatly so. You have erred in supposing him not attached to her. He loved her, I am persuaded, as well as it was possible for him to – We have not all, you know, the same tenderness of disposition – and

I will not pretend to say that while she lived, she might not often have had much to bear, but though his temper injured her, his judgment never did. His value of her was sincere; and, if not permanently, he was truly afflicted by her death.'

'I am very glad of it,' said Catherine, 'it would have been very shocking!' –

'If I understand you rightly, you had formed a surmise of such horror as I have hardly words to – Dear Miss Morland, consider the dreadful nature of the suspicions you have entertained. What have you been judging from? Remembering the country and the age in which we live. Remember that we are English, that we are Christians. Consult your own understanding, your own sense of the probable, your own observation of what is passing around you – Does our education prepare us for such atrocities? Do our laws connive at them? Could they be perpetrated without being known, in a country like this, where social and literary intercourse is on such a footing; where every man is surrounded by a neighbourhood of voluntary spies, and where roads and newspapers lay every thing open? Dearest Miss Morland, what ideas have you been admitting?'

They had reached the end of the gallery; and with tears of shame she ran off to her own room.

Chapter 10

The visions of romance were over. Catherine was completely awakened. Henry's address, short as it had been, had more thoroughly opened her eyes to the extravagance of her late fancies than all their several disappointments had done. Most grievously was she humbled. Most bitterly did she cry. It was not only with herself that she was sunk – but with Henry. Her folly, which now seemed even criminal, was all exposed to him, and he must despise her for ever. The liberty which her imagination had dared to take with the character of his father, could he ever forgive it? The absurdity of her curiosity and her fears, could they ever be forgotten? She hated herself more than she could express. He had – she thought he had, once or twice before this fatal morning, shewn something like affection for her. – But now – in short, she made herself as miserable as possible for about half an hour, went down when the clock struck five, with a broken heart, and could scarcely give an intelligible answer to Eleanor's inquiry, if she was well. The formidable Henry soon followed her into the room, and the only difference in his behaviour to her, was that he paid her rather more attention than usual. Catherine had never wanted comfort more, and he looked as if he was aware of it.

The evening wore away with no abatement of this

soothing politeness; and her spirits were gradually raised to a modest tranquillity. She did not learn either to forget or defend the past; but she learned to hope that it would never transpire farther, and that it might not cost her Henry's entire regard. Her thoughts being still chiefly fixed on what she had with such causeless terror felt and done, nothing could shortly be clearer, than that it had been all a voluntary, self-created delusion, each trifling circumstance receiving importance from an imagination resolved on alarm, and every thing forced to bend to one purpose by a mind which, before she entered the Abbey, had been craving to be frightened. She remembered with what feelings she had prepared for a knowledge of Northanger. She saw that the infatuation had been created, the mischief settled long before her quitting Bath, and it seemed as if the whole might be traced to the influence of that sort of reading which she had there indulged.

Charming as were all Mrs Radcliffe's works, and charming even as were the works of all her imitators, it was not in them perhaps that human nature, at least in the midland counties of England, was to be looked for. Of the Alps and Pyrenees, with their pine forests and their vices, they might give a faithful delineation; and Italy, Switzerland, and the South of France, might be as fruitful in horrors as they were there represented. Catherine dared not doubt beyond her own country, and even of that, if hard pressed, would have yielded the northern and western extremities. But in the central part of England there was surely some security for the existence even of a wife not beloved, in the laws of the land, and the manners of the age. Murder was not tolerated, servants were not slaves, and neither poison nor sleeping potions to be procured, like rhubarb, from every druggist. Among the Alps and Pyrenees, perhaps, there were no mixed characters. There, such as were not as spotless as an angel, might have the dispositions of a fiend. But in England it was not so; among the English, she believed, in their hearts and habits, there was a general though unequal mixture of good and bad. Upon this conviction, she would not be surprized if even in Henry and Eleanor Tilney, some slight imperfection might hereafter appear; and upon this conviction she need not fear to acknowledge some actual specks in the character of their father, who, though cleared from the grossly injurious suspicions which she must ever blush to have entertained, she did believe, upon serious consideration, to be not perfectly amiable.

Her mind made up on these several points, and her resolution formed, of always judging and acting in future with the greatest good sense, she had nothing to do but to forgive herself and be happier than ever; and the lenient hand of time did much for her by insensible gradations in the course of another day. Henry's astonishing generosity and nobleness of conduct, in never alluding in the slightest way to what had passed, was of the greatest assistance to her; and sooner than she could have supposed it possible in the beginning of her distress, her spirits became absolutely comfortable, and capable, as heretofore, of continual improvement by any thing he said. There were still some subjects indeed, under which she believed they must always tremble; – the mention of a chest or a cabinet, for instance – and she did not love the sight of japan in any shape: but even *she* could allow, that an occasional memento of past folly, however painful, might not be without use.

The anxieties of common life began soon to succeed to the alarms of romance. Her desire of hearing from Isabella grew every day greater. She was quite impatient to know how the Bath world went on, and how the Rooms were attended; and especially was she anxious to be assured of Isabella's having matched some fine netting-cotton, on which she had left her intent; and of her continuing on the best terms with James. Her only dependence for information of any kind was on Isabella. James had protested against writing to her till his return to Oxford; and Mrs Allen had given her no hopes of a letter till she had got back to Fullerton. – But Isabella had promised and promised again; and when she promised a thing, she was so scrupulous in performing it! this made it so particularly strange!

For nine successive mornings, Catherine wondered over the repetition of a disappointment, which each morning became more severe: but, on the tenth, when she entered the breakfast-room, her first object was a letter, held out by Henry's willing hand. She thanked him as heartily as if he had written it himself. ''Tis only from James, however,' as she looked at the direction. She opened it; it was from Oxford; and to this purpose: –

'Dear Catherine,
    'Though, God knows, with little inclination for writing, I think it my duty to tell you, that every thing is at an end between Miss Thorpe and me. – I left her and Bath yesterday, never to see either again. I shall not enter into particulars, they would only pain you

*more. You will soon hear enough from another quarter
to know where lies the blame; and I hope will acquit
your brother of every thing but the folly of too easily
thinking his affection returned. Thank God! I am
undeceived in time! But it is a heavy blow! – After my
father's consent had been so kindly given – but no more
of this. She has made me miserable for ever! Let me
soon hear from you, dear Catherine; you are my only
friend; your love I do build upon. I wish your visit at
Northanger may be over before Captain Tilney makes
his engagement known, or you will be uncomfortably
circumstanced. – Poor Thorpe is in town: I dread the
sight of him; his honest heart would feel so much. I
have written to him and my father. Her duplicity hurts
me more than all; till the very last, if I reasoned with
her, she declared herself as much attached to me as
ever, and laughed at my fears. I am ashamed to think
how long I bore with it; but if ever man had reason to
believe himself loved, I was that man. I cannot
understand even now what she would be at, for there
could be no need of my being played off to make her
secure of Tilney. We parted at last by mutual consent –
happy for me had we never met! I can never expect to
know such another woman! Dearest Catherine, beware
how you give your heart.*

> *'Believe me,' &c.*

Catherine had not read three lines before her sudden
change of countenance, and short exclamations of sor-
rowing wonder, declared her to be receiving unpleasant
news; and Henry, earnestly watching her through the
whole letter, saw plainly that it ended no better than it

began. He was prevented, however, from even looking his surprize by his father's entrance. They went to breakfast directly; but Catherine could hardly eat any thing. Tears filled her eyes, and even ran down her cheeks as she sat. The letter was one moment in her hand, then in her lap, and then in her pocket; and she looked as if she knew not what she did. The General, between his cocoa and his newspaper, had luckily no leisure for noticing her; but to the other two her distress was equally visible. As soon as she dared leave the table she hurried away to her own room; but the house-maids were busy in it, and she was obliged to come down again. She turned into the drawing-room for privacy, but Henry and Eleanor had likewise retreated thither, and were at that moment deep in consultation about her. She drew back, trying to beg their pardon, but was, with gentle violence, forced to return; and the others withdrew, after Eleanor had affectionately expressed a wish of being of use or comfort to her.

After half an hour's free indulgence of grief and reflection, Catherine felt equal to encountering her friends; but whether she should make her distress known to them was another consideration. Perhaps, if particularly questioned, she might just give an idea – just distantly hint at it – but not more. To expose a friend, such a friend as Isabella had been to her – and then their own brother so closely concerned in it! – She believed she must wave the subject altogether. Henry and Eleanor were by themselves in the breakfast-room; and each, as she entered it, looked at her anxiously. Catherine took her place at the table, and, after a short silence, Eleanor said, 'No bad news from Fullerton, I hope? Mr and Mrs

Morland – your brothers and sisters – I hope they are none of them ill?'

'No, I thank you,' (sighing as she spoke,) 'they are all very well. My letter was from my brother at Oxford.'

Nothing further was said for a few minutes; and then speaking through her tears, she added, 'I do not think I shall ever wish for a letter again!'

'I am sorry,' said Henry, closing the book he had just opened; 'if I had suspected the letter of containing any thing unwelcome, I should have given it with very different feelings.'

'It contained something worse than any body could suppose! – Poor James is so unhappy! – You will soon know why.'

'To have so kind-hearted, so affectionate a sister,' replied Henry, warmly, 'must be a comfort to him under any distress.'

'I have one favour to beg,' said Catherine, shortly afterwards, in an agitated manner, 'that, if your brother should be coming here, you will give me notice of it, that I may go away.'

'Our brother! – Frederick!'

'Yes; I am sure I should be very sorry to leave you so soon, but something has happened that would make it very dreadful for me to be in the same house with Captain Tilney.'

Eleanor's work was suspended while she gazed with increasing astonishment; but Henry began to suspect the truth, and something, in which Miss Thorpe's name was included, passed his lips.

'How quick you are!' cried Catherine: 'you have guessed it, I declare! – And yet, when we talked about it in Bath, you little thought of its ending so. Isabella – no wonder *now* I have not heard from her – Isabella has deserted my brother, and is to marry your's! Could you have believed there had been such inconstancy and fickleness, and every thing that is bad in the world?'

'I hope, so far as concerns my brother, you are misinformed. I hope he has not had any material share in bringing on Mr Morland's disappointment. His marrying Miss Thorpe is not probable. I think you must be deceived so far. I am very sorry for Mr Morland – sorry that any one you love should be unhappy; but my surprize would be greater at Frederick's marrying her, than at any other part of the story.'

'It is very true, however; you shall read James's letter yourself. – Stay – there is one part –' recollecting with a blush the last line.

'Will you take the trouble of reading to us the passages which concern my brother?'

'No, read it yourself,' cried Catherine, whose second thoughts were clearer. 'I do not know what I was thinking of,' (blushing again that she had blushed before,) – 'James only means to give me good advice.'

He gladly received the letter; and, having read it through, with close attention, returned it saying, 'Well, if it is to be so, I can only say that I am sorry for it. Frederick will not be the first man who has chosen a wife with less sense than his family expected. I do not envy his situation, either as a lover or a son.'

Miss Tilney, at Catherine's invitation, now read the letter likewise; and, having expressed also her concern and surprize, began to inquire into Miss Thorpe's connexions and fortune.

'Her mother is a very good sort of woman,' was Catherine's answer.

'What was her father?'

'A lawyer, I believe. – They live at Putney.'

'Are they a wealthy family?'

'No, not very. I do not believe Isabella has any fortune at all: but that will not signify in your family. – Your father is so very liberal! He told me the other day, that he only valued money as it allowed him to promote the happiness of his children.' The brother and sister looked at each other. 'But,' said Eleanor, after a short pause, 'would it be to promote his happiness, to enable him to marry such a girl? – She must be an unprincipled one, or she could not have used your brother so. – And how strange an infatuation on Frederick's side! A girl who, before his eyes, is violating an engagement voluntarily entered into with another man! Is not it inconceivable, Henry? Frederick too, who always wore his heart so proudly! who found no woman good enough to be loved!'

'That is the most unpromising circumstance, the strongest presumption against him. When I think of his past declarations, I give him up. – Moreover, I have too good an opinion of Miss Thorpe's prudence, to suppose that she would part with one gentleman before the other was secured. It is all over with Frederick indeed! He is a deceased man – defunct in understanding. Prepare for your sister-in-law, Eleanor, and such a sister-in-law as you must delight in! – Open, candid, artless, guileless, with affections strong but simple, forming no pretensions, and knowing no disguise.'

'Such a sister-in-law, Henry, I should delight in,' said Eleanor, with a smile.

'But perhaps,' observed Catherine, 'though she has behaved so ill by our family, she may behave better by your's. Now she has really got the man she likes, she may be constant.'

'Indeed I am afraid she will,' replied Henry; 'I am afraid she will be very constant, unless a baronet should come in her way; that is Frederick's only chance. – I will get the Bath paper, and look over the arrivals.'

'You think it is all for ambition then? – And, upon my word, there are some things that seem very like it. I cannot forget, that, when she first knew what my father would do for them, she seemed quite disappointed that it was not more. I never was so deceived in any one's character in my life before.'

'Among all the great variety that you have known and studied.'

'My own disappointment and loss in her is very great; but, as for poor James, I suppose he will hardly ever recover it.'

'Your brother is certainly very much to be pitied at present; but we must not, in our concern for his sufferings, undervalue your's. You feel, I suppose, that, in losing Isabella, you lose half yourself: you feel a void in your heart which nothing else can occupy. Society is becoming irksome; and as for the amusements in which you were wont to share at Bath, the very idea of them without her is abhorrent. You would not, for instance, now go to a ball for the world. You feel that you have no longer any friend to whom you can speak with unreserve; on whose regard you can place dependence; or whose counsel, in any difficulty, you could rely on. You feel all this?'

'No,' said Catherine, after a few moments' reflection, 'I do not – ought I? To say the truth, though I am hurt and grieved, that I cannot still love her, that I am never to hear from her, perhaps never to see her again, I do not feel so very, very much afflicted as one would have thought.'

'You feel, as you always do, what is most to the credit of human nature. – Such feeling ought to be investigated, that they may know themselves.'

Catherine, by some chance or other, found her spirits so very much relieved by this conversation, that she could not regret her being led on, though so un-accountably, to mention the circumstance which had produced it.

Chapter 11

From this time, the subject was frequently canvassed by the three young people; and Catherine found, with some surprize, that her two young friends were perfectly agreed in considering Isabella's want of consequence and fortune as likely to throw great difficulties in the way of her marrying their brother. Their persuasion that the General would, upon this ground alone, independent of the objection that might be raised against her character, oppose the connexion, turned her feelings moreover with some alarm towards herself. She was as insignificant, and perhaps as portionless as Isabella; and if the heir of the Tilney property had not grandeur and wealth enough in himself, at what point of interest were the demands of his younger brother to rest? The very painful reflections to which this thought led, could only be dispersed by a dependence on the effect of that particular partiality, which, as she was given to understand by his words as well as his actions, she had from the first been so fortunate as to excite in the General; and by a recollection of some most generous and disinterested sentiments on the subject of money, which she had more than once heard him utter, and which tempted her to think his disposition in such matters misunderstood by his children.

They were so fully convinced, however, that their brother would not have the courage to apply in person for his father's consent, and so repeatedly assured her that he had never in his life been less likely to come to Northanger than at the present time, that she suffered her mind to be at ease as to the necessity of any sudden removal of her own. But as it was not to be supposed that Captain Tilney, whenever he made his application, would give his father any just idea of Isabella's conduct, it occurred to her as highly expedient that Henry should lay the whole business before him as it really was, enabling the General by that means to form a cool and impartial opinion, and prepare his objections on a fairer ground than inequality of situations. She proposed it to him accordingly; but he did not catch at the measure so eagerly as she had expected. 'No,' said he, 'my father's hands need not be strengthened, and Frederick's confession of folly need not be forestalled. He must tell his own story.'

'But he will tell only half of it.'

'A quarter would be enough.'

A day or two passed away and brought no tidings of Captain Tilney. His brother and sister knew not what to think. Sometimes it appeared to them as if his silence would be the natural result of the suspected engagement, and at others that it was wholly incompatible with it. The General, meanwhile, though offended every morning by Frederick's remissness in writing, was free from any real anxiety about him; and had no more pressing solicitude than that of making Miss Morland's time at Northanger pass pleasantly. He often expressed his uneasiness on this head, feared the sameness of every day's society and employments would disgust her with the place, wished the Lady Frasers had been in the country, talked every now and then of having a large party to dinner, and once or twice began even to calculate the number of young dancing people in the neighbourhood. But then it was such a dead time of year, no wild-fowl, no game, and the Lady Frasers were not in the country. And it all ended, at last, in his telling Henry one morning, that when he next went to Woodston, they would take him by surprize there some day or other, and eat their mutton with him. Henry was greatly honoured and very happy, and Catherine was quite delighted with the scheme. 'And when do you think, sir, I may look forward to this pleasure? – I must be at Woodston on Monday to attend the parish meeting, and shall probably be obliged to stay two or three days.'

'Well, well, we will take our chance some one of those days. There is no need to fix. You are not to put yourself at all out of your way. Whatever you may happen to have in the house will be enough. I think I can answer for the young ladies making allowance for a bachelor's table. Let me see; Monday will be a busy day with you, we will not come on Monday; and Tuesday will be a busy one with me. I expect my surveyor from Brockham with his report in the morning; and afterwards I cannot in decency fail attending the club. I really could not face my acquaintance if I staid away now; for, as I am known to be in the country, it would be taken exceedingly amiss; and it is a rule with me, Miss Morland, never to give offence to any of my neighbours, if a small sacrifice of time and attention can prevent it. They are a set of very worthy men. They have half a buck from Northanger twice a year; and I dine with them whenever I can. Tuesday, therefore, we may say is out of the question.

But on Wednesday, I think, Henry, you may expect us; and we shall be with you early, that we may have time to look about us. Two hours and three quarters will carry us to Woodston, I suppose; we shall be in the carriage by ten; so, about a quarter before one on Wednesday, you may look for us.'

A ball itself could not have been more welcome to Catherine than this little excursion, so strong was her desire to be acquainted with Woodston; and her heart was still bounding with joy, when Henry, about an hour afterwards, came booted and great coated into the room where she and Eleanor were sitting, and said, 'I am come, young ladies, in a very moralizing strain, to observe that our pleasures in this world are always to be paid for, and that we often purchase them at a great disadvantage, giving ready-monied actual happiness for a draft on the future, that may not be honoured. Witness myself, at this present hour. Because I am to hope for the satisfaction of seeing you at Woodston on Wednesday, which bad weather, or twenty other causes may prevent, I must go away directly, two days before I intended it.'

'Go away!' said Catherine, with a very long face; 'and why?'

'Why! – How can you ask the question? – Because no time is to be lost in frightening my old housekeeper out of her wits, – because I must go and prepare a dinner for you to be sure.'

'Oh! not seriously!'

'Aye, and sadly too – for I had much rather stay.'

'But how can you think of such a thing, after what the General said? when he so particularly desired you not to give yourself any trouble, because *any thing* would do.'

Henry only smiled. 'I am sure it is quite unnecessary upon your sister's account and mine. You must know it to be so; and the General made such a point of your providing nothing extraordinary: – besides, if he had not said half so much as he did, he has always such an excellent dinner at home, that sitting down to a middling one for one day could not signify.'

'I wish I could reason like you, for his sake and my own. Good bye. As to-morrow is Sunday, Eleanor, I shall not return.'

He went; and, it being at any time a much simpler operation to Catherine to doubt her own judgment than Henry's, she was very soon obliged to give him credit for being right, however disagreeable to her his going. But the inexplicability of the General's conduct dwelt much on her thoughts. That he was very particular in his eating, she had, by her own unassisted observation, already discovered; but why he should say one thing so positively, and mean another all the while, was most unaccountable! How were people, at that rate, to be understood? Who but Henry could have been aware of what his father was at?

From Saturday to Wednesday, however, they were now to be without Henry. This was the sad finale of every reflection: – and Captain Tilney's letter would certainly come in his absence; and Wednesday she was very sure would be wet. The past, present, and future, were all equally in gloom. Her brother so unhappy, and her loss in Isabella so great; and Eleanor's spirits always affected by Henry's absence! What was there to interest or amuse her? She was tired of the woods and the shrubberies – always so smooth and so dry; and the

Abbey in itself was no more to her now than any other house. The painful remembrance of the folly it had helped to nourish and perfect, was the only emotion which could spring from a consideration of the building. What a revolution in her ideas! she, who had so longed to be in an abbey! Now, there was nothing so charming to her imagination as the unpretending comfort of a well-connected Parsonage, something like Fullerton, but better: Fullerton had its faults, but Woodston probably had none. – If Wednesday should ever come!

It did come, and exactly when it might be reasonably looked for. It came – it was fine – and Catherine trod on air. By ten o'clock, the chaise-and-four conveyed the trio from the Abbey; and, after an agreeable drive of almost twenty miles, they entered Woodston, a large and populous village, in a situation not unpleasant. Catherine was ashamed to say how pretty she thought it, as the General seemed to think an apology necessary for the flatness of the country, and the size of the village; but in her heart she preferred it to any place she had ever been at, and looked with great admiration at every neat house above the rank of a cottage, and at all the little chandler's shops which they passed. At the further end of the village, and tolerably disengaged from the rest of it, stood the Parsonage, a new-built substantial stone house, with its semi-circular sweep and green gates; and, as they drove up to the door, Henry, with the friends of his solitude, a large Newfoundland puppy and two or three terriers, was ready to receive and make much of them.

Catherine's mind was too full, as she entered the house, for her either to observe or to say a great deal; and, till called on by the General for her opinion of it, she had very little idea of the room in which she was sitting. Upon looking round it then, she perceived in a moment that it was the most comfortable room in the world; but she was too guarded to say so, and the coldness of her praise disappointed him.

'We are not calling it a good house,' said he. – 'We are not comparing it with Fullerton and Northanger – We are considering it as a mere Parsonage, small and confined, we allow, but decent perhaps, and habitable; and altogether not inferior to the generality; – or, in other words, I believe there are few country parsonages in England half so good. It may admit of improvement, however. Far be it from me to say otherwise; and any thing in reason – a bow thrown out, perhaps – though, between ourselves, if there is one thing more than another my aversion, it is a patched-on bow.'

Catherine did not hear enough of this speech to understand or be pained by it; and other subjects being studiously brought forward and supported by Henry, at the same time that a tray full of refreshments was introduced by his servant, the General was shortly restored to his complacency, and Catherine to all her usual ease of spirits.

The room in question was of a commodious, well-proportioned size, and handsomely fitted up as a dining parlour; and on their quitting it to walk round the grounds, she was shewn, first into a smaller apartment, belonging peculiarly to the master of the house, and made unusually tidy on the occasion; and afterwards into what was to be the drawing-room, with the appearance of which, though unfurnished, Catherine was delighted enough even to satisfy the General. It was a prettily-shaped room, the windows reaching to the ground, and the view from them pleasant, though only over green meadows; and she expressed her admiration at the moment with all the honest simplicity with which she felt it. 'Oh! why do not you fit up this room, Mr Tilney? What a pity not to have it fitted up! It is the prettiest room I ever saw; – it is the prettiest room in the world!'

'I trust,' said the General, with a most satisfied smile, 'that it will very speedily be furnished: it waits only for a lady's taste!'

'Well, if it was my house, I should never sit any where else. Oh! what a sweet little cottage there is among the trees – apple trees too! It is the prettiest cottage!' –

'You like it – you approve it as an object; – it is enough. Henry, remember that Robinson is spoken to about it. The cottage remains.'

Such a compliment recalled all Catherine's consciousness, and silenced her directly; and, though pointedly applied to by the General for her choice of the prevailing colour of the paper and hangings, nothing like an opinion on the subject could be drawn from her. The influence of fresh objects and fresh air, however, was of great use in dissipating these embarrassing associations; and, having reached the ornamental part of the premises, consisting of a walk round two sides of a meadow, on which Henry's genius had begun to act about half a year ago, she was sufficiently recovered to think it prettier than any pleasure-ground she had ever been in before, though there was not a shrub in it higher than the green bench in the corner.

A saunter into other meadows, and through part of

the village, with a visit to the stables to examine some improvements, and a charming game of play with a litter of puppies just able to roll about, brought them to four o'clock, when Catherine scarcely thought it could be three. At four they were to dine, and at six to set off on their return. Never had any day passed so quickly!

She could not but observe that the abundance of the dinner did not seem to create the smallest astonishment in the General; nay, that he was even looking at the side-table for cold meat which was not there. His son and daughter's observations were of a different kind. They had seldom seen him eat so heartily at any table but his own; and never before known him so little disconcerted by the melted butter's being oiled.

At six o'clock, the General having taken his coffee, the carriage again received them; and so gratifying had been the tenor of his conduct throughout the whole visit, so well assured was her mind on the subject of his expectations, that, could she have felt equally confident of the wishes of his son, Catherine would have quitted Woodston with little anxiety as to the How or the When she might return to it.

Chapter 12

The next morning brought the following very unexpected letter from Isabella: –

> *Bath, April –*
>
> My dearest Catherine,
>
> *I received your two kind letters with the greatest delight, and have a thousand apologies to make for not answering them sooner. I really am quite ashamed of my idleness; but in this horrid place one can find time for nothing. I have had my pen in my hand to begin a letter to you almost every day since you left Bath, but have always been prevented by some silly trifler or other. Pray write to me soon, and direct to my own home. Thank God! we leave this vile place to-morrow. Since you went away, I have had no pleasure in it – the dust is beyond any thing; and every body one cares for is gone. I believe if I could see you I should not mind the rest, for you are dearer to me than any body can conceive. I am quite uneasy about your dear brother, not having heard from him since he went to Oxford; and am fearful of some misunderstanding. Your kind offices will set all right: – he is the only man I ever did or could love, and I trust you will convince him of it. The spring fashions are partly down; and the hats the most frightful you can imagine. I hope you spend your time pleasantly, but am afraid you never*

think of me. I will not say all that I could of the family you are with, because I would not be ungenerous, or set you against those you esteem; but it is very difficult to know whom to trust, and young men never know their minds two days together. I rejoice to say, that the young man whom, of all others, I particularly abhor, has left Bath. You will know, from this description, I must mean Captain Tilney, who, as you may remember, was amazingly disposed to follow and tease me, before you went away. Afterwards he got worse, and became quite my shadow. Many girls might have been taken in, for never were such attentions; but I knew the fickle sex too well. He went away to his regiment two days ago, and I trust I shall never be plagued with him again. He is the greatest coxcomb I ever saw, and amazingly disagreeable. The last two days he was always by the side of Charlotte Davis: I pitied his taste, but took no notice of him. The last time we met was in Bath-street, and I turned directly into a shop that he might not speak to me; – I would not even look at him. He went into the Pump-room afterwards; but I would not have followed him for all the world. Such a contrast between him and your brother! – pray send me some news of the latter – I am quite unhappy about him, he seemed so uncomfortable when he went away, with a cold, or something that affected his spirits. I would write to him myself, but have mislaid his direction; and, as I hinted above, am afraid he took something in my conduct amiss. Pray explain every thing to his satisfaction; or, if he still harbours any doubt, a line from himself to me, or a call at Putney when next in town, might set all to rights.

I have not been to the Rooms this age, nor to the Play,
except going in last night with the Hodges's, for a
frolic, at half-price: they teased me into it; and I was
determined they should not say I shut myself up
because Tilney was gone. We happened to sit by the
Mitchells, and they pretended to be quite surprized to
see me out. I knew their spite: – at one time they could
not be civil to me, but now they are all friendship; but
I am not such a fool as to be taken in by them. You
know I have a pretty good spirit of my own. Anne
Mitchell had tried to put on a turban like mine, as
I wore it the week before at the Concert, but made
wretched work of it – it happened to become my odd
face I believe, at least Tilney told me so at the time,
and said every eye was upon me; but he is the last
man whose word I would take. I wear nothing but
purple now: I know I look hideous in it, but no matter
– it is your dear brother's favourite colour. Lose no
time, my dearest, sweetest Catherine, in writing to him
and to me,

Who ever am, &c.

Such a strain of shallow artifice could not impose even
upon Catherine. Its inconsistencies, contradictions, and
falsehood, struck her from the very first. She was
ashamed of Isabella, and ashamed of having ever loved
her. Her professions of attachment were now as disgust-
ing as her excuses were empty, and her demands impudent. 'Write to James on her behalf! – No, James should
never hear Isabella's name mentioned by her again.'

On Henry's arrival from Woodston, she made known
to him and Eleanor their brother's safety, congratulating

them with sincerity on it, and reading aloud the most material passages of her letter with strong indignation. When she had finished it, – 'So much for Isabella,' she cried, 'and for all our intimacy! She must think me an idiot, or she could not have written so; but perhaps this has served to make her character better known to me than mine is to her. I see what she has been about. She is a vain coquette, and her tricks have not answered. I do not believe she had ever any regard either for James or for me, and I wish I had never known her.'

'It will soon be as if you never had,' said Henry.

'There is but one thing that I cannot understand. I see that she has had designs on Captain Tilney, which have not succeeded; but I do not understand what Captain Tilney has been about all this time. Why should he pay her such attentions as to make her quarrel with my brother, and then fly off himself?'

'I have very little to say for Frederick's motives, such as I believe them to have been. He has his vanities as well as Miss Thorpe, and the chief difference is, that, having a stronger head, they have not yet injured himself. If the *effect* of his behaviour does not justify him with you, we had better not seek after the cause.'

'Then you do not suppose he ever really cared about her?'

'I am persuaded that he never did.'

'And only made believe to do so for mischief's sake?'

Henry bowed his assent.

'Well, then, I must say that I do not like him at all. Though it has turned out so well for us, I do not like him at all. As it happens, there is no great harm done, because I do not think Isabella has any heart to lose. But, suppose he had made her very much in love with him?'

'But we must first suppose Isabella to have had a heart to lose, – consequently to have been a very different creature; and, in that case, she would have met with very different treatment.'

'It is very right that you should stand by your brother.'

'And if you would stand by *your's*, you would not be much distressed by the disappointment of Miss Thorpe. But your mind is warped by an innate principle of general integrity, and therefore not accessible to the cool reasonings of family partiality, or a desire of revenge.'

Catherine was complimented out of further bitterness. Frederick could not be unpardonably guilty, while Henry made himself so agreeable. She resolved on not answering Isabella's letter; and tried to think no more of it.

Chapter 13

Soon after this, the General found himself obliged to go to London for a week; and he left Northanger earnestly regretting that any necessity should rob him even for an hour of Miss Morland's company, and anxiously recommending the study of her comfort and amusement to his children as their chief object in his absence. His departure gave Catherine the first experimental conviction that a loss may be sometimes a gain. The happiness with which their time now passed, every employment voluntary, every laugh indulged, every meal a scene of ease and good-humour, walking where they liked and when they liked, their hours, pleasures and fatigues at their own command, made her thoroughly sensible of the restraint which the General's presence had imposed, and most thankfully feel their present release from it. Such ease and such delights made her love the place and the people more and more every day; and had it not been for a dread of its soon becoming expedient to leave the one, and an apprehension of not being equally beloved by the other, she would at each moment of each day have been perfectly happy; but she was now in the fourth week of her visit; before the General came home, the fourth week would be turned, and perhaps it might seem an intrusion if she staid much longer. This was a painful consideration whenever it occurred; and eager to get rid of such a weight on her mind, she very soon resolved to speak to Eleanor about it at once, propose going away, and be guided in her conduct by the manner in which her proposal might be taken.

Aware that if she gave herself much time, she might feel it difficult to bring forward so unpleasant a subject, she took the first opportunity of being suddenly alone with Eleanor, and of Eleanor's being in the middle of a speech about something very different, to start forth her obligation of going away very soon. Eleanor looked and declared herself much concerned. She had 'hoped for the pleasure of her company for a much longer time – had been misled (perhaps by her wishes) to suppose that a much longer visit had been promised – and could not but think that if Mr and Mrs Morland were aware of the pleasure it was to her to have her there, they would be too generous to hasten her return.' – Catherine explained. – 'Oh! as to *that*, papa and mamma were in no hurry at all. As long as she was happy, they would always be satisfied.'

'Then why, might she ask, in such a hurry herself to leave them?'

'Oh! because she had been there so long.'

'Nay, if you can use such a word, I can urge you no farther. If you think it long –'

'Oh! no, I do not indeed. For my own pleasure, I could stay with you as long again.' – And it was directly settled that, till she had, her leaving them was not even to be thought of. In having this cause of uneasiness so pleasantly removed, the force of the other was likewise weakened. The kindness, the earnestness of Eleanor's manner in pressing her to stay, and Henry's gratified look on being told that her stay was determined, were such sweet proofs of her importance with them, as left her only just so much solicitude as the human mind can never do comfortably without. She did – almost always – believe that Henry loved her, and quite always that his father and sister loved and even wished her to belong to them; and believing so far, her doubts and anxieties were merely sportive irritations.

Henry was not able to obey his father's injunction of remaining wholly at Northanger in attendance on the ladies, during his absence in London; the engagements of his curate at Woodston obliging him to leave them on Saturday for a couple of nights. His loss was not now what it had been while the General was at home; it lessened their gaiety, but did not ruin their comfort; and the two girls agreeing in occupation, and improving in intimacy, found themselves so well-sufficient for the time to themselves, that it was eleven o'clock, rather a late hour at the Abbey, before they quitted the supper-room on the day of Henry's departure. They had just reached the head of the stairs, when it seemed, as far as the thickness of the walls would allow them to judge, that a carriage was driving up to the door, and the next moment confirmed the idea by the loud noise of the house-bell. After the first perturbation of surprize had passed away, in a 'Good Heaven! what can be the matter?' it was quickly decided by Eleanor to be her eldest brother, whose arrival was often as sudden, if not quite so unseasonable, and accordingly she hurried down to welcome him.

Catherine walked on to her chamber, making up her mind as well as she could, to a further acquaintance with Captain Tilney, and comforting herself under the unpleasant impression his conduct had given her, and the persuasion of his being by far too fine a gentleman to approve of her, that at least they should not meet under such circumstances as would make their meeting materially painful. She trusted he would never speak of Miss Thorpe; and indeed, as he must by this time be ashamed of the part he had acted, there could be no danger of it; and as long as all mention of Bath scenes were avoided, she thought she could behave to him very civilly. In such considerations time passed away, and it was certainly in his favour that Eleanor should be so glad to see him, and have so much to say, for half an hour was almost gone since his arrival, and Eleanor did not come up.

At that moment Catherine thought she heard her step in the gallery, and listened for its continuance; but all was silent. Scarcely, however, had she convicted her fancy of error, when the noise of something moving close to her door made her start; it seemed as if some one was touching the very doorway – and in another moment a slight motion of the lock proved that some hand must be on it. She trembled a little at the idea of any one's approaching so cautiously; but resolving not to be again overcome by trivial appearances of alarm, or misled by a raised imagination, she stepped quietly forward, and opened the door. Eleanor, and only Eleanor, stood there. Catherine's spirits however were tranquillized but for an instant, for Eleanor's cheeks were pale, and her manner greatly agitated. Though evidently intending to come in, it seemed an effort to enter the room, and a still greater to speak when there. Catherine, supposing some uneasiness on Captain Tilney's account, could only express her concern by silent attention; obliged her to be seated, rubbed her temples with lavender-water, and hung over her with affectionate solicitude. 'My dear Catherine, you must not – you must not indeed –' were Eleanor's first connected words. 'I am quite well. This kindness distracts me – I cannot bear it – I come to you on such an errand!'

'Errand! – to me!'

'How shall I tell you! – Oh! how shall I tell you!'

A new idea now darted into Catherine's mind, and turning as pale as her friend, she exclaimed, ''Tis a messenger from Woodston!'

'You are mistaken, indeed,' returned Eleanor, looking at her most compassionately – 'it is no one from Woodston. It is my father himself.' Her voice faltered, and her eyes were turned to the ground as she mentioned his name. His unlooked-for return was enough in itself to make Catherine's heart sink, and for a few moments she hardly supposed there were any thing worse to be told. She said nothing; and Eleanor endeavouring to collect herself and speak with firmness, but with eyes still cast down, soon went on. 'You are too good, I am sure, to think the worse of me for the part I am obliged to perform. I am indeed a most unwilling messenger. After what has so lately passed, so lately been settled between us – how joyfully, how thankfully on my side! – as to your continuing here as I hoped for many, many weeks longer, how can I tell you that your kindness is not to be accepted – and that the happiness your company has hitherto given us is to be repaid by – but I must not trust myself with words. My dear Catherine, we are to part. My father has recollected an engagement that takes our whole family away on Monday. We are going to Lord Longtown's, near Hereford, for a fortnight. Explanation and apology are equally impossible. I cannot attempt either.'

'My dear Eleanor,' cried Catherine, suppressing her feelings as well as she could, 'do not be so distressed. A second engagement must give way to a first. I am very, very sorry we are to part – so soon, and so suddenly too; but I am not offended, indeed I am not. I can finish my visit here you know at any time; or I hope you will come to me. Can you, when you return from this lord's, come to Fullerton?'

'It will not be in my power, Catherine.'

'Come when you can, then.' –

Eleanor made no answer; and Catherine's thoughts recurring to something more directly interesting, she added, thinking aloud, 'Monday – so soon as Monday; – and you *all* go. Well, I am certain of – I shall be able to take leave however. I need not go till just before you do, you know. Do not be distressed, Eleanor, I can go on Monday very well. My father and mother's having no notice of it is of very little consequence. The General will send a servant with me, I dare say, half the way – and then I shall soon be at Salisbury, and then I am only nine miles from home.'

'Ah, Catherine! were it settled so, it would be somewhat less intolerable, though in such common attentions you would have received but half what you ought. But – how can I tell you? – To-morrow morning is fixed for your leaving us, and not even the hour is left to your choice; the very carriage is ordered, and will be here at seven o'clock, and no servant will be offered you.'

Catherine sat down, breathless and speechless. 'I could hardly believe my senses, when I heard it; – and no displeasure, no resentment that you can feel at this moment, however justly great, can be more than I myself – but I must not talk of what I felt. Oh! that I could suggest any thing in extenuation! Good God! what will your father and mother say! After courting you from the protection of real friends to this – almost double distance from your home, to have you driven out of the house, without the considerations even of decent civility! Dear, dear Catherine, in being the bearer of such a message, I seem guilty myself of all its insult; yet, I trust you will acquit me, for you must have been long enough in this house to see that I am but a nominal mistress of it, that my real power is nothing.'

'Have I offended the General?' said Catherine in a faltering voice.

'Alas! for my feelings as a daughter, all that I know, all that I answer for is, that you can have given him no just cause of offence. He certainly is greatly, very greatly discomposed; I have seldom seen him more so. His temper is not happy, and something has now occurred to ruffle it in an uncommon degree; some disappointment, some vexation, which just at this moment seems important; but which I can hardly suppose you to have any concern in, for how is it possible?'

It was with pain that Catherine could speak at all; and it was only for Eleanor's sake that she attempted it. 'I am sure,' said she, 'I am very sorry if I have offended him. It was the last thing I would willingly have done. But do not be unhappy, Eleanor. An engagement you know must be kept. I am only sorry it was not recollected sooner, that I might have written home. But it is of very little consequence.'

'I hope, I earnestly hope that to your real safety it will be of none; but to every thing else it is of the greatest consequence; to comfort, appearance, propriety, to your family, to the world. Were your friends, the Allens, still in Bath, you might go to them with comparative ease; a few hours would take you there; but a journey of seventy miles, to be taken post by you, at your age, alone, unattended!'

'Oh, the journey is nothing. Do not think about that. And if we are to part, a few hours sooner or later, you know, makes no difference. I can be ready by seven. Let me be called in time.' Eleanor saw that she wished to be alone; and believing it better for each that they should avoid any further conversation, now left her with 'I shall see you in the morning.'

Catherine's swelling heart needed relief. In Eleanor's presence friendship and pride had equally restrained her tears, but no sooner was she gone than they burst forth in torrents. Turned from the house, and in such a way! – Without any reason that could justify, any apology that could atone for the abruptness, the rudeness, nay, the insolence of it. Henry at a distance – not able even to bid him farewell. Every hope, every expectation from him suspended, at least, and who could say how long? – Who could say when they might meet again? – And all this by such a man as General Tilney, so polite, so well-bred, and heretofore so particularly fond of her! It was as incomprehensible as it was mortifying and grievous. From what it could arise, and where it would end, were considerations of equal perplexity and alarm.

The manner in which it was done so grossly uncivil; hurrying her away without any reference to her own convenience, or allowing her even the appearance of choice as to the time or mode of her travelling; of two days, the earliest fixed on, and of that almost the earliest hour, as if resolved to have her gone before he was stirring in the morning, that he might not be obliged even to see her. What could all this mean but an intentional affront? By some means or other she must have had the misfortune to offend him. Eleanor had wished to spare her from so painful a notion, but Catherine could not believe it possible that any injury or any misfortune could provoke such ill-will against a person not connected, or, at least, not supposed to be connected with it.

Heavily past the night. Sleep, or repose that deserved the name of sleep, was out of the question. That room, in which her disturbed imagination had tormented her on her first arrival, was again the scene of agitated spirits and unquiet slumbers. Yet how different now the source of her inquietude from what it had been then – how mournfully superior in reality and substance! Her anxiety had foundation in fact, her fears in probability; and with a mind so occupied in the contemplation of actual and natural evil, the solitude of her situation, the darkness of her chamber, the antiquity of the building were felt and considered without the smallest emotion; and though the wind was high, and often produced strange and sudden noises throughout the house, she heard it all as she lay awake, hour after hour, without curiosity or terror.

Soon after six Eleanor entered her room, eager to show attention or give assistance where it was possible;

but very little remained to be done. Catherine had not loitered; she was almost dressed, and her packing almost finished. The possibility of some conciliatory message from the General occurred to her as his daughter appeared. What so natural, as that anger should pass away and repentance succeed it? and she only wanted to know how far, after what had passed, an apology might properly be received by her. But the knowledge would have been useless here, it was not called for; neither clemency nor dignity was put to the trial – Eleanor brought no message. Very little passed between them on meeting; each found her greatest safety in silence, and few and trivial were the sentences exchanged while they remained up stairs, Catherine in busy agitation completing her dress, and Eleanor with more good-will than experience intent upon filling the trunk. When every thing was done they left the room, Catherine lingering only half a minute behind her friend to throw a parting glance on every well-known cherished object, and went down to the breakfast-parlour, where breakfast was prepared. She tried to eat, as well to save herself from the pain of being urged, as to make her friend comfortable; but she had no appetite, and could not swallow many mouthfuls. The contrast between this and her last breakfast in that room, gave her fresh misery, and strengthened her distaste for every thing before her. It was not four-and-twenty hours ago since they had met there to the same repast, but in circumstances how different! With what cheerful ease, what happy, though false security, had she then looked around her, enjoying every thing present, and fearing little in future, beyond Henry's going to Woodston for a day! Happy, happy breakfast! for Henry had been there, Henry had sat by her and helped her. These reflections were long indulged undisturbed by any address from her companion, who sat as deep in thought as herself; and the appearance of the carriage was the first thing to startle and recall them to the present moment. Catherine's colour rose at the sight of it; and the indignity with which she was treated striking at that instant on her mind with peculiar force, made her for a short time sensible only of resentment. Eleanor seemed now impelled into resolution and speech.

'You *must* write to me, Catherine,' she cried, 'you *must* let me hear from you as soon as possible. Till I know you to be safe at home, I shall not have an hour's comfort. For *one* letter, at all risks, all hazards, I must entreat. Let me have the satisfaction of knowing that you are safe at Fullerton, and have found your family well, and then, till I can ask for your correspondence as I ought to do, I will not expect more. Direct to me at Lord Longtown's, and, I must ask it, under cover to Alice.'

'No, Eleanor, if you are not allowed to receive a letter from me, I am sure I had better not write. There can be no doubt of my getting home safe.'

Eleanor only replied, 'I cannot wonder at your feelings. I will not importune you. I will trust to your own kindness of heart when I am at a distance from you.' But this, with the look of sorrow accompanying it, was enough to melt Catherine's pride in a moment, and she instantly said, 'Oh, Eleanor, I *will* write to you indeed.'

There was yet another point which Miss Tilney was anxious to settle, though somewhat embarrassed in speaking of. It had occurred to her, that after so long an absence from home, Catherine might not be provided with money enough for the expenses of her journey, and, upon suggesting it to her with most affectionate offers of accommodation, it proved to be exactly the case. Catherine had never thought on the subject till that moment; but, upon examining her purse, was convinced that but for this kindness of her friend, she might have been turned from the house without even the means of getting home; and the distress in which she must have been thereby involved filling the minds of both, scarcely another word was said by either during the time of their remaining together. Short, however, was that time. The carriage was soon announced to be ready; and Catherine, instantly rising, a long and affectionate embrace supplied the place of language in bidding each other adieu; and, as they entered the hall, unable to leave the house without some mention of one whose name had not yet been spoken by either, she paused a moment, and with quivering lips just made it intelligible that she left 'her kind remembrance for her absent friend.' But with this approach to his name ended all possibility of restraining her feelings; and, hiding her face as well as she could with her handkerchief, she darted across the hall, jumped into the chaise, and in a moment was driven from the door.

Chapter 14

Catherine was too wretched to be fearful. The journey in itself had no terrors for her; and she began it without either dreading its length, or feeling its solitariness. Leaning back in one corner of the carriage, in a violent burst of tears, she was conveyed some miles beyond the walls of the Abbey before she raised her head; and the highest point of ground within the park was almost closed from her view before she was capable of turning her eyes towards it. Unfortunately, the road she now travelled was the same which only ten days ago she had so happily passed along in going to and from Woodston; and, for fourteen miles, every bitter feeling was rendered more severe by the review of objects on which she had first looked under impressions so different. Every mile, as it brought her nearer Woodston, added to her sufferings, and when within the distance of five, she passed the turning which led to it, and thought of Henry, so near, yet so unconscious, her grief and agitation were excessive.

The day which she had spent at that place had been one of the happiest of her life. It was there, it was on that day that the General had made use of such expressions with regard to Henry and herself, had so spoken and so looked as to give her the most positive conviction of his actually wishing their marriage. Yes, only ten days ago had he elated her by his pointed regard – had he even confused her by his too significant reference! And now – what had she done, or what had she omitted to do, to merit such a change?

The only offence against him of which she could accuse herself, had been such as was scarcely possible to reach his knowledge. Henry and her own heart only were privy to the shocking suspicions which she had so idly entertained; and equally safe did she believe her secret with each. Designedly, at least, Henry could not have betrayed her. If, indeed, by any strange mischance his father should have gained intelligence of what she had dared to think and look for, of her causeless fancies and injurious examinations, she could not wonder at any degree of his indignation. If aware of her having viewed him as a murderer, she could not wonder at his even turning her from his house. But a justification so full of torture to herself, she trusted would not be in his power.

Anxious as were all her conjectures on this point, it was not, however, the one on which she dwelt most. There was a thought yet nearer, a more prevailing, more impetuous concern. How Henry would think, and feel, and look, when he returned on the morrow to Northanger and heard of her being gone, was a question of force and interest to rise over every other, to be never ceasing, alternately irritating and soothing; it sometimes suggested the dread of his calm acquiescence, and at others was answered by the sweetest confidence in his regret and resentment. To the General, of course, he would not dare to speak; but to Eleanor – what might he not say to Eleanor about her?

In this unceasing recurrence of doubts and inquiries, on any one article of which her mind was incapable of more than momentary repose, the hours passed away, and her journey advanced much faster than she looked for. The pressing anxieties of thought, which prevented her from noticing any thing before her, when once beyond the neighbourhood of Woodston, saved her at the same time from watching her progress; and though no object on the road could engage a moment's attention, she found no stage of it tedious. From this, she was preserved too by another cause, by feeling no eagerness for her journey's conclusion; for to return in such a manner to Fullerton was almost to destroy the pleasure of a meeting with those she loved best, even after an absence such as her's – an eleven weeks absence. What had she to say that would not humble herself and pain her family; that would not increase her own grief by the confession of it, extend an useless resentment, and perhaps involve the innocent with the guilty in undistinguishing ill-will? She could never do justice to Henry and Eleanor's merit; she felt it too strongly for expression; and should a dislike be taken against them, should they be thought of unfavourably, on their father's account, it would cut her to the heart.

With these feelings, she rather dreaded than sought for the first view of that well-known spire which would announce her within twenty miles of home. Salisbury she had known to be her point on leaving Northanger; but after the first stage she had been indebted to the post-masters for the names of the places which were then to conduct her to it; so great had been her ignorance of her route. She met with nothing, however, to distress or frighten her. Her youth, civil manners and liberal pay, procured her all the attention that a traveller like herself could require; and stopping only to change horses, she travelled on for about eleven hours without accident or alarm, and between six and seven o'clock in the evening found herself entering Fullerton.

A heroine returning, at the close of her career, to her native village, in all the triumph of recovered reputation, and all the dignity of a countess, with a long train of noble relations in their several phaetons, and three waiting-maids in a travelling chaise-and-four, behind her, is an event on which the pen of the contriver may well delight to dwell; it gives credit to every conclusion, and the author must share in the glory she so liberally bestows. – But my affair is widely different; I bring back my heroine to her home in solitude and disgrace; and no sweet elation of spirits can lead me into minuteness. A heroine in a hack post-chaise, is such a blow upon sentiment, as no attempt at grandeur or pathos can withstand. Swiftly therefore shall her post-boy drive through the village, amid the gaze of Sunday groups, and speedy shall be her descent from it.

But, whatever might be the distress of Catherine's mind, as she thus advanced towards the Parsonage, and whatever the humiliation of her biographer in relating it, she was preparing enjoyment of no every-day nature for those to whom she went; first, in the appearance of her carriage – and secondly, in herself. The chaise of a traveller being a rare sight in Fullerton, the whole family were immediately at the window; and to have it stop at the sweep-gate was a pleasure to brighten every eye and occupy every fancy – a pleasure quite unlooked for by all but the two youngest children, a boy and girl of six and four years old, who expected a brother or sister in every carriage. Happy the glance that first distinguished

Catherine! – Happy the voice that proclaimed the discovery! – But whether such happiness were the lawful property of George or Harriet could never be exactly understood.

Her father, mother, Sarah, George, and Harriet, all assembled at the door, to welcome her with affectionate eagerness, was a sight to awaken the best feelings of Catherine's heart; and in the embrace of each, as she stepped from the carriage, she found herself soothed beyond any thing that she had believed possible. So surrounded, so caressed, she was even happy! In the joyfulness of family love every thing for a short time was subdued, and the pleasure of seeing her, leaving them at first little leisure for calm curiosity, they were all seated round the tea-table, which Mrs Morland had hurried for the comfort of the poor traveller, whose pale and jaded looks soon caught her notice, before any inquiry so direct as to demand a positive answer was addressed to her.

Reluctantly, and with much hesitation, did she then begin what might perhaps, at the end of half an hour, be termed by the courtesy of her hearers, an explanation; but scarcely, within that time, could they at all discover the cause, or collect the particulars of her sudden return. They were far from being an irritable race; far from any quickness in catching, or bitterness in resenting affronts: – but here, when the whole was unfolded, was an insult not to be overlooked, nor, for the first half hour, to be easily pardoned. Without suffering any romantic alarm, in the consideration of their daughter's long and lonely journey, Mr and Mrs Morland could not but feel that it might have been productive of much unpleasantness to her; that it was what they could never have voluntarily suffered; and that, in forcing her on such a measure, General Tilney had acted neither honourably nor feelingly – neither as a gentleman nor as a parent. Why he had done it, what could have provoked him to such a breach of hospitality, and so suddenly turned all his partial regard for their daughter into actual ill-will, was a matter which they were at least as far from divining as Catherine herself; but it did not oppress them by any means so long; and, after a due course of useless conjecture, that, 'it was a strange business, and that he must be a very strange man,' grew enough for all their indignation and wonder; though Sarah indeed still indulged in the sweets of incomprehensibility, exclaiming and conjecturing with youthful ardour. – 'My dear, you give yourself a great deal of needless trouble,' said her mother at last; 'depend upon it, it is something not at all worth understanding.'

'I can allow for his wishing Catherine away, when he recollected this engagement,' said Sarah, 'but why not do it civilly?'

'I am sorry for the young people,' returned Mrs Morland; 'they must have a sad time of it; but as for any thing else, it is no matter now; Catherine is safe at home, and our comfort does not depend upon General Tilney.' Catherine sighed. 'Well,' continued her philosophic mother, 'I am glad I did not know of your journey at the time; but now it is all over perhaps there is no great harm done. It is always good for young people to be put upon exerting themselves; and you know, my dear Catherine, you always were a sad little shatter-brained creature; but now you must have been forced to have your wits about you, with so much changing of chaises and so forth; and I hope it will appear that you have not left any thing behind you in any of the pockets.'

Catherine hoped so too, and tried to feel an interest in her own amendment, but her spirits were quite worn down; and, to be silent and alone becoming soon her only wish, she readily agreed to her mother's next counsel of going early to bed. Her parents seeing nothing in her ill-looks and agitation but the natural consequence of mortified feelings, and of the unusual exertion and fatigue of such a journey, parted from her without any doubt of their being soon slept away; and though, when they all met the next morning, her recovery was not equal to their hopes, they were still perfectly unsuspicious of there being any deeper evil. They never once thought of her heart, which, for the parents of a young lady of seventeen, just returned from her first excursion from home, was odd enough!

As soon as breakfast was over, she sat down to fulfil her promise to Miss Tilney, whose trust in the effect of time and distance on her friend's disposition was already justified, for already did Catherine reproach herself with having parted from Eleanor coldly; with having never enough valued her merits or kindness; and never enough commiserated her for what she had been yesterday left to endure. The strength of these feelings, however, was far from assisting her pen; and never had it been harder for her to write than in addressing Eleanor Tilney. To compose a letter which might at once do justice to her sentiments and her situation, convey gratitude without servile regret, be guarded without coldness, and honest without resentment – a letter which Eleanor might not be pained by the perusal of – and, above all, which she might not blush herself, if Henry should chance to see, was an undertaking to frighten away all her powers of performance; and, after long thought and much perplexity, to be very brief was all that she could determine on with any confidence of safety. The money therefore which Eleanor had advanced was inclosed with little more than grateful thanks, and the thousand good wishes of a most affectionate heart.

'This has been a strange acquaintance,' observed Mrs Morland, as the letter was finished; 'soon made and soon ended. – I am sorry it happens so, for Mrs Allen thought them very pretty kind of young people; and you were sadly out of luck too in your Isabella. Ah! poor James! Well, we must live and learn; and the next new friends you make I hope will be better worth keeping.'

Catherine coloured as she warmly answered, 'No friend can be better worth keeping than Eleanor.'

'If so, my dear, I dare say you will meet again some time or other; do not be uneasy. It is ten to one but you are thrown together again in the course of a few years; and then what a pleasure it will be!'

Mrs Morland was not happy in her attempt at consolation. The hope of meeting again in the course of a few years could only put into Catherine's head what might happen within that time to make a meeting dreadful to her. She could never forget Henry Tilney, or think of him with less tenderness than she did at that moment; but he might forget her; and in that case to meet! – Her eyes filled with tears as she pictured her acquaintance so renewed; and her mother, perceiving her comfortable suggestions to have had no good effect, proposed, as another expedient for restoring her spirits, that they should call on Mrs Allen.

The two houses were only a quarter of a mile apart; and, as they walked, Mrs Morland quickly dispatched all that she felt on the score of James's disappointment. 'We are sorry for him,' said she; 'but otherwise there is no harm done in the match going off; for it could not be a desirable thing to have him engaged to a girl whom we had not the smallest acquaintance with, and who was so entirely without fortune; and now, after such behaviour, we cannot think at all well of her. Just at present it comes hard to poor James; but that will not last for ever; and I dare say he will be a discreeter man all his life, for the foolishness of his first choice.'

This was just such a summary view of the affair as Catherine could listen to; another sentence might have endangered her complaisance, and made her reply less rational; for soon were all her thinking powers swallowed up in the reflection of her own change of feelings and spirits since last she had trodden that well-known road. It was not three months ago since, wild with joyful expectation, she had there run backwards and forwards some ten times a-day, with an heart light, gay, and independent; looking forward to pleasures untasted and unalloyed, and free from the apprehension of evil as from the knowledge of it. Three months ago had seen her all this; and now, how altered a being did she return!

She was received by the Allens with all the kindness which her unlooked-for appearance, acting on a steady affection, would naturally call forth; and great was their surprize, and warm their displeasure, on hearing how she had been treated, – though Mrs Morland's account of it was no inflated representation, no studied appeal to their passions. 'Catherine took us quite by surprize yesterday evening,' said she. 'She travelled all the way post by herself, and knew nothing of coming till Saturday night; for General Tilney, from some odd fancy or other, all of a sudden grew tired of having her there, and almost turned her out of the house. Very unfriendly, certainly; and he must be a very odd man; – but we are so glad to have her amongst us again! And it is a great comfort to find that she is not a poor helpless creature, but can shift very well for herself.'

Mr Allen expressed himself on the occasion with the reasonable resentment of a sensible friend; and Mrs Allen thought his expressions quite good enough to be immediately made use of again by herself. His wonder, his conjectures, and his explanations, became in succession her's, with the addition of this single remark – 'I really have not patience with the General' – to fill up every accidental pause. And, 'I really have not patience with the General,' was uttered twice after Mr Allen left the room, without any relaxation of anger, or any material digression of thought. A more considerable degree of wandering attended the third repetition; and, after completing the fourth, she immediately added, 'Only think, my dear, of my having got that frightful great rent in my best Mechlin so charmingly mended, before I left Bath, that one can hardly see where it was. I must shew it you some day or other. Bath is a nice place, Catherine, after all. I assure you I did not above half like coming away. Mrs Thorpe's being there was such a comfort to us, was not it? You know you and I were quite forlorn at first.'

'Yes, but *that* did not last long,' said Catherine, her eyes brightening at the recollection of what had first given spirit to her existence there.

'Very true: we soon met with Mrs Thorpe, and then we wanted for nothing. My dear, do not you think these silk gloves wear very well? I put them on new the first time of our going to the Lower Rooms, you know, and I have worn them a great deal since. Do you remember that evening?'

'Do I! Oh! perfectly.'

'It was very agreeable, was not it? Mr Tilney drank tea with us, and I always thought him a great addition, he is so very agreeable. I have a notion you danced with him, but am not quite sure. I remember I had my favourite gown on.'

Catherine could not answer; and, after a short trial of other subjects, Mrs Allen again returned to – 'I really have not patience with the General! Such an agreeable, worthy man as he seemed to be! I do not suppose, Mrs Morland, you ever saw a better-bred man in your life. His lodgings were taken the very day after he left them, Catherine. But no wonder; Milsom-street you know.' –

As they walked home again, Mrs Morland endeavoured to impress on her daughter's mind the happiness of having such steady well-wishers as Mr and Mrs Allen, and the very little consideration which the neglect or unkindness of slight acquaintance like the Tilneys ought to have with her, while she could preserve the good opinion and affection of her earliest friends. There was a great deal of good sense in all this; but there are some situations of the human mind in which good sense has very little power; and Catherine's feelings contradicted almost every position her mother advanced. It was upon the behaviour of these very slight acquaintance that all her present happiness depended; and while Mrs Morland was successfully confirming her own opinions by the justness of her own representations, Catherine was silently reflecting that *now* Henry must have arrived at Northanger; *now* he must have heard of her departure; and *now*, perhaps, they were all setting off for Hereford.

Chapter 15

Catherine's disposition was not naturally sedentary, nor had her habits been ever very industrious; but whatever might hitherto have been her defects of that sort, her mother could not but perceive them now to be greatly increased. She could neither sit still, nor employ herself for ten minutes together, walking round the garden and orchard again and again, as if nothing but motion was voluntary; and it seemed as if she would even walk about the house rather than remain fixed for any time in the parlour. Her loss of spirits was a yet greater alteration. In her rambling and her idleness she might only be a caricature of herself; but in her silence and sadness she was the very reverse of all that she had been before.

For two days Mrs Morland allowed it to pass even without a hint; but when a third night's rest had neither restored her cheerfulness, improved her in useful activity, nor given her a greater inclination for needle-work, she could no longer refrain from the gentle reproof of, 'My dear Catherine, I am afraid you are growing quite a fine lady. I do not know when poor Richard's cravats would be done, if he had no friend but you. Your head runs too much upon Bath; but there is a time for every thing – a time for balls and plays, and a time for work. You have had a long run of amusement, and now you must try to be useful.'

Catherine took up her work directly, saying, in a

dejected voice, that 'her head did not run upon Bath –
much.'

'Then you are fretting about General Tilney, and that
is very simple of you; for ten to one whether you ever
see him again. You should never fret about trifles.' After
a short silence – 'I hope, my Catherine, you are not
getting out of humour with home because it is not so
grand as Northanger. That would be turning your visit
into an evil indeed. Wherever you are you should always
be contented, but especially at home, because there you
must spend the most of your time. I did not quite
like, at breakfast, to hear you talk so much about the
French-bread at Northanger.'

'I am sure I do not care about the bread. It is all the
same to me what I eat.'

'There is a very clever Essay in one of the books up
stairs upon much such a subject, about young girls that
have been spoilt for home by great acquaintance – "The
Mirror," I think. I will look it out for you some day or
other, because I am sure it will do you good.'

Catherine said no more, and, with an endeavour to
do right, applied to her work; but, after a few minutes,
sunk again, without knowing it herself, into languor
and listlessness, moving herself in her chair, from the
irritation of weariness, much oftener than she moved
her needle. – Mrs Morland watched the progress of
this relapse; and seeing, in her daughter's absent and
dissatisfied look, the full proof of that repining spirit to
which she had now begun to attribute her want of
cheerfulness, hastily left the room to fetch the book in
question, anxious to lose no time in attacking so dreadful
a malady. It was some time before she could find what

she looked for; and other family matters occurring to detain her, a quarter of an hour had elapsed ere she returned down stairs with the volume from which so much was hoped. Her avocations above having shut out all noise but what she created herself, she knew not that a visitor had arrived within the last few minutes, till, on entering the room, the first object she beheld was a young man whom she had never seen before. With a look of much respect, he immediately rose, and being introduced to her by her conscious daughter as 'Mr Henry Tilney,' with the embarrassment of real sensibility began to apologize for his appearance there, acknowledging that after what had passed he had little right to expect a welcome at Fullerton, and stating his impatience to be assured of Miss Morland's having reached her home in safety, as the cause of his intrusion. He did not address himself to an uncandid judge or a resentful heart. Far from comprehending him or his sister in their father's misconduct, Mrs Morland had been always kindly disposed towards each, and instantly, pleased by his appearance, received him with the simple professions of unaffected benevolence; thanking him for such an attention to her daughter, assuring him that the friends of her children were always welcome there, and intreating him to say not another word of the past.

He was not ill inclined to obey this request, for, though his heart was greatly relieved by such unlooked-for mildness, it was not just at that moment in his power to say any thing to the purpose. Returning in silence to his seat, therefore, he remained for some minutes most civilly answering all Mrs Morland's common remarks about the weather and roads. Catherine meanwhile, – the anxious, agitated, happy, feverish Catherine, – said not a word; but her glowing cheek and brightened eye made her mother trust that this good-natured visit would at least set her heart at ease for a time, and gladly therefore did she lay aside the first volume of the Mirror for a future hour.

Desirous of Mr Morland's assistance, as well in giving encouragement, as in finding conversation for her guest, whose embarrassment on his father's account she earnestly pitied, Mrs Morland had very early dispatched one of the children to summon him; but Mr Morland was from home – and being thus without any support, at the end of a quarter of an hour she had nothing to say. After a couple of minutes unbroken silence, Henry, turning to Catherine for the first time since her mother's entrance, asked her, with sudden alacrity, if Mr and Mrs Allen were now at Fullerton? and on developing, from amidst all her perplexity of words in reply, the meaning, which one short syllable would have given, immediately expressed his intention of paying his respects to them, and, with a rising colour, asked her if she would have the goodness to shew him the way. 'You may see the house from this window, sir,' was information on Sarah's side, which produced only a bow of acknowledgment from the gentleman, and a silencing nod from her mother; for Mrs Morland, thinking it probable, as a secondary consideration in his wish of waiting on their worthy neighbours, that he might have some explanation to give of his father's behaviour, which it must be more pleasant for him to communicate only to Catherine, would not on any account prevent her accompanying him. They began their walk, and Mrs Morland was not entirely mistaken in his object in wishing it. Some explanation on his father's account he had to give; but his first purpose was to explain himself, and before they reached Mr Allen's grounds he had done it so well, that Catherine did not think it could ever be repeated too often. She was assured of his affection; and that heart in return was solicited, which, perhaps, they pretty equally knew was already entirely his own; for, though Henry was now sincerely attached to her, though he felt and delighted in all the excellencies of her character and truly loved her society, I must confess that his affection originated in nothing better than gratitude, or, in other words, that a persuasion of her partiality for him had been the only cause of giving her a serious thought. It is a new circumstance in romance, I acknowledge, and dreadfully derogatory of an heroine's dignity; but if it be as new in common life, the credit of a wild imagination will at least be all my own.

A very short visit to Mrs Allen, in which Henry talked at random, without sense or connection, and Catherine, wrapt in the contemplation of her own unutterable happiness, scarcely opened her lips, dismissed them to the extasies of another tête-à-tête; and before it was suffered to close, she was enabled to judge how far he was sanctioned by parental authority in his present application. On his return from Woodston, two days before, he had been met near the Abbey by his impatient father, hastily informed in angry terms of Miss Morland's departure, and ordered to think of her no more.

Such was the permission upon which he had now offered her his hand. The affrighted Catherine, amidst all the terrors of expectation, as she listened to this account, could not but rejoice in the kind caution with which Henry had saved her from the necessity of a conscientious rejection, by engaging her faith before he mentioned the subject; and as he proceeded to give the particulars, and explain the motives of his father's conduct, her feelings soon hardened into even a triumphant delight. The General had had nothing to accuse her of, nothing to lay to her charge, but her being the involuntary, unconscious object of a deception which his pride could not pardon, and which a better pride would have been ashamed to own. She was guilty only of being less rich than he had supposed her to be. Under a mistaken persuasion of her possessions and claims, he had courted her acquaintance in Bath, solicited her company at Northanger, and designed her for his daughter in law. On discovering his error, to turn her from the house seemed the best, though to his feelings an inadequate proof of his resentment towards herself, and his contempt of her family.

John Thorpe had first misled him. The General, perceiving his son one night at the theatre to be paying considerable attention to Miss Morland, had accidentally inquired of Thorpe, if he knew more of her than her name. Thorpe, most happy to be on speaking terms with a man of General Tilney's importance, had been joyfully and proudly communicative; – and being at that time not only in daily expectation of Morland's engaging Isabella, but likewise pretty well resolved upon marrying Catherine himself, his vanity induced him to represent the family as yet more wealthy than his vanity and avarice had made him believe them. With whomsoever he was, or was likely to be connected, his own consequence always required that theirs should be great, and as his intimacy with any acquaintance grew, so regularly grew their fortune. The expectations of his friend Morland, therefore, from the first over-rated, had ever since his introduction to Isabella, been gradually increasing; and by merely adding twice as much for the grandeur of the moment, by doubling what he chose to think the amount of Mr Morland's preferment, trebling his private fortune, bestowing a rich aunt, and sinking half the children, he was able to represent the whole family to the General in a most respectable light. For Catherine, however, the peculiar object of the General's curiosity, and his own speculations, he had yet something more in reserve, and the ten or fifteen thousand pounds which her father could give her, would be a pretty addition to Mr Allen's estate. Her intimacy there had made him seriously determine on her being handsomely legacied hereafter; and to speak of her therefore as the almost acknowledged future heiress of Fullerton natur-ally followed. Upon such intelligence the General had proceeded; for never had it occurred to him to doubt its authority. Thorpe's interest in the family, by his sister's approaching connection with one of its members, and his own views on another, (circumstances of which he boasted with almost equal openness,) seemed sufficient vouchers for his truth; and to these were added the absolute facts of the Allens being wealthy and childless, of Miss Morland's being under their care, and – as soon as his acquaintance allowed him to judge – of their treating her with parental kindness. His resolution was soon formed. Already had he discerned a liking towards Miss Morland in the countenance of his son; and thankful for Mr Thorpe's communication, he almost instantly determined to spare no pains in weakening his boasted interest and ruining his dearest hopes. Catherine herself could not be more ignorant at the time of all this, than his own children. Henry and Eleanor, perceiving nothing in her situation likely to engage their father's particular respect, had seen with astonishment the suddenness, continuance and extent of his attention; and though latterly, from some hints which had accompanied an almost positive command to his son of doing every thing in his power to attach her, Henry was convinced of his father's believing it to be an advantageous connection, it was not till the late explanation at Northanger that they had the smallest idea of the false calculations which had hurried him on. That they were false, the General had learnt from the very person who had suggested them, from Thorpe himself, whom he had chanced to meet again in town, and who, under the influence of exactly opposite feelings, irritated by Catherine's refusal, and yet more by the failure of a very recent endeavour to accomplish a reconciliation between Morland and Isabella, convinced that they were separated for ever, and spurning a friendship which could be no longer serviceable, hastened to contradict all that he had said before to the advantage of the Morlands; – confessed himself to have been totally mistaken in his opinion of their circumstances and character, misled by the rhodo-montade of his friend to believe his father a man of substance and credit, whereas the transactions of the two or three last weeks proved him to be neither; for after coming eagerly forward on the first overture of a marriage between the families, with the most liberal proposals, he had, on being brought to the point by the shrewdness of the relator, been constrained to acknowledge himself incapable of giving the young people even a decent support. They were, in fact, a necessitous family; numerous too almost beyond example; by no means respected in their own neighbourhood, as he had lately had particular opportunities of discovering; aiming at a style of life which their fortune could not warrant; seeking to better themselves by wealthy connexions; a forward, bragging, scheming race.

The terrified General pronounced the name of Allen with an inquiring look; and here too Thorpe had learnt his error. The Allens, he believed, had lived near them too long, and he knew the young man on whom the Fullerton estate must devolve. The General needed no more. Enraged with almost every body in the world but himself, he set out the next day for the Abbey, where his performances have been seen.

I leave it to my reader's sagacity to determine how much of all this it was possible for Henry to communicate at this time to Catherine, how much of it he could have learnt from his father, in what points his own conjectures might assist him, and what portion must yet remain to be told in a letter from James. I have united for their ease what they must divide for mine. Catherine, at any rate, heard enough to feel, that in suspecting General Tilney of either murdering or shutting up his wife, she had scarcely sinned against his character, or magnified his cruelty.

Henry, in having such things to relate of his father, was almost as pitiable as in their first avowal to himself. He blushed for the narrow-minded counsel which he was obliged to expose. The conversation between them at Northanger had been of the most unfriendly kind. Henry's indignation on hearing how Catherine had been treated, on comprehending his father's views, and being ordered to acquiesce in them, had been open and bold. The General, accustomed on every ordinary occasion to give the law in his family, prepared for no reluctance but of feeling, no opposing desire that should dare to clothe itself in words, could ill brook the opposition of his son, steady as the sanction of reason and the dictate of conscience could make it. But, in such a cause, his anger, though it must shock, could not intimidate Henry, who was sustained in his purpose by a conviction of its justice. He felt himself bound as much in honour as in affection to Miss Morland, and believing that heart to be his own which he had been directed to gain, no unworthy retraction of a tacit consent, no reversing decree of unjustifiable anger, could shake his fidelity, or influence the resolutions it prompted.

He steadily refused to accompany his father into Herefordshire, an engagement formed almost at the moment, to promote the dismissal of Catherine, and as steadily declared his intention of offering her his hand. The General was furious in his anger, and they parted in dreadful disagreement. Henry, in an agitation of mind which many solitary hours were required to compose, had returned almost instantly to Woodston; and, on the afternoon of the following day, had begun his journey to Fullerton.

Chapter 16

Mr and Mrs Morland's surprize on being applied to by Mr Tilney, for their consent to his marrying their daughter, was, for a few minutes, considerable; it having never entered their heads to suspect an attachment on either side; but as nothing, after all, could be more natural than Catherine's being beloved, they soon learnt to consider it with only the happy agitation of gratified pride, and, as far as they alone were concerned, had not a single objection to start. His pleasing manners and good sense were self-evident recommendations; and having never heard evil of him, it was not their way to suppose any evil could be told. Good-will supplying the place of experience, his character needed no attestation. 'Catherine would make a sad heedless young house-keeper to be sure,' was her mother's foreboding remark; but quick was the consolation of there being nothing like practice.

There was but one obstacle, in short, to be mentioned; but till that one was removed, it must be impossible for them to sanction the engagement. Their tempers were mild, but their principles were steady, and while his parent so expressly forbad the connexion, they could not allow themselves to encourage it. That the General should come forward to solicit the alliance, or that he should even very heartily approve it, they were not refined enough to make any parading stipulation; but the decent appearance of consent must be yielded, and that once obtained – and their own hearts made them trust that it could not be very long denied – their willing approbation was instantly to follow. His *consent* was all that they wished for. They were no more inclined than entitled to demand his *money*. Of a very considerable fortune, his son was, by marriage settlements, eventually secure; his present income was an income of independence and comfort, and under every pecuniary view, it was a match beyond the claims of their daughter.

The young people could not be surprized at a decision like this. They felt and they deplored – but they could not resent it; and they parted, endeavouring to hope that such a change in the General, as each believed almost impossible, might speedily take place, to unite them again in the fullness of privileged affection. Henry returned to what was now his only home, to watch over his young plantations, and extend his improvements for her sake, to whose share in them he looked anxiously forward; and Catherine remained at Fullerton to cry. Whether the torments of absence were softened by a clandestine correspondence, let us not inquire. Mr and Mrs Morland never did – they had been too kind to exact any promise; and whenever Catherine received a letter, as, at that time, happened pretty often, they always looked another way.

The anxiety, which in this state of their attachment must be the portion of Henry and Catherine, and of all who loved either, as to its final event, can hardly extend, I fear, to the bosom of my readers, who will see in the tell-tale compression of the pages before them, that we are all hastening together to perfect felicity. The means by which their early marriage was effected can be the only doubt: what probable circumstance could work upon a temper like the General's? The circumstance which chiefly availed, was the marriage of his daughter with a man of fortune and consequence, which took place in the course of the summer – an accession of dignity that threw him into a fit of good-humour, from which he did not recover till after Eleanor had obtained his forgiveness of Henry, and his permission for him 'to be a fool if he liked it!'

The marriage of Eleanor Tilney, her removal from all the evils of such a home as Northanger had been made by Henry's banishment, to the home of her choice and the man of her choice, is an event which I expect to give general satisfaction among all her acquaintance. My own joy on the occasion is very sincere. I know no one more entitled, by unpretending merit, or better prepared by habitual suffering, to receive and enjoy felicity. Her partiality for this gentleman was not of recent origin; and he had been long withheld only by inferiority of situation from addressing her. His unexpected accession to title and fortune had removed all his difficulties; and never had the General loved his daughter so well in all her hours of companionship, utility, and patient endurance, as when he first hailed her, 'Your Ladyship!' Her husband was really deserving of her; independent of his peerage, his wealth, and his attachment, being to a precision the most charming young man in the world. Any further definition of his merits must be unnecessary; the most charming young man in the world is instantly before the imagination of us all. Concerning the one in question therefore I have only to add – (aware that the rules of composition forbid the introduction of a character not connected with my fable) – that this was the very gentleman whose negligent servant left behind him that collection of washing-bills, resulting from a long visit at Northanger, by which my heroine was involved in one of her most alarming adventures.

The influence of the Viscount and Viscountess in their brother's behalf was assisted by that right understanding of Mr Morland's circumstances which, as soon as the General would allow himself to be informed, they were qualified to give. It taught him that he had been scarcely more misled by Thorpe's first boast of the family wealth, than by his subsequent malicious overthrow of it; that in no sense of the word were they necessitous or poor, and that Catherine would have three thousand pounds. This was so material an amendment of his late expectations, that it greatly contributed to smooth the descent of his pride; and by no means without its effect was the private intelligence, which he was at some pains to procure, that the Fullerton estate, being entirely at the disposal of its present proprietor, was consequently open to every greedy speculation.

On the strength of this, the General, soon after Eleanor's marriage, permitted his son to return to Northanger, and thence made him the bearer of his consent, very courteously worded in a page full of empty professions to Mr Morland. The event which it author-ized soon followed: Henry and Catherine were married, the bells rang and every body smiled; and, as this took place within a twelvemonth from the first day of their meeting, it will not appear, after all the dreadful delays occasioned by the General's cruelty, that they were essentially hurt by it. To begin perfect happiness at the respective ages of twenty-six and eighteen, is to do pretty well; and professing myself moreover convinced, that the General's unjust interference, so far from being really injurious to their felicity, was perhaps rather conducive to it, by improving their knowledge of each other, and adding strength to their attachment, I leave it to be settled by whomsoever it may concern, whether the tendency of this work be altogether to recommend parental tyranny, or reward filial disobedience.

END OF VOL. II

Bronwyn Scott is a communications instructor at Pierce College in the United States, and the proud mother of three wonderful children—one boy and two girls. When she's not teaching or writing she enjoys playing the piano, travelling—especially to Florence, Italy—and studying history and foreign languages. Readers can stay in touch via Facebook at facebook.com/bronwynwrites, or on her blog, bronwynswriting.blogspot.com. She loves to hear from readers.

A WAGER TO TEMPT
THE RUNAWAY

Bronwyn Scott

MILLS & BOON

First Published in Great Britain 2021
by Mills & Boon, an imprint of HarperCollins*Publishers* Ltd,
1 London Bridge Street, London, SE1 9GF

www.harpercollins.co.uk

HarperCollins*Publishers*
1st Floor, Watermarque Building,
Ringsend Road, Dublin 4, Ireland

A Wager to Tempt the Runaway © 2021 Nikki Poppen

ISBN: 978-0-263-28401-0

05/21

MIX
Paper from
responsible sources
FSC™ C007454

Printed and bound in Spain
by CPI, Barcelona

For Carol, who lived and loved to the fullest, who put family above all else, and who convinced me to buy the red dress in the window. We'll always have Italy.

Chapter One

Seasalter, Kent

Wildness born of midnight and madness coursed through Josefina, filling her with the hot, exhilarating thrill of a mission accomplished, and beneath a full moon no less! She threw back her head and howled in victory at that bright moon as the last of the crates were offloaded from the boats on to the discreet beach of Shucker's Cove.

Padraig O'Malley, the smuggling captain, laughed and tossed her a bag. 'Josefina, catch.'

Josefina hefted the little washed leather bag in her hand with an appraising glee. One could never have too much money. A year on the road, painting from town to town, had taught her that. She tested the weight of the coins within. Enough. There was enough inside to make a nice addition to the stash of coins she had hidden beneath her mattress back at the art school.

'Well, Fina, is it enough? Do you want to count it out in front of me?' Padraig the Irishman chuckled at her obvious assessment of the payment. He flung a casual arm about her and took a swig from his flask. He was in high humour; the shipment had come in easily and without trouble. 'You'll notice the other boys, Fina. They take their payment without question.' He laughed.

'Well, I'm not one of the boys, now am I?' Josefina gave her hair a coy toss over her shoulder, flirting. Padraig was the leader of the Seasalter gang. He decided what shipments they took and when. He also decided how they were dispersed, what they were sold for and who got what share of the take. It paid to be friendly to him.

'No, you're certainly not.' He passed her the flask and she took a healthy swallow. 'Although you can drink like them.'

Josefina shoved the flask back at him against the hard breadth of his chest. Padraig was all muscle and brawn, a burly man. 'You like that about me,' she flirted, dancing away from him. She was aware there was a great deal more he liked about her. It was best to keep him at arm's length when he was flush with drink and success. Nights like tonight, men like Padraig thought themselves kings of the world and all those in it. She knew how to handle such men, but she'd prefer not to have to.

Josefina ducked away into the night, losing herself among the dispersing crew members. 'Goodnight, Charlie, goodnight, Thomas, goodnight, Ned,' she called until she was out of sight, alone on the Faversham Road leading to the art school, where her bed waited for her. She had her very own room and three warm meals a day until May and all she had to do was paint one picture.

Josefina tossed the little bag in her hand, listening to the coins clink. How satisfying to have money of her own, a roof over her head and food for the winter, all provided by her own efforts. And how different. Her life was not the one she'd led a year ago. Life was simpler now, freer. She was her own master. She went where she chose and stayed as long as she chose. She ate, she drank, she painted what she chose. She saw the world in all of its raw beauty, not the rose-filtered version she'd been raised on. She was twenty-four, a child no more. No one told her what to do, although there were plenty of people from her past life who had tried, who would still try. Men like Signor Bartolli. Only no one knew where she was.

She liked it that way. Liked it enough to have walked away from the luxury of her father's villa and all the comforts provided by his wealth and fame. His death had freed her and she'd fled the moment the cage door was open. If she'd learned anything from her father's life, it was that gilded cages were still cages. He'd spent his life kowtowing to patrons, painting what they desired in order to secure his wealth and reputation. He lived where they lived. He did not get to travel as he desired and had never seen the places of his own dreams: the pyramids of Egypt, the tropical islands of the Caribbean, the painted natives of the Americas. But she would. She would see it all, paint it all for him. Just as she'd promised him before he died.

Josefina looked to the stars, indulging in the fantasy that her father looked down on her from the lofty heavens. What would he think if he really could see her now? Would he applaud her decision to disappear, to seize and shape her own destiny? Would he be appalled that she'd walked out on the luxury he'd spent his life providing to live the life of a vagabond, wandering the dirt roads of a backwater like Seasalter at midnight, her worldly wealth clutched in her hand?

She hoped not. She hoped he would understand her choice. She'd chosen to keep her promise to him and to herself. She was never going back, even if it meant she had fewer dresses to wear and none so fine as the ones left behind in her wardrobe. Even if it meant she had to count her pennies and join smuggling rings, working her way through her adventures from place to place. She didn't want to be the pampered daughter or wife of a rich man, a princess in a tower. She wanted to be free.

That's what she told herself late at night in her warm dormitory room when the doubts crept in. She *wanted* to be free. Freedom was *her* choice. Only lately, it didn't seem to be enough. She tossed the bag again. She had shelter, food, the chance to make some money. In exchange, come May, she was free to go, free to set sail for the Americas. She had everything she desired. What more was there? She had enough. More than enough.

He had seen enough. The little fool thought to compound a crime against the Crown with walking home alone at midnight. Owen Gann didn't need a telescope to see the stupidity in that, not even from the distance of the widow's walk atop his Seasalter manor house situated along the marshy Kent coast. Tonight, he stood atop the walk and kept his own discreet vigil as Padraig O'Malley's free-traders unloaded their monthly shipment, his telescope never leaving the deep pocket of his greatcoat.

He had no quarrel with smuggling. Growing up in Seasalter, he understood intrinsically that for many it was a necessity in order to make ends meet. Once, he'd been one of them. These days, he preferred to make his money honestly by daylight and without fear of criminal repercussions. Apparently, that was just one of the many differences between him and *her*. He was full of caution and restraint. She was without either.

From the cove, her laughter carried up to him, proof that she lacked all caution, all fear. The moonlight caught her in profile, her head thrown back to the evening light, her silhouette lithe and dark, dressed in trousers that flattered her figure even at a distance, her identity unmistakable against the moon: Josefina Ricci, the Italian protégée of Seasalter's leading artist, Artemisia Stansfield, the Lady St Helier. Damn and double damn. She was the last person who needed to be on the beach tonight engaged in illegal transactions beneath a full moon for all to see, excisemen and riding officers included.

Josefina Ricci was a thrill seeker, that had been clear about her from the start. But Owen had not thought she'd go as far, however, as to embrace crime. He might be understanding of smuggling, but the Crown was not. He reached into his pocket for the telescope, sweeping the beach once more to be sure the smugglers were safe. The cove was hidden and there were no excisemen on duty in this part of

Kent at present. He knew the smugglers' informants must have reported that no trouble was expected, but still, one couldn't be too careful. And someone *did* have to be careful on Josefina's behalf if she wouldn't be careful on her own. That person wasn't going to be Padraig O'Malley. O'Malley was notorious for his daring, although 'daring' wasn't what Owen called it—he called it recklessness. He looked to the sky and swore again. Padraig should have known better. The night was too bright for any but the most intrepid of free-traders or the most desperate.

Given that it was January and seas were rough, the Seasalter smuggling company surely fit the latter if not the former. Winter was slow for free-traders, the Channel a chancy proposition, storm ridden for months with dangerous gales, one of the two main sources of income for Seasalter families. Oysters were the other. While oysters could be harvested in January if the seas cooperated, the lack of reliable winter smuggling income—also weather dependent—made for long, empty stretches around here, broken up only by the art school's annual Christmas party and his own 'Oyster Ball' in

February to provide the folks with enough gaiety to get through the final phase of winter.

Assured the beach was secure, Owen put away the telescope. Safe beach or not, it didn't change his opinion. The landing tonight was too dangerous, but then, he had the luxury of such an opinion. O'Malley did not. Owen remembered the days when he didn't have the luxury either, of the long winters growing up when his family struggled through the cold harvesting months, October to April, augmenting the off-season of spring and summer with smuggling and some fishing, and then the years when support for his family had fallen singly on his own young shoulders.

In those days, the fraternity of smugglers had been the saving of his family. He would not turn his back on them now that he had money of his own and no need of their services. They had been there for him and he'd be there for them. Those men out there on the beach tonight might not have a choice, but *she* did. He'd like to know what possessed Josefina Ricci to be out there howling at the moon—an action as incautious as the landing itself.

And the sight of her doing so called to him, deep down in his bones.

Even though he didn't want to admit it.

Even though part of him was angered by her recklessness in joining O'Malley—how *dare* she take such a chance after all Artemisia had done in bringing her here?—the other part of him revelled, albeit cautiously, in it. The part of him that had made a habit of taking to his widow's walk with his telescope on smuggling nights to protect the gangs from a distance. He liked to tell himself he'd adopted the ritual because he owed the smugglers, because he had a reckless younger brother whom he'd nearly lost. But he suspected there was more to his increased recent vigilance than that.

Josefina reminded him of his brother, Simon. She, too, was a free spirit, a breath of fresh air in any room she entered. Like Simon, she was reckless. She simply couldn't help it. Recklessness was part of who she was. Even the circumstances surrounding her arrival had been reckless—her presence in Seasalter the result of a wager Artemisia Stansfield, the art academy's headmistress, had made with her arch nemesis, Sir Aldred Gray, over female talent when it came to painting.

The tale was Artemisia and her sister, Adelaide, had plucked Josefina at random from among the Covent Garden street artists for rehabilitation, for redemption, and for revenge after Sir Aldred had remarked a woman couldn't paint as well as a man—and a woman *certainly* couldn't instruct another to paint as well as a man could. It had been meant as a slur against Artemisia's academy and Artemisia had reacted immediately, wagering Sir Aldred on the spot that she could take an itinerant artist from the market and turn them into an artist capable of winning a prize at the Academy's spring show. A hundred pounds was on the line, but Owen knew it was about more than money. Pride and reputation were on the line, as well.

Watching Josefina tonight, Owen wondered, though, if the redoubtable Artemisia had finally bitten off more than she could proverbially chew. Did she know that her new protégée was running with Padraig O'Malley's smuggling gang? Looking back, perhaps he shouldn't be so surprised. Certainly, the signs of wildness had been there since her arrival.

The first night he'd seen her had been at the school's welcome-back-from-the-holiday gathering. She'd been a veritable spark, the heart of the party. Everywhere he'd looked, she was there, the red of her dress always catching the corner of his eye, her laughter bright and clear, cutting across myriad conversations to reach his ears. He'd stood up with her for a few of the informal country dances that night after furniture had been pushed back and carpet rolled up.

She'd been a laughing, living flame that night, igniting anything in her path and she'd done it every day since. It was rumoured she'd drunk freely at a local gathering at the Crown, Seasalter's only inn, after a successful smuggling run, danced on the tables with Padraig O'Malley and even let the smuggling captain kiss her. It had been a public kiss surrounded by laughter, nothing a man ought to be jealous of, yet it had stirred him. Owen wanted to be the one dancing on scarred tables with her, the one sharing a flask of cheap spirits with her, the one kissing her at midnight. He knew it was not well done of him, but there it was. He was jealous of her, of Padraig. He was likely ten years her senior; he didn't swig from flasks and take chances beneath a full moon. But sometimes when the moon was full like tonight and the heft of his burdens weighed upon him, he wished he could.

What would it be like to be that young again? That free? No one counting on you? Able to go where you wanted, when you wanted? To howl at the moon and not care what anyone thought? These days he was closer to forty than he was thirty. He ran an oyster empire that shipped shellfish to London *and* the Hapsburg Court. He had a string of oyster factories along the Kent coast: Seasalter, Whitstable, Haversham.

He'd come a long way from the boy who'd run with smugglers at fifteen so he could buy medicines for his sick mother, harvesting the Gann family oyster beds at sixteen alongside his father and taking on the responsibility of raising his brother at seventeen when his father died. He spent his twenties enacting the possibilities he saw around him, adding another link to the heavy chain of responsibilities he already carried.

He was no longer Owen Gann, the Oyster Man, but Owen Gann, the Oyster *King* of Seasalter, of all of Kent—a title he'd worked his life for so that no one under his care would ever suffer for the lack of money as his mother had suffered. But even noble goals had their price. That goal had cost him—a price he was reminded of when he looked at Josefina Ricci and his blood began to sing and his mind began to hum with yearning. Not for days gone by to be repeated, but for the days ahead to be different—less ledger work and more…something else. Something he couldn't put a name to, something the wild Josefina Ricci had come to embody.

A cloud crossed the moon, blocking his view of the smugglers below, Josefina's vibrant flame lost from sight as she took to the road leading to the art school a full two miles away. Owen stood awhile longer in the dark, debating his options, although he was already sure of his conclusion. He would not rest easy while Artemisia's protégée was abroad in the night. He ought to be working. He had an enormous investment underway to complete a process of vertical acquisitions that had been years in the making, but his ledgers would get nothing from him until she was safely home. He would not be able to live with his conscience otherwise.

Owen turned and made his way down the steps. If he was quick, he could intercept her at the Faversham fork. Surely his ledgers could survive one night without him. Evening accounting was what rich men did, he'd come to learn. They counted their money and then figured out how to make more. He wished the prospect of that still stirred him the way it used to. But at some point, maybe a man had enough and maybe he'd reached it.

Chapter Two

Josefina had reached the fork in the road when a form stepped across her path, blocking the moon with its size, a tall, broad-shouldered man. For a moment, a sense of alert caution swept her. Her first instinct was that Padraig had followed her. Josefina gripped the handle of the knife worn at her waist. She wouldn't call her caution fear; she refused to be afraid of a man—it gave him too much power. Moonlight picked at his hair, glinting white gold, and the grip on her knife relaxed. She knew this man and he wasn't Padraig. In fact, he was quite Padraig's opposite.

'Mr Gann, what an odd time of night to be abroad.' He was dressed in boots, a greatcoat and waistcoat, but beneath those layers his shirt was undone, open at the neck as if he'd already been in for the night. In where? In a mistress's bed? Was he coming home from somewhere? It wasn't impossible that Kent's most eligible bachelor had a lover squirrelled away somewhere, just perhaps…improbable? He was as upstanding as they came. One could not imagine he would allow himself to engage in anything as sinful or delightful as carnal pleasure. Neither concept seemed to be in his vocabulary.

'You as well, Signorina Ricci.' He gave the pointed reply and fell into step beside her. They might have been out for an afternoon stroll. 'Does Lady St Helier know one of her students is abroad in the night?'

Josefina tossed her head. 'I am hardly one of the girls. The oldest among them is sixteen.'

'And you are so much older, is that it? Worldly wise enough to be out alone on the Faversham Road in the dark?' Gann chuckled, a low, dubious baritone in the night. 'What would you have done if I was a less than honourable character?' He leaned close to her ear in a conspiratorial gesture and she smelled the sage and rosemary of his soap. He was honourable *and* fastidious. 'What if I'd been an exciseman? Or Padraig O'Malley? A pretty head toss is seldom enough to convince their sort to stand down.'

Josefina grimaced. 'You saw?' Her mind played back all that was included in that statement. He'd seen not just smuggling, but Padraig on the beach with his flask and his familiarity.

Gann gave a negligent shrug that lifted his wide shoulders. He wasn't built like a gentleman; he was big, broad and blond. 'Anyone could have seen. Only the desperate take a shipment under a full moon. Are you desperate, *signorina*, or merely reckless?' His words were tinged with derision and rebuke.

'You disapprove,' Josefina challenged. Disapproved of smugglers. Disapproved of Padraig O'Malley, perhaps even of sucking a little joy from life in a moment's thrill. They'd come to the place where the path to the school veered from the road. He disapproved and yet he was here. 'Did you come to scold me or to see me home safe?'

'Perhaps both, *signorina*.' Gann gave her a small smile as he stepped away from her. 'I assume you can make it from here without falling into any trouble?'

It was on the tip of her ready tongue to say she could have made it all the way without help, but he'd already left her, his broad back and blond hair disappearing into the night. Josefina wished he'd disappear from her thoughts as easily, but he seemed insistent on remaining, all of which focused on the single salient point that he'd come to walk her home at midnight. How interesting. He barely knew her. What he did know of her was through Lady St Helier and limited to a dance or two at the welcome-back party, hardly the stuff on which to build anything beyond an acquaintanceship. Certainly not enough on which to make demands of protection.

Not that she was looking for protection or for anything other than passing acquaintance. She had her knife for protection and her time in Seasalter was limited to mere months. She had a world to see come May when the weather cleared and now she had money for travel. She was not looking for attachment. *Was he?* Had something more than acquaintanceship prompted his nocturnal outing? Was that something more of the decent or indecent variety?

A woman must always ask these questions, even if the man appeared upstanding. It was one way in which a smart woman could shield herself. Back at home, disappointing interactions with Signor Bartolli, a man she'd thought was her friend, had taught her that. *Disappointing* was a mild word for what had ultimately happened between them. He'd offered marriage in exchange for access to her father's name and reputation posthumously. He'd been more interested in her connection to fame than he had been in her. He'd definitely not been interested in no as an answer, making it clear in several ways including threat and force that his offer was merely a rhetorical question. Men offered nothing, not even protection, for free. She did not think *free* was a word that figured in Gann's vocabulary either. He was wealthy and men with wealth knew its worth and the worth of all things. Everything was endowed with a price. The world was one giant ledger book to such men. But the world was so much more than that.

Gann was not her type at all. The scold in his voice tonight was proof enough of that. Owen Gann hadn't an adventurous bone in his body.

He liked sure things. Businessmen didn't become rich because they took risks. Their risks were calculated, hedged against careful odds. She knew he'd spent his life in Kent. She was out seeing the world. He opposed recklessness for its own sake; she embraced it. He could not be less like her if he tried. And yet she fell asleep with one thought whispering across her reasoning: he'd come to walk her home.

He'd come to tattle on her! The next morning, the sound of voices in the school's receiving parlour stopped Josefina in her tracks, her breath catching in alarm. She flattened herself against the hall wall, careful not to be seen from the parlour—at least not until she was ready. She needed to have her arguments in place first. From her vantage point, however, she could see them—Lady St Helier and *him*: Owen Gann. What a queer sense of gentlemanly honour he had to walk her home last night and betray her the next day. A gentleman was supposed to keep a lady's secrets.

Was this why Lady St Helier had asked her to come to the parlour? So that Gann could confront her with her crimes? What would

Lady St Helier think? Would she ask her to leave? Josefina experienced a moment of panic over the prospect. She didn't want to leave the security of the school in the dead of winter. She was miles from anywhere. It would take a few days to walk to London, although a horse or coach could make the trip in a long day. It would be an inconvenience to be sure. She would end up spending her hard-earned savings surviving the winter with little left over for travel in the spring.

These were very practical reasons, she told herself, for not wanting to leave Seasalter yet. But her conscience forced her to be honest. Was it only practical reasons that prompted her panic? Or was it that after three weeks here, she was already getting comfortable? Lulled into complacency by hot meals and a warm bed? Surely not. She dismissed the notion. She had a promise to keep to her father. She would not falter now, not after coming so far, and neither would Lady St Helier. She squared her shoulders with resolve. The wager meant too much to her tutor. To turn out her hand-picked protégée would be to concede. From what Josefina knew of Lady St Helier, she was not a woman who conceded anything, especially to a man. Josefina blew out a steadying breath. She was not going to be expelled, no matter what Owen Gann had come to say.

'I don't know what could be keeping Josefina. I told her to be prompt.' Lady St Helier's voice drifted into the hall.

'It's no matter. I have time.' Gann paused. 'Perhaps it is the proposition that delays her. Perhaps she is opposed to it?'

Proposition? Josefina furrowed her brow. She knew of no such thing. What she did know, though, was that the conversation didn't sound as if Gann had come to tattle. Her curiosity was piqued, too much to claim a headache and send her regrets with a maid. She could not walk away from the parlour door now. Josefina smoothed her skirts and stepped into the parlour, mustering a polite apology as she entered. 'Lady St Helier, my apologies for being late.' She made a little curtsy, keeping her eyes on the floor. Her father always said a little display of humility never went amiss. At any rate, it was far better to look at the floor than to catch Owen Gann's eye. There was always the possibility he might intend to expose her later.

Lady St Helier gestured for her to take a seat. 'Do you remember our guest, Mr Gann? You met him at our little party when you first arrived.'

'Yes, I remember him.' Now she had no choice but to look his way. He was dressed most properly today; his shirt was done up, his patterned waistcoat buttoned, his cravat tied intricately. Gone was the man in haphazard dishabille who had walked beside her at midnight. This man's boots were polished, his breeches pressed and... Well, never mind about his breeches. A girl ought not to notice how tight a man's breeches were or how muscular his thighs might look showcased in all that well-fitted buckskin. One could not notice such things in the dark at midnight. Daylight, however, changed all that. In the daylight, without the length of a greatcoat to disguise anything, she was finding it difficult *not* to notice those thighs.

Josefina forced her gaze to remain on his face—surely that ought to be safer. But there was no safety in the late-morning gleam of

perfectly styled gold hair, or the sharply chis-
elled angle of a clean-shaven jaw. There certainly was no safety in the blue gaze that met
hers, steady, even and laughing. She stiffened.
He was laughing at her, very secretly, but it
was there in those eyes. She took the upper
hand, letting him see she was not bothered by
his presence. 'What brings you out this morning, Mr Gann?'

'You do, actually, Signorina Ricci.' He
smiled, his eyes continuing to spark.

'I can't imagine why,' she replied coolly.
This was all a game to him. He was teasing her, dangling her secret between them in
this private contest that reshaped basic conversation with innuendo. She would not have
thought he possessed a teasing spirit, stick-
in-the-mud that he was. Except for when he'd
danced with her, he'd spent the night of the
party talking with the older men in a corner.

'Can't you, now?' He chuckled and let the silence linger too long for comfort, long enough
to draw attention to the tension between them.

Lady St Helier's gaze moved between them
over the rim of her teacup. She set it down and
cleared her throat. 'I've been thinking about

the painting for the wager with Sir Aldred, Josefina. After assessing your work, I've decided you should do a portrait. It would allow for the best showcasing of your natural and acquired talents. Mr Gann has agreed to serve as your subject.'

Josefina stared at Lady St Helier, disappointment washing through her. 'I'd thought to do a landscape.' Landscapes were her specialty.

'I want a portrait for the wager. It is *my* wager, after all.' Lady St Helier's answer was politely pointed and Josefina's temper flared despite having known the conditions. Of course, it was Lady St Helier's decision. But that did not ease the sting of memory. How many times had her father been given similar commands? This was what it meant to have a patron. One took orders, one set aside their own creativity in exchange for room and board and occasionally fame.

'Certainly, my lady. It was just a suggestion.' Josefina fixed her gaze on her lap. Perhaps this was just the prick she needed to ensure she didn't become complacent. She'd not come all this way to fall prey to the same predicament that had trapped her father. Seasalter was a short-term arrangement. She would help Lady St Helier win the blasted wager and be on her way in the spring. As she'd planned. As she'd *promised.*

'Lady St Helier won the portrait category a few years back.' Gann tried to make peace. 'You could not ask for a better mentor.' She speared him with her gaze for his efforts. She'd had mentors before. Her father's artistic circle had been full of them, men she'd looked upon as uncles, helping her hone her craft. Those same men had offered her positions in their workshops when her father had fallen ill. One or two of them, Signor Bartolli among them, had offered more. But she'd not been interested in either apprenticeship or marriage. Both led to the same result, a surrender of her freedom. She'd end up as her father had, beholden to others for her livelihood.

Lady St Helier rose to make her exit. 'Now that's settled, I'll leave you two to work out the details. Once the setting and some initial sketches have been done, you and I can consult on your approach, Josefina.'

Gann waited to speak until Lady St Helier

had gone. 'Perhaps it's not the portrait you object to, but the subject.'

'Not disappointed, merely surprised by the…um…nature of your business here this morning,' she put it delicately.

'You find a social call odd?' He grinned. He was playing with her again, but she was ready for him this time.

She nodded towards the two unused teacups on the tray. 'Social calls in England require the drinking of tea. You had none.'

'I never drink the stuff.' Gann chuckled, that same edgy baritone that had rumbled near her ear on the road last night. 'By the time I could afford such a luxury, I had no taste for it. And you, *signorina*? Is tea not an Italian taste?'

'Not really. It's coffee we like, done in the Turkish style.' Turkish coffee, strong and hot, drunk from the Venetian cafés lining the canals with her father's friends as they watched gondolas glide past. The world came to Venice, even these days when people whispered of its decline. Perhaps that's why her father loved Venice above all other places. Venice brought the world to him when he could not go out to the world.

'I've heard of it.' Gann gave her a slow smile, his gaze contemplative. 'From the look on your face, I can tell it is a pleasure not to be missed.' He grew serious. 'You thought I came to tell Artemisia about your prank last night.' His voice was low, private, so that they would not be overheard. Even now, he was being careful with her secret.

'Yes, I did.' Josefina met his gaze openly. 'It's not a prank, though. It's work.'

He did not flinch from her scold. 'It's dangerous, whatever you call it. You are not from here, perhaps you do not understand. Smugglers can be hung or transported and there is little mercy for them. The Crown has hung children for smuggling. It will not hesitate over a woman, especially one who isn't English. The Crown does not care to have money taken from its treasury and that's what smuggling does.'

Josefina gave a toss of her head. 'I can hardly imagine the sum is so substantial.'

Gann fixed her with an arched blond brow. 'A few years back, smuggled tea alone cost the Crown as much as seven million pounds in lost revenues.' *Touché*. The sum was staggering. She should have known better than to challenge him on a money matter.

'Perhaps that will give you pause, *signorina*, the next time O'Malley asks you to go out. This is not trivial business to the Crown. They catch so few smugglers that they must make harsh examples of those they do catch.' He paused and reached for a lemon cream cake from the tea tray. 'I don't come for the tea, but I do like the cakes. My sister-in-law, Elianora, makes them at the bakery. I confess to a bit of a sweet tooth.'

A baker? Josefina found that interesting. A rich man had a baker for a sister-in-law? But then, he hadn't always been rich, had he? That had been an interesting note dropped into the conversation and then glossed over.

He bit into the spongy cake and watched her in the ensuing silence. 'I want your word that you won't go out with the crew again. It's not safe.'

'We won't be caught,' Josefina argued, reluctant to admit to the danger he called out. 'The cove is hidden and Padraig says the riding officer is in our pocket.'

'One of them is,' Owen corrected, finishing the little cake. 'Not all of them are. Lieu-tenant Hawthorne certainly is not. He's new, he's ambitious and, at the moment, he's alone in his command without our fellow to tem-per him. Meanwhile our man is wintering in town on orders of the Crown. He won't be back until spring.' Owen grimaced. 'That's not the only reason it's not safe. I would not recom-mend running around anywhere with Padraig O'Malley at midnight. It could lead to all na-ture of unintended consequences.'

Such as informing Lady St Helier? Josefina's temper flared. He was trying to order her life with a bit of patriarchal blackmail. She would not tolerate it. She rose, putting an end to their conversation. 'For future reference, Mr Gann, I do not like to be told what to do, especially by someone who has no right to tell me. I am painting your portrait. That is all.'

'You misunderstand, *signorina*.' His tone was stern as he rose to meet her challenge, his height towering in the small room. 'I do not mean to impose my will, but since Lady St Helier is not aware of your associations she cannot offer any guidance or caution, which I am sure she would if she knew what you were up to. In her absence, I feel it is imperative to remind you that you are a representative of this school and of her. She has given you a great opportunity. Do not make her regret it.'

That reminder did make her conscience fidget, not that she would ever let Gann see it. She did not want to bring scandal to the school, but she needed the money and she needed the thrill. 'I appreciate your concern, Mr Gann. I assure you I can take care of myself on all accounts.' She gave him a nod and turned to go, stopping at the door. 'Last night, Mr Gann, you asked me what I would have done if the man in the road had not been yourself.' She looked over her shoulder, meeting Owen Gann's impenetrable blue gaze. 'I would have gutted him.'

Chapter Three

'I hear you're having your portrait painted.'
Simon Gann lowered his large fisherman's
frame into the leather chair across from Owen's
desk. A cosy fire popped in the hearth behind
him as the carved mahogany mantel clock
chimed a peaceful eight in the evening. All
was well, or nearly so. Owen did admit to some
curiosity and concern over his brother's visit.

'Isn't it a bit late for a social call?' Owen
joked once he was assured the call had nothing
to do with ill news regarding his sister-in-law
and newborn niece, just weeks old. He saw less
of his brother than he'd like these days. Simon
was busy with his life as a baker, a husband
and now a father.

'It was Ellie's idea that I come.' Simon still
grinned at the mention of his wife's name a

year after the wedding. 'She says a man needs a little time away from his daily routine.'

That was generous of her, given that the bakery opened before dawn to bake the morning bread and she had a newborn on her hands. It was insightful, too, Owen thought. Simon and Ellie lived in the set of rooms above the bakery with Ellie's father. It was a comfortable but small space, made smaller by the arrival of an infant. 'I imagine it feels good to have a moment to yourself,' Owen said. 'Babies are sometimes noisy blessings.' That didn't stop him from smiling, too, over the thought of his little niece. She wasn't even a month old and she was already breaking hearts.

Simon's brow frowned for a moment. Realisation struck and he laughed. 'Oh, no, Ellie didn't mean me. She meant you. She thinks you're working too hard.'

It wasn't untrue. Between the upcoming Oyster Ball in February and the vertical acquisitions project, his ready resources, both mentally and fiscally, were stretched at the moment. 'I always work hard,' Owen dismissed the concern. 'Are you sure she didn't mean you?' he teased and Simon chuckled.

'Well, she might mean us both, at that. My Ellie is a perceptive woman. It is nice to have a moment's peace with another man for company,' Simon confessed. 'Even with the squalling, I've no complaints. My daughter is an angel and my wife is a saint. She's up twice a night with the babe and still rises to see to the morning bread and the rest of us.' He shook his head in fond disbelief that such a paragon was his. 'I don't know how she does it.'

'I could make it easier for her, for both of you. My offer is still good. There's plenty of room here for a family,' Owen said. 'Ellie wouldn't have to worry about housekeeping and there'd be help with the baby.'

'We wouldn't want to be underfoot,' Simon refused politely.

'You wouldn't be and it would only be temporary if that's what you're worried about.' Owen could argue as amicably as Simon could refuse. He strode to the decanters on the sideboard and poured two glasses of brandy, handing one to his brother. 'We can build you a house in the spring. The lot near the church is still for sale and it would be close to the bakery, too.'

Simon shook his head. 'I appreciate it, but

Ellie and I are happy as we are.' He took a swallow of the brandy and smiled thoughtfully. 'Do you remember growing up, you and I thought the baker's quarters were the most luxurious accommodations we'd ever seen. The Foakeses had four whole rooms, they were always warm from the oven, and smelled like biscuits and bread.'

Owen nodded. In their youth, the Foakes house had been all a home should be, warm and yeasty, where no one went hungry. There was always the assurance of bread, even the assurance of dessert after supper every night. How different that was compared to the dark, often cold one-room fisherman's hut he and Simon were raised in where there was no assurance of supper, let alone dessert.

Simon stretched expansively in his chair, his arms wide. 'Now I'm living that dream, Owen.' He winked contentedly. 'And I have the bonus of going to bed with the baker's daughter every night. I wouldn't trade my lot for all the tea in China.'

Although he almost had. Owen sipped his own drink, leaning against the sideboard. Simon had travelled the Near East looking for spices, looking to make his own fortune a few years ago rather than go into business with his brother and ride off Owen's coattails. Such a foray had nearly cost Simon his life. His ship had gone down and Simon had been marooned on an island off the east coast of Africa long enough to be thought dead. His brother had been through hell in those months, trying to survive. Owen did not begrudge him an ounce of the happiness he now had.

'Have you and Ellie given any more thought to opening a bakery in London?' Simon and Ellie had hopes of establishing Ellie as a premiere provider of sweet delicacies to the ladies of London. Ellie was an extraordinary baker. The idea was sound. If Simon wouldn't take money or a home from him, perhaps he could at least give his brother some business advice. 'I could have my man in town look for a property. There's plenty of time to be ready for the Season.'

'Yes, we're still thinking about it, but, no, you needn't put your man on it. We can handle that, too,' Simon demurred. 'I think Ellie was right. You do need to get out if all you do is spend your nights worrying over me and

Ellie. You need something or some*one* to occupy your time or you'll nag me to death.' It
was said good-naturedly, but Owen recognised
it wasn't necessarily untrue. He was in a rut.
Life lacked a certain spark these days. Making money and looking for ways to make more
had lost some of its lustre—even his coveted
vertical acquisitions project had lost some of
its shine and he was desperate to reclaim it.

Simon leaned forward. 'You're used to taking care of people, Owen. You've been doing
it since you were a boy. First Mother, then me.
Now it's your workers, the smugglers. You take
care of all of us. Perhaps it's time to see to
yourself.' He gave Owen the knowing look of
happily married men everywhere as he offered
his advice. 'A wife and children would fill this
house right up and your life, too. No more long
nights alone with only your ledgers for company.' Simon had never put it so bluntly before.

'I have a family, Simon. You, Ellie and the
baby.' They were the only people in the entire
world he trusted to love him for himself, the
people who knew him in all his incarnations,
rich or poor, and they loved him regardless.
There were others for whom he could not say

as much. 'Besides, I think it might be rather difficult to find someone who will suit me, who would be happy living a life "between."' For women seeking status—the daughters of baronets and second sons—to marry him meant to have access to the wealth and comfort that eluded their fathers, but his wife would not possess a title. No matter how much money he made, they would always live outside the *ton*. Sons of oystermen could rise only so far. To the *ton*, he'd always be a novelty, someone to invite and gape at. On the other hand, a hardy woman like Simon's Ellie would be too intimidated. The oystermen of Seasalter thought him a demi-god, too lofty to approach on a daily basis, too different from them despite his lowly origins, yet for London society he'd never be lofty enough.

Simon made a derisive noise in the back of his throat. 'You're still not smarting from Alyse Newton's snub years ago, are you?' He tossed back the remainder of his drink in a show of solidarity. 'You came out the winner there. You're far wealthier now than you were when you were courting her. She probably regrets it every night.'

Owen gave his brother a wry smile. Alyse

Newton might regret certain aspects. She was Lady Stanley now, wife to a diplomat who hauled her from post to post every two years doing England's business in the most inclement corners of the empire, although rumour had it Lord and Lady Stanley were in town this year between posts. Inclement posts aside, she had her title. He did not wish her ill. He hoped whatever sacrifice she'd made, it was worth it. A title was the one thing Owen couldn't give her, although he'd been prepared to give her so much more: his heart, his love. He'd not put them on offer since. He'd not been enough for a woman like Alyse.

Simon rose and glanced at the clock. 'Why don't you come down to the Crown with me for a nightcap? We've drunk the good stuff, now let's go drink the bad like the old days. I thought I'd look in on the men down there before heading home.'

The offer was tempting. A cold walk, more time with his brother, a chance to rub elbows with the ordinary men of Seasalter, to try to prove yet again he was one of them. Owen shook his head. 'I can't afford another night away from the ledgers.'

Simon raised a blond brow. 'You took a night off?'

'Last night. The smugglers were running.' Simon knew of his vigil.

'Ah, taking care of all of us again.' Simon grinned.

'They took care of us once,' Owen said, feeling as if he had to defend his decision.

'Yes, they did and thank goodness for them or we might have starved.' Simon cocked his head. 'It's more than that, though, isn't it? You miss them.'

Owen gave a snort. 'I *owe* them. I do not miss making illegal money when I have plenty of ways to make it legally.' He clapped his brother on the shoulder. 'I thank you for the visit and the invite. You can tell your wife I am fine and that you've discharged your duty admirably. Be sure to kiss that niece of mine for me.'

Simon slanted him a dubious look. 'Are you sure you won't come?'

Owen nodded. 'I'm sure.'

The house was quiet after Simon left. Owen was acutely aware of every crackle of fire, every tick of the clock. Sounds that had intimated cosiness when Simon had been there now emphasised how alone he was. He wasn't just alone, he was lonely, which was quite a different thing altogether.

The columns of the ledgers blurred before him. Owen passed a weary hand over his eyes. What was all this for if Simon would not take a pound from him? If Simon didn't need his money, didn't need all he'd worked for? After all, Simon had his own funds set aside from his voyage, driven by his own need for self-sufficiency. There was no mother or father for Owen to support in their old age. His wealth had come too late for that. There was his niece, little Rose, of course. Perhaps Simon would allow him to spoil her.

Maybe this was the reason his business ventures had lost their appeal, becoming merely perfunctory. There was no *need* for more money. He had enough for whatever might come his way. There was no one to spend it on, no one who needed him. Well, that wasn't quite true. His workers needed him. They relied on his factories and the oyster harvest to see them through. But deep down, he knew it wasn't the same. His workers needed what he could provide for them. They didn't need *him*. Anyone with money would do. He could sell the factories to another fair-minded man and that man would suffice for them.

It was a sobering thought to realise he was merely an interchangeable piece for many. It was just as disconcerting to have reached the pinnacle of one's success and wonder what it had all been for. It was akin to forgetting why you'd wanted to climb the mountain in the first place after reaching the summit. Owen shook himself and rose, pushing away the megrims with the ledgers. This was the night talking, nothing more. He would get no more work done this evening. He would read something edifying and turn in with the hopes of rising early and concluding his work before his appointment with Josefina Ricci tomorrow.

The thought of Josefina brought a wry smile to his face as he climbed the stairs, a book tucked under one arm, a lamp in the other. Was she retiring early tonight as well in anticipation of a busy day tomorrow? Somehow, he doubted it. She seemed to live in the present, to move from moment to moment, not looking too far ahead. Perhaps even now she was at the Crown amid those drinking to Simon's new daughter. Perhaps Padraig O'Malley was there, too, an arm slung about her as it had been on the beach. Would she be flirting with him? Stealing his flask? Would O'Malley follow her home and end up gutted for his efforts?

'I would have gutted him.'

Owen could still see her face, all seriousness, as she'd offered her parting shot this morning. There'd been no hesitation. In the moment of danger, she seemed very certain of herself. Her answer had been in deadly, doubtless earnestness. Did she know her response from experience? He hoped not, yet she was very much a woman alone who had no one to rely on but herself. The world could be a very unforgiving place for such a woman. It was such a woman who perhaps needed a protector more than anyone else. He thrust the thought aside at the top of the stairs before it could take on dangerous proportions. He would *not* be that protector. She'd made it clear she didn't feel the need for one. She'd also made it clear that he had no claim to her. Of course. Sitting for a portrait did not qualify him to a claim in any regard. Still, perhaps he could keep watch at a distance, like he did for the smugglers. He would be waiting. Just in case.

Chapter Four

She did not want to keep him waiting. It wasn't professional and she'd already done it once. She didn't like to be predictable. Josefina trudged up the gravel drive leading to Owen Gann's home, trying to avoid most of the mud and puddles that populated the winter roads in Seasalter—a near impossibility, she was coming to learn. English winters were vastly different from Venetian winters: colder, wetter, damper. It was true San Marco's piazza flooded at times, but she'd never felt a wetness like England's, that went straight to a person's bones and stayed there. Today, the rain had relented, leaving the sky heavy with steel-grey clouds that promised a few hours reprieve at most.

Sometimes she wondered if she'd ever be warm again. Josefina sidestepped a puddle, laughing at herself. But of course she would, in May, when she set sail for the Americas and the Caribbean with its fabled turquoise waters and white sand beaches. For now, though, blue sky and bluer water seemed a fantasy.

She rounded a turn in the drive and Owen Gann's house came into view, a brick structure that only nominally answered to the description of 'farmhouse.' Manse was more appropriate. Her artist's eye took in the symmetry of the building; the balance of the home was broken in equal halves by a portico at the centre for coaches to drive beneath and disgorge their passengers. Each side sported six perfectly spaced white-shuttered windows, three up and three down, with the left side of the home ending in a single-storeyed brick square denoting the kitchen. Certainly an elegant building for a place like this. It even outshone the farmhouse Lady St Helier and her husband called home.

It was clean, too. She could see that close up as she approached the front doors, white without a speck of mud on their pristine panels and the brass knocker on the right gleamed. Even the white shutters on the windows were clean and the ivy that framed the windows did so in a controlled crawl. Owen Gann took pride in his home. The home of his adulthood. This was not a poor man's manse if she'd understood the brief reference he'd made earlier. She supposed in some places an ancestral home might linger in a family even after the coffers were depleted, but not here in Seasalter, where there weren't any noble families or country squires. Josefina made a mental note as she raised the brass knocker. This was a home he'd acquired.

A man dressed in the uniform of a country butler answered her knock and ushered her into a drawing room, where a fire burned and Owen Gann waited. She'd hoped to be the one waiting on him. To be alone in the drawing room would have given her a chance to take his measure in more subtle ways.

He rose as the butler announced her. 'Signorina Ricci, welcome.' He gestured that she should take the seat opposite him by the fire. 'Coffee, please, Pease,' he ordered, tossing a wry smile her direction. 'No tea for us, isn't that correct, *signorina*?' He settled into his chair and crossed a long leg over his knee, studying the small satchel she set beside her chair. 'Is your equipment outside?'

'No, it's all right here.' She drew a notebook from her bag and smiled at his surprise. 'Not everything about painting occurs on an easel, Mr Gann. I can't paint what I don't know and I don't know you, not well enough to paint at any rate.' Here was a man who had everything—wealth and status—yet he strode midnight roads in order to walk home a woman he didn't know beyond passing acquaintance. Here was a man who dressed expensively, but sported a build more commonly found among manual labourers and fishermen, a man who chided her for her risks, but kept her secrets when given the opportunity to expose them. Here was a stick-in-the-mud who had become interesting. None of those pieces added up to anything cohesive. How was she to paint someone who didn't make sense?

The coffee tray appeared, complete with rolls stuffed with a chocolate creme worthy of a Parisian patisserie. 'It isn't Turkish coffee, but perhaps it will do.' Gann poured from a silver pot into two expensive creamware porcelain cups. Their very simplicity made them elegant. Much like the man himself. The expensiveness of his clothes did not equate with gaudiness. No brightly patterned waistcoats for him. She made a note in her book.

'Shall we start as we drink our coffee? I am sure you must be a busy man. Tell me about yourself. What do you do?'

'I sell oysters, *signorina*. I sell them all over England and I ship them to royal courts like the Hapsburgs where English oysters are considered the best in the world.' The stick-in-the-mud was back. How was she to paint a man who sold *oysters*? All she knew of oysters was that her father's friends sometimes joked that oysters were nature's aphrodisiac. Great. That would hardly impress anyone.

'Oysters are how you made your fortune?' Perhaps painting a rich man would be a better angle. She tried to imagine how she would paint him in this house surrounded by his silver service and Wedgwood creamware. Would she position him at the fireplace in the heavily masculine chair he currently sat in, all dark leather and wood? 'Do you have a dog?' She interrupted as the inspiration struck. A dog would be nice, a big one, perhaps a black-and-tan hound whose head reached the arm of the chair, tall and regal and alert like his master.

'No.' Gann speared her with a blue stare that would have rendered the hardiest of debaters speechless. 'I do *not* have a dog.' Too bad. Dogs made unapproachable men seem more human and uninteresting sticks-in-the-mud less so. 'Shall I continue? I believe I was explaining the beginnings of my fortune to you, because you *asked*.' He was scolding her for the rude interruption. It was poorly done of her, Josefina recognised, but somewhere between his dissertation on supply and demand in the oyster fields and buying his first boat, her thoughts had simply strayed away from the conversation and when they'd come back they'd brought a dog with them.

'I'm afraid money matters are hardly interesting to the general public,' Gann apologised, but coldly. He wasn't apologising for himself, but for her.

'Show me around the house.' Josefina jumped up, eager to change the pathetic trajectory of the interview. One could learn a lot about another person by looking at their home and the things they surrounded themselves with.

Gann rose, apparently finding the topic a suitable substitute for his boring fortune. 'I acquired the house in 1812 when it came on the market. It's the nicest house of its kind in this area and it had been owned by a man much like myself, a local rags-to-riches fellow named William Baldock. He herded cows and eventually was an innkeeper, but he died with a fortune some estimate to be worth over a million pounds.'

Now *that* was interesting. 'How did he make *his* money?' she felt compelled to ask. Certainly cows and innkeeping didn't account for it.

Gann gave his low baritone laugh. 'How do you think a man makes that kind of money in the isolated reaches of Kent? I'll give you a hint—it wasn't oysters.' He ushered her through into the dining room, sliding back the doors that separated it from the drawing room. She was aware of his hand, light at her back as he allowed her to step through ahead of him. Whatever his rough beginnings, Gann had acquired good manners somewhere along the way and good grooming, too. She could smell the clean scent of soap on him and the undertones of starched linen.

A glass-fronted hutch displaying eye-catching

pieces of china sat on one wall, a sideboard on the other, and a gleaming table that could seat twelve dominated the centre of the room. Very elegant for the country. Probably the largest table on this end of the Kent coast. Surely he didn't eat in here alone? 'Who do you entertain here?' Josefina was trying to place him in this room and couldn't.

'No one.' He strolled the perimeter, studying the space as if seeing it for the first time. 'This room is seldom used. I think the last time I opened it up was a year ago for Simon and Elianora's wedding. They were married on Christmas Day, a very impromptu affair given that Simon didn't return until Christmas Eve.' He smiled at the memory and then sobered. 'To date, it is the grandest surprise of my life, to have my brother back from the dead. Of course, my new niece runs a very close second.'

Josefina nodded. Artemisia had told her about Simon Gann's miraculous return. She liked Simon. He was gregarious and always had a smile when she saw him at the bakery. He might look like his brother, both of them tall, broad and blond in the best tradition of

Vikings and Saxons, but he lived out loud whereas Owen Gann lived 'within,' she supposed. She'd hoped the interview today might shed some light on that. So far, she was failing to find that light.

They left the dining room, Gann shutting the doors behind them. There were other rooms; the kitchen, a small sitting room at the back of the house that appeared as pristine, as elegant and as unused as the dining room. They toured the enormous, barren, currently unused cellar beneath the house, where Gann speculated a large part of the Baldock fortune had been earned, then a smaller wine cellar close to the kitchen. The final room was his private office and he'd saved it for last as they returned to the front of the house—Gann was too much of a gentleman to suggest they tour the private bedchambers upstairs. She had hopes for the office, the place where his work happened. Surely, this room would reflect his heart.

She stepped inside and breathed in the masculine smell of the study, the remnants of smoke from the fire, the scent of leather-covered furniture. The room had potential, more so than the others. Deep turquoise velvet curtains trimmed in heavy gold fringe framed the windows, a wide, polished desk bearing a stack of open ledgers testified to its use as more than a decoration. Two tall wing-backed armchairs faced the fireplace, an oil of the English countryside hung over it, the only nod to pictures in the room. The requisite sideboard with decanters stood against one wall. A full-length bookcase lined the other, filled with expensively bound tomes, the books on the shelves interrupted occasionally by the showcasing of a costly ornament: a paperweight, a small globe with lapis-lazuli oceans.

Josefina crossed the floor on a hunch, noting the quality woven carpet beneath her feet, another nod to the room's luxury. She gave the lapis-lazuli globe a spin on its gold axis. 'This is pretty, tell me about it.'

She watched Gann give a dismissive shrug. 'What is there to tell? It was here with the house. It was something of Baldock's. I paid extra to the family to purchase the house with all its furnishings.' He gave her one of his wry smiles. 'More efficient that way. I don't have the time or the eye to decorate an entire house.'

She'd thought as much about the furnishings.

There was nothing of *him* here, nothing of his taste, nothing of his history. He'd bought and borrowed his status. All legitimately, of course. She gave the globe a final spin and turned to face him. 'Is there anything of *you* in this house, sir? A hobby? A favourite piece of furniture? Do you play the pianoforte in the drawing room? Is there an addition you've made to the house or the gardens?' Hope flared briefly. Perhaps he'd put in a folly or a fountain outside?

'No, the house was quite perfect the way it was. There was no need to change anything.' He gave her a sharp look as he squashed the last of her hopes for useful conversation. She couldn't paint supply-and-demand charts. 'As for pianofortes, music lessons weren't on the agenda in my childhood. We were lucky to have food to eat.'

'You must have had some education. You read and write and work sums,' she argued. Owen Gann was a shrewd, educated business-man. He might not have attended university, but he had far more learning than most.

'Thanks to the generosity of the curate at St Alphege's I was able to receive private tutelage long after most boys around here left school.' The words were as sharp as his look. 'I am sorry you find me of little interest, after all.' He was more stubborn than most. Usually men enjoyed the opportunity to talk about themselves. He was proving reluctant. Defensive almost. She wondered why.

Josefina flipped her little notebook shut, sensing the interview had come to an end. Normally, she would give a client encouragement, but Gann was being intentionally oblique. 'It's not that I find you uninteresting, it's that I find you bland, sir, and a bland portrait will not win any prizes no matter how well executed it might be.'

He gave her a curt nod. 'Forgive me for not being forthcoming enough. I am not in the habit of baring my soul to all and sundry.'

That would have to change if she was to paint something meaningful. She held his gaze, refusing to be rebuked for her probing. 'You don't have to share yourself with everyone, Mr Gann. Just with me. We'll try again tomorrow.' She saw herself out and made her way down the drive to the road, glancing back at the house just once to catch Gann's blond head already bent over his ledgers at his desk. He probably wouldn't leave the office, spending all day in there or, if he did, he'd merely trade that office for another at the factory. Then back to the estate office for the evening. It sounded like a lonely existence.

She began to speculate. Perhaps he took supper on a tray in there as well since he wasn't using the dining room. The man had a large house at his disposal and he only lived in two rooms, his office and presumably his unseen bedchamber. Or perhaps, she mused, he slept in there, too. No matter where he slept, it begged the question of why he'd bought the house in the first place. But that, like so much else about the man, remained shrouded in mystery, assuming there was anything else. Perhaps he *was* bland, a handsome, well-built man with nothing going on inside. She'd met men like that before. But this man was a successful businessman. That didn't happen on its own. One could not be bland about money and be successful. There was more to Owen Gann than met the eye, but how did she find it? How did she paint it?

'He's being difficult,' she complained to Artemisia over a lively supper with the St Heliers.

Artemisia had invited her to dine at the farmhouse so they could discuss the interview. Like
herself, Lady St Helier believed in the importance of setting the stage for an exceptional
painting with excellent research beforehand.
'Either he is truly uninteresting or he is deliberately hiding himself.'

Artemisia's handsome husband gave a short
laugh, his eyes sparking. 'I assure you, I've
worked with Gann and the man is *not* bland.
But he is private.'

'You're not helping,' Artemisia scolded him
playfully and something shimmered, palpable
in the air between them. Josefina recognised
the need to make this a short night.

Darius sobered and fixed his gaze on her.
'You said he gave you a tour of the house.' Josefina made a face. He chuckled. 'Oh, I agree.
The public rooms are of no use. William Baldock could come back from the dead and still
recognise the place right down to where that
little globe sits on the shelf. It hasn't moved in
over a decade.' He leaned a little closer. 'Make
him take you up to the widow's walk. Make
him tell you what he does up there.'

'Why don't you just tell me?' Josefina replied. 'It would save time.' Especially as the Viscount clearly already knew.

St Helier shook his head. 'No, it's not my story to tell. It's his and it's your job to root it out of him.'

Artemisia rose. 'Come with me, Josefina. Let me show you something.' Josefina followed her to the back of the farmhouse where a long glass-walled room had been converted into an artist's studio. Artemisia sorted through a pile of sketches until she found the one she wanted and lit a lamp. 'Do you recognise this?'

Josefina studied the pencil drawing. Even in a rough draft, she envied Artemisia's eye for detail. There was no doubting that the woman who'd set herself up as her mentor was an accomplished artist. 'This is a preliminary of the woman with her horse.' Josefina couldn't recall the names.

'Yes, tell me about the woman.'

'I don't know her,' Josefina stammered.

'Look at the drawing. What do you know of her from that? Look carefully,' Artemisia coached.

For the first time since coming to Seasalter, Josefina felt nervous about her own skill.

Would it measure up to the genius of Lady St Helier? She took her time, letting her eyes study the drawing by section, moving slowly from the top left to the bottom right. 'She's defiant, you see it in her eyes. She's a horse-woman, her posture is turned towards the horse as if they are one, as if they understand each other. She is not the horse's master. The pro-portions suggest they are each other's equal. They are a pair in all ways.' She dropped her eyes to the woman's hands. 'She's unmarried, further proof that she's defiant. She is standing on her own without the shelter of a husband's name or title to protect her from censure. Fur-thermore, she's wearing breeches, you can just see that at the bottom of the painting, enough to know she's not wearing a riding habit.'

Artemisia smiled approvingly and Josefina felt a warm stab of pride in having pleased her. 'Now, tell me why this painting won its cat-egory that year.' That was a little harder to do having only the sketch to go on.

'Because it tells a story.' She knew that, though. Painting was a type of storytelling, history-recording, record-keeping. The problem was Owen Gann wasn't giving her a story *to* tell.

'How do you think I unearthed that story? I will tell you Lady Basingstoke, as she is known now, was not the most forthcoming of subjects until I got her in the stables. I travelled north up to her family's seat and spent a week following her around the stable. When we were in the stables, she never stopped talking about this horse and that, which ones were hot and which one was lame and which one was in foal, and the bloodlines of each. When she came to Warbourne, the horse in the picture, her voice would drop and become soft. One day she said to me, "We saved each other, Warbourne and I. We were both lost causes. In many ways I bet my life on him and he bet his on mine."' Artemisia paused, her own eyes soft on the drawing. 'She told me she pawned the only piece of jewellery she had from her mother to purchase him at auction, that she'd taken the bidding paddle away from her brother and stared down a whole tent of men for that horse. Her brother had been furious. She'd made a spectacle of herself.'

Artemisia turned to her. 'That's the woman

I wanted everyone to see in the portrait, a woman who challenged conventions to engage her passion. The point is, Josefina, I had to discover that woman. Lady Basingstoke did not just divulge all of that to me. I had to uncover it by going to the places that meant the most to her. I had to get into her world. You need to get into Owen Gann's. When you do, you'll see who and what he really is. You'll find the story you need to tell.'

'I went to his home,' Josefina protested. Artemisia's lesson wasn't wrong, but she'd done all that today.

'A home is a man's castle,' Artemisia quoted. 'It's not necessarily his heart.'

St Helier appeared at the studio door, their son in his arms. 'Somebody wanted to say goodnight.' St Helier jiggled the baby in his arms and he giggled at his father's attentions. Artemisia went to them and for a moment the threesome was a circle unto themselves, cohesive and unbreakable as she took the baby from St Helier. The sight made Josefina's throat constrict. It had been a long time since she'd seen a family up close, even longer since she'd been part of one. Even then, it had never been like this for her. It had only been she and her father. But that had been family enough until it wasn't.

'I'm the one that needs to say goodnight.' Josefina could take a cue. St Helier was looking at his wife as if he could hardly wait for his son to go to sleep and his wife's protégée to leave.

'Let me know how it goes with Gann tomorrow.' The baby began to fuss and root at his mother's bodice.

'I will. I'll see myself out,' Josefina offered. 'Thank you for a wonderful evening.' But it was hardly over for her. The St Helier family might be going upstairs to put the day to bed, but not she. She couldn't sleep until she figured out how to get the reticent Owen Gann to reveal himself to her, bared soul notwithstanding.

Chapter Five

He'd been deliberately taciturn with her, making her job difficult, all in order to protect himself. Owen poured himself a late-night brandy and settled into his favourite chair near the fire in his office, declaring surrender as rain battered the windows of Baldock House. No ledger work would get done tonight. Again. His thoughts preferred to roam over the interview—or more to the point the *interviewer*—instead of bank balances.

He'd been rude today. He hadn't wanted her to pretend to be interested, to pretend to care, to pretend this was a real conversation, not an interview for the sake of conducting her business of portrait painting. It would have been too easy for him to get caught up in the flash of her dark eyes, the toss of her black hair, to mistake her natural ebullience for a more personalised flirtation. For heaven's sake, he was thirty-eight years old. He knew how the world worked. Women like Josefina Ricci weren't interested in men like him. He was reserved, conservative, something of a recluse not by choice, but by the necessity of living between worlds, a man who worked hard for his living, his fortune. A man who took only calculated risks. A man who was honest with himself when it came to the fairer sex.

Women wanted more. Alyse Newton certainly had. He had not been enough for her. His fortune had not been enough to override her disgust for his lowly origins. The amount of time he devoted to the necessary maintenance and growing of that fortune had not impressed her. She didn't understand it. As such, they'd had nothing in common. Just as he had nothing in common with Josefina Ricci, a woman who embraced adventure, who never calculated her risks, she merely took them, a woman who travelled, who danced on tabletops. Josefina had been bored by his explanations today about his house and his oysters. A little voice whispered a scold in his head. Perhaps that had been his fault. Perhaps he'd made it boring on purpose. Maybe he hadn't given her a chance.

And rightly so. Giving her a chance was tantamount to all hell breaking loose. He shifted in his chair and took a fierce swallow of brandy. What did giving her a chance get him but trouble and heartache? Giving her a chance to do what? Get under his skin? Torment his body with every toss of her head, every look? Torment his mind with fantasies more appropriate for a younger man? He'd had a taste of that the night of Artemisia's welcome-back party, dancing with her in the parlour, the feel of her in his arms. He'd had another, different taste of her today, a taste of her temper as she'd challenged him, trying to provoke him into startling revelations. It had been just as heady. He'd spent too much time today staring at her mouth while she harangued him, too much time following her about the rooms of his house, too much time fighting a case of rising arousal.

His body was most definitely and inconveniently attracted to her and his mind was not far behind as evidenced by his choices these last few nights: midnight escorts and evenings spent daydreaming into the flames instead of updating ledgers when he had an enormous investment deal looming. She occupied his every thought. Perhaps he could live with that if it went no further than his imagination. He knew better than to let those feelings manifest into something else. He'd convinced himself once that he'd been in love, only to have those feelings quashed with a brutal reminder he couldn't possibly ever be enough for a daughter of a peer. Josefina Ricci might not be the daughter of a peer, but she'd expect a man to be enough in other ways. She'd want a man who matched her in adventure, in live-out-loud passion. She'd made it plain today what she thought about a man who lived in an empty house and curled up with ledgers every night.

It's because she doesn't know you, the little voice whispered. *You can't be mad at her disdain when you didn't give her a chance.*

If she knew him, would she love him? That was the logical question that followed. To what end? She would leave in May, off on another adventure. Not even love was permanent with her. Best not to venture down that path at all and save himself a world of unnecessary hurt. That meant taking certain precautions. He needed to limit his exposure to her. No more days like today where they were alone. Surely, they could conduct their portrait work up in the public vicinity of the school instead of here at Baldock House. In truth, how much time with him did she really need? Just enough time to get a few sketches. He knew enough about portrait painting to know that quite a lot of the process was completed without the subject needing to be present.

The wind howled down the chimney, gusting over the flames in the fireplace. The weather was ratcheting up another notch, enough to worry him. He'd have to go out tomorrow and check the oyster beds. Owen rose and made his way upstairs. Perhaps checking the beds would be a blessing in disguise. He could spend the day on the water engaged in the labour of hard rowing and it would have the added benefit of keeping him out of Josefina's way. He need only see her for a few moments as he explained why he had to break their appointment.

He was waiting for her in the drawing room again, but she noticed the difference in this meeting immediately. These were not drawing room clothes. These were workmen's clothes. Gann was dressed in rough trousers, old boots, a linsey-woolsey shirt open at the neck beneath a shabby hacking jacket, with no cravat or waistcoat in sight. There was, however, worn leather gloves and a knit muffler in his lap, proof that he had other plans this morning.

'Going somewhere, Mr Gann?' Josefina gave a pointed stare to the muffler and gloves.

He rose, unapologetically pulling on the gloves. 'As a matter of fact, I am, *signorina*. After last night's weather, I need to check on the oyster beds.'

'Today? You have to go today? Right now?' Josefina challenged. It sounded like a preposterous excuse for getting out of their appointment. She didn't have time for this.

'I'm afraid so.' Owen Gann was already moving towards the door, already leaving as if his departure was a foregone conclusion simply because he'd decided to break the appointment.

No. Josefina stepped slightly to the right, putting herself between him and the door ever so subtly. If he dismissed her now, it would just prove to him that he could dismiss her again.

Seasalter's leading citizen or not, he wasn't going to manoeuvre his way out of their appointment. 'It's no problem,' she said smartly. 'I can see there's no arguing with you.'

'I'm glad you understand, *signorina*.' He had reached her and now found himself in need of stepping around her. 'Perhaps if there's anything you'd like to see here, my man can show you about?' It was an effort at a peace offering—unfettered roaming privileges in Owen Gann's home, but she already knew why he'd offered it. There was nothing here to see, except perhaps the widow's walk, but she sensed it would mean little without him.

'That's not necessary.' Josefina smiled brightly, looping her arm through his as she sprung her snare. 'I am coming with you.' The inspiration had come to her the moment he'd said he was going out. This would be her chance to see inside his world, his real world, not the world he'd purchased from the Baldock estate for display. She moved towards the front door, towing him with her and forestalling any protest he was sure to make. 'I won't be in the way at all. You'll hardly know I'm there.' He gave her a look that said he didn't quite believe that and she shrugged. Well, maybe he was right, but she did promise herself to be on her best behaviour.

She kept that promise, walking beside him quietly, looking at the surroundings, until they reached the shoreline. The waters were grey and choppy today, at least they looked that way to her eye. Owen waded into the water to untie one of the rowboats used by the oystermen to go out to the beds. When it became apparent he expected her to board one of them she could stay quiet no longer. 'We're going out in *that*?' She eyed the water askance, her reference extending to both the boat and the waves. This was far different from the gondolas that glided down the smooth, narrow canals of Venice. But Gann was unfazed.

'Yes, or rather, *I* am going out. You can wait here, although it will be a while.'

'Is it safe?' The boat size didn't seem commensurate to the waves. She might have taken on more than she'd anticipated.

'Yes, I assure you it is. This is nothing. Are you coming?' He was growing impatient.

She didn't dare let this chance slip away. 'Of course I'm coming.'

'Wait right there, I'll carry you.' Gann

strode back to the shore and swept her up in his arms before she could protest. She'd promised to not be a burden and now here she was, a literal one. It was hardly the stuff of fairy tales. She'd never been lifted so perfunctorily before and yet she was aware of the effortless strength behind the act as he deposited her over the side of the rowboat and then levered himself in, a reminder that Owen Gann was a big man and a strong one.

He took the oars and they set out, Josefina gripping the gunwales as the boat rode the waves. 'How far are the oyster beds?' Already the shore seemed excessively far away.

'Just a mile out.' Gann nodded to empty, larger boats moored nearby as he rowed, making small talk between the pulls on the oars. 'Normally, we row the boats to those hoys and then take the hoys the rest of the way. But today we don't have the manpower to crew one and we aren't bringing in a large load.'

She was starting to get used to the motion of the boat on the water and her mind began to function again. She wasn't going to drown out here. Gann was too competent and too much of a gentleman to allow it. She told herself Gann wouldn't have gone to the effort of saving her skirts from a wetting at the shore just to let her get entirely soaked now. 'What is so important about the beds?' she asked as he pulled hard on the oars. Winter waters required strenuous effort to keep the boat on course. His strength was on display one more time. Impressive.

'It's been a wet year,' he explained as he rowed. 'There's flooding along the Thames which feeds the estuary and the marshes here and flooding at Maidenhead. We've not experienced the flooding as badly because of the oyster beds. They've built up over the years and made a reef of sorts. But there's been so much rain, I need to be sure the reef has held.' He gave a hard pull on the oars as the boat rose on a grey wave and she fixed him with an enquiring stare. That did not explain the urgency in going out today.

He continued, 'The men who work these beds need me to assure them our harvest will be intact, that their livelihood has not washed out to sea after last night's deluge. Understand, this is not an issue of a single downpour, but an accumulation of them.

'We're here.' Gann pulled the boat to a halt

and set the oars. Josefina looked back towards shore. They were a long way out. The only two people in the world. Gann reached for a cage behind him and sent it down into the waters. 'I'd prefer to dive in and see for myself, but given the weather, this will have to do.' He laughed at the look of disbelief she shot him. Dive in indeed.

'Do you dive often?' Perhaps Owen Gann had a crazy side, after all.

'Only when the weather permits. We dive in the summer, those of us who swim. Mostly for fun.' *For fun.* It was difficult to think of him doing anything for fun, yet it was all too easy to let images came to mind of Owen Gann stripped to the skin, his chest bare in the sun— did they get sun in England? She hadn't seen much evidence of it, but in her imaginings the scene was all sunlight and muscle, the muscles that had lifted her into the boat, muscles that rowed against the waves, and hefted the oyster cage into the depths. 'Nothing like the pearl divers off the shores of Arabia.' He laughed and his eyes lit. Another insight and interesting juxtaposition—the oysterman was also a connoisseur of the world. One did not usually equate a worldly education with a simple oysterman, but Owen Gann was proving to be far more.

'Do you find pearls in your oysters?' Josefina wanted to know. He was interesting today and her questions flowed easily as a result. His guard was down. Did he realise?

'Ah, not often. But I have found some, enough over the years to make a decent string. Actually, it's a string started by my great-grandfather, the first Gann oysterman. They're not all matched, of course, it's not like a fancy string you might see in a jeweller's shop.' Suddenly, Josefina wanted nothing more than to see Owen Gann's pearl string. He was being far too modest, far too dismissive of it. Yesterday, when he'd been dismissive, he'd been protecting himself, she saw that now. She had no idea from what, though. Now he was protecting his string of pearls. Why?

'What do we do now?' Josefina gripped the sides of the boat as a wave rocked them. This was far rougher water than the narrow canals of Venice.

'Now we wait.' Owen smiled in assurance. She was only partially reassured. Perhaps this was nothing for an oysterman who spent his life on the water. To such a man the waters were calm enough today. But to someone who hadn't lived on the water, the wide, grey depths so far from shore were daunting. Still, he wouldn't have brought her out if he'd been worried about the weather.

'Are these your oyster fields or are they open to whoever wants to fish them?' Talking kept her mind off all the dangers that could befall them out here.

'My factory doesn't own the beds, if that's what you're asking. But we are in the Gann bed. An oysterman has his own bed to harvest. His son can take on rights to fish the bed at sixteen. That means he can harvest and sell the oysters.'

'Is that when you started?' She could see him, sixteen, towheaded and gangly, come into his full height but not his full breadth, perhaps more carefree than he was now.

'Yes, on my sixteenth birthday I stood before the oyster guild and claimed my rights to harvest from the Gann bed.'

'It must have been a proud day,' Josefina coaxed, expecting his face to shine perhaps with the memory, a mile marker on the way to manhood, and she wanted to hear more of this story of a younger Owen Gann. But his face remained stern as he momentarily flicked his gaze in her direction before returning to the task of levering the oyster cage from the water.

'It was a necessary one.' The brief words effectively ended that avenue of conversation. More dismissal. More protection. There was something here, something that she'd missed. It was too late to go back for it now. She would make a note to try again later.

Gann set the oyster cage between them and studied its contents, relief spreading across his face. 'Look, everything is fine. The only thing the cage brought up were oysters, as it should. If the reef was breaking, there would be pieces of old, broken shell here, having come loose from whatever they'd attached themselves to.' His excitement grew with his relief. 'Oyster reefs protect the mainland, but also provide a place for other sea life to live.' His blue eyes sparked. 'They're quite beneficial for more than just oyster harvesting.' He broke off with a laugh. 'Have I succeeded in boring you again, *signorina*?'

Hardly. Not today. This man was a revelation. 'I like you this way,' Josefina said honestly. 'Much better than the man yesterday.' This man might even have bordered on fascinating. Not because oysters were fascinating, but because a man explaining his passion, the thing that gave his life purpose, *was* interesting. That man had layers she wanted to peel away, to see the man within, and his secrets, the things he was trying to protect, to hide.

'Watch this.' Gann pulled a small knife from a pocket and selected an oyster from the cage. In two lightning flicks of his blade, the oyster shell lay open in his palm.

'How did you do that?' Josefina's eyes were riveted on his hands. 'Do it again?' He took another oyster and repeated the process. 'Amazing, you're so fast. Slow it down. I want to learn how you do it.' She leaned closer in her curiosity.

'*I'll hardly know you're here.* I think those were your exact words.' He wasn't upset, though. 'You've been full of questions since we set out.' Gann chuckled, but he relented and showed her again. 'You take this little knife and insert it at the back hinge, until you've made a slit and then…' he paused and gave

her a serious look '...this is critical, you have
to turn your hand so that the blade lifts the
shell, like this. Then, you wiggle the flat blade
back and forth until you've opened the shell
entirely and separated the oyster muscle from
the top of the shell.' He presented the oyster to
her. 'There you go, that's how it's done. You
might come back with the knife for one more
pass underneath to sever the oyster from the
bottom shell, just so. Now it's ready.'

Josefina met Gann's gaze. 'Ready for what?'

'For eating. Have you not eaten live, raw
oysters? Some circles consider them quite the
delicacy.' He was daring her again. He'd dared
her to get in the boat and now he was daring her
to eat this...thing...*raw*. It was the price for his
stories, she realised. He'd given her a glimpse
into his past today and now she must pay for
it. So be it. How bad could it be if people considered it a delicacy? After all, the French ate
snails. This could hardly be worse.

She straightened her shoulders, meeting the
challenge. 'How do you eat it?'

'Slurp it off the wide end. Chew it perhaps
once or twice and then swallow.' He shucked
an oyster for himself and held up the shell to

demonstrate, slurping down the oyster, liquid and all with enviable ease. 'Your turn.'

She would not be outdone by him. Josefina held his gaze steady and tipped up the shell. She chewed once, the briny taste of it filling her mouth, and she swallowed fast before she could think too much about what she was doing.

Gann clapped his hands. 'Bravo, *signorina*. Well done. So, what do you think of our local gold?'

Josefina wiped her mouth with the back of her hand. 'I think they are an acquired taste.'

Gann laughed. 'All the best delicacies are. Escargot, caviar.'

Josefina smiled. 'Perhaps I will get used to it, then. Do you harvest oysters all year?'

'You can. I'm not sure it's the best idea if there's concern over sustaining the beds.' Owen furrowed his brow. 'Beds can be overharvested just like land can be overworked. Oysters need time to breed, which they do usually from May to September. There's an old saying that oysters should be eaten only in months with an 'r' in their names, which indicates harvesting between September and April. Sometimes the weather forces us to take

January off. It did last year and this year we are being cautious.'

He made a gesture to the waves. 'As you might guess, harvesting in winter out here can be dangerous. While we *can* harvest in the winter, it's often difficult and I do limit it for that reason. I've been experimenting with borrowing some agricultural techniques like fallow fields. We don't harvest during the re-productive season. We harvest October through December out there, then modestly harvest through the winter and make a final push through March and April. It's not what every-one does, but it's what I'm doing for the sake of the oyster crop, the health of our waters and the safety of our workers.' He grinned. 'Have I bored you yet? I failed to bore you earlier, so I felt compelled to try again.'

'A businessman with a conscience, I like that.' Josefina smiled.

He reached for the oars. 'Time to go back and report the good news.'

Chapter Six

On shore, oystermen milled about the beach, waiting for word. At the sight of Owen's rowboat, a few waded into the water to pull it in. Padraig O'Malley swung her up into his arms and carried her to shore while Gann strode through the water among the men. 'If you're looking for adventure, dear girl, he's not the man to give it to you.' Padraig set her down on the pebbly shingle that passed for a beach. 'We've got another drop coming in a week or so,' he murmured. 'I can use you if you're up for it.' He gave her a wink, his hand surreptitiously on her bottom.

'I'm up for it,' she whispered, pointedly removing his hand. 'The smuggling, that is.'

Padraig stepped away good-naturedly, a wide, teasing smile on his face as he moved towards the men to hear Gann's news. 'Let me know when you're up for a bit more—you wouldn't be sorry.'

No, probably not sorry. Padraig O'Malley seemed very capable of showing a certain kind of girl a good time, being big and broad, as big as Owen Gann. But she wasn't sure she was that girl. She'd had lovers like O'Malley before, men who were interested in the pursuit, in a one-night encounter. Those interludes had their purpose. She'd indulged once or twice since leaving home to keep loneliness and grief at bay. But for a woman, such indulgences too often were too risky to become habit. The last thing she needed was an unwanted child or disease now that she was alone in the world with no one to fall back on should she suffer a setback. Padraig O'Malley would soon give up on her and find easier conquests.

Josefina smoothed her skirts and lingered on the fringes of the little gathering, trying to keep her word not to be in the way. Gann would not like her interfering now and calling attention to her presence. But he could not escape drawing her attention. The men gathered about him, interested in every word although his report was short.

They looked to him not just for jobs, she realised, but for leadership, even though such a role put him beyond them. He'd been one of them, once. He understood the oystering life far better than a man who ran his factory from afar. This was yet another image to add to her collection today: the oysterman at the oars, the shucker with deft hands even on a bobbing sea, the young man standing before the guild, now the grown man standing before men who might have been his peers if things had been different. Today, he stood before them not as a peer, but as their leader—an inadequate word, Josefina thought. The men respected him, but he was in some way removed from them. Even in his workman's clothes, he moved in an echelon above mere leader. Yet, their hope was in him, that was plain to see. Owen Gann carried the weight of the community on his shoulders. So went the harvest, so went the community. Only he stood between them and desolation.

After a while, it began to rain, the grey clouds no longer willing to hold off. The men dispersed, back to their huts, back to the Crown.

There would be no oystering today, but they'd go out tomorrow. Gann strode back to her side after the last man left. 'I'd offer to see you home to the art school, but with the rain coming down hard, perhaps it would be best to return to my home, which is decidedly closer, and wait for a break in the weather. We can continue our conversation and perhaps have something to eat.'

She'd like that, she realised. The day had passed, the light starting to fade with the coming storm. She wasn't ready to let him go. There were more stories to hear and today he was in the mood to tell them. She wondered if that would change once they returned to the house that was his, but not his, and once he changed out of his workman's clothes. Would the informality that had marked their day disappear amid the formality of his home?

There was one place in Baldock House where informality still reigned. The kitchen. After refreshing herself, Josefina found him there, shirtsleeves rolled up, large competent hands slicing a thick loaf of bread at the long worktable. Something delicious simmered on the stove, filling the room with a fragrant, welcoming warmth. Kitchens were the heart of a home and she thought, seeing him here at work, that this kitchen might be at the heart of Owen Gann in a way the rest of his house wasn't. The warmth here wasn't entirely due to the natural kitchen ambience: worktable, hearth, stove, overhead rack with dangling pots for easy access. How odd to find *any* man comfortable in his kitchen, let alone a man like Gann, who had money to spare for the best of cooks.

Josefina gave an appreciative sniff and let the door swing shut behind her. 'You've been busy.' While she'd been upstairs in a guest room tidying herself and changing out of her damp clothes, Gann had changed quickly and seen to their supper.

He looked up from his bread slicing. 'Cook's day off. She has a sister in Whitstable with a new baby.' His gaze lingered on her longer than usual before he spoke. 'I see you found something to wear.'

Josefina gave a laugh and twirled in her borrowed plum skirts. She liked that reaction, catching him off guard, invoking a response from a man who was so cool, so in control of himself. 'Will it do?' The wardrobe upstairs in the guest chamber had been full of ladies' dresses. The plum gown had fit almost perfectly. She'd also managed to find a hairbrush and a few accessories, too, to tackle her wavy curls made even more so by the rain, and a plum hair ribbon to hold them back.

Gann looked up again from the bread. 'You'll do.' As would he. She rather liked, objectively of course, this version of Owen Gann who wasn't dressed either as a worker or a gentleman, but somewhere in between. Just a man. In a kitchen. An odd juxtaposition, to be sure, and an intoxicating one in its own right. How many women did she know who wouldn't mind having a blond Viking of a man toasting their evening bread? Perhaps she ought to paint him like this. But she discarded the notion as quickly as she formed it. She doubted an upper-crust audience would be attuned to the nuanced messages of such a painting.

Josefina pulled a stool up to the worktable and leaned in on her elbows, teasing him just a bit with a smile. What would he do if she flirted with him? Would it soften him up? Would he laugh with her as he had out in the boat now that his duty and responsibilities for the day were discharged? What might she learn if he let his guard down again for a few more precious moments? 'If you don't like the plum, there's a forest-green gown upstairs I could change into.'

Gann stopped slicing and set down his knife. 'The plum is fine,' he said decisively, almost sternly. 'Are you fishing for compliments?'

'Not compliments. I *am* fishing for answers.' She cocked her head to one side and met his gaze with a coy smile. 'It does make a girl wonder as to why an unmarried gentleman has a closet full of clothes at the ready for a female guest.' She'd speculated on the answer upstairs, of course, after seeing the wardrobe full and functioning. She might even have dallied over selecting a gown. It had been a long time since she'd had clothes to fuss over or choose from. She had precisely three outfits, all of them for work and travel. There'd been triple that many upstairs. 'Do you entertain women in damp clothes often?' Or perhaps he just entertained one woman. The gowns had all been of a size. She liked the plum gown less at the thought it might belong to his mistress.

She ought not to care who the gowns belonged to. Gann was allowed his affairs.

Gann reached for a tray and loaded it with the sliced bread for toasting. He deftly slid it into the oven before answering her question. 'I see your sordid little imagination at work, *signorina*.' He gave her one of his wry smiles, the one that said her imaginings were unworthy of her and of him. 'I fear your curiosity will be disappointed. The dresses came with the house. They belonged to one of Baldock's female relations.' He turned to the stove and puttered with the pot, stirring and tasting and stirring some more. Her first impression hadn't been wrong. He was definitely at home in this space.

'You really meant it, then. You did buy this place lock, stock and barrel,' Josefina mused, watching his rather adroit moves. He bent to the oven to check the toast, his buckskins pulling taut across the muscled expanse of his buttocks as he squatted. Gann had an exquisite backside, a discovery previously obscured by his coats. But dressed in only a shirt and buckskins, *very tight buckskins*, there was nothing to keep her eyes from roaming over that particular feature now.

'I did.' He shut the oven, satisfied with the toast's progress, and turned around. 'Fancy that. Did you think I would lie?'

'Most men do.' Signor Bartolli had been willing to promise her the moon in order to win her hand, but she'd learned soon enough he didn't intend to keep those promises.

'I don't.' Gann fixed her with a hard blue stare for a long moment before returning to the mystery pot. She'd offended him.

She believed him, despite what she knew to be a contrary truth in the world—men lied to get what they wanted. A tense silence stretched thin between them. 'What's in the pot?'

The tension eased. Gann grinned, this one a full genuine smile instead of a wry scold as he announced, 'Oyster stew, made fresh from our catch today.' She gave him a dubious look and he laughed. 'Have faith, *signorina*. Oyster stew is far better than raw oysters. It's creamy, warm and filling. More of a soup than a stew, really.'

'You sound like an expert on oyster stew.' In truth, he sounded like a mystery. For every single thing she'd learned about him today, more questions had abounded. Beneath his stuffy exterior, Owen Gann was a riddle of interesting proportions. He *was* stuffy, but he was also proving to be more than that.

'I was raised on it. If it can be done with an oyster, I can do it.' He began laying out dinner things: two sturdy bowls, plates, utensils, a crock of butter, a plate of unshucked oysters, a bottle of cold white wine and two plain goblets. Rustic and domestic. Gann ladled the creamy stew into the bowls and a sense of comfort settled over the kitchen that she hadn't known since she left home.

'Can you teach me to shuck oysters?' She picked one up from the plate and tossed it in her hand. She reached for the shucking knife and awkwardly tried to simulate his movements from the boat.

'No, wait, you have to be careful!' Owen came around to her side of the worktable, swift with concern. 'Wrap your other hand with a towel or you're likely to slice it open.' He was all grim efficiency as he came up behind her and brought his hands over hers, directing her grip. She felt her pulse give a little kick at the nearness and intimacy of their bodies. He smelled of kitchen and clean male. What would he do if she wiggled backwards just a bit? Perhaps she ought not find out when there was a knife involved. But the intrigue remained. Her attempts at flirting earlier had been rebuffed with sternness. For a moment the old Owen Gann had returned. Was he afraid of flirting? Of her? Was it himself he was trying to protect?

'Wedge it under the hinge like so.' His hands directed hers, his strong fingers expertly prising the shell gently apart and working the blade along its length. The shell opened. 'There, we did it.' He set aside the knife and held out his hand. 'Always use a towel. Look, I learned the hard way.' He held up his pinkie where a thin white line ran down the centre.

'Ouch, it looks like that hurt.' Josefina grimaced.

'It did. I didn't listen to my father and nearly sliced myself down to the bone.' Owen stepped away and returned to his side of the worktable. If the closeness of the interaction affected him, he covered it well doing little tasks. He filled the wine glasses and slid the toasted bread and cheese on to their plates. He nodded towards the door. 'Shall we go through to the dining room with our feast?'

'No, let's stay here.' She didn't want to exchange the cosiness of the kitchen for the cold formality of the dining room. She wasn't ready to give up the comfort she felt here and she wasn't ready to give up him. If they went to the dining room, this version of Owen Gann might be replaced by the cold boor she'd encountered yesterday.

Gann nodded, approving of the choice. 'In that case, we'll need this.' He reached for a lamp and brought it to the worktable, setting it in the centre and turning up the wick. 'There, candlelight.' The flame lent another type of ambience to the space, making the kitchen into an intimate space where two people might partake of meal together and more, where secrets might be exchanged.

'Were you raised to cook, as well?' Josefina enquired taking a first, tentative sip of her soup.

'I learned to cook out of necessity.' She recognised that line from earlier. He'd used those words before. 'An oysterman can't stand on ceremony. He has to be able to provide for himself in all ways. A man should be able to cook and sew for himself at least enough to get by. He never knows when he might need the skills.'

'A stew and stitches?' Josefina laughed softly in the candlelit darkness.

'Exactly. Try this...' Gann reached for a small bottle and dribbled a few drops of brown liquid into her stew '...it's sherry.'

'Oh, that's delicious.' Josefina savoured the swallow and took another spoonful, eating in earnest now that she'd decided she *liked* oyster stew. She studied Gann as he applied himself to his own bowl, taking hearty spoonsful and eating with the well-mannered gusto of a man who appreciated a hot meal. She tried to reconcile all she knew of him and failed. 'I admit to having trouble imagining you as a stew-and-stitches man, cooking on a hob over a fire in a fisher's hut.' They'd passed the huts today on the beach, draughty, mean hovels, the most rudimentary of shelters.

'Yet those were my humble beginnings.' Gann's gaze was serious in the candlelight, the flame turning his blue gaze a dark sapphire.

Josefina reached for the wine and refilled

their glasses. This was the moment to push forward, to ask about those humble beginnings. What else could she add to the puzzle of Owen Gann, not just for the painting, but for herself? She was aware, sitting here in the lamplit kitchen, that something had subtly shifted for her today. She'd become interested in him, not solely for the extrinsic reward of the painting, but for the intrinsic reward of simply knowing who he was. 'Tell me about those beginnings.'

Gann shook his head as if he were clearing cobwebs. 'Not tonight. You shan't have all my secrets out of me at once. Besides, I don't have company for dinner often. I'd hate to ruin a good meal and good wine with a sad story.' Ah, so he'd noticed her efforts. She'd not been as deft with the wine as she'd hoped or with her questions.

Perhaps he was right, though. The meal was going well and it was indeed a delight to eat with someone. Of course she ate with sixteen someones every night in the great hall at the school, but it wasn't like this. The great hall was noisy, filled with the chatter of sixteen young girls all talking at once. Gann's kitchen was quiet, warm, intimate and it reminded her of home. 'My father and I would eat like this in our kitchen of an evening when his work was done.' Josefina helped herself to another slice of bread and dipped it in her bowl. 'Hearty food and a chance to talk over the day, just the two of us.' How she'd looked forward to that precious hour. No apprentices from her father's workshop running in with messages, no imperious orders from a patron over time-lines and expenses. Her throat tightened at the unexpected memory.

'Your father?' Gann asked the question quietly, a thousand other questions underlying it. How did a father allow a daughter to wander the world at will? What caused an Italian girl to make her way to England on her own?

'My father passed away last year.' It was difficult to speak through the tightness in her throat. She'd given up thinking it would ever get easier.

Gann gave a slow nod of understanding. 'I *am* sorry.'

'I am, too.' Josefina took a swallow of wine, letting the coldness ease her throat. She'd lost everything when she lost her father: her family, her home, her position in society and in the community. Even her name, although that had been—to borrow Gann's word—of necessity. Who was she if she wasn't Felipe Zanetti's daughter? She wasn't sure she knew yet. But she couldn't be Josefina Zanetti and roam Europe unheeded. Josefina Zanetti could be found by the likes of Signor Bartolli. She *had* to be someone else and so Josefina Ricci was born. Ricci had been her mother's name and a common name in Italy, unexceptional and unlikely to draw interest.

Gann was studying her intently, his gaze prying into her with methodical certainty like the shucking knife had prised into the oyster. It was a reminder to be careful. The less people knew of her, the more secure her dreams were. How was she to see the world and fulfil her promise to her father, if people knew who she was and where she was? There were those who would think she was better off at home. They would look for her if they knew where to start. She'd confounded them so far. Josefina Zanetti had disappeared the day of her father's funeral. She didn't need Gann or Artemisia getting too curious about her antecedents. 'I don't mean to be intrusive, but why did you leave? Was there no way to stay?'

She met his gaze evenly. 'Not any way that was acceptable to me.' His thoughtful stare was discomfiting. She was used to men being more interested in her face than in who she was. She'd expected the same from Owen Gann when she'd twirled into the room in her plum skirts. Men told pretty girls their secrets all the time and far too easily. But here in this kitchen, he had turned the tables on her. It was she telling him her secrets. It was time to get back to business.

She rose and half leaned over the worktable, letting the flame pick out the mischief in her eye, mischief not even a man like Owen Gann would miss. 'I hear you have an interesting widow's walk, Mr Gann.' She snatched up the wine bottle. 'Perhaps you'd like to show me or will I have to find my way on my own?' Gann wouldn't refuse. He wouldn't want her wandering around his house unescorted, despite the fact that she'd been alone upstairs for quite some time when she'd changed.

'Are you sure you want to see it in the dark?' Gann prevaricated. Ah, he was protecting himself again. He wasn't sure going upstairs with her was in his best interest. Perhaps he wasn't as immune to her flirting as she'd thought. Frankly, neither was she.

'Yes, most definitely.' She came around the table and hooked her arm through his before he could come up with other arguments. 'Lead on, sir.' When he wasn't being a boor, Owen Gann was an attractive man. The widow's walk was turning into a compelling proposition for reasons that had little to do with her painting.

Chapter Seven

The view from the top was breathtaking and cold. One could see across the water to the Isle of Sheppey. The steeple of St Alphege's gleamed white in the distance against the dark sky. The clouds had blown away after the rain and a few stars peeked out. Josefina raised an arm. 'The stars are so close, it's like I can almost pick them. I like that here, I can see the stars. You can't see stars in London.' One could see stars and Sheppey, and something else far more interesting. 'That's Shucker's Cove.' The hidden cove wasn't so hidden from above. A gust of wind blew across the widow's walk and she shivered, the plum wool of her gown no match for a late January wind off the water.

'Shall we go in?' Gann enquired, noting her shiver.

'Please, no, I'm fine.' She wasn't ready to go in yet. The idea that he could see Shucker's Cove from here was interesting. She needed to think of a different word. She'd overused it today with regard to Gann.

He moved away from her momentarily to a trunk set in the corner of the walk and returned with a blanket. He shook it out and wrapped it about her. 'You'll need this if we're to stay up here.'

'You can see the smugglers from here.' She was thinking out loud now. 'You watched us from the widow's walk last time.' That's how he'd known to meet her on the road. 'Do you always watch the smugglers?' But she answered her own question. 'Of course you do. The house is perfectly situated.' She gave a pleased laugh. 'Baldock made his fortune smuggling, didn't he?' She could see it now, how a smuggler could protect his investment from here. One could see Shucker's Cove *and* the surrounding area. From here, one could see the approaching Coast Guard from the water or riding officers approaching from land.

'You're very astute, *signorina*.' Gann made her a little bow.

But that wasn't all. 'I know why Baldock would have found this useful, but why do you? Why do you watch the smugglers? You're not one of them.' Another gust swept over them and she pulled the blanket tighter. It was cold and late. She'd have to go soon before Artemisia worried, but not before she solved this particular mystery.

'No, not any more.' He leaned on the railing, looking out into the distance. 'I used to be, though.' He shot her a glance, perhaps measuring how she took the news.

'You? A smuggler?' She smiled, wanting to coax the story from him. He turned away, his gaze looking out over the cove.

'When I was about fifteen, my mother needed medicines we couldn't afford on an oysterman's salary. I wasn't old enough to work the beds. But I could work with the smugglers.'

Josefina processed that information in silence for a long while. There was so much there—his warning to her about smuggling, a further glimpse into the tales he'd told her today and a glimpse into those humble beginnings he'd refused to tell her about. And a glimpse into tragedy. 'Was it enough? Did the medicines save her?' Fifteen-year-old Owen had loved his mother enough to risk his own neck.

Owen shook his head. 'Not in the end. Perhaps the medicines bought her a little more time with us. I'll never really know, though.' She heard the hurt in his voice. He'd risked everything for no guarantees. Perhaps that was why he was so reserved, so calculated now about what risks he took, what he revealed. 'I stopped smuggling then, after she died. I'm not one of them any more, but they are my men, my fishers. Who will harvest the oysters that feed my business empire if they're in prison? Who will care for their families if they are taken?'

He was retreating, she heard it in his words. He made his support of the smugglers sound more practical than he meant it, but she wasn't fooled. Owen Gann was an honourable man. His next words proved it. 'I pay a decent wage, but they need smuggling to make ends meet in the off-season. It's a way of life here. Everyone is part of it even if they're *not* a part of it, do you understand? That doesn't make it less dangerous, though.' He gave a stern lift of his eyebrow. '*You* do not have to be part of it. There's no reason for you to take unnecessary risks.'

'Yet *you* continue to align yourself with them.' Josefina gave a defiant toss of her head, challenging him and the wind. She did not like being told what to do, especially by a man who had taken the risks he was advising her against.

'I can afford to. I dare say you cannot.'

'Do they know you watch them?'

'No, but now that you've figured it out, I'd prefer you not say anything to them. It's better that way.' Owen Gann, the silent protector, watching over his people from a distance, just as he'd watched over them today, rowing out to the oyster beds to assure them their harvest was intact.

'I'll keep your secret,' she whispered softly beneath the wind. The concept of a chieftain had died out centuries ago in these parts, but in Owen Gann, she sensed the role was alive and well. If Seasalter had a chieftain, it would be him. She'd not expected to find this discovery beneath the stuffy exterior of her subject when she'd set out this morning. What else might she unveil if she pushed hard enough? Temptation rose with the wind.

'You're a good man, Owen Gann.' Good men were rarities and inspired a certain intoxication all their own. The wine and the late hour moved her to a recklessness she struggled to keep leashed. Late hours were dangerous. The night interposed a false sense of intimacy that lured one towards impulsive gestures often regretted by morning. And yet, what was life without a little temptation? 'Thank you for a lovely evening, the nicest I've had in a long while.'

Josefina stretched up on her tiptoes to reach him and gave in to impulse. She kissed him, once on each cheek, the stubble of his beard brushing her skin with its roughness, the smell of him—sweet sherry and sharp wine—in her nose. It was tempting to kiss his lips, to drink in all of him. She held it in check and stepped back.

'Why did you do that?' His hand went absently to his right cheek, unsure what to make of it.

'It's how Italians say goodnight.' She smiled. The kiss was ambiguous to Englishmen. The French had *la bise*, but the cold, reserved English had nothing like it. She would let him read into it however he liked as she made her exit.

* * *

What should he make of it? Everything? Nothing? Was it just flirting? Was it something more or was that just his heated imagination? The power of the moment? Owen played the brief scene back in his mind over and over as he sat before the fire in his chamber, remembrance dancing in the flames.

She'd moved against him without warning, her arms about his neck, her mouth brushing his cheek, once, twice. The rosewater on her skin had been a borrowed scent, perhaps from the guest chamber, not her own. Her own scent was something wilder, like the woman herself.

For a moment he had contemplated the outrageous, taking the kiss from her, capturing her mouth with his. There had been a slight hesitation in her movements, as if the thought had occurred to her as well, and then it had been gone. She'd stepped back and the evening had been over.

The episode had lasted seconds, but his mind slowed it down, dissected it, savoured it like the tender morsel it was. Good lord, what was the matter with him? He was acting like a moony village boy, building a fantasy out of a simple gesture and a few words. *This is how Italians say goodnight.* A bold gesture and bold words. Englishwomen didn't kiss men of their acquaintance goodnight. Neither did they tramp through mud and row out to oyster beds alone with a gentleman they barely knew. Or slurp raw oysters on the half-shell in a rowboat. His mind flooded with images of the day, of her, each scene imprinted in vivid detail.

He'd *enjoyed* today. It was quite an admission given the strategy he'd devised last night to avoid her and beginning the day trying to leave her behind. Neither stratagem had lasted long. He could not recall the last time he'd enjoyed an ordinary work day or an ordinary meal; his own company had paled ages ago. Then she'd kissed him. Sweet Heavens, he was back to that again. His mind seemed to have it on a perpetual loop.

Somewhere in the depths of Baldock House, the hall clock struck midnight. He'd best get to bed. Tomorrow was another work day at the factory and here at home. Downstairs there was a pile of paperwork waiting for him to complete the purchase of a fleet of ships that would take his oysters throughout Europe. No longer would he have to pay exorbitant shipping fees or rely on others' schedules. It had taken three years to arrange the financing, to arrange the deal that would complete his vertical empire.

Owen waited for the joy of acquisition, the glee of accomplishment, to fill him. No glee, no joy came. There was only a sense of relief, a very different feeling than joy and a slightly emptier one. Perhaps that was the price one paid to keep those he cared about safe.

It doesn't have to be. The little voice spoke in his head. *You're lonely. Why not do something about it?*

Perhaps there could be joy of a short-term nature with Josefina Ricci. She'd expect nothing but comfort. He could offer that. She'd made no secret she was leaving in May. By May, he'd be in London, doing business, shipping oysters, making deals. He wouldn't have time for comfort or anything else then. What had been a detriment last night was suddenly an advantage.

Shame on him! Was he really so lonely he was thinking of propositioning a woman who might feel obliged to him because of her work? All because she'd kissed his cheek? It was midnight foolishness at best. She might be the sort of beauty a man dreamed about, but she wasn't for him. He'd been through this last night with himself, as well. What would he do with all that wildness, all that passion even if he dared to claim it? That was for the Padraig O'Malleys of the world, not the Owen Ganns. *But once she might have been.* Once, he'd burned with that same passion, that same drive to drink fully from life's cup. Responsibility had made that a rather short-lived period. He rose and made ready for bed, determined to put her out of mind.

Padraig O'Malley's expression bordered on fiercely determined as he faced the group assembled in the Crown's parlour. Private business required a private space, it seemed. His eyes lingered on her a little longer than necessary. Josefina smiled back out of a need to lend him support. The big Irishman appeared to need it tonight. He seemed agitated as he brought the meeting to order. It made her sit up a little taller, take sharper notice of his words. Or was that because of Owen Gann?

These are risks you don't need to take.

Gann would be furious if he knew she was

here. No, not furious. She didn't think Owen Gann was ever furious. He was calmness itself. He did not deal in extremes and intensities. Then again, his world was well ordered. Except for that moment two nights ago when she'd kissed him. There'd been disorder then, the potential for passion in the moment. She'd seen that potential flare in his eyes. An instant only.

'We have news from our source.' The words dragged Josefina back to the meeting. 'He says the coast from Seasalter to Whitstable is being watched more heavily after the last drop. The Frenchies weren't as careful as they should have been. Their ship was spotted. It eluded the Coast Guard, but it's alerted them all the same. This is a problem with regard to the next shipment.' A large order of brandy that the gang was counting on for a big sale in London. Usually, Josefina learned, those large shipments made berth at Shoreham because of its close proximity to London, but Shoreham was being heavily watched. When plans had been laid, the obscurity of Seasalter had seemed a good substitute.

'With such a large order, we'll need a different place to store the tubs while we cut the brandy and get it ready to transport. We can't use the cave. It will be the first place anyone looks.' Padraig faced the group squarely, hands on hips. 'That means we'll need to have the Frenchies put in several miles up the coast.'

There were grumbles. Miles up coast meant a journey, time away from home and more risk of discovery. It would look odd for a large part of a small village to suddenly be absent. 'If we don't risk ourselves, we risk the shipment,' Padraig argued with the dissension in the room. 'There's no place here large enough.' He was gruff and, for a moment, Josefina thought he and one of the men might come to blows. Then Padraig softened. 'Perhaps if it's too risky all around, we should bow out. There's still time to reach the French.'

The loss of anticipated income silenced the group. Josefina's gaze flitted from man to man, each one processing what the loss of the delivery would mean to them, to their families: shoes that wouldn't be bought for growing children, clothes, medicines. That money wouldn't be spent on luxuries, but on necessities. They had to take the shipment. If Gann knew of the dilemma, he'd want to help, she reasoned. But these men would never ask for that help so it had to be offered in a way that served Owen's desire for secrecy about his midnight vigils and serve Padraig's pride, too. The words were out of her mouth before she thought better of them. 'What about Baldock House? The cellar was used for storing smuggled brandy before.'

'It hasn't been Baldock's house for years now. Gann isn't a smuggler. I don't think he'd approve.' Padraig gave her a smile that bordered on patronising, it said he didn't expect her to understand the nuances of their community, let alone their history. It was a reminder that she was an outsider. 'I appreciate the idea, though, Fina.'

Josefina rose, not willing to be dismissed. 'Wait, here me out, Padraig.' The men around her murmured. Someone stifled a guffaw. Stupid men, assuming she had feathers for brains. 'Gann doesn't need to know.' His ignorance would keep them all safe. 'The night of the drop is the Oyster Ball. He'll be out of the house and he's not bound to wander down there until you can move the barrels. He doesn't use the cellar. Gann keeps his wines in a different place. No one will even know the barrels are down there. They can stay as long as we need them to. Then we can arrange to distil and move the brandy while he's out on another night.' The more she thought about it, the more sense it made. It kept the drop local and didn't require the men to travel a long distance to meet the ship. 'The cellar door is unlocked and can be accessed from outside the home.' Even better. There was no need to steal a key or to arrange to have the door propped open.

Padraig's gaze had become thoughtful. 'It could work,' he said slowly, starting to think out loud. 'A lot will ride on you, Fina. You need to guarantee he'll be out when we need him to be out. Can you do that? You have time, the drop isn't for another two weeks.'

'He'll be too busy dancing.' She laughed, a bit of warmth flooding her at the acceptance. Men who'd laughed at her earlier were nodding now. Never mind they were taking their cue from Padraig. It felt good to feel like she belonged, no longer just the pretty outsider.

Charlie remained sceptical. 'What about getting it out? We can distil the brandy during the day once it's stored without being seen, but we can't haul it out in daylight or even by moonlight if he's home.'

'I could arrange to have Gann come dine with Lady St Helier and the Viscount,' Josefina spoke up. It was a bold offer, but surely it wouldn't be that hard to arrange, followed by an evening of cards? 'You would have to move quickly, though.' Cards would only last so long and Artemisia and Darius tended to retire early on account of their infant son.

'Fair enough.' Padraig looked pleased with her response and Charlie looked appeased. Padraig gave her a wink. 'We'll count on our lovely Josefina to keep Gann too busy to notice us coming or going. He'll return home none the wiser.'

Which was all to the good, Josefina thought. The less Gann knew, the more help he could be if anything went wrong. He'd be entirely innocent of the whole operation should anyone question him. And he'd approve if he knew. He'd said as much, hadn't he? He felt it was his job to watch over the people of Seasalter, to care for them. He understood how important the smuggling money was to them. If he could have offered, he would have.

'Now that's settled—' Padraig beamed at the crew '—let's drink, first to our success, then we'll find something else to drink to.' He threw an arm about her as a cheer went up at the notion of an impromptu party. 'Well done, Fina. I knew you'd bring us good luck the moment I saw you.'

He pulled out his flask and offered it to her. Gann would hate that, too. She took a defiant swallow as a fiddle tuned up in the common room. It was going to be a loud, raucous night. There'd be drinking and dancing and she was determined to enjoy herself, determined not to think of a quieter evening spent with a quieter sort of man, who, probably, right now, was tucked up behind his big desk, writing in his ledgers while the clock ticked somnolently in the hall, punctuating the stillness of the house. Why ever would she want to be there, when she could be here? And yet, when Padraig grabbed her about the waist and twirled her into a country dance, she couldn't shake the notion this felt wrong. This wasn't where she wanted to be.

Chapter Eight

The sketches weren't right. Josefina stepped back from the drafting table, hoping distance might bring a different perspective and re-assurance that she'd only imagined the imperfections. It didn't help. Taken separately, parts of the sketches were right. His hands were right: big, capable hands, roughened by weather and work, devoid of a gentleman's ornamentation—no rings even though he could afford them. But his eyes were wrong. The setting around him was wrong.

She'd drawn him at his desk, beside his desk, the long elegant turquoise curtains in the background, in the chair in the drawing room, but they were just places. They didn't offer any useful insight into him. A setting ought to do that. It ought to tell the subject's story. The person in these backdrops could be any rich man. The Academy would find the work generic and unworthy of a prize. She had to do better. Perhaps she needed some more inspiration. Perhaps she needed to study her subject in his natural habitat again since the unnatural habitat had failed to do him justice. Or perhaps she just needed a walk, some air to clear her head.

Josefina put the sketches away and grabbed her cloak from a peg in the work room and her ever-ready satchel and set out for the shore. She wouldn't dare think of calling on Gann unannounced. He wouldn't approve of such disorderly conduct as an unscheduled call. But maybe she didn't need to see him to be inspired. Perhaps it would be enough to walk in his footsteps.

The shore was busy despite the cold. Children played tag on the pebbly shingle, men worked on boats and nets. Women went about chores and child-watching, all out of doors. Where else were they to do the work of living? As she watched them, it occurred to Josefina there was no choice but to live outside. The huts could hardly be lived in around the clock. Even the few row cottages would be too small for a family of any size to enjoy the indoors for any long period of time. These homes sufficed for evening meals and shelters when the weather gave them no choice.

It occurred to her, too, that this was how Owen had grown up. He and his brother, Simon, had played as these children played: in ragged breeks and thin coats, with pebbles, sticks and shell shards washed ashore and fashioned into whatever their imaginations could conjure. He had lived like this, wild, free, poor, unlikely to rise above whatever his father had been. And yet he had. He had not only risen above his father's humble station, he'd fashioned a life that was the complete antithesis of the one he'd had. No more poverty, but also no more freedom, no more wildness. What had he been like? The wild boy, Owen Gann? It made her smile to imagine the restrained, reclusive businessman as an extroverted boy.

She stopped to chat with a few women, but the usually talkative women were taciturn and distracted today as they gathered together. Their gazes drifted towards the water edge and the group of men gathered there. Two blond heads stood out among the crowd. Simon and Owen. The Gann brothers. The other men, she did not recognise. They were not Seasalter men. Their coats were too fine, their boots too clean. And there were soldiers among them. 'Who are they?' Josefina asked. The sight of soldiers made her as uneasy as the women.

'Some fancy men from London, business partners of Mr Gann's,' Charlie's wife whispered in awe. Another whispered in disdain, 'And some redcoats.' The woman spat on the ground. 'That Lieutenant Hawthorne is too nosy for his own good and ours.'

'What are they doing here?' She could guess. Did it have something to do with the highly anticipated brandy run? Or perhaps it had to do with the prior run and the French boat that had nearly been caught. Her stomach tightened, Owen's warnings coming back to her.

'The businessmen want assurances that Gann's reputation is clean before they close a big deal. The soldiers are here to ensure Seasalter isn't a hotbed of smuggling,' Charlie's wife explained. The meeting down by the shore had broken up. Men paired up in groups and headed back to the Crown. There was a rustling among the women as they suddenly drifted apart and tried to look busy. Josefina felt exposed, left alone. She froze with a moment's indecision. Did she want Owen to see her or should she hurry back the way she'd come?

Too late. Owen and Simon strode towards her. 'Miss Ricci, what a pleasant surprise. Have you come to sketch the fishermen?' Simon was all cheerfulness next to his brother's more subdued demeanour.

Josefina laughed and gave a toss of her head. 'No, I've come for inspiration. How is your baby girl?'

'Inspiration enough for me. Elianora and I have decided to rent a shop space in London for the Season to sell her cakes.' Simon was in high spirits. 'You must excuse me, Elianora is expecting me at the bakery. Owen, I will see you tonight.'

Simon's departure left her alone with Owen for the first time since their supper together. 'Today's a big day, I hear.' It stung to think the whole village had known of this big day and the purpose for it and yet she hadn't. She'd spent an entire day with him, eaten a meal with him, and he hadn't mentioned it once.

'Yes, it is. I am closing a deal for a purchase of ships, a small shipping line, if you will.' Gann looked every inch the prosperous businessman today with his pristine cravat and expensively cut jacket peeping from beneath a dark blue, many-caped wool greatcoat with polished brass buttons that rivalled military perfection.

She felt dishevelled in her work skirts and warm but well-worn cloak beside his sartorial elegance. Not that he was looking at her. He seemed to be looking beyond her to a point over her shoulder. 'Did you find what you were looking for, *signorina*?' His gaze met hers only briefly before returning to the point over her shoulder. His demeanour was stiff. He was trying very hard to be aloof as if they were still in his drawing room, as if they hadn't shared a meal in his kitchen or experienced a fleeting moment of intimacy during a goodnight kiss on his widow's walk. Was that kiss still on his mind? She wasn't sure that any man had ever thought about her kisses days later.

'Yes. I was looking for you, actually. I was walking in your footsteps.' She looped her arm through his and continued her stroll. 'Tell me, which of these huts was yours?'

He didn't have time for this. He needed to be back at the house overseeing Pease, who was overseeing Cook, who was overseeing the dinner that would be on the table at seven o'clock sharp tonight after a half-hour of preprandial drinks in the drawing room. But here he was, strolling the shingle with Josefina Ricci as if he had all the time in the world. He wished he did. There was something about being in her company that made him forget his cares, as if nothing mattered but this moment and the next. It made her dangerous to him.

She'd taken his arm, but now it was he leading her through the warren of row cottages and huts that comprised the main part of what nominally passed as the village. They came to a stop next to a hut, as ordinary and as ramshackle as the rest. It was nothing special. It hadn't been then and it wasn't now. It was set back, apart from the rest. No one was home, not that he had any intention of knocking and asking to come in. It would put pressure on the family to want to entertain him with resources they couldn't spare and it would bring back memories he didn't want to engage with, not today. He didn't want to step into the one-room abode and see the bed where his mother had died still standing in one corner, or the hearth where he'd cooked so many inadequate meals and fallen asleep next to on so many nights, exhausted to the bone.

'Four generations of Ganns lived here,' Owen said. All the way back to his father's grandfather. Oystermen their entire lives. 'My mother died there.' He was aware of Josefina squeezing his hand, lending her compassion, but the rest of him was in the past, remembering, filling in the pieces. 'My father died two years later of hard work and a broken heart. I raised my brother in that hut after that. Working the oyster beds in season, working odd jobs out of season, cooking meals, keeping us fed.' Those had been hard, but inspiring, years. They'd been the catalyst for wanting to do more, for seeing the potential to do better.

'I am sorry to raise the dead.' Josefina's voice was quiet, her earlier teasing subdued.

No doubt she was regretting it. She'd likely got more than she asked for, but once he'd started remembering, started talking, he had not been able to hold back. She made divulgence as irresistible in daylight as she had on the widow's walk the other night. Today he could not blame it on the wine or the hour.

'Who lives here now?' Josefina was studying him with her dark eyes.

'A family named Bexley with three children under the age of six, at least they were when they moved in, but that was years ago.' Before he'd bought Baldock House. He'd been renting a house a little way up the coast that had belonged to a squire who favoured London. Goodness, those children would be full grown now. The daughter would be old enough to marry, the little boy nearly old enough to claim his rights to fish the oyster beds. Three children grown to adulthood in that single room, like he and his brother.

They moved on, a thoughtful silence between them. 'Why don't you do something about it?' Josefina spoke quietly but there was a challenge in the question.

He didn't like the underlying assumption,

that somehow he'd turned a blind eye to the situation. He stopped and faced her slowly, giving himself time to put his temper in check. 'Do you think I haven't tried? It's not as easy as you might believe. I can't just throw money at it. If I could just build them all houses, I would.' Goodness knew he'd tried just such a strategy several years back when he was new to the dynamics of money and pride. His money had come up hard against a stone wall.

'They say it's not fitting. How can oystermen live like equals to foremen and managers?' New houses struck a dangerous blow to the social order that had sustained their little community for centuries. Everyone understood their place. Still, he didn't want Josefina to think he'd simply given up. He was made of sterner stuff than that and he wanted her to know it for reasons he couldn't quite fathom or didn't want to.

'I do what I can. If someone has an ill grandmother, I send medicine, if a family is bad off, I try to see they have what they need, but even then I have to be discreet. A man's pride is a formidable object even when his family stands to benefit.' He had a hundred examples of times when his outright help had been turned down. He'd had to find other more subtle ways to offer it through the church or another third party. 'I was young and brash. I thought money could fix anything, but sometimes it creates more problems than it solves.'

Josefina nodded. 'I know.' It was said in commiseration, sympathetically, as if she did indeed know and it made him wonder—how would she know such a thing? It was a reminder of all he didn't know about her and wanted to.

'How? How do you know?' It was a frank, rude question. One never asked so directly about another's financial background.

Josefina threw him a coy look as they began to walk again. 'That's very direct, Mr Gann. I'll give you points for boldness.'

'I'd rather have an answer.' He smiled back, enjoying the banter. He was good at this, direct negotiating. He'd honed his teeth on such strategy in the boardrooms of London's businessmen. He'd learned early not to take no for an answer if one expected to get anywhere and he'd been rewarded. Businessmen had liked the scrapper from Kent. Women liked it, too, up to a point—a point he'd never be able to cross.

'There's a lot of things I'd rather have, Mr Gann.' She laughed, to divert him, darting ahead with a quick little half-step. It only made him more determined.

He lengthened his stride and caught up to her. 'Call me Owen. No more of this "Mr Gann" business. Were you always an itinerant artist?' There were suddenly a million questions he wanted to ask her, wanted to know.

'No, I wasn't.' She danced away, walking backwards now so she could face him with that teasing smile of hers. The cold air had pinkened her cheeks and the wind had picked her hair free. She was beautiful and out of reach. 'But that's all I'll tell you for now. The rest will cost you.'

They'd left the village and had reached the road. It was decision time. He didn't want her to go. 'Come to dinner tonight, Josefina.' *That* stopped her in her dancing tracks. She pushed an errant strand of hair out of her face.

'I don't have anything to wear. I didn't pack my ball gowns when I left home.' She tried for a joke. He'd caught her off guard and now she was grasping for an excuse.

'There are gowns upstairs at the house. I'm sure there's something suitable among them, or that Lady St Helier could loan you.'

She shook her head. 'You don't want me at your very important party.' But he did. He was already imagining her at the table, charming the businessmen with her smile, her wit and her boldness. And afterwards, they might go up to the widow's walk, they might continue their conversation and other things.

'I do. Lady St Helier and the Viscount are coming. She's agreed to act as my hostess. You wouldn't be alone at the table.' Now that he'd invited her, now that he'd thought about it, he *wanted* her to be at his dinner tonight.

'I can't.' She was firmer in her response this time.

'Why? What are you doing that precludes an evening of socialising and good food?' He recognised that he was pushing hard now. It was not well done of him. She hesitated and he *knew*. He stepped forward, compelled to stop her with words, with whatever he had. He grabbed her wrist. 'Don't go to him. Don't…'

Don't pick Padraig O'Malley over me, don't go with the smugglers.

It wasn't just the danger he wanted her to reject. There was no run tonight, but they would all gather to drink and dance and get up to general mischief at the Crown. Owen resorted to bribery. 'I think you might find an association with Lieutenant Hawthorne insightful and potentially useful.' Perhaps if he could give her a reason to come besides simply coming for him he could sway her.

She studied him, reading the implied message that there might be help for the smugglers in her attendance. 'Well, when you put it that way, perhaps I might avail myself of a dress from your guest chamber after all.'

The dinner was starting to look more enjoyable. 'I'll send the dress down to the school right away.'

Chapter Nine

Inviting her was the most impetuous, most selfish thing Owen had done in a long while and he did not regret it. Josefina was dazzling. The rose silk brought out the black of her hair and the dark of her eyes. Gold earbobs in the shape of tiny leaves teased at her lobes as her laughter teased from the other end of the table, where she sat beside Lieutenant Hawthorne. Watching her made it difficult to keep his attentions on the dry banker, a Mr Matthews, who sat to his left. Thank goodness St Helier was doing that for him with a few well-placed questions to keep the conversation going.

'You set a superior table, Gann. Quite a surprise to find such culinary excellence is such an isolated place.' The banker's gaze twitched down the table. 'It seems Seasalter has other pleasant surprises, as well. Who knows, this might become the next Brighton. First the art school and the St Heliers taking up full-time residence, now the Italian protégée.' Owen didn't care for the way the banker's glance moved down the table and lingered, the object of his gaze evident. The man was taken with Josefina. 'Quite the community you've got here, Gann. A little undiscovered gem if I don't say so myself.'

Owen didn't like the direction of either of Matthew's insinuations. 'The art community here is all Lady St Helier's doing.' He would insist on credit being given where it was due.

'Seasalter would make a fine resort town,' Matthews said. 'Just a day's carriage drive from London makes it accessible. You could really develop this place. Throw up a few middle-class hotels and inns, get a few bathing machines and just like that you have another seaside resort,' he mused out loud. He leaned towards Owen confidentially. 'Let me know if you ever want to go in on it.'

'No, Matthews, I am afraid it would be a poor investment from beginning to end,' Owen said firmly. He motioned for Pease to refill the man's goblet, hoping to redirect the man's thoughts. 'The beach is too pebbly. It's a working man's beach, hardly conducive to luxurious picnics, and the shoreline isn't right for a harbour. We're more estuary and marsh than open sea,' he reminded Matthews. They'd discussed this today, the importance of eventually building their own harbour for the fleet at Whitstable for just that reason. Even if such things were possible, development of Seasalter was the last thing Owen wanted.

Matthews shrugged, undaunted by Owen's reservations. 'That's what sea walls and promenades are for. Structures can be built to overcome geographic limitations.'

Owen raised a brow. 'And risk jeopardising the wildlife Lady St Helier draws in the marshes? I don't think that would go over well.' Lady St Helier wouldn't want the intrusion of tourists and crowds. Neither would the smugglers. Summer travellers and boaters were not conducive to discreet drops in Shucker's Cove. More importantly, such tourism could negatively affect the oyster beds and jeopardise the livelihood of those who counted on them. No, the charm of Seasalter depended on it being left alone. He was relieved when Artemisia rose from the other end of the table and signalled for the ladies to depart with her to the drawing room. The evening could move forward towards more pleasant topics.

He didn't keep the men long at the table. They'd spent the day together and business had been settled. In truth, the main concern of their business had been settled before the visit. They were here to ensure his money was good enough for them, that Owen Gann wasn't a gauche fisherman. Having a viscount to dine and a table that rivalled any table of the *ton* had sealed that concern. That the table was graced with the refined company of Lady St Helier and the alluring Signorina Ricci had further reinforced for them that his money and his person was good enough for their association. They could comfortably overlook his humble antecedents.

That wasn't to say it didn't gall him that such measures were still necessary a decade after having made the first steps towards his substantial wealth. Money was money. Technically, his pounds spent as well as a duke's, perhaps better since it seemed so many of the aristocracy was perpetually burdened by debt. But he knew better. Money was not money. It mattered who had it. The brine of the sea would follow him always.

In the drawing room, Lady St Helier invited the bankers' wives to take turns at the piano and a polite musicale evening ensued. Matthews, it turned out, was a passable tenor who sang with his wife. Josefina was the last of the women to take a turn. She rose and made her way to the piano and Owen felt as if every man in the room watched her. Or was he the only one who was aware of each movement she made?

She sat down at the instrument, adjusting her skirts. 'This is a Venetian serenade sung by the gondoliers as they pole through the canals of an evening,' she offered by way of introduction, tossing Lieutenant Hawthorne a little smile that had the man positively drooling in his chair. What an imbecile, Owen thought. The King's Finest had his head easily turned. Perhaps it took one to know one. She'd certainly turned *his* head.

Josefina began to sing in soft gentle Italian and soon Lieutenant Hawthorne wasn't the only man in the room entranced. If there'd been any question of her refinement, Josefina's performance would have confirmed it. It was as if they were in Venice itself when she sang. Owen had never been, but he could imagine it: a city built of canals instead of roads, lanterns bobbing on long narrow boats that slid peacefully between the watery lanes, a soft breeze of an evening carrying the gondolier's songs throughout the town. What magic that must be.

But it provoked questions, too. Why would someone ever leave such a place? What was so unacceptable about the offers that would have allowed her to stay? What sort of woman was she that she painted, spoke two languages and played the pianoforte? She possessed the refinements of a well-brought-up young woman, not a street rat. She'd not always been an itinerant artist.

His thoughts had wandered far afield when she finished and he was loath to give them up when the song ended. He would have liked to have stayed in his imaginary Venice awhile longer, but it was time to end the evening and she'd given him the perfect note on which to do it.

* * *

'I think it went well,' Josefina said as he shut the door behind the St Heliers. They had lingered a short while after the last guests departed to assure him the evening had been a success. But they were eager to get home to their infant son and Josefina, it seemed, was eager to stay. She'd been the one to encourage them to go, assuring them she would follow shortly. She had portrait business she wanted to discuss first. Owen thought it more likely there was smuggling business she'd want to discuss. Whatever the reason, he was more than happy to have her stay behind.

'I think so, too, thanks to you. I am glad you decided to come.' Owen gave her an easy smile. 'Would you like a drink? A nightcap, perhaps?' How natural it seemed to have her here after just a few visits. How right it seemed to debrief the evening with her as he might with a wife and how foolish it seemed to entertain such fantasies.

'If it's up on the widow's walk, you have a deal.' Josefina tossed him one of her wide smiles and swished her skirts as she set out ahead of him for the stairs. He followed, decanter in one hand, two glasses in the other as those rose silk skirts led him out on to the walk.

There were no stars tonight. The clouds hung low and cold. He poured for them as she hunted out the blanket. 'It would be a good night for smuggling,' he said once they'd settled against the railing, drinks in hand, the blanket about her shoulders. 'I'm sure Lieutenant Hawthorne gave you a useful earful of information tonight.' He clinked his glass against hers, but she seemed subdued.

'He did, but that's not why I wanted to come up here.' The smile she gave him was soft, almost sad. There was a different light to her eyes. 'Tonight reminded me of home and I would linger in the memory awhile longer.'

'To home, then.' Owen nodded. In a way, the evening reminded him of home, too. Not a home he'd lost or left, but a home he'd not possessed and perhaps never would. Tonight had been a glimpse into the what could have been, or what might yet still be if he tried for it again. His unused dining room had been transformed into a beautiful setting for a beautiful meal, people lining the sides of his pol-

ished table, silver shining, crystal catching the
light, china clinking. What would his mother
have given to sit at such a table, to eat such
food? Could she even have pictured such luxury? And yet, he wasn't entirely sure when he
looked at Josefina that the home he imagined
tonight was a place.

'To home,' Josefina whispered and he whispered back in the intimacy of the night, hungry for the pictures she would paint with her
words of places he'd never seen and people
he'd never meet, 'Tell me about it, tell me about
Italy, about your father, about nights like this.'

At his words, the memories rushed forth,
needing no further invitation. She'd not been
aware they'd swum so close to the surface.
Tonight they would not be denied. 'We would
host supper parties on the balcony of our town
house. We lived on the Cannaregio Canal and
the balcony ran the length of the house.'

She could remember that house down to the
minutest detail, the peeling pink stucco, the
long country table on the balcony, the benches
and chairs they cobbled together up and down
its length, the mishmash of second-hand dishes

her father made look eccentrically artistic instead of incongruous. After enough wine, no one much cared if the china matched. In truth, no one had cared before. They cared only for good food and good friends. 'Those evenings went on late into the night, sometimes even until the sun came up. A few nights, we served breakfast before they all went home.' Josefina gave a little laugh at the remembrance.

'It sounds wonderful.' Owen grinned in the darkness.

'It was.' She was warming to the topic now, the memories seeming to lose their sadness. 'I played the hostess. We'd sit for hours, talking about art, arguing about this technique or that or who made more important contributions to the medium: Caravaggio or Tintoretto.' She'd cut her teeth on those discussions. Her education had not been as formalised perhaps as Artemisia's, who'd had the Royal Academy to fall back on, but she'd argue it was just as good. Her education had taken place informally at the hands of her father and his friends. At their knees, she'd learned of the Renaissance masters, how to recognise a Titian, how to mix paint, how to develop perspective. 'The gondoliers would push their boats past, singing, a perfect accompaniment for our evenings. Sometimes we sketched the people in their boats and sent the drawings down. Someone always had a pad of paper at the table.'

'You miss it. You speak of it with such passion. I can imagine I'm there, at the table with you.' Owen's words were soft in the darkness. 'I would miss such a magical place.'

'I miss *him*. He made it magical.'

Had she really said that out loud? She should have said, *It stinks in the summer. There are fevers.* Why hadn't she said something witty to lighten the mood or disabuse him of the magic of Venice? Josefina peered into her nearly empty glass and set it aside. Perhaps she could blame it on the wine and the brandy, but she suspected she would have told him anyway. Owen Gann had a way of bringing out her secrets, things she talked about with no one.

Owen leaned against the rail, his big body angled to face her. 'What was he like, your father?'

'He was an artist, romantic, scatterbrained at times. He'd get lost in his work and forget to eat. He might not pay the bills for months on end. He was eccentric, sporadic, brilliant, loving, kind. He wasn't a usual father, but he was a good one. He bought me my first evening gown and my first pearls. He wasn't afraid of me growing up like some parents are. He encouraged me to embrace my talents and dreams.' She reached for his free hand and matched her fingers to his, lacing them through. She needed to stop this conversation before she told him too much. 'What of your father? Did he encourage you to dream of all this?'

'No, my father didn't know how to dream, only how to work and it killed him when I was seventeen. It was a hard dose of reality. I realised that could be me in twenty years, leaving behind a family who needed looking after if things didn't change and why would they change? They hadn't changed for generations. If anything was going to change, I had to do it. No one was going to do it for me.'

She heard the resolution that lingered in his voice still. After all these years, he was still changing things, for himself, for his people. She heard the angst, too, the boy who'd become the family's breadwinner. At seventeen, she'd been living blissfully in her father's studio while he'd been dredging oysters, doing a man's work. 'He would be amazed at what you've done, this empire you've built.'

Owen's gaze met hers, sharp and shrewd. She'd made a misstep. 'Would he? I think he would say, "Owen, you've forgotten where you came from. We are oyster people."'

'You're still oyster people, aren't you?' she argued gently. That won her a rueful smile.

'Yes, I am still oyster people, but not the way my father understood it and, unfortunately, not in the way bankers like Elias Matthews understand.' He looked out over the quiet waters of Shucker's Cove. 'Tonight was a success, but it should not have been necessary. They came to judge me. My money wasn't good enough on its own. They didn't want to be tainted by associating with an oysterman, a mere fisherman even if he could make them money.' He gave a harsh chuckle.

'You were more than equal to the task.' He'd been a revelation tonight in his fine clothes, at his fine table, his manners as impeccable as his wine. What a chameleon Owen Gann was—one day a cool businessman eager to be rid of her, the next, a simple man in a rowboat, a man who could cook, and a man who could entertain as if he'd never seen the inside of his own kitchen. But it was easy to be a chameleon when one belonged everywhere and nowhere, wasn't it? Who knew this better than she?

She could be anything she said she was. There was no one to gainsay her, no one who knew better, no one who could divine her lies from truths. It was the blessing and the curse of being free. She filed it away with all the other images of Owen, this new image of the man caught in between worlds. Too good for one and not deemed good enough by the other. It was a dichotomy she, as a female artist, was all too familiar with. Too good to be ignored, but too controversial to be accepted—unless she was someone's wife. One couldn't have all that talent running around unleashed, unaccounted for. If not, she'd simply have to be ignored, brushed away like a nuisance of a fly until she was forgotten or lost amid a workshop of apprentices who were more memorable and more male. But the price of that freedom was high, the price of not belonging, of only pretending to for a short time. His eyes held hers and in that moment

she understood one thing with raw, unadulter-
ated clarity.

He knew.

Owen shared that price with her. It rocketed
through her with all the electrical charge of a
lightning bolt. They were both people caught
between worlds. The space betwixt was the
only space in which they could be free. That
he knew and understood undid her. In the face
of the evening, the memories it invoked, the
sharing of those memories here with him, of
realising she was not alone in her isolation,
were too much. *She need not be alone.* What
if he was also desperate to set aside the seclu-
sion he lived in? A little thrum began to hum
through her, the thrum of mutual attraction,
of mutual acknowledgement, of anticipation,
of expectation and easing. She licked her lips.
'Why did you invite me tonight?'

His eyes lingered on her face, hot blue
flames in the cold dark. 'Shall I tell you the
truth?' His voice was a low baritone of a whisper. 'You will think me selfish.' His hand
skimmed her cheek with its knuckles, an intimate gesture that sent a slow river of warmth
straight to her belly. 'I didn't want to be alone.'

'And now?' She hardly dared to breathe for fear of breaking the spell woven by their words, the night and his touch.

'I still don't want to be alone.'

She turned her cheek into his palm, caressing it with the whisper of her words. 'Neither do I.' Invitation accepted. His mouth found hers then in a long, slow kiss that sipped from her as if she were the finest of wines. It turned her insides to *marmelatta* and her knees to a trembling *panna cotta* held together only by the cream that might collapse at any time. Who would have thought the solid, solitary Owen Gann would kiss like Casanova? Or that a simple dinner party would end in his arms and in his bed—there was no mistaking what they'd committed to here on the widow's walk. There would be no hasty tupping against the railing and a walk home in the dark, the space between her legs sore from rough, hurried use.

Owen swung her up into his arms as if she were weightless. She looped an arm about his neck and teased her lover—yes, her lover... he would be that very soon. 'Where are you taking me?'

'To bed.'

The two words sent a shot of excitement through her. Were there any two more thrilling words in the English language?

'Very well then, carry on.' She laughed up at him softly, seductively, noting the way his eyes darkened in response. A different sort of tremor went through her, a reminder that Owen Gann was not a man who made love for pleasure's whim alone.

Chapter Ten

It was a reminder borne out in the bedroom. He placed her on the wide four-poster bed and stepped back to undress with intentional care. First, laying aside his masculine accoutrements: the sapphire pin in his snowy cravat, the gold pocket watch and chain, the matching cuff-links that glinted in their trifle tray, the way his eyes had glinted on the widow's walk with hot, deliberate desire. His coats followed: dark evening jacket, waistcoat of damask ivory… sombre colours compared to this year's brighter hues she'd seen in London. But Owen Gann was a serious man, as sober in the boardroom as he was in the bedroom, it seemed.

The thought of all that seriousness brought to bear in lovemaking made her mouth go dry as deft fingers made short work of his shirt buttons with the same dexterity with which they'd wielded a shucking knife on a rocking boat. She sucked in her breath as his shirt joined his jacket. Sweet heavens, he was a beautiful man, a Viking in the raw indeed. Years of hard labour had left him with a smooth, sculpted expanse of pectoral muscles that tapered to lean hips and an exquisitely defined iliac girdle that disappeared into the waistband of his trousers.

His hands rested there, angling downwards, drawing her gaze towards the manly core of him. His arousal was evident despite the dimness of the room and the dark fabric of his trousers. She licked her lips in anticipation and encouragement, the flick of her tongue saying *Go on, don't make me wait too long.* A hint of mischief flashed in his eyes as if he knew precisely what he was doing and what she thought about it.

'Good things come, Josefina…' His voice was a raw chuckle.

'To those who wait?' she concluded for him, her own voice husky. She liked this seductive glimpse of Owen Gann as a lover, a man who could tease, who could tempt a woman to abject distraction with a look, with a single line.

She watched, hungrily, as he slid those trousers over lean hips and muscled thighs, revealing himself inch by erotic inch. Her own desire ratcheted, a desire to look, to lick, to possess and be possessed by the powerful promise of the body on display. He kicked his trousers aside and she burned with greedy need. He was blond, golden, smooth, so unlike the men of southern Europe. She was hungry for contact, her body starving to assuage the loneliness unleashed inside her. If she could touch him, lie with him, let him fill her, somehow it would drive away the loss that swamped her—it would appease his devils, too. She wanted that, for both of them.

Josefina rose and went to him, plucking at the decorative ribbon at the bodice of her gown as she approached, her voice a whisper of want. 'Undress me, touch me, Owen.' She wanted those big, deft hands on her skin.

He did not disappoint. He made short work of the gown's buttons, his mouth pressing kisses against the column of her neck, her undergarments followed, his hands as quick on lacing as they'd been on buttons, skimming bare skin in tantalising touches until she was left in her chemise. She stepped away then and turned back to face him. She would be the author of this final reveal herself. 'Watch me, Owen.' She gave the low, throaty command as she took the hem of the chemise and pulled it over her head. The fluid movement brought her breasts into high relief and she heard Owen's breath hitch. Then she stood before him gloriously nude, her own desire heightened by his.

She closed the distance between them and placed the flat of her hands on his chest. 'Good lord, you are like marble,' she breathed in erotic appreciation.

'That I am. I'm marble everywhere,' Owen growled, dancing her back towards the bed. She went willingly, feeling the mattress give under his weight as he followed her down, his mouth finding hers in a hot kiss that tasted of brandy and promise and craving. 'I want, I need, Josefina.' There was desperation in his hungry plea that matched her own.

Her arms were about his neck, pulling him close against her, her body thrilling to the strength, the proximity of his. '*I* want, *I* need, Owen. Come and feast with me.'

'Josefina, are you sure?' Owen's sense of decency asserted itself even now amid unbridled passion. It was sweet of him to think she had a reputation to protect and that he should be the one to do it even at such a moment.

She smiled. 'Yes, I choose for myself, Owen, and I choose you.' Wanderers had the freedom to not worry about such things. She kissed him on the mouth in assurance. Desire was driving her hard now—had any feast ever been so needed? His mouth moved down the length of her, from throat column to breasts, sucking, licking its way down to her navel, his hands bracketing her hips, holding her steady as he went lower still, his tongue finding the discreet cove between her folds.

He licked at her, his big shoulders heaving beneath her hands as she clutched at him, desperate to anchor herself against the pleasure that shook her. Yet, this exquisite pleasure was not enough. 'Come inside, Owen,' she begged, breathless but not sated.

The words had barely left her before he moved between her legs, his big body levered over her, his phallus at the crux of her thighs, eager and hard against her entrance, finding

her more than ready. The damp evidence of
that readiness nearly undid him, proof that her
want was as great as his. A guttural exhalation
took him and all restraint fled.

They fell to the feast together. This was what
he wanted, what his body needed, this joining, her arms about his neck, her legs wrapped
tight about his hips as he plunged deep into her
depths. She met him there in the deep. Passion did not frighten her. She welcomed it and
him with a recklessness his body answered to.
Her body arched into him, head thrown back,
throat exposed, and he took it, his mouth rav-
enous for the taste of her. Her nails raked his
back, his teeth bit into her skin, until it wasn't
clear who was driving whom, their pleasures
interdependent and inseparable.

He thrust hard again and deeper still, letting her recklessness enfold them both until
he felt her clench about him, felt his own body
gather for a final effort and they fell together
from impossible heights, a free fall into pleasure's abyss. By the heavens, had anything
ever been so satisfying? Had anything ever
filled him with such completion he wanted
to do nothing but lie here with her and let it

wash over them? 'I've made love with a sensual angel.' He sighed contentedly, feeling her nestle against him in the crook of his arm.

She gave a throaty, drowsy laugh. 'No, just a woman, a mere mortal, although for a few moments we might have touched the heavens.'

'Hmm.' Owen pondered the thought, a hand playing idly through her hair, sifting the silky dark strands. He was learning her, her body and her mind, piece by piece tonight, and the process was intoxicating and addicting. He wanted to know all of her. 'You're a woman from Venice. A woman who has traversed the Continent. My oysters have travelled further than I have.' He laughed. 'I suppose I envy you that. What's your favourite place? The most interesting place you've been?'

She gave a thoughtful sigh. He could almost hear her sorting through her memories. 'If I had to choose a city, I'd choose Marseilles. It's a confluence of culture and trade, like Venice. But it's older, so much older. People from all over the Mediterranean have done business there since the days before Christ. You can hear languages spoken from Turkish and Arabic to Greek and French and Italian. Russian, too. And some languages I don't even have names for. In some ways all that culture reminded me of Venice, at least what Venice must have been at its height. But Marseilles still bustles. The streets are narrow, the buildings are weathered but there are treasures inside them. There's a church, the Church of St Laurent of Marseilles, on top of a hill and it commands a view of the old port. I sat up there for afternoons on end, painting and imagining the city in ancient times when the Greeks controlled it.'

He could imagine it, too. Old streets, bustling with modern life. He could smell the fishy wharves and hear the cries of fishmongers. It came to life through her words as Venice had come to life tonight in her song. 'But if you didn't choose a city?' Owen prompted. 'What would you choose then?'

'Anything in the Alps,' she answered without hesitation. 'I spent time at a castle with a lake on one side of it and a mountain on the other. I was there in the spring, of course, otherwise it wouldn't have been accessible. It was beautiful, rugged majesty cloaked in wildflowers and the bluest skies above it. I painted a few landscapes for the Count who lived there.'

Jealousy pricked. Owen didn't want to think about the Count. He opted to talk about the art instead. 'You're a very talented artist if Counts are giving you commissions. Does Artemisia know?' He was thinking about his friend's wager now and about the hidden trove of talents Josefina possessed.

'No.' She traced a design around his aureole and his flat nipple pimpled into erectness. 'It doesn't signify. I am just a street artist here, an itinerant traveller who will move on to fulfil other dreams in May.'

He stilled her hand, aware that perhaps she was deliberately distracting him. Not yet. He wanted clarity for a moment more. 'But you're not really a street artist. Your father was an artist, you lived well in Venice, well enough to acquire a genteel education that left you fluent in English and music along with painting.'

Josefina raised up on one elbow and smiled, her hair falling over her shoulder. 'I have what one might call a wide-ranging, haphazard education acquired from whatever tutors were on hand and my father when he could spare the time. My mathematics are atrocious, by the way. My father's patrons weren't interested in numbers and science.' He felt her eyes linger on him. 'What are you worried about, Owen?'

He might as well be honest with her. 'Deception. Artemisia's wager is about turning a street artist into something finer, but you're already quite fine.'

She chuckled. 'I was chosen at random for better or worse, with whatever bad habits and whatever training I might already have acquired. That was the point of the wager, I believe. To take a diamond in the rough and transform it.'

'But you're already transformed,' Owen argued, only to be met with her laughter in the dark as she reached for him.

'Hardly. I am learning plenty from Artemisia. She's a genius and portraiture is not where I excel.' She kissed him softly. 'You'd be surprised by the amount of talent in the pool of street artists—and the stories, too. My background isn't so unusual.' Her hand found him beneath the covers. 'Speaking of transformations, however, this one seems to be coming along nicely.' Indeed it was. When her hand encircled his shaft and began to stroke, he was far more interested in what was happening here and now between them than anything that had gone before.

They made love twice more that night, each time bringing a slightly different variation to their pace and appreciation as they learned one another's bodies. If it had been up to him, Owen would have never got out of bed. He would have traded all his worldly positions to hold on to those precious minutes when there was nothing but peace and pleasure and possibility. After all, he could make another fortune. But this, he thought drowsily as dawn encroached, was more precious than pearls: Josefina asleep in his arms, her dark hair draped across his chest, her naked breast pressed to him, his body and his mind replete. He did not know if he could make this night happen again.

He didn't want to wake up, not fully. He wanted to linger here in this world of impossible fantasy. But the morning had other ideas. The house would soon begin to stir. The cook in the kitchen, the maid to lay fires, Pease to oversee the post-mortem clean-up from the dinner party. Owen's eyes forced themselves open and he groaned against reality.

Had the dinner party only been last night? It seemed a lifetime had passed since then. When he thought of last night, dinner didn't come to mind. He thought instead of the first desperate, thundering coupling, of his body pouring its need into hers, of her body offering rough succour in return, of Josefina's hot words, *Come inside, Owen*. God, yes. His body stirred even now at the echo of that memory. Then he thought of the playfulness that engendered the time after that, and the tenderness of the time after that.

He had not planned for this to happen. He'd not invited her for a drink on the widow's walk with the intention of bedding her any more than he'd intended on inviting her to the dinner party when he'd left the house yesterday with nothing but business on his mind. But there she was, on the shore, the wind pulling her hair loose and her hand pulling him down memory lane, her smile beguiling stories from him. He hadn't wanted to leave her, so he'd invited her to the party and it still hadn't been enough. Like recognised like, two hungry souls in the night had come together. Quite explosively. Quite repeatedly.

Artemisia was going to kill him for this. She'd trusted him with her protégée and he'd seduced her. By no stretch of the imagination did 'I'll be along shortly' cover coming home the next morning after the sun was up. There was nothing for it. Owen shook Josefina awake gently. 'Wake up, love, I have to take you home.' He gave another groan and swung himself out of bed. There was going to be hell to pay. He'd best get on with it. But even that realisation wasn't enough to extinguish a little flame that had begun to burn inside him, something warm that he hadn't felt for a long time.

Chapter Eleven

She'd not been that reckless for a long while. Josefina didn't allow herself to examine exactly *how* reckless she'd been until she was in the privacy of her little studio late the next morning. What she examined made her cheeks flame. She'd not gone to the dinner party with any intention of revealing so much of herself to Owen or of going to bed with him—the host. Not just the host, she'd gone to bed *with the subject of her upcoming portrait*.

It was hardly professional and it ought to be cringeworthy. Recklessness was usually followed with regret and she could not summon any. This was perhaps more shocking than the impetuosity of the act itself. She'd *enjoyed* the night with Owen, more than enjoyed. The word seemed too tepid to describe how she felt about the encounter. It was far *more* than an encounter. *Allora*—not even that word was right. What a dry, objective word, *encounter*.

She sighed and absently laid out her brushes. Her English was failing her this morning. *Colpo di fulmine*. There, that was better. The thunderbolt. Love falling on someone suddenly, intensely. Only last night hadn't been about love. She would not pretend it had been. It had been about need, want and loneliness overcome. She wanted another. That was yet an additional layer of shock. The spontaneous needy act had created not the desire to regret it, but the desire to repeat it. Owen had been a thorough lover and a thoughtful one who had seen to her pleasure even as he'd claimed his own.

Such attentiveness amid the wild throes of passions begged the question: Why hadn't he been snatched up? She spread out her sketches, laying them side by side on a long table as her mind sorted through the question. A man who was as thorough in bed as he was with his ledgers was a rare find. In her experience, the better the lover, the worse his finances. Not that it had ever mattered. She was gone before such things as finances became relevant.

Oh, she liked this sketch, Owen at the shore in his workman's clothes. The eyes were better. She picked it up for closer scrutiny, but it was thoughts of last night that were examined: his insistent mouth on her, everywhere, the strength of the arms that had carried her downstairs to the bedroom, the exquisite body displayed in lamplight, the power of him as he'd thrust into her.

Sweet heavens, she couldn't help but smile at herself. Her body was rousing just from the memory of him. Owen Gann in the grip of his passion was a spectacular sight to behold. He'd given his all, he'd been entirely vulnerable in the last moments of his pleasure, entirely on display. Perhaps that was the reason, she mused, that he was so alone, by choice. A man who made love like that wouldn't put it on display for just anyone to see.

He let you see it. The warning whispered on the fringes of memory. Danger lurked there. What would such a man want in return for his vulnerability? She ought to take warning from it. Perhaps she would, later. For now, she just wanted to savour it while she could. She did not kid herself; the savouring wouldn't last.

There would be a price for last night, for letting the hours fly past, for letting Owen walk her home in dawn's early light and kiss her goodbye before she sneaked into the dormitory to tidy herself up before going downstairs for breakfast with the girls as if nothing had happened.

'What happened last night?' Artemisia's voice cut across her thoughts in slicing tones. Josefina nearly dropped the sketch in startlement—not because she was surprised to see Artemisia, her arrival had only been a matter of time, but because her thoughts had been that far away, lost in the remembered raptures of last night's passion and her own reaction to it.

Josefina hugged the sketch to her in a reflexive gesture of protection, of him, of her, of what they'd shared. 'That's private. It's no one's business but mine.'

Artemisia speared her with a sharp look. 'So, you slept with him.' It was not a question.

'I did not say that,' Josefina snapped.

'You didn't have to.' Artemisia moved through the studio, stopping to casually study drafts of work Josefina had spread throughout the room. 'If you hadn't, you wouldn't be wor-

ried about what was private and what wasn't.'
She looked up with a shake of her head. 'I don't
know what to do with you, Josefina. On the
one hand, you're a very talented artist. I like
this landscape, by the way. You've captured
the beauty and the isolation of Seasalter perfectly. It takes a sophisticated eye to see beyond the mud and the marshes. On the other
hand, you're going to drive yourself to ruin
with your recklessness.'

'I'm not reckless.' Josefina felt obliged to
make the demur. Artemisia raised a dark eyebrow in disbelief.

'I know what you are. You're sneaking out
to meet with O'Malley's smuggling gang and
now you've taken a shine to Seasalter's leading citizen. You crave adventure.' Artemisia
gave a half-laugh. 'I know because I was like
that. But it wasn't adventure I craved. It was
something far deeper. I spent a lot of years not
realising that and I made mistakes because of
it.' Artemisia's tone softened, as did her gaze.
'I would warn you off those mistakes so you
don't need to make them for yourself.'

She could handle an angry Artemisia. An
empathic Artemisia was more difficult. Josefina was wary. 'You're not mad?'

Artemisia frowned and took a seat. Josefina winced. Taking a seat presaged at longer conversation. She'd hoped they'd almost been done. 'I am mad. Your recklessness could reflect poorly on the school. When you go out with the smugglers you set a poor example. The other girls look up to you. They find your lifestyle glamorous—a single girl tramping about Europe with her paints.' Artemisia gave her a knowing smile. 'You and I know differently. It's not glamorous. It's hard. The inns are poor quality, the food worse, the guarantee of work non-existent and there's the inherent risks of being a woman alone. But they are young and impressionable. They're still holding on to fairy tales and we need to be careful with that. So, yes, when you jeopardise what I am trying to build here, I am angry. When you stay out all night with a man and sneak back in with your stockings in one hand at dawn, I am angry. What if one of the girls had seen you instead of Mrs Harris on her way up to the house to start the fires?' Mrs Harris was the redoubtable housekeeper at the farmhouse which served as the St Heliers' residence.

'I'll be more careful—' Josefina didn't complete her sentence, realising the trap she'd laid for herself.

'There'll be a next time, then?' Artemisia didn't miss the implication. Of course there would be. The smugglers were counting on her and she wanted another night with Owen. The women's eyes met and an awkward silence followed. Artemisia gave a sigh, making a decision with herself. 'Do you need a preservative?'

Josefina eased. Artemisia understood the limits of her control. 'No, I can take care of that.'

Artemisia rose and smoothed her skirts. 'Good, because Owen is not the sort of man who would ever let the mother of his child leave him.' She paused and Josefina felt the weight of her gaze settle firmly on her. 'Unless…that's what you're angling for? A rich, lonely man would look like an easy solution to a girl who's tired of running.'

Josefina bristled at the insinuation. 'That is not what I am angling for. I am gone in May.'

Artemisia nodded. 'Then I hope you'll stay safe long enough to make your getaway. We need to discuss sketches, but not today. We'll do it tomorrow when tempers aren't so hot.'

Josefina gritted her teeth and bit back a growl in the empty studio after Artemisia left. The English were so blasted composed even when they were seething. She'd much rather have had a full-blown argument with Artemisia complete with raised voices and loud epithets like any good Venetian instead of Artemisia coolly asking bold, blunt questions and establishing inconvenient truths like the risk to the school. She'd not thought of that, only of the danger to herself. On the road, there was just herself to consider. One more reason to make sure she was gone in May. Putting down roots meant being responsible for others, letting those others know her and making herself open to the possibility of hurt and disappointment that came from long-term attachments. Losing her father was all the loss she wanted to withstand. When spring came, she would move on, pursuing dreams, keeping promises, staying one step ahead of the hurt. This reminder, coming in the wake of a soft night in a man's arms when her guard was down as a result, was exactly what she needed to steel her resolve.

* * *

Artemisia with her resolve in full force was, in a word, intimidating to most men. Owen did not consider himself one of them. However, he could easily believe everything that had ever been said of her as she paced his study. 'Did she seduce you?'

Ah, so Artemisia knew. Owen chuckled. 'Is that what she told you?' He'd have preferred to have his interlude kept private, but he also knew how impossible such a wish was in a small village. It didn't get any smaller than Seasalter. Still, he'd rather enjoyed the laconic nature of today. He'd let his mind leisurely replay the night before as he'd looked over the contracts for the boats.

'No, she said nothing. I guessed.' Artemisia huffed. 'She was quite keen to not kiss and tell, if you must know.'

That was gratifying. He liked the idea that Josefina had been protective of what had passed between them. There was something sacred about the night despite its unplanned nature. 'She did not seduce me, to set the record straight. Do you think I'm such a stick-in-the-mud I can't manage a bit of romance on my own?' He flashed his old friend a smile and then sobered. 'No one else knows, do they?' He did not want it dissected as cheap gossip. It would do little to him, but it would besmirch Josefina's reputation and that could not be what Artemisia wanted for her school. Was that why she was here? To protect her school?

'No, and I want to keep it that way.' Artemisia's fury abated. 'Owen, the school doesn't need a scandal. But it isn't just the school I've come about.'

'Then take a seat and tell me about it before you wear a hole in my carpet.' Owen gestured to the spare chair. She was pacing before the fireplace incessantly. This agitation was about more than a truant student. Artemisia was no prude and he was a grown man capable of managing his own affairs discreetly. 'If you're worried I'll hurt her, you needn't. We'll be careful, in all ways. No one will know and I won't leave her with a child.' He paused, wondering if that was a promise he could keep. They hadn't been that careful last night, but going forward, he'd see to it. 'If there was a child, you know I would do the right thing.' Marriage. To Josefina. To have last night, every night, to wake up to a family, the empty halls of this house filled with running feet and raised voices. Josefina would not have a quiet home.

'Get your head out of the clouds, Owen,' Artemisia snapped. 'She's not looking for that.' Owen gave her a quelling look. Friend or not, she had no right to charge in here and shatter his daydreams. She bit her lip, taking his look to heart. 'I'm sorry. I'm out of sorts today. I know you wouldn't hurt her. It's not her I'm worried about. It's us.' She pulled a letter from her pocket. 'Addy's written. Sir Aldred Gray has been asking questions about Josefina. Hazard says Gray's hired a Bow Street Runner.' Hazard would know. Before marrying Addy, he'd been a Runner himself. His connections were likely very well informed.

Owen read the short note, his mouth pursed in a grim line. 'He means to discredit her, to paint her as a loose woman if she wins and by extension to cast aspersions on the school. If she loses, it's all matter of fact that, of course, you can't turn a sow's ear into a silk purse. Neither way is incredibly flattering to you or the school.'

'My deduction exactly.' Artemisia sighed. 'I'm starting to think my wager with him was foolhardy.'

'It's not the first time you've done something rash.' Owen handed the letter back to her. 'You'll sort it out.'

'Usually the truth is on my side, though, while I'm doing the sorting.' Artemisia shook her head. 'Not this time. I don't know anything about her. Sir Aldred Gray could make up whatever he liked and who would gainsay him?' She sighed. 'What a mess. I *assumed* he would play fair. I *assumed* she was just a starving artist, that she would be so thrilled to be here with a roof over her head that she wouldn't engage in anything illicit. I was wrong on both accounts. I made a classic mistake. I'm only just now starting to ask questions I should have asked weeks ago. Who is she, where did she come from, why is she here and not there? Who are her people? Everyone has a story, I just assumed I knew hers.' Artemisia sighed. 'Then last night, I had to rethink that. I couldn't ignore the evidence before me. She plays the pianoforte. She was more than up to sitting at a formal table. I can't protect her if I don't know.'

Ah, so he wasn't the only one trying to put pieces together.

'Have you asked her?' Owen played with the paperweight, feeling uncomfortable with where this was going. He *could* enlighten Artemisia, but the things Josefina had told him in the confidence of the post-coital bed weren't for general consumption. They were private, personal, things just between them.

'Yes, she's been very closed. She doesn't talk about her life before. She's from Venice.' Artemisia gave a half-smile. 'I learned that last night. It was something of a surprise when she sang.'

Owen shifted in his seat. This was a deuced awkward position to be in. He knew some of the answers Artemisia was looking for, but obviously Josefina had withheld that information except from him. It didn't matter the reasons. He was hardly going to sell her secrets. But at the same time, he could not let his friend worry more than she already was.

'She's good. She's had prior training, that much is evident. Addy chose a highly qualified candidate for our wager,' Artemisia mused out loud, slanting an enquiring gaze at him as she fished for information.

'Perhaps her family were artists, like the Stansfields.' Owen could give Artemisia that much without feeling as if he were betraying Josefina's confidences.

'Were?' Artemisia asked. 'Do you think they're all gone?'

Owen evaded the question by calling for Artemisia's coat. 'I don't know much at all,' he said, helping Artemisia into her outerwear and escorting her to the door. He knew only that he wanted to see Josefina again, wanted to burn again, wanted to feel that for a brief time there was a place for him again.

While he was musing over the last of the paperwork, wondering how he might arrange seeing her, she came to him armed only with her sketchpad and satchel for subterfuge. 'Miss Ricci, to see you, sir,' Pease announced, with mild distaste over the spontaneous visit. Unscheduled arrivals meant disruption to Pease's carefully cultivated routine. Owen, who usually disliked disruption as much as Pease, simply didn't care. He wanted only to drink her in, the sight of her enough to set his body stirring with memories of the night and hopes for what might yet come.

'What are you doing here?' Owen rose from behind the desk. He took her satchel and helped her out of her coat, taking any excuse to touch her, to breathe her in.

'I need a few more sketches. I can just sit and watch you work. I'll be quiet.' She'd not been quiet last night, nor still. There was a small chunk out of the wall behind the head-board this morning in testimony.

'I don't like you quiet, Josefina,' he murmured at her ear, 'or still.' Did he imagine it or did her pulse jump at the base of her throat? 'Is that all you came for? Sketches?'

'No, not all.' It was her turn to flirt as she took up her station in a chair beside the fire. 'I came to see what else you can make with oysters.' She licked at her bottom lip, a quick, coy flicking motion that drew the eye to her mouth. 'Or are you just a one-trick wonder?'

Chapter Twelve

Owen leaned back in his chair, hands behind his head, and favoured her with a devilish smile, one that she was coming to believe was just for her alone, then he began. 'There's fried oysters, pan oysters, baked, broiled or smoked oysters. Roasted oysters. Steamed oysters. Stewed oysters: cream stew, plain stew, dry stew, box stew on toast with cream sauce. Are you hungry yet? If not, there's more. There's devilled oysters, glazed oysters on toast, scalloped, sauce coated, there's fancy fry, there's croustade of oysters.'

'Stop!' Josefina laughed, throwing up her hands in mock surrender. She liked him this way, his stern demeanour set aside. 'All right, I'm convinced, oysters aren't a one-trick wonder— for now.' She gave him a teasing smile and rose from her chair to approach the desk. She rested her hip on the edge. 'What of yourself? Are your skills limited to...oyster stew?' His eyes lingered on her face in a long stare that suggested he understood her innuendo. But he did not take the bait.

'I can cook a variety of oyster dishes. I'll do a croustade for you sometime.' Sometime. Would that be before May? Before she had to leave? To move on and keep promises?

'It sounds complicated. I like things simple and straightforward. Box stew on toast sounds more like me,' Josefina pressed. She'd come for more than oysters and sketches. She'd come to see if the passion between them could live now that the edge of loneliness was gone or to determine if the edge had been sufficiently blunted. She wanted more of last night, but perhaps more didn't exist. Perhaps it was just a single, brilliant flame, meant to burn only once like a falling star.

Owen rose from the desk and moved towards the bookshelves and the door, away from her. Josefina resisted the urge to follow him. She needed to be patient and let her words do the work for her. He knew very well what she was talking about. He wanted to make things between them complicated like a croustade, when they needn't be. She needed to show him how simple it was. At the door, he stopped and pulled it shut, the lock snicking into place. 'Josefina, we should talk.'

Oh, this sounded dangerous and disappointing. 'I disagree.' Josefina was quick to head the conversation off that path. They ought to do something, but talking wasn't it. 'I didn't come for conversation, Owen. I came for you.' She sat on the desk, legs crossed, willing him to come to her. She was not going to cross the room to him and beg. He was going to own what he wanted and come to her. She held his gaze with her own, steady and strong, letting her need reflect in her eyes. 'I don't want for ever, Owen. I want a few nights, a few months. I want your mouth on me, I want your hands on me, your kisses at my neck, I want you inside me, filling me until I can think about nothing else, until I can do nothing else but scream your name when the pleasure takes me. I want you, Owen, just you.'

Everything he'd ever wanted was sitting on his desk in a workaday blue wool skirt and a high-collared white blouse, the standard uniform of the art school, wanton words falling from red lips. *I want you, Owen, just you.* The words had him hard with yearning. Josefina couldn't possibly know how those words were a balm to a wounded soul, to a man who'd given his heart to a woman who'd stomped on it and treated his very touch with contempt. Alyse Newton had acted as if the very nearness of him dirtied her. It had been a long while before he'd been able to not take her rejection personally, to believe that he could be enough for a woman, to realise the problem was with her, not with him. But the incident had certainly made him wary of trying again. Holed up in Seasalter, he'd found there was very little temptation to gainsay that wariness. It had been a comfortable isolation, until now.

Temptation leaned back on her hands and licked her lips with her wicked tongue. 'Well? Owen, will you have me?'

It was a rhetorical question at best, which she likely well knew. Josefina was confident with a capital *C*. Did he want her? Yes, he'd thought of little else today, which explained the stack of work still on his desk. Would he have her? He answered with his body. The throaty words had him crossing the room, his mind in sudden agreement with his body. She was right. It didn't need to be complicated. A few nights, a few months to hold the long lonely winter at bay and the memories to keep afterwards.

'Do I want you?' He gave an incredulous growl. 'I want you like I want to breathe.' Her legs parted as he approached and he moved within the vee of her skirts. He could feel the heat of her, smell the early scent of rising arousal. His mouth bent to hers and he was lost to reason, lost to restraint, the embers of last night easily prodded to flames. Her arms were about his neck, her mouth open beneath his, her tongue tangling with his, proof that her want had not been words alone. She moved against him, her hand on the length of his cock where it jutted up hard against his trousers, and Owen was nearly undone.

Recklessness was contagious and heady. He pushed back her skirts, his hands on warm bare skin high at her thighs. Her hips pressed into him as her hand stroked him through the barrier of his clothing, her mouth at his ear now, whispering decadent prompts. 'I want you inside me again, Owen.' He wouldn't last long at this rate. This was nothing like last night's slow, deliberate lovemaking. This was a fast-moving storm. There was no time for beds and disrobing. There was time only to appease the aches of their bodies, brought to a fine point after a day of denial.

'Free me.' His request was guttural and hoarse. Josefina's hands worked open his fall, her hand closing around his hot, aroused flesh at last. If he'd entertained any thoughts of relief at being freed from the confines of his trousers, his body to be soothed by her touch, they were short-lived. Her touch only inflamed him further. She brought him to her core, nudging his head against the dampness of her entrance. He bit at her neck. 'I know where it goes, my dear.' He'd demonstrated that quite aptly last night.

He thrust into her hard, honouring her request and his overwhelming need. He was thankful for the foresight of the locked door. He couldn't have stopped and given a pretence of normality if his life depended on it. Pease would have had to just stand there and wait until he was finished. Impatience and want were driving them both frantically now, the peak rising fast before them. This would be over in a matter of moments, their bodies already gathering to summit that peak. Josefina's head was thrown back, her legs clenching tightly around his waist, cleaving to him like a drowning man to driftwood. He thrust once, twice more, felt her shudder, heard her cry out as his own pleasure let down and he pulled away, releasing against her thigh with a thundering pulse.

Josefina breathed a sigh of relieved contentment at his ear, as if a great weight had been lifted from her. He wrapped his arms tight around her, holding her close. *This*. Whatever this was, he wanted it for now and always. His body hummed the incoherent, indefinable thought in the wake of his own contentment. He could stand here joined with her for evermore. It was an impossible thought, but one he didn't feel inclined to argue with at the moment, not with her dark head resting on his shoulders, not with perfection so near to hand.

She sighed against him. 'The night didn't lie.'

'No, I suppose it didn't.' Owen stepped away

reluctantly and righted himself. Then he lifted her in his arms and carried her to the divan set before the fire. He sat and gathered her to him, liking the way she snuggled into him as if she'd always belonged there, as if their bodies had always known how to fit together, how to be together.

'So, this is the room where you work your magic?' She peered up at him, her eyes still misty with the haze of happy completion, her voice soft.

'Yes. I've shown it to you before.' But not like this. The kind of magic he associated with this room might be drastically altered by what had just transpired. He wasn't sure he'd ever be able to work from behind that desk again without seeing her sitting on his polished surface, her legs and lips inviting him to indulge right there among the ledgers. And indulge he had, *they had*, madly, deeply, ferociously right there on his desktop. He had not been alone in that and the realisation filled him with a sense of awed hindsight. Reckless Josefina Ricci had got into more than his trousers. She'd gotten beneath his skin and into his mind.

She'd become…*important*…to him in a

shockingly short span of time. He no longer reviled her recklessness, but revelled in it. How had that happened? Why had he *allowed* it to happen, he who kept himself carefully guarded? Who'd learned painful lessons well. And why *now* should an itinerant artist tempt him to match her in recklessness when he was on the brink of achieving his ambitions, when business was requiring all his attentions, financially and otherwise. It was not the most ideal of times to find those attentions dragged away from his ledgers.

'Tell me about the deal you are masterminding. I've realised I don't know a thing about it, only that it involves ships.' Josefina snuggled in more comfortably, content to let him talk.

Owen chuckled into her hair, breathing in the scent of it. 'You weren't so interested in economics the last time we discussed it. I believe you found me rather boring.'

'Not forthcoming. Those are two different things,' Josefina corrected, sitting up. 'Besides, you were being stiff and obtuse on purpose.' She leaned in to give him a quick peck on the cheek, her eyes dancing merrily. 'I know you better now.' She snuggled back down. 'Tell me about your latest venture.'

Knew him better? The idea that someone might seek to know him filled him with warmth. How long had it been since anyone had sought to understand him? His father hadn't understood his dreams. His mother had smiled patiently at them, but she hadn't believed in them no matter how much she believed in him. Simon understood, but in a world of nearly a billion souls, one person who believed in him seemed a measly number. Perhaps it was the idea of adding a second person to that short list that brought the warmth. 'Well, if you really want to know, I'll indulge you,' Owen said drily.

'Indulge me, please.' She wiggled against him, making him think of other indulgences he might enjoy.

'It's the final piece in a vertical building scheme of mine. Several years ago, I realised I could be more efficient and make more profit if I wasn't reliant on other people to fulfil parts of my supply chain. I started with the oystermen. Instead of relying on oystermen to sell to me, I went to them. I offered them a regular salary so they weren't reliant on the poundage they brought in. This was good for business; I had a consistent supply without overharvesting for short term gain and it was beneficial for them. They didn't have to settle for whatever the other buyers were willing to pay by weight, especially in years when the harvest was lean. They had a guaranteed wage from me. Next, I bought boats for rowing out to the hoys and I bought hoys to sail out to the beds. Then I bought the factory at Seasalter, then another at Whitstable and another at Faversham. After that, I bought a line of transport drays that could take barrels of oysters up the road to London to sell in the markets instead of paying other teamsters to haul for me.'

'And now, you are buying a fleet of ships to send your oysters to the Continent and beyond?' Josefina surmised.

'Yes. The royal courts of Europe love oysters from the Kentish coast.'

'Such acquisition is expensive.'

'Yes.' Owen sighed. 'This last has me stretched at the moment, but it's always that way in the beginning of a big new step. I'm not worried.' At least he wouldn't be once the first batch to the Hapsburg court was sent off in a few months. By July, money would be flowing again. Until then, though, he tried not to worry overmuch.

The room had grown dark, a reminder of how much time had passed since she'd walked through his door, satchel in hand. 'Are you hungry? I am sure it's well past supper.' It was an effort for Owen to rouse himself from the divan. 'We can raid the kitchen. The cook always leaves something from lunch behind.'

The kitchen was warm and Owen made a quick assembly of bread and cheese to slide into the oven. 'No oysters tonight.' He grinned over his shoulder, aware that she was watching his every move.

'How is it that you haven't been snatched up by a woman who recognises the rare treat of a man who cooks?' Josefina leaned on the worktable, her gaze intent on him. His body liked her scrutiny.

'Not every woman finds cooking a desirable quality in a husband.' He tried to make light of it as he laid out plates and set out a bottle of wine.

'Ah, I see. My mistake.' Josefina fell quiet. She took the bottle and struggled to work the cork free, her brow knit, her mouth a tight line of concentration. 'You are looking for a wife of high birth. A final piece to your vertical empire perhaps?'

'I *was* looking,' Owen corrected, refusing to be offended by her implication. He took the bottle from her and gently wrestled the cork free. He poured, the sound of wine filling the glasses seeming abnormally loud in the space left by her silence. 'I decided I wanted more from a marriage than a mere acquisition.' He paused. Best to be honest. 'Which worked out for the best since it seemed titled women were averse to an oysterman.' He reached for the tray of bread and cheese from the oven and deposited it on the table between them. 'I didn't want a wife who was repulsed by her husband's money-making tendencies.'

'I'm sure that wasn't the case,' Josefina said, but he cut her off with a shake of his head.

'I assure you it was. My heart was in it, but hers was not. I am thankful I discovered that before it was too late.' He flashed her a smile. 'Too many complications, as you like to say.'

'Well, I'm sorry. It couldn't have been easy if your heart was engaged.' She took a slow sip of her wine, her eyes holding his over the rim of the goblet. A sharp stab of want pierced him. Good lord, she could burn him to cinders or rouse him to flames with a single look.

'Now you have my secret. Turnabout is fair play. Have you ever been in love?' Owen leaned across the table, closing the distance between them. He hoped not. It was an irrational realisation and a selfish one that rather surprised him. Why did he care? She'd had lovers, that was one thing. But to be *in* love, that was another, a more sacred place.

She shook her head and he let out a breath he hadn't realised he was holding. 'No, not in love. Flirtations certainly, men I've felt great respect and admiration for, but not love, not like you mean it when my heart was engaged.'

'Is that why you left Venice? A man loved you, but you didn't love him? I remember you said you didn't have a reason to stay that was palatable to you.'

'No, he didn't love me. He loved what I could do for him.' She gave him a slow smile. 'Perhaps, like you, I, too, felt that marriage should be something that involved the heart. When that was not on offer, I made other decisions.'

Darkness settled, offset only by the lamp on the table. He watched as she finished her bread and cheese, washing it down with a final swallow of wine before she answered. She ate deliberately and slowly, gathering her thoughts. He'd hit upon a delicate matter, then. 'There was a man, a friend of my father's. He offered to marry me. But as I said, he did not love me, not like that. He wanted me in his bed, he expected children, he expected a lot of things— let's just leave it at that—and in exchange I'd have the protection of his wealth, his name, his social standing. A lot of women would have thought it a good trade. But I expected more and he would not give it.'

'More?' Owen had forgotten his own bread, mesmerised with her tale here in the dark, lamplight flickering over her face, the flames highlighting her features, the fine cheekbones, the dark eyes, the elegant length of her nose. 'Like love?' What more would there be?

'Not love. I wasn't in love with him.' She favoured him with a slow smile. 'I wanted a place in his workshop, I wanted him to support me as a wife *and* an artist in my own right.' She reached for her glass, only to find it empty.

Owen poured, cautious of his rising feelings. He should not exult in the fact that the man didn't offer her a love match or that she'd not wanted one. 'What happened?'

'My father died and this man became more insistent, thinking I was vulnerable. But my father's death changed everything for me, my priorities, my possibilities.' She took a swallow of wine and explained, 'When my father knew he was dying, he asked me to promise him that I would not tie myself to patrons, to people who would steal my dreams in pursuit of theirs. My father spent his life wanting to travel, wanting to paint the wonders of the world, but he hadn't the freedom to do it. I promised him I would go in his stead. After such a promise, I could hardly limit myself to working in a workshop, let alone being a wife. But this man felt otherwise, that my father's request was unreasonable and that I should give up the quest. He pressed me for an answer the morning of the funeral.' The way she said 'pressed' made Owen's anger rise. This man had not pressed her with words alone. Josefina's voice was low, matter of fact, in the quiet of the kitchen. 'I knew he would not relent until he had what he wanted. There would be no reasoning with him. I promised him an answer after the funeral.'

'And what was that?' Owen could guess. She was here, after all.

'I never went back,' Josefina whispered quietly. 'After the funeral, I simply walked away from the grave, down the road, and kept on walking.'

He could imagine it. Josefina, straight-shouldered, turning her back on everything and everyone, walking down the road and disappearing without a backward glance. The temerity of it almost made him smile until he realised one day she'd do the same to him—walk away without a backward glance. She *would* leave. She'd said as much and she'd said why. She was off to see the world. Her father's predicament resonated too well with him. He, too, had spent his own life building safety, security for those around him at the expense of his own freedom.

The wick burnt low on the lamp and their

meal was long done. 'Shall I walk you home?' Owen offered, although letting her go was the last thing he wanted to do. What he wanted was…

She gave him a coy smile and he felt his body tighten in anticipation of a wish about to be granted. 'No, but you may walk me upstairs and in the morning I'll make you Turkish coffee.'

Chapter Thirteen

She made him coffee the next morning and the morning after that and the one after that until their days fell into a rhythm of discretion: long nights in Owen's bed, followed by early morning walks back to the school, hands interlocked; days spent in her studio painting until she could sneak off again to Owen, to passion.

Not only passion. To say this affair was based solely on lust was to demean it, to not understand it. It was fast becoming something more than what it had begun as. It was hard to describe, not even *colpo di fulmine* would suffice. Whatever 'this' was, it far exceeded the thunderclap of sudden, overwhelming desire. This was deep and abiding, something that transcended physical need, a fulfilment of a different sort.

To be with Owen, to lay in bed with him and talk of anything and everything, was like finding sanctuary. With him, she could talk of her father, of her life in Venice, of her art—things she'd not talked of with another since she'd left home for fear of giving in to grief and for fear of leaving too many breadcrumbs behind if anyone was looking for her. It was as if she could set aside fear in Owen's bed.

In the days leading up to the Oyster Ball, Josefina was happy, content, in a way she had not felt in a long while, or perhaps ever, and it worried her. Happiness, contentment, was changing her. It dulled the edge of her recklessness. She no longer felt the keen need to slice through life, taking herself and others by surprise, always seeking the next thrill. Some might call this new order peace.

Josefina snuggled against Owen's warm body in the early morning hours, testing to see if he was awake. His hand tightened reflexively at her hip in answer. If this was peace, it was imperfect, her new contentment tinged with a guilt that hadn't plagued her old reckless self. She was riddled with regret, a relatively new experience.

She was regretting the promise she'd made to Padraig about using Owen's cellar, regretting involving Owen unknowingly in the smuggler's plans, regretting that she could not change the trajectory of Padraig's plans now with the cargo planning to drop at Shucker's Cove tonight, regretting that she could not tell Owen, for his own safety. There were too many moving parts to this plan to call it off now and they were all counting on the money. With the money from tonight's drop, her travel plans in May would be secure. She would be able to afford passage to the Americas, afford rent on a small house where she could paint once she arrived in the Caribbean. All she could do now was to dance Owen's feet off tonight at the Oyster Ball, keep him oblivious and keep him safe. It would all be fine. It would go off without any trouble.

She'd been repeating that litany for days now and sometimes she managed to convince herself it *would* be fine. It was *always* fine. Padraig hadn't been caught *ever*. Worry couldn't change anything now. The Josefina who'd come to Seasalter in January would have thought nothing about tonight's upcoming escapades. But the Josefina she was becoming saw the lark in an entirely different light. It did not sit comfortably—what was she to do with this new Josefina?

There was an hour or so left before she had to go back and she didn't want to spend it alone with her thoughts. If this new peace of hers was tinged with the guilt of a secret, it was also tinged with complication, something she was reminded of every morning when she left Owen. He walked as far as he could with her, but the final length was always a distance she had to walk on her own. It was an apt metaphor that lived in her mind each morning. One day in spring, she'd walk away from him for the last time. He would have come as far as he could on her journey and she would be alone, again.

The thought made her restless. 'Owen,' she whispered his name, wishing him awake.

Maybe this was why she made a point of blowing through places like a storm, never staying anywhere too long. Staying was dangerous. Staying risked missing some place or someone. Staying risked being found, in case anyone was looking. Staying risked forgetting her promises, forgetting the dreams she'd shouldered on her father's behalf. Staying risked her freedom. There were so many reasons to go, to keep moving, and only one reason to stay—this warm, virile man beside her, who worshipped her body with a reverence that astonished her, who'd revealed himself layer by careful layer, showing her the poor boy who'd grown up on the beaches, who'd taken on the work of a smuggler at fifteen and the work of a man at sixteen, who'd grown an empire from the simplest of beginnings armed only with a quick mind, who made love with the same single-minded intensity he devoted to his business.

'Josefina?' Owen's voice was gravelly with morning's drowsy rasp.

She turned into him, her head on his shoulder. 'You're awake.' She ran a hand down his chest. She never tired of touching him, of feeling his muscles ripple beneath her fingertips.

'Yes, you minx. Don't act surprised,' Owen chuckled. 'You woke me. Don't think I didn't notice your wiggles and whispers.'

'I haven't the faintest idea of what you're talking about.' She laughed, her fingertip drawing an idle circle around the aureole of his flat nipple, raising gooseflesh in its wake.

His arm tightened about her, pulling her close. She felt safe, wrapped in the cocoon of blankets and his body. Would that she could stay here for ever. *For ever.* The words were as dangerous as the idea of staying. This wasn't supposed to be about for ever. For ever implied expectations, and she remembered very clearly that night on the widow's walk when she'd insisted there was nothing to lose, nothing to expect beyond the moment. Had that only been a short two weeks ago? It seemed a lifetime ago, they'd been different people then. She didn't like it. She *couldn't* like it.

'You're thinking this morning, Josefina. Did you wake me to share your thoughts? Have you some grand scheme?' He chuckled, lazy and carefree before the day settled its burdens on him.

'I woke you because I didn't want to think.' She rolled on top of him, straddling him between her thighs. His hands framed her hips and desperation seized her: desperation to have him inside her, to fill her, to thrust her worries away, to distract her from the thoughts haunting her mind. She levered up over him and slid down his length. He was more than willing, but he was less than convinced. Even as she made quick, frantic work of finding pleasure, she was aware of his eyes on her, his gaze not quite as lost to passion as their bodies.

Afterwards, he gathered her to him and let her float in the slice of oblivion she'd found before he whispered, 'Are your demons back in their cages?'

She sighed. 'Chained, at least.' She hadn't been subtle at all, another regret to add to her list. 'I'm sorry.' It was poorly done of her. She'd used him selfishly this morning for pleasure, for release, as a place to run and hide.

'Tell me?' he prompted. He wouldn't thank her for it, but perhaps it was what both of them needed—a dose of reality, a reminder that they were just playing.

'I was thinking this can't last.' It wasn't speculation, it was simply fact. She levered herself up enough to watch his face. What would he say to that? Owen the protector, Owen the fixer who tried to make life better, safer for his people even when they didn't know it. Would he do the same for her? Offer her platitudes about how things could change, how they could decide to redefine their association when the time came? What would she say if he did? It would all be just an extension of the current fantasy. There could be no real redefinition. She could not stay.

She waited for the platitudes, but they didn't come. Owen said simply, 'We never thought it could last, Josefina. That doesn't mean it will be easy when you go. I, for one, prefer not to think about it yet.' He paused and gave her a considering look. 'Are *you* thinking about it? Do you *want* to leave?' She thought she heard a note of panic in his voice, a note quickly subdued. Perhaps she'd imagined it. Owen Gann never panicked. He was the embodiment of stability to her storm.

'I am *not* thinking about it,' she said resolutely, settling down into the crook of his arm. She envied him his control, his ability to tamp down worry. He took life's bumps in his stride, consuming them with his power; he'd risen above poverty and rejection. He'd rise above her, too, when she left. She needn't worry about him. That should be relieving. She didn't want to hurt him. And yet, part of her wanted to be remembered, wanted to leave her mark because she knew already that he would leave his on her.

The room was getting brighter. She found the willpower to roll away and swing her legs over the side of the bed. She needed to get dressed and he did, too. This was a big day. He would be busy with final preparations for the Oyster Ball tonight. She had her own arrangements to make.

Owen reached for her. 'Don't go yet.'

She moved beyond the temptation of his arm. 'I have to. Artemisia might turn a blind eye to my leaving, but she expects me back. It's part of our tacit bargain. She doesn't complain and I don't disappoint her.' Artemisia hadn't broached the topic of Owen with her since that first day. Josefina had been grateful for her discretion and she'd done her best to repay Artemisia with discretion of her own. 'You have the Oyster Ball to oversee.' She slipped into her clothes and put her hair into a hasty braid. Owen moved about the room, putting on his own clothes. She helped him with his cravat, giving it a final pat.

'Speaking of the ball...' Owen captured

her hands before she could step away. 'Shall we pick a gown for tonight from the wardrobe in the guest room?' He was feeling playful this morning, a bright juxtaposition to the gloom that haunted her. 'There's a red gown that would be beautiful on you. You can take it with you. There's slippers, too.'

'I thought I would just wear the gown from the dinner with the bankers.' Josefina hesitated, her earlier guilt pinching at her. She was not entitled to more from this man. He'd put his heart on offer to a woman before to great disappointment. She did not want it to get that far again. Bodies on offer were one thing. Hearts were another.

He dropped her hands and moved to his bureau with a glint of mischief in his eyes—there were many such glints these days as his walls came down. She also noticed he'd ignored her polite protest about the dress. He pulled open a drawer and withdrew a velvet bag. 'There are these, too. I've been meaning to show them to you, but I haven't found the right moment.'

Josefina moved closer to him with a smile. 'And dawn is the right time?' she teased.

'It seems so.' Owen laughed and opened the

little drawstring sack. He poured its contents into his hand and held them up for her to see. 'The Gann pearls, the ones I was telling you about.' He studied them with a wry grin. 'Not much to look at, as I mentioned.' It was true. The strand was not perfectly matched like the one she'd left behind in Venice, the first piece of jewellery her father had bought her when she'd turned eighteen.

'It has character, though, a collection of generations, history on a string,' Josefina said softly. She touched a pearl at the top of the string. 'Tell me about them. Which one is this?'

'That's the primary pearl, we call it. The first one, found by my great-grandfather. In fact, these seven are all primaries. He found them over twenty years of working the beds. No one has ever found as many pearls as he did.' Owen nodded to the next set. 'Those were found by my grandfather, these by my father, and these last three were found by me.' He paused. 'There were four, but I sold one for a doctor and medicines for my mother.' The remark sobered the joy of the morning. He'd smuggled and sold a family heirloom for his mother. There was no length this man would not go to for those who held his heart. Josefina curled her hand over his.

'I should have insisted we sell the pearl sooner. I should have pushed to have sold them all. We waited too long. She argued she'd get well, that it was just a cough, that we needn't spend money on her. By the time we did, it was too late. That's when everything changed for me. Money would have protected her if we'd had it sooner. Watching her waste away unnecessarily, I vowed I'd never let those I loved go without again.' Owen gave her a rueful smile. 'Enough of that, though. I didn't show these to you to be morbid. I wanted to ask, will you wear them tonight?'

Josefina's smile faded and she took an involuntary step back. Men bearing jewellery were to be avoided. Men bearing family jewels especially. She'd left the Swiss Count the night he'd presented her with an emerald tiara that had belonged to his grandmother. 'I couldn't, Owen. It wouldn't be right.' Hadn't they both just agreed this was never meant to last? And now here he was, pushing pearls on her as if this was more than a secret *affaire*. It wouldn't be secret much longer if she showed up in his pearls.

'What wouldn't be right about it?' Owen was already moving behind her, placing the pearls about her neck and fastening the clasp, his hands sending a warm trill shooting through her where they rested on her shoulders.

Her hand couldn't help itself from touching the pearls at her neck. They were warm and smooth beneath her fingers, like the man himself. 'These should be worn by...' She couldn't finish the sentence. It was too dangerous. *By someone you love. By your wife.* She didn't want to put impossible ideas in his head. She could be neither of those things to him. She didn't want him to love her, not enough to hurt, and she certainly couldn't marry him. She cleared her throat and tried again. 'They should be worn by someone who isn't me.' It was the best she could do.

'Nonsense, it's not as if they're diamonds.' Owen remained stubborn, refusing to remove them. 'It's just for the night. Consider them on loan, like the dress and the slippers.' He smiled broadly. 'The next time I see you, you'll be my lady in red, wearing the Gann pearls.'

The earlier pinch of guilt became a gouge.

Here she was, helping smugglers sneak illegal goods into his home, and he was heaping her with 'riches,' a gown, slippers, all to make her the belle of the ball, *his* ball. She would be on his arm tonight, everyone would see her with him. 'Are you sure? People will speculate about us.'

Owen tucked her arm through his as they left the room. 'People have been speculating about me for years.' He paused, considering. 'Do *you* mind?'

'No.' Josefina let him usher her into the guest room and fill her arms with the red gown and all its accessories. The dress was a bright ruby shade. No one would overlook her in it. That was all to the good. If anything went wrong tonight, everyone would know Owen had no part in it. No one would dare accuse him of having been anywhere but on the dance floor with his lady in red. It was a significant consolation to hold on to and she clung to it gladly as something to offset her guilt and restore her peace. Everything would be fine tonight. Nothing would go wrong.

Something had been wrong with Josefina that morning. The thought niggled at Owen, refusing to let go throughout the day despite the busy agenda of overseeing refreshment tables and the unloading of food. She'd been distracted and desperate, that desperation evident in her lovemaking. Not that he hadn't enjoyed her desperate ride astride him in the dawn. There was something intoxicating about frantic lovemaking and the reckless speed of it. He'd willingly given her whatever succour she could find from his body. But this morning, he thought it hadn't quite been enough. Her demons still rattled their cages, still claimed her attentions. Whatever they might be.

'Bring the barrels of ale over here,' Owen instructed as men began to unload beverages. He wandered over to the chairs being set out for the older folks who preferred talking to dancing and then up to the dais being erected for the musicians, trying not to give in to the temptation of thinking through those demons. He failed to keep his thoughts away from them. The list of options was short: their relationship or leaving their relationship. What else might be on her mind? Perhaps he was missing something because their relationship was on *his* mind, occupying more mental space than even the vertical acquisition.

'Brother!' Simon called to him, waving from the factory door. Simon strode forward. 'Your head's in the clouds. I've called to you three times now.' Simon looked around. 'But it seems you have things well in hand as usual: chairs, tables, beverages, musicians.' He grinned in high spirits and clapped him on the shoulder. 'Elianora and I are looking forward to it. Her father is going to stay with the baby.' Simon paused. 'May I venture to guess what you were thinking about so intently you didn't hear me come in? Perhaps dancing with the delectable Miss Ricci?'

Owen smiled. There was no sense in hiding it from his brother. 'Perhaps I am.'

'My brother in love is a happy sight to see.' Simon's grin widened but Owen's vanished. Simon's gaze questioned his. 'Don't like the *L* word, dear brother?'

'I think that overstates the situation. We have become…friends. She is painting my portrait, we are spending time together as I show her around Seasalter, giving her a sense of my background. But that should not be misconstrued as something more.' He was rambling now, perhaps making the argument more for himself than for his brother.

Simon sobered. 'I didn't mean to bring up a touchy subject.'

Owen made a gesture to suggest it was of no import. But it was. He felt a fraud to disavow the relationship, as if it did Josefina a disservice and himself. He was *lying* to his brother. In the name of discretion and honour, of course, he reminded himself. To tell the truth was to be indiscreet, to risk rumour about Artemisia's school, to risk Josefina's honour and his own. He would be expected to do the right thing by her.

Simon looked uncomfortable despite his absolution and Owen relented. He directed Simon to a quiet corner, his voice hushed among the hubbub of workers. 'It's complicated because it's not complicated. She's here until May and that's it.' He was less sanguine about that then he'd made out to be with Josefina. She would leave sooner than May, that was merely the date of the show in London. Artemisia would want to go up earlier in April and open the town house and take care of a hundred details.

'That's it? You'll let her walk away?' Simon pressed in quiet tones.

'What else can I do?'

'Give her a reason to stay, for starters,' Simon argued. 'What's she in a hurry to get to, after all?'

It was a good question. In all the conversations they'd had, where she went next hadn't come up. Not surprisingly so. After all, to talk about where she went next meant talking about a future they didn't share. He was in no hurry to have that conversation. Josefina had changed his world in a very short time. She'd brought companionship, passion and a new delight to every day that had been missing. He could share with her. She was not put off by his humble beginnings. She embraced him as he was. Perhaps that was because their association wasn't permanent. But for now, he didn't want to question it. He wanted to enjoy it. He'd spent years looking ahead, looking down the road and for once, he just wanted to live in the moment.

Simon looked as if he wanted to pose another question. Owen shook his head, warding it off. 'Say nothing more, please.' Although the damage might already be done. His mind was beginning to spin with intriguing possibilities. What if things could be different? What if there was a future where he and Josefina could be together? Would he want it? Would he fight for it? How might he win her over? These were dangerous thoughts. He pushed them aside. 'I just want to enjoy tonight, Simon. I don't want to look beyond it, not yet.'

Chapter Fourteen

He could not look beyond her. Josefina was radiant and he simply could not tear his gaze away from the moment she entered to the moment she reached his side, weaving her way through the crowd, a bright scarlet thread amid a sea of more sensible blues, greys and greens. Even when she stood before him, he could not look away, his eyes lingering at the pearls at her neck. *His*, they seemed to say. She was his.

'You've outdone yourself, my dear.' He was glad he'd dressed the part as host more formally, choosing dark evening wear that would pass muster in London. The guests expected it of him, and tonight Josefina's appearance demanded it, her inky dark hair piled in ringlets and threaded with a ribbon, gold earbobs dancing at her ears, her gown pressed to perfection. Even if it was from a collection at least ten years old, the cut was excellent and the fabric expensive. It deserved, *she* deserved, to be partnered with its equal. She held up the hem of her skirts to show off the matching scarlet slippers with a mischievous smile.

'You look quite fine yourself, sir.' She made a little curtsy, her cheeks high with colour. 'What a party this is! Look at all of the food, I hardly know what to do first: eat, drink or dance.'

He offered her his arm. 'Let's dance and work up an appetite.'

She slid her arm through his and flashed him a naughty smile. 'What sort of appetite would that be, Mr Gann?'

Owen laughed. 'A hearty one, *signorina*.' He led her to the dance floor and found them a place in a set for the scotch reel, a lively circle country dance. He closed his hand around hers as the music began and she smiled at him. Not a bedroom smile, but a smile of simple joy. She *wanted* to be here with him. The thought warmed him as the music began. There was a rightness to being here with her like this, in his factory, among his people, in the place he was raised. The dance was fast, a series of half-steps and heel clicks as the circle went left and then right, couples moving to form a star and then reforming the circle and passing partners.

He acknowledged his new partner, but his eyes were riveted on Josefina across the circle from him. She sparkled, dazzling her partner with her smile, her laugh. She was grace itself as she went through the steps, her skirts swishing, her slippers flashing on her feet. How many nights could be like this? Dancing with Josefina, watching her with his people? What a hostess she'd make, bringing life and excitement everywhere she went.

Just a hostess? His conscience laughed at him. *You are not so selfless*, it said. *This is not just about serving your people. She'd serve you well, too. You want her by your side, regardless.*

He did want her by his side. He hadn't even realised how dead he'd been inside until she'd shown him with her flashing eyes and her arguments what it meant to be alive, to move away from his lonely isolation. The dance ended, but they stayed on the floor, moving into a speedy country galop of a dance that left them laughing and winded, but still they danced on, neither of them interested in leaving the dance floor, or interested in relinquishing each other. He relished his hand at her waist, the nearness of her body as they moved around the dance floor, her face turned up to his, her eyes alight. Good lord, he would give the world to hold on for ever to the feelings she stirred in him, for holding *her* for ever. What would he give for *this*?

Elation buoyed him across the floor, speeding their steps. Thank goodness this wasn't London. Such freedom would not be possible there. But, oh, how she'd shine in town, gracing the ballrooms with that smile, in fashionable gowns, pearls about her neck—matched pearls, perhaps, a better quality than his own string. He could afford the best.

'You are floating somewhere, Owen. Care to take me along?' Josefina laughed up at him.

'I'm just happy.' And that was more than enough. The music stopped, the musicians taking a mid-evening break. 'Let's get something to eat, I am told the oysters are spectacular.' Owen winked at her, ushering her through the crowd. They filled their plates at the tables laid out buffet-style and filled mugs with foaming ale from the barrels. Owen found them a quiet place beneath the stairs. It was tempting to go upstairs to his offices, but he'd not be able to manage it without everyone noticing.

'Do you really think oysters are an aphrodisiac?' Josefina slurped an oyster off the half-shell with easy dexterity.

Owen laughed. 'I think they could be. A scientist friend of mine told me there was a lot of zinc in oysters and zinc inspires one's libido. So, perhaps there's some legitimacy to the idea. But I think one can make an aphrodisiac out of anything.' He tapped his head with a finger. 'It's all in one's mind. Though, it's good for business. Men are impressed with its…um… certain properties.' He leaned close, breathing her in. 'You in a red dress, though, are all the aphrodisiac I need.' He caught her lips and stole a kiss, tasting the sweet ale on her tongue. She moved into him, all soft, warm, willing woman. Her arms twined about his neck and he wanted to be anywhere but here, preferably in his bed, with her. Owen whispered between heated kisses, 'I wish all these people were gone. I wish we were home.'

'I don't.' Josefina slipped a hand between

their bodies, finding his member fighting a rather public display of arousal. 'Intimacy in a crowd can be rather erotic.' She kissed him full on the mouth.

'Josefina, have a care. I might feel like marble, but I assure you I am merely a man,' he breathed against her, his member firm beneath her hand, beneath his trousers. 'I'll have to go back out there. I can't possibly do that in this condition you have me in.' At least his trousers were dark, but his evening coat was cut rather unhelpfully in that regard, sitting square and short at his waist. So much for being fashionable. He was missing the folds of his greatcoat.

She licked her lips, leaving them red and glistening in the dimness of the stairwell as she whispered her temptation. 'I can take care of that, if you're up for it.' The minx was daring him. His body wanted to take that dare, but his mind knew better. What sort of host took his pleasure in a dark corner while his guests partied? He'd been a poor enough host already, devoting himself singularly to just one guest. Although, after enough ale and full bellies, his guests were likely not to notice.

'Am I up for it?' Owen gave a hoarse chuckle.

'What do you think?' He'd never done anything so outrageous in a public venue and the thought was rather intoxicating. 'You're rubbing off on me, Josefina. I'm becoming reckless.'

'I like it, Owen. All work and no play makes for a dull man. Shall I take you with my hand right here or do you want to step outside?'

Outside would be safer, but in for a penny, in for a pound. 'Here, Josefina. Right here.' He kissed her then, drinking all of her as she opened the fall of his trousers and slipped her hand inside, circling his swollen member. He didn't last long, he hadn't been meant to. By the time she'd got her hand on him, the anticipation of the act and very thought of where it was taking place had already done much of the work, his arousal rock hard and complete, needing only the lightest of coaxings towards release.

'Better?' She flirted up at him, taking his offered handkerchief. She was right, stolen intimacy in public carried an eroticism of its own that lived beyond the act. When they went back out there and joined the others, whenever their eyes met the rest of the evening, they would think of this, of these decadent moments apart from the crowd.

'Yes, thank you.' He smiled, trying to match her playfulness and falling short. He could not forget the desperation she'd awakened with this morning, how she'd sought oblivion with his body, her thoughts worrying over the future, not unlike his own thoughts perhaps. Had she, too, played the 'what if' game?

Josefina moved as if to return to the party. He put a hand on her wrist, gently stalling. 'Wait, I want to ask you something.' He'd not planned to do it this way, but the moment seemed right and momentum was on his side. He drew her to him, into the vee of his thighs, his hands gripping hers. 'It's about what you said this morning.' He gave her a moment to think back to that conversation, his gaze intent on hers. 'Josefina, what if you stayed? What if you didn't leave in May?'

She worried her lower lip with her teeth. He'd caught her by surprise, something he didn't think happened often, not when it came to men. 'What are you saying, Owen?'

'What if you didn't leave in May? What if you never left? What if you stayed with me, here?'

Her finger was soft against his lips. 'That's not the plan. I don't need you to play the gallant, Owen. We said no expectations.'

He moved her finger aside in a gentle gesture. 'Plans change and an absence of expectations doesn't rule out surprises, only anticipated prospects.' He needed to be careful here; there was a thin line between persuading and begging. He would not beg. She would not respect a beggar, a man with no self-respect. 'Tell me you don't want to stay. Tell me you don't want more of this.'

'It's not about want, Owen. Of course I *want* more of this. But I *need* to go. I have promises to keep.'

Owen took a deep breath, steadying himself, and she stepped back, a bad omen, surely. 'We should not discuss such things tonight. This evening is for fun and revelry. I dare say we're not in our best minds. We should dance and feast and enjoy each other's company to the full, not make plans for an uncertain future.'

He reached for her hand. She hadn't stepped so far from him that he couldn't touch her. He raised it to his lips, unwilling to leave the discussion with nothing. He needed a token of her commitment to allay the knot of panic that had tied itself in his stomach, his intuition screaming that amid all that was right, something was wrong. He didn't know what, only that the wrongness was there, a nugget hidden among the hoard of his happiness. He turned her hand over, palm up and kissed it. 'You're right. Tonight is not the night. We have time. Tell me you'll think about it, though. Promise me that much at least.'

She gave him a soft smile and the words he needed. 'I will, but you need to do something for me.'

'Anything.' The ill-fated words of Richard III played through his head, *my kingdom for a horse*. He'd give it all for her. Economically, it was a poor trade, but his heart wasn't buying it at all. Perhaps Simon was right and he was on the brink of falling in love.

His conscience laughed. *On the brink, my boy? Oh, heavens, no, you've already jumped into the abyss.*

And he was still falling. If there was a bottom he hadn't found it.

She flashed him a smile. 'I want to dance

and dance until the sun comes up and my slippers are worn through.' Ah, *that* he could manage.

He did manage it: circle dances, reels, dashing polkas. The headiness of the evening returned, unmarred by his error beneath the stairs. He had misjudged the situation. He had pushed for too much against his own good sense. He should have stuck to what he'd told Simon this afternoon: he was looking to enjoy the evening and not beyond it. Besides, he knew how the evening would end—with Josefina in his bed. That was enough for now and for the weeks to come.

Half-past eleven there was a commotion at the factory door. His instincts had him leaving the dance floor and crossing the wide room before Simon could signal him. Josefina trailed behind him. 'What is it? What's going on?'

'I don't know.' He turned to her, his hands on her shoulders, feeling the slickness of silk beneath his fingers. 'Stay here, my dear. I'll be back in a moment. It seems some business has arisen. It will be a minute, nothing more. I can't imagine anything serious on party night.'

At the door, he recognised Lieutenant Hawthorne. 'Lieutenant, how can I help you?' He ushered the man outdoors into the dark where they might have privacy. 'Has anyone given you some ale? Food? There's plenty.' He felt for the man, having drawn the short straw on party night.

The Lieutenant didn't smile. 'I've not come for entertainment, Mr Gann. I will need to pull you away from the party, in fact. There was a cargo unloaded this evening on the cove not far from your home.' The Lieutenant waited, watching him. The Lieutenant expected a reaction, Owen realised. The cargo was supposed to mean something to him.

'I am surprised to hear that, Lieutenant.' All revelry fled, his mind shifting gears into twin modes of protection and predation. Whatever the Lieutenant was hunting for he would not find it here. The Lieutenant might, however, find that he was not the hunter any longer, that he was on foreign ground.

'Are you?' The Lieutenant had become grim. Owen racked his mind for any mention of a drop tonight. There'd been none. There wasn't likely to be any more until spring, in fact. There had been talk, though, a couple of weeks ago, about a large cargo of French brandy, but no place to land it and store it until it could go up to London. Talk of it had disappeared. Had it resurfaced and he'd missed it somehow? He'd been wrapped up in his vertical venture and in Josefina, his mind elsewhere these past weeks—it was entirely possible, but that assumed arrangements had been made, that the earlier obstacles had been overcome. If so, he should have been on his roof tonight. He would have seen Lieutenant Hawthorne's men.

'Perhaps you will also be "surprised" to know that Padraig O'Malley and five other men are under our supervision at present and that twenty barrels of brandy are currently in your cellar.'

Owen didn't even need to feign surprise. That was positively shocking and impossible. 'I've been here all night. Everyone will tell you that. Padraig O'Malley has been here, as well.' Only not all night. He began to sort through the evening in his mind, stealthily, not to give any hint of doubt to the Lieutenant. Padraig had been at the party. But for how long? Up until he and Josefina had stepped behind the stairs. Owen wasn't sure he could recall seeing the man after he and Josefina had returned. Even more interesting, the man hadn't sought to dance with her. Odd, given that Owen knew Padraig and Josefina had danced often at the Crown. Of course, that was before her relationship with him. Still, at an informal party, one might have thought Padraig would seek one dance at least, or perhaps not. Owen had not thought overmuch about it until now.

'I will need you to come with me to Baldock House and sort this out.'

'I'll be right with you, let me leave word with my brother.' Owen turned to go inside, and a flash of red glinted on his periphery. Josefina in the dark.

'No.' Lieutenant Hawthorne's tone was authoritative and definitive. 'I don't think you understand, Mr Gann. Your home is holding illegal goods and you are potentially moments away from being arrested on the grounds of dealing in contraband. You are in no position to negotiate.'

That was a mistake. One was always in a position to negotiate. Some positions were just better than others. Owen drew himself up to his full height and breadth. 'And you forget, Lieutenant Hawthorne, that you most recently dined at my table as my guest.'

Lieutenant Hawthorne stiffened at the reminder of hospitality and the idea that his behaviour at present was in violation of that hospitality. 'That, sir, was when I thought you were an honest man.' Hawthorne had gumption, Owen would give him that and he would remember it. This would not be the only negotiation tonight. There were men counting on him to untangle this mess.

Owen hazarded a quick look to the left where he'd seen the flash of red gown. Their gazes met in a swift moment, her eyes wide with concern. He wanted to go to her, assure her all would be well, but there was no time. Hawthorne was insistent. He gave thanks that Josefina hadn't been among the smugglers tonight or she would have been taken, too, the very nightmare he'd warned her about. That was a stroke of luck, at least.

Was it? Luck? A happy coincidence? His conscience teased with cynical disregard for his feelings.

Perhaps she'd been playing her part? His

heart gave a cry in the dark, *for how long?* Had it been a part she'd played behind the stairs so Padraig could sneak out? Had she been playing that part all night? For weeks?

And then he knew, this was the nugget. This was what was wrong. He and Josefina. Oh, God. He wanted to collapse, wanted to slink away and sort through it, understand it, but he couldn't even think about it now because five men needed him to save them from the hangman. After one final look, he turned to follow the Lieutenant.

Chapter Fifteen

She had to save him. Josefina stepped back into the shadows, bracing herself against the wall for support as she watched Owen follow Lieutenant Hawthorne into the night, into disaster. Her mind was a frantic mess. This wasn't how it was supposed to be. Owen was innocent. Being with her tonight was supposed to have deflected any guilt away from him should things go awry and keep him in the dark if they went right. Just the opposite had happened. Padraig and the men had been caught at the house and, by extension, their presence at the house itself had made Owen guilty. Oh, what a mess this was and it was all her fault. There was no escaping her part in this and Owen had known it.

That last gaze, when their eyes had met

before he turned away, had made her nau-
seous. He knew; he knew that she'd known
about the drop, that perhaps she'd known they
were using his house, and the speculation that
this evening had been planned. It had bordered on condemnation. It wouldn't take long
for that condemnation to become full blown.
His mind was fast—he would soon figure
out what had happened and what she'd done.
He would doubt her, doubt them, and then
he would hate her. Perhaps even see her as
a woman worse than the one who'd rejected
him those years ago.

The enormity of what that meant sent her
sliding down the length of the wall, the cold
of it seeping through the back of her gown and
into her skin, stealing all the warmth from the
night, a night that had, up to that point, been
quite warm. A moan escaped her, the realisation providing as much physical anguish as
mental. She covered her mouth with her hands,
lest someone hear her. It was all gone. Everything was gone: the warm nights in his bed,
the worship in his eyes when he looked at her,
the reverence of his hands on her body, the way
he listened to her, the way he talked to her,

spilling tales of his boyhood over the kitchen counter as he cooked for her.

She rocked herself in the dark, her arms wrapped around her waist, trying to subdue the pain, trying to keep the hurt in. In her recklessness, in her desire to belong, she'd endangered a good man. More than that, she'd endangered a man who *loved* her. She saw that now even if that word hadn't been used. He'd asked her to stay, tonight. He didn't want her to leave. He'd given her part of himself—the stories of his childhood, the tragedies of that childhood as well, the heartbreak of early adulthood, the hard realisations that no matter how much money he made, he'd always belong to a place between two worlds.

A man did not make himself vulnerable on a whim, not to any woman, not if he'd been burned by love before. What had it taken for him to open himself so completely to her? Look what she'd done with it. She'd betrayed him. Would he believe she'd betrayed him in all ways, that everything between them had been tied up in this one betrayal? Would he think tonight, those vital moments behind the stairs, had been nothing more than a distraction? Would he think her a trollop, a woman who had used her body in exchange for smuggler's money? That all of this had been her earning her pay, her cut of tonight's ambitious drop?

The factory door opened, a shaft of light piercing the darkness, the raucous sounds of the party filling the silent night. She wanted it gone, she wanted no reminders of the joy she'd felt only minutes ago. A shadow stepped across the light. 'Josefina, what are you doing out here? Where's Owen?'

Simon! Josefina swiped at her cheeks and scrambled to her feet, events falling from her lips in a mad, incoherent rush. 'Lieutenant Hawthorne was here—there was a smuggling run tonight and he caught Padraig at Owen's house, hiding the barrels in the basement. The Lieutenant made Owen go with him.' She gripped Simon's arm. 'He thinks Owen is guilty, that Owen had something to do with it. Owen doesn't, though. He was here all night.'

'Being here doesn't mean he hadn't had a hand in organising it.' Simon's face wore a grim expression. 'It will be hard to prove that he hasn't masterminded this.'

Terror gripped her. That thought had not crossed her mind in all the planning. 'He is innocent, Simon. He didn't plan this. He didn't even know Padraig was going to store the barrels there.'

'I'll go at once. Perhaps you might go in and tell Lady St Helier? It wouldn't hurt to have a viscount on Owen's side.' Then he relaxed and he forced a smile. 'Don't worry, Josefina, I am sure by the time I get there Owen will have it all smoothed over.' But Simon set off into the dark after his brother with great speed, a sign that he, too, was worried. Smuggling was a grave offence, in all ways.

Josefina went back inside and found Artemisia and Darius. She pulled them aside and delivered the news, but speculation was already running through the crowd. People had begun slipping off to their homes, or gathering together in tight knots. Everyone had seen Lieutenant Hawthorne at the door, even though Owen had tried to escort him outside quickly before panic could set in. Redcoats weren't welcome around here. They meant only one thing—trouble. In these parts, trouble was smuggling.

The party was effectively over. Owen hadn't been the only one involved in tonight's cargo. Josefina looked about the emptying room; Charlie's wife, white-faced and stoic, as she comforted Ned's pregnant bride; Thomas's wife slipping out the door alone, no doubt going home to make the house safe, to prepare for whatever came next. For the first time since Lieutenant Hawthorne had taken Owen, Josefina found the strength to move beyond her own fear. What would happen to these women's men? Men who were husbands and fathers? Would Owen be able to save them? She knew he would try. He would not let his men, his workers, go to the gallows.

Artemisia was asking her questions in low, rapid tones. 'What happened?'

'I don't know. Someone must have told Hawthorne about the drop. Somehow he found out. He's got everyone at Baldock House. Even Owen.' Tears were starting again. She turned her gaze to the Viscount. 'Please say you'll go. You cannot let them blame Owen. He didn't know anything.'

Artemisia pursed her lips. 'Don't be naive, Josefina. The barrels are in his basement.

He likely knew everything. How else would O'Malley have got in? I have no quarrel with smuggling. It's how things are done here. However, I didn't know Owen still dabbled in it. I thought he'd left it years ago. That's fine. It's his choice, after all. But we can't make ridiculous arguments of innocence with the Lieutenant. He won't believe them and we'll look foolish.'

'The cellar door is an outside door and it's unlocked.' Josefina's voice was a whisper as the folly of what she'd done overwhelmed her. What had she been thinking to risk Owen like this? Owen had warned her, hadn't he? That day in the parlour? But she'd not taken his words to heart. Then, he'd been nothing but a stuffy man without an adventurous bone in his body. How wrong she'd been and now he was going to hang for her if she didn't set the record straight.

Artemisia shook her head, unconvinced. 'Further proof that Owen is part of this. Doors aren't just left unlocked. No doubt Owen and Padraig arranged it between them. How else would Padraig have known the door was open?'

Josefina met Artemisia's gaze, steady and

even. 'The reason Padraig knew the door was open is because I was the one who arranged for him to use the cellars. Owen knows nothing about it.' She swallowed hard, trying not to think of the consequences of her confession, only of what must be done. 'I will tell the Lieutenant. Owen *is* innocent.'

'You will do no such thing!' Artemisia snapped sotto voce, flashing a speaking look at Darius, who gave a curt nod and headed towards the door. Artemisia's grip on her arm hurt. 'Do you want to be hung? Transported? To admit to such a thing is to condemn them all.'

'I would do it to save him,' Josefina whispered fiercely. She would sell them all to Lieutenant Hawthorne if it made a difference. They'd all made terms with the risks of their endeavours. Owen had not. Owen had not asked for any of this.

'It won't come to that,' Artemisia said staunchly and Josefina desperately wanted to believe her. She looked longingly towards the door. She should be out there, at Baldock House, arguing with the Lieutenant. She wanted to see Owen, wanted to explain everything to him, to assure him. Of what? That she loved him, too? Did she love him? She feared she did, but she'd not acted like a very good lover. Lovers didn't betray one another. He would be hard pressed to find her protestations believable.

'Absolutely not.' Artemisia read her mind. 'The best thing you can do now is to come home with me and wait.'

'I want to do something,' Josefina argued.

'You will be. No sneaking out, no going over to Baldock House. You are to stay as far away from that mess as possible. For Owen's sake, for your own sake and for the school's sake, I need you to follow directions this once.' She looped her arm through Josefina's. 'Let's go home. There's nothing more we can do now except hope that St Helier can work some magic.' The room for doubt in Artemisia's words caused her to worry anew.

'Simon says Owen will have it sorted out,' Josefina offered, but Artemisia's gaze was dubious.

'Smuggling is serious, it's not easily sorted, Josefina. So few are actually caught, the Crown is dedicated to making a very good example of those they do catch as a reminder of just how grave an offence it is to steal from the King.' That was when it truly dawned on her how much trouble Owen was in. He could hang. Not just hang. He could die. Because of her. A grave offence indeed.

'Smuggling is a grave offence, Mr Gann.' Lieutenant Hawthorne had the audacity to sit behind *his* desk. The man had wasted no time commandeering the office at Baldock House as his own. Two eager young Corporals stood at attention at the door while Hawthorne's men had established a perimeter guard about the house. The place was like an armed camp and, in Owen's opinion, a bit over the top for the situation. Then again, Hawthorne was likely bucking for promotion, a hard task in peacetime. Owen was not sympathetic. The Lieutenant had locked him in the cellar with the others until the Lieutenant was ready to 'interview the prisoners,' as he put it.

'As is an obstruction of justice.' Owen strolled to the sideboard, *his sideboard*, and poured himself a drink just to prove he was still in charge of his domain, no matter who sat behind the desk. He did not offer Hawthorne one. He'd offered the man enough of his hospitality. 'I would be careful how you proceed, Lieutenant. You cannot go about throwing citizens into cellars without a warrant. Neither can you go about assuming people are guilty until proven innocent. I believe it works the other way around.' He took a swallow of the brandy, letting it burn down his throat in a slow, fiery river.

'The barrels are in your cellar,' the Lieutenant reminded him coolly. 'I am not sure how much more proof I need to demonstrate.' That was, of course, something of a surprise and a stumbling block. Certainly, Padraig knew what the barrels were doing there, but Padraig had said nothing down in the cellar. Perhaps he'd been worried about being overheard or self-incriminating. Whatever the reason, the big Irishman had barely spared him a glance, which spoke of layers of guilt Owen wasn't ready to contemplate. First things first. That meant getting these charges removed and getting these men home to worried families.

'A man cannot have liquor in his cellar? Where else would he keep it?' Owen queried.

He set down his glass and strode to a drawered cabinet where he kept his cheques. Casually, he opened the drawer and took out his chequebook.

The Lieutenant gave a tired sigh. 'You and I both know the liquor is illegal.'

'It's illegal to drink brandy?'

'It's illegal to have brandy that has not cleared customs. You are being tedious, Mr Gann. You and I both know there is a tax on brandy. Not paying that import tax is akin to stealing from the Crown.'

Owen approached the desk, his gaze hard as steel. 'Get yourself a drink, Lieutenant. I need to sit down and you're in my chair. It's difficult to conduct business standing up.' The Lieutenant met his gaze for an uncomfortable moment. Owen did not flinch. This was his house, dammit, and these were his men in the cellar. He was not going to let a promotion-hungry lieutenant ruin their lives. Lieutenant Hawthorne's Adam's apple bobbed and then he rose. 'Thank you.' Owen slid into his chair and took out a fountain pen. He dipped it and began to write. 'There you are, Lieutenant.' He pushed the cheque across the desk.

'What is this?' Hawthorne's eyes narrowed and then widened at the amount. It was a rather staggering sum, one that would deplete his ready resources for a time. 'Is this a bribe, sir? Because I assure you that a King's Officer does *not* take bribes as a substitute for justice.'

'Hardly a bribe.' Owen managed to look coolly offended. Under other circumstances, he would have liked to have debated the Lieutenant's assertion. 'I am making the brandy legal. As you are aware, I was not at home when it arrived. I had no chance to pay. Given the chance, as is clearly evidenced by this cheque, I am more than willing to pay the taxes on it and, in fact, had always intended to do so.'

Hawthorne would not touch the cheque. 'There is no customs house in Seasalter. *Legal* brandy comes to London. It does not come here. Seasalter is a hotbed of smuggling activity.'

'Says who?' Owen stared him down. 'I know of no smugglers. No one has been caught, to my knowledge. So how would you know if there was any smuggling happening here?' He furrowed his brow in puzzlement. 'I'm afraid I don't follow your logic.'

'There was a French ship last month,' Hawthorne sputtered. Owen hid a smile.

'The war is over. The French are allowed to sail these waters. I heard about that ship. I believe it was empty, nothing of note was found aboard. I'm not sure what that proves, Lieutenant.'

'That we caught it after it unloaded its cargo. Right here.'

'But no cargo was found,' Owen persisted. 'An empty ship off the coast of Seasalter, a fishing village with no harbour, I might add, does not make a strong correlation, let alone offer proof of anything.' Hawthorne's frustration was evident. There was a moment in every negotiation when it became important to claim what you wanted and that moment had arrived. Owen smiled empathetically. 'I appreciate your commitment, Lieutenant. Truly. But this is not your night. Surely even you can hear how ridiculous your claims are as you talk through the situation right now. I shudder to think of how much weaker a professional barrister would make those claims sound in front of a judge and a packed courtroom.' He paused to let that last piece sink in. A man hoping for promotion could hardly risk being the centrepiece to a farce.

He let Hawthorne imagine it—*a man tried to pay his legitimate taxes on brandy and you refused his money.* It wouldn't sound like smuggling as much as stupidity on Hawthorne's part, especially when the man in question was Owen Gann, a man with plenty of money who didn't need to skirt taxes.

Hawthorne took a nervous swallow of his drink. Owen pressed his advantage. 'Now, I am sure you are disappointed. It is hard to get advancement during peacetime, nearly as hard as your impossible assignment of catching smugglers. Take the cheque, see to it that my honest money for honest brandy goes into the King's coffers.' Or not. Owen didn't particularly care if Hawthorne pocketed the sum. Either way, the man wouldn't be able to inform on him. If he kept the money and tried to convict Owen, Owen would have the cheque number and the draw on his bank to show he'd paid the taxes.

'This isn't right, Gann, and you know it,' Hawthorne huffed, but he took the cheque.

Owen shrugged. 'No, Lieutenant, I don't

know it. What I do know, though, is that innocent men are locked in my cellar for a non-existent crime. I'll go let them out and send them home. Meanwhile, I'll expect your men gone within the next quarter-hour. There's no reason for them to stay and I'm sure they'll welcome their own beds. It's been a long night.' It would be longer still for Owen. There was more to be done, more to be reckoned with. Confronting Lieutenant Hawthorne had been the first of many confrontations. There was still Padraig to deal with, and Josefina. He would save her for last because she would take all the strength he had left.

Chapter Sixteen

Owen faced Padraig man to man after he'd sent the others home. 'I would like my cellar back as soon as you can move the brandy.' He'd like a lot more than his cellar back; he'd like his heart back, his self-respect back. His money back. Josefina back. But all of those things were beyond his reach. He had to settle for what he *could* have back. In the immediacy, that meant a dark, empty space he never used. The money would come later. He could always make more. His self-respect might take a bit longer, but he'd put that back together once before, too. He could certainly do it again. As for Josefina, that was likely unsalvageable, nor should he tempt himself in that direction again even if it was, not when he knew such disastrous truths.

To his credit, Padraig didn't make excuses. 'We can have it distilled and ready to move out in two days.' Owen nodded. They could take as long as they liked, technically. After all, the brandy was legal now, paid for twice over. But the sooner any sign of his folly was removed from his house, the better.

Regret was written plainly on Padraig's face. 'It wasn't supposed to turn out this way.'

'What went wrong?' Owen asked directly.

'Hawthorne knew.' Padraig shrugged. 'I don't know how, but I will find out. If it was a leak, if someone here betrayed us, I will put a stop to it,' he said grimly. 'Thank you for what you did tonight. We can never repay you.' Owen knew he meant it quite literally. The sum had been exorbitant. An oysterman would never see that much money in his entire life.

Owen clapped the man on the shoulder. 'I can't lose my best harvesters, not with the season about to peak. Now that the liquor is legal, you boys can cut it at leisure in the cellar and sell it without worry.'

'That's very generous.' Padraig hesitated. 'I'm sorry about her, too, Gann. I should not have let her do it.' Ah. Bitter confirmation of his suspicions. Another nail in the coffin of his hopes. He could not ignore the truth now. She had offered up Baldock House without his knowledge, behind his back. He could not pretend otherwise, not with Padraig's confirmation. He'd made it easy for her. He hadn't even tried to resist her.

Owen gave a short nod. 'Well, if you hadn't used my cellars you couldn't have taken the delivery.' It was best to think about the practicalities and not the motives behind them. The best way to get through a crisis was to simply put one foot in front of the other, to do the next thing, to not look too far afield. If he gave himself permission to think about her, he would break and that was not something he could allow yet.

'She's a lot of woman to handle,' Padraig commiserated, not taking the hint Owen would like to leave the subject of Josefina alone. She wasn't meant to be handled. That was any man's first mistake, Owen thought. Josefina was meant to be *enjoyed*. Preferably from afar, like a brilliant lightning storm at sea. He should have followed his own advice in that regard. He never should have walked her home that night in January when he'd spied her on the beach. He never should have agreed to sit for the portrait. Josefina was something a man might look at but did not touch except at risk to himself.

He gave Padraig another short nod and excused himself. There was still more work to be done before his night was over. There was Simon to see, instructions to leave, trunks to pack—he could not stay here. There was Josefina to deal with. He did try to talk himself out of the latter. Why not just get in his coach and leave? He did not owe her a goodbye. He owed her nothing after tonight. That was the coward's way out. He was no coward. He would face her, he wanted her to know that he knew what she'd done, to him and to them. She'd broken his heart and taken his trust. Those were no small things to do to a man. Then, when he was in his coach on the way to London, he would let himself grieve for all that could have been.

He came to her well after sunrise, unkempt, still dressed in his evening clothes, his cravat undone, his shirt open at the neck, stubble on his cheek, his blond hair falling forward on to his face so that he had to push it back every few minutes. Perhaps he should have changed and shaved, but his horses were as fresh as his pain and he wanted to be gone, on to the next thing that needed tackling to keep the pain at bay. If he could stay busy enough, perhaps he might avoid grieving altogether.

She was at the farmhouse with Darius and Artemisia, all of whom had kept vigil throughout the night. The night had not been kind to her. She was pale and drawn, dark circles beneath her eyes, an old shawl wrapped about her shoulders. Her hair was down and she still wore the red dress. The two of them had turned into pumpkins, she with her wilted gown and old shawl, he with his dishevelled clothes. Gone was the girl who'd dazzled him hours ago, yet his eyes were drawn to her. He had no attention for Artemisia and Darius.

At the sight of him, she was on her feet, a cry of relief on her lips. 'Owen!' She crossed the parlour at a run, dodging furniture edges in her haste. She flung her arms about him and pressed close, her lips spilling questions and information all at once. 'You're safe, Hawthorne's let you go? I was so worried. I saw him take you away. I sent Simon and Darius after you, but they were turned back. Hawthorne had guards all about the place and I feared the worst.' It took her a moment to realise he had not hugged her back, had not wrapped his arms about her, but had stood there aloof while she'd showered him with affection. He did not want her to guess how hard it was not to give in, not to hold her close and breathe her in as if nothing had changed. He supposed he could. He could pretend he didn't know, that Padraig had kept her secret. But what point was there in rebuilding a relationship on a lie?

She quieted, her eyes stilling on his as she stepped back and smoothed her rumpled skirts. 'Owen, I am so sorry. I didn't mean to hurt you. What I did was wrong, so wrong.' Her dark eyes filled with tears that tore at his heart, but he strengthened his resolve. If he allowed himself to be won over by a few tears, he would never get his self-respect back.

'Hurt me? By that, are you referring to breaking my heart or nearly breaking my neck? There are, after all, only so many ways to hurt a man. I have saved my neck for the time being.' But his heart was clearly still hers and might always be. He'd have to find a way to go on without it, then, because there was no question of putting himself through this again. He was aware of Darius and Artemisia discreetly leaving the room. He waited to hear the soft snick of the door shutting behind them.

'You could have got me killed.' He let the quiet words fill the room, more potent for the muted volume of his voice than if he'd yelled them. He wanted to yell, though, wanted to throw something, several somethings for the satisfaction of watching them shatter like his heart. But that would accomplish nothing.

'Your absence, your ignorance of the plan, was supposed to keep you safe.' She reached for him again, wanting to put her hands on his shoulders, wanting to reason with him through her touch. He stepped away.

'Quite the opposite occurred. Fortunately, I was able to pay the taxes due on the brandy and legitimise it. Everyone is safe and the smugglers still have a product to sell.' He laid out the facts with the objective efficiency of a barrister. It was easier to talk to her that way. 'Padraig explained everything.'

A little smile of relief—of hope?—hovered on her lips. Did she view this as some sort of absolution? 'Then the worst is over.' Her smile widened. 'No harm done in the final analysis.'

He cut her off almost savagely. 'No harm done? You lied to me. You made me believe you—' *love you*—no, he wouldn't say the words '—you *cared* for me. I told you things, showed you things that I've not ever shared with another person and all the while you were stealing from me: my home, my heart. You are reckless, Josefina, with yourself and with others. You were reckless with me.'

She shook her head, pleading, 'I made a mistake, Owen. I should have told you. I should have asked you to help. I was trying to keep you safe.' He'd never been more unsafe in his life than when he'd been with her. He'd been exposed, vulnerable, and that had been used against him.

'How much of it was a lie, Josefina?' He ground out the words. 'All of it? When we were behind the staircase last night was that just a ploy, a cover so Padraig and the others could slip out of the party unnoticed?' When he replayed those moments, he felt the complete fool, a love-sick schoolboy led by the ear, overwhelmed by the elation of intimacy that had surged through him, the recklessness. He'd begged her to stay; he'd nearly proposed. And she'd refused. He understood why now.

Josefina blanched at the accusation, her face white with shock and fury. Ah, so she had followed those words to their logical implication. 'If you are suggesting I slept with you only for the purpose of helping the smugglers, then I am not the only one in this room who needs to apologise.' He'd hurt her. His heart kicked. What a beastly thing to do, to *say*, and yet sometimes beastly things were true. She hadn't denied his claims.

She put her hand in her pocket and pulled out a familiar velvet bag to hand to him. 'These are yours, of course.' He took the pearls and stuffed them into his pocket. It would be ages before he would be able to look at them again without seeing her in them, the way they'd lain around her neck, the way they'd seemed to belong on her. She gave a toss of her head, a gesture he'd seen her make countless times. 'I am disappointed in you, Owen Gann.'

That made two of them. Disappointment

wasn't in short supply this morning. He was disappointed in her, in himself. 'Perhaps I should not have come.'

She nodded. 'Perhaps you should not have.' She was all coolness now, ice protecting her flame. Somewhere in the past few moments she'd moved beyond the girl pleading for reconciliation in a rumpled red dress.

Owen took a final look at her. Less than a day ago he'd been in love with her, had wanted to marry her. Those were dangerous feelings, feelings that still lingered, mingled now with the devastation of betrayal, leaving him confused. How could he still want a woman who'd betrayed him? Those were feelings that could ruin a man, if he let them. It was right to leave. His feelings would go away over time, and over distance. If he stayed, he'd be tempted to give in. He could not afford another disaster. 'Goodbye, Josefina.'

He turned on his heel and exited the room, his body aware that she'd taken one last step towards him and stopped, perhaps by her pride. He shut the door behind him. Halfway down the hall, a strangled cry reached him, followed by the sound of china shattering against a wall.

That was the difference between them, wasn't it? How had he ever thought such opposites could fit together?

Josefina was on the floor, scrabbling for pieces of the broken shepherdess when Artemisia found her. The figurine had shattered quite thoroughly into shards too tiny for repair, but she had to try. If she could piece the shepherdess together perhaps she could piece her heart, her world, Owen back together. Her hands trembled as she fitted three pieces of the shepherdess's skirt together, a sharp edge pricking the pad of her finger.

'My dear girl, what have you done?' Artemisia was on the floor beside her, taking the pieces from her.

'I broke your figurine.' She sucked on her finger, the tears she'd held back in front of Owen beginning to fall. He was right. She was reckless. With other people and their things. She'd broken Artemisia's figurine and she'd broken Owen's heart. She'd not meant to do either any more than she'd meant to break her own.

Artemisia took her good hand in her own.

'It seems you've broken more than that. Care to tell me about it?'

She shook her head, but the words tumbled out anyway. 'He loved me. He wanted me to stay.' That had been the worst of the visit, listening to Owen lay himself bare, confess to his feelings. Another man, a lesser sort of man would have made a show of bravado, insisting that she meant nothing to him to save his own pride. But Owen had said she'd stolen his heart, that she'd made him believe she cared for him. She turned a tear-stained face to Artemisia. 'He *loved* me.' He'd not said the word per se. A man like Owen would not use that word easily, not when he'd already lost in love once.

Oh, God. How he must be suffering. She rocked a little, choking back sobs, for her, for him. He'd trusted her enough to try again. Artemisia's arm was about her. 'Is there no way back for you and Owen?' she asked softly.

'How could there be? He thinks I betrayed him.' Which she had. She could not pretend it was all a misunderstanding. She had betrayed him. It was the motive behind it that was the sticking point. She could barely bring herself to say the words. 'He thinks all that was between us was a lie, that I slept with him for the sake of the smugglers' cache. I didn't, Artemisia. I swear it.' She was suddenly frantic to be believed, by someone, anyone. 'I did it because I wanted to, because I wanted him.' Like she'd wanted no other and now he was broken. Owen would repair himself. He was a strong man in all ways. She envied him that. Perhaps this morning, he'd already been trying to heal himself.

'Shh, hush, my dear girl, you remind me so much of myself.' Artemisia held her, a soft hand in her hair, soothing. 'It always hurts like this at the beginning.'

'What will I do?'

'You will finish your painting and in the spring we will go to London as we planned. After that, you will carry on, just as *you* planned. Losing one's self in one's work does wonders to ease the pain. Distance and time will do the rest.' She hoped Artemisia was right, although she noted Artemisia hadn't said it would cure the pain, only ease it.

Chapter Seventeen

Owen arrived in London just in time. He'd been in residence at his town house for three days before the first letter came. Mr Matthews had written to say there'd been a change of plans. He was no longer able to recommend that his bank invest in the proposed shipping venture. He was very sorry, of course, and wished him the best of luck. Letters from the other investors arrived in short order. By the end of the week, they had all withdrawn with polite, vague apologies citing a change in plans, except for the last one, which helpfully suggested that unsavoury rumours surrounding his reputation had arisen. It confirmed for Owen what he'd feared: that Lieutenant Hawthorne had discovered there was more than one way to hang a man. Owen crumpled the letter in his hand, letting reality sink in. He was going to lose the fleet, the apex of his vertical empire, the final piece in his ability to control all aspects of his industry, three years of work ruined. Along with everything else he'd lost in the last few days, he was going to lose that, too, at least a part of it. Unless…

Unless he lost himself in his business instead. It had worked once before. When Alyse had left him, he'd buried himself in building the business to unprecedented heights. Business had saved him, but he hadn't loved Alyse, he saw that now. Against the backdrop of the passion he'd shared with Josefina, his feelings for Alyse showed for what they'd been: lukewarm at best. He'd liked the idea of what she represented, the placeholder she filled. He'd wanted the entrée she could provide him.

It would have been a poor reason to wed, in his estimation. She'd done him a favour in jilting him, although it had taken years to realise it and longer to believe it. Perhaps in time, he would see Josefina's betrayal as a favour as well, perhaps he would be thankful he'd seen what her wildness could lead to before he'd done anything foolish like marrying her.

Right now, it was hard to believe that would be the case with Josefina. But he could try. He couldn't save what had existed between he and Josefina, because it had never been real, just an illusion of something wonderful, but he could save his business.

Losing one's self in work did wonders for the pain. Goodness knew there was plenty of it— pain and work. Neither ever went away entirely, but the one numbed the other. There were enquiries to make about Hawthorne, about what Hawthorne had done with the cheque; there were oysters to send, beautifully displayed on perfectly shucked half-shells on ice in elegantly carved gift boxes, accompanied by expensive champagne, to the bankers and private investors who'd once sat at his table and toasted the shipping venture.

He would deal with Hawthorne and he would win the investors back. These were things he knew how to handle, men he knew how to handle. He had a plan for them. He could meet them on the battlefield of the boardroom. But love's battlefield? There was no one to fight there but himself and he wasn't sure he wanted to win. Winning meant forgetting her, forgetting how he'd felt. He'd felt *good*, *free*, *cherished*.

Late at night, once the letters were written, the correspondence read, and he was alone in his bed, it was easy to convince himself it would be better to keep the pain if it meant keeping the memory of her, of how they'd been together, for as long as he could stand it. It gave him an excuse to remember the feel of her touch on his body, the smell of summer roses on her skin, the press of her mouth on his, her laughter, the toss of her head, the red of her lips, the way she moved through the world as if it was hers for the taking, all ardour and audacity. He would fall asleep with those memories, dream them into existence and wake up hard, paying the price.

It didn't stop there. Throughout the day, he'd catch himself staring off into space, beyond ledgers and letters, imagining her at her easel. She would be painting, painting him. There was a bittersweet quality to the knowledge of that. She'd be faced with him every day. Was she still in tears as he'd left her or had she, like him, harnessed her emotions into something more productive? Was she watching the calendar pages turn? Counting the days to the show, the days until she was free of England? Did she think leaving England would free her from him or was she already free? Had she already forgiven herself? Already forgotten him? After all, she'd had what she wanted from him—access to his house for the smugglers.

His heart refused to accept that. *Unless, unless*, it would pound out, unless their time together had been more than that. What if it had? It didn't really matter. Betrayal or not, she was leaving in May. It would only have prolonged the agony of losing her. Yet his heart would not accept that either, the same way his mind would not accept no as an answer from his investors.

His mind was right. Owen sat back in the chair behind his desk, allowing himself a smug smile of victory, the recent letter open on his desk. He'd been correct in not taking no for an answer, in persisting with gifts of oysters and champagne. The board at the bank was willing to meet with him. Tomorrow at noon. He'd been right about Hawthorne, too, the bastard.

Owen reached for the second letter from his bank, confirming that Hawthorne had cashed the cheque. It had not gone to the King's coffers, but Hawthorne's own personal accounts. That was fine. Either way, the money had accomplished what Owen needed it to. He was free, his men were free. The gallows were thwarted and Owen had leverage. Now that Hawthorne had pocketed the money, he'd have to retract the rumours. Hawthorne had no proof and, if he persisted otherwise, Owen would threaten to expose what he'd done with the cheque.

But Hawthorne would be on the watch in the future. Shucker's Cove was no longer a hidden entity. O'Malley would need to lay low for a while, and, when he did resume smuggling activity, he'd need to be extra-vigilant. Owen wouldn't be there to watch from the widow's walk at Baldock House, not for a long while. It would be some time before he could walk the halls of his house with any peace, let alone his roof. Oh, Lord, his *roof.* Just thinking of those nights up there was enough to render him hard—the first night he'd carried her downstairs and made love to her in his bed, and the night they couldn't wait.

Focus, man. You have a presentation to make, a fleet to win. Your heart has already sailed.

* * *

Owen entered the boardroom at noon sharp, dressed soberly like the cohort assembled before him. 'Thank you for meeting, gentlemen.' They'd left the chair at the foot of the table open for him and he took it, looking each of them in the eye, letting them see his appreciation and his confidence that he fully expected this to end well. 'I want to begin by speaking frankly and addressing some unfounded rumours that I believe may have led to your reconsideration.' He laid out his case, firmly and directly, making no attempt to shield Lieutenant Hawthorne from actions that had been proven in hindsight to be precipitous and unnecessarily damning. He kept it simple. 'There was no illegal brandy brought in by me, as Lieutenant Hawthorne led you to believe. I understand your unwillingness to want to associate with free trading—however, I assure you, as I assured you upon your visit to Seasalter, that I am not involved. I assure you as well, that the proposal, as presented to you, still stands to make a profit. That hasn't changed, which is why your investment should not change.' He watched a look ripple around the table, passing from man to man.

'Would you excuse us, Mr Gann? I think we'd like to converse among ourselves.' Mr Matthews was all pleasantness. Owen stepped out of the room and waited. He didn't have to wait long, which had to be a good sign. He tugged once at his cuffs and stepped back inside. A folded sheet of paper sat at his place at the table. Another good sign. For the first time in weeks, something was finally going his way.

Mr Matthews nodded towards the paper. 'We are pleased to make you an offer, Mr Gann. We hope you are amenable to continuing our association.' He understood there would be no negotiation. The sum on the sheet would not be a starting place but a final offer, an only offer.

Owen smiled, politely, and picked up the paper. He unfolded it and stared, masking his disappointment. This was a compromise and it simply wouldn't do, as perhaps they'd been well aware. However, it did allow them to save face for allowing rumours to cause them to retract their original offer. No one could say they hadn't tried to participate in the venture. Owen folded the sheet calmly and put it back on the table. 'Gentlemen, it simply isn't enough. I thank you for your time. Good day.'

He was preternaturally calm as he exited the building into bright April sunshine. Spring was out today in London. He waved off his carriage, choosing to walk the distance home, buying himself time to think, time to grieve. He'd lost the fleet. Not him, actually, but Josefina. Her recklessness had cost him the fleet, the dream. He waited for sadness over the loss to fill him. He waited for resentment. He wanted to be angry with her. Perhaps anger would free him from her lingering spell.

Anger didn't come, sadness didn't come. Tenacity came, the determination to survive against the odds came, the same determination that had got him through the loss of a father and a mother, and through the raising of a younger brother, through the early beginnings of founding his company. He could not have a fleet, he needed help for that. But he could have one ship. He could do that on his own. A new dream formed. It was a start. It would keep him busy, perhaps busy enough to ignore that it was April, that she would be in town soon. London was big, the Season crowded and bustling. He needn't see her. Not unless he wanted to, which Owen feared would very much be the case. He would need to steel his resolve one more time. He just had to get through another month and she would be beyond him, out there, somewhere unknown in the wide, wild world. But not here. Surely, the distance would solve what burying himself in his work could not subdue.

Josefina could not subdue the nervous flutter in her stomach as she dressed for the evening, her first evening out in London under Artemisia and Darius's aegis. A maid tightened her corset and tied her petticoat tapes before slipping a sapphire-blue gown over her head. Josefina loved the way the expensive fabric felt sliding over her skin like a lover's hand, decadent and sure. Under other circumstances, she'd revel in the fine evening that laid before her, the opera and then a rout at the Duke of Boscastle's afterwards—the Duke was an art friend of Darius's. It would be an introduction of her to London society and to those who were interested in the Royal Academy as well as those who were carefully following the progress of Artemisia's wager with Gray. Some would argue that securing Boscastle's support was a victory all its own, regardless of how the wager turned out. Yes, indeed, under other circumstances, this would be an exciting evening, a milestone in which she would celebrate having stepped out on her own as an artist.

But under *these* circumstances, she felt more nerves than excitement. Not over dancing, not over meeting noblemen—she'd attended balls and masques with her father through his patrons and she'd dazzled plenty of noblemen in Venice. No, most of her nerves centred around one question: Would Owen be there? And then all the questions that followed that one: What would it be like to see him again? Would he acknowledge her? Had he forgiven her?

'Sit down, miss, and let me put up your hair.' The maid had finished with the dress. It was the shade of Owen's eyes when they burned bright with passion. She might have chosen a different colour. She could do with fewer reminders, but Artemisia had insisted. Her wardrobe had been carefully curated and created with an eye to how the St Heliers wanted to present her to society—not as a poor woman rescued from the streets, nor as a debutante feigning a certain innocence, but as a sophisticated young woman. Artemisia felt such an image would help others take her work more seriously. 'You want to look as sophisticated as your painting,' Artemisia had said.

The result had been a whirlwind of shopping that had occupied her first weeks in town. Artemisia had seen her supplied with everything a young woman about town would need to participate in the Season. She'd protested, of course. She didn't need that much. She wasn't even going to be here for the whole Season, just until the show on the first of May. Artemisia's argument had simply been, 'You never know what might happen.'

But she did know. Josefina stifled a sigh as she sat still for the maid. She studied her reflection in the mirror while the maid worked, pinning up tresses and curling locks. She could stay. Even if she didn't win the competition between Gray and Artemisia, she would win recognition. Her work was good. She would get commissions if she wanted them. Artemisia would see to it, as she would likely see to a spot at the school. With her sister leaving shortly for Florence, Artemisia was in need of an instructor. *She could stay.* The three words formed a dangerous litany.

For what? Seasalter was dead to her. When she'd left for London, she'd said goodbye to the little place. She wouldn't be going back. She would go to London and keep on going. Seasalter without Owen held too much pain. March had been proof of that. She'd spent it in her studio painting Owen, faced with his image daily, and his ghost haunted her rambles when she went out. She couldn't get away from him. He was there when she looked out over the water or walked the shoreline or wound her way through the little streets of village huts.

Everywhere she looked, there was a story, a remembrance of something they'd done, of something he had said. Her feet had a habit of turning towards Baldock House, shuttered, pristine and utterly empty now. She'd not understood the last day she'd seen him that he'd meant to leave town. It had taken a week before she realised he was physically gone. Darius had finally told her over supper. He'd gone to London to try to save the business. The news had stolen her appetite. She'd cost him even that, his beloved vertical acquisition.

Chances of forgiveness seemed slim. If she stayed, she'd have to face him, or worry about facing him, day after day.

Staying would be painful. Staying would be another betrayal. This time of her father. She'd promised him on his deathbed to be his dream. Staying would contradict that promise entirely, it would commit her to a life of relying on patrons. She would be tied to London, tied to society. She'd left Venice to avoid any scenario that tied her to another, that fettered her freedom. Patrons and marriage weren't that different in that regard.

There was a knock on her door and Artemisia slipped in, gowned in an exquisite coral silk. 'Are you ready? You look stunning. Darius has the carriage ready downstairs. We need to pick up Addy and Hazard at half past and we want everyone to get a good look at you in our box before the opera starts. Don't forget your gloves.' She paused. 'What is it? Aren't you excited?'

Josefina stood up and smoothed her sapphire skirts. 'Just nervous.' She hesitated and then opted for boldness. 'Will Owen be there?' It sounded like both a plea and a prayer. What would she say to him?

Artemisia shook her head, the pearl earbobs dancing. 'I don't know, honestly. He could be. London is a big town, but the upper circles are smaller than one might think.' Artemisia reached for her hand. 'It is inevitable that you will encounter him, it's just a matter of when and where. But you needn't worry. Whether he is or isn't there this evening, tonight is the first night of the next chapter of your life. You will meet people who will create opportunities for you.' She smiled. 'It's nice to have choices, Josefina, even if you think you don't want them. Not every woman gets such a luxury. Enjoy the moment.'

Josefina wished it was that easy, but all she could think of throughout the evening, watching Artemisia with Darius and Addy with her husband, Hazard, was that she'd enjoy the moment so much more if Owen was with her. There were times when she caught herself looking for him in the crowd, at the theatre and later at Boscastle's. Other times when she felt as if his eyes were on her. Once, she even turned around, expecting to see him. But it was only her imagination. Owen was gone from her.

Chapter Eighteen

He was *here*. She'd not imagined his presence after all. Josefina's gaze snagged on a pair of broad shoulders and a blond head that towered above the rest of Boscastle's guests. She'd know that build anywhere. She'd spent hours at her easel, figuring out how to show it to advantage, and hours in bed, tracing that body with her fingers until it was intimately imprinted on her mind. She didn't need to see his face to know it was him. Artemisia discreetly stepped on her toe, dragging her attention back to the conversation. One ignored the Duke of Boscastle at one's own peril.

Josefina made a point to nod and smile. She liked the Duke and his son, Inigo, both of them friends of Darius and supporters of the arts. Boscastle had mentioned he had several of Artemisia's pieces. She made sure to follow the general gist of the conversation, but her mind insisted on being allowed to disengage long enough to follow its own train of thought. How long had Owen been there? Had he been here all night? Had he seen her? Surely, if she'd felt his gaze, he must have. If he turned, he would see her now, dressed in fashionable silks, talking to a duke, his handsome heir to her right and Viscount St Helier on her left. Quite a different setting than Seasalter. No more borrowed ten-year-old dresses and smugglers for company.

They were both far from home. Even Owen looked different beneath the chandeliers of Boscastle's ballroom, although she'd seen him in evening clothes before. Tonight, he was more polished. There was an urbanity to him she'd not seen before. There was a mask, as well. This was a different version of Owen and an incomplete one. London was not allowed to see the man who shucked oysters with a knife at lightning speed, or the man who walked among the oystermen as if he were one of them. They saw only the successful businessman with a fortune that exceeded many of their own and they were jealous of it. A woman in his group leaned forward and tapped his arm with a fan. She was pretty in a worldly way, with her knowing eyes and teasing mouth. Whatever look he gave her, seemed only to spur her on.

'That's Lady Stanley... Alyse Newton as she was known before her marriage,' Artemisia whispered. 'Apparently she finds Owen more attractive now that's she married to someone else.' The edge to Artemisia's tone was unmistakable. This was the woman who'd thrown him over for a man with a title. Josefina disliked her instantly and she disliked the idea of Owen spending time with her, even in a group under bright lights.

She watched as Owen's head made a short nod and his broad shoulders set to turn. She froze with the knowledge that within moments he couldn't help but see her. This was not to be feared. This was her chance to apologise again, to convince him she'd not used him, that what they'd had was real.

She stepped backwards, out of the circle of conversation, and met Owen's gaze. She skirted the circle in a bold approach, making it clear that she intended to meet him. Her palms were sweaty inside her gloves. She didn't want to do this. But she had to. If she ran now, she'd be in hiding the whole time she was in London. Worse, she'd know herself for a coward. She'd made this mess, she could very well brazen it out. 'Owen, it's good to see you.' She didn't hold out her hands, didn't want to see if he'd deign to touch her. The last time they'd met, he had not.

He made her a small bow, his own address more formal. '*Signorina*, are you enjoying the evening? Did you find the opera on par with Venetian standards?' Ah, so he had been there. Perhaps her thoughts had not been so fanciful after all.

'I enjoyed it very much.' She stepped closer, her skirts brushing the leg of his trousers. She didn't want to talk about the opera or the evening. She wanted to talk about him. 'How are you? Are you well? I heard—'

Owen interrupted, his hand at her elbow, nothing more than a gentleman's guiding touch and yet it sent lightning through her. Her body knew this touch, craved it. 'Not here, *signorina*,' he chastised. 'Perhaps I might escort you outside for a bit of air?' It was a reminder that she'd been indiscreet, about to ask him personal questions where anyone could overhear.

She let him escort her outside to join other strolling couples. Boscastle's town house boasted a rare-sized garden for the city, complete with gravelled pathways and a fountain at its centre. For an event held before the official start of the Season next week, the event couldn't be described as a crush, but the garden traffic was significant. Still, there were fewer ears to overhear out here than indoors.

They strolled in silence to the fountain at the garden's centre. Perhaps he, too, was marshalling his thoughts, organising himself for the encounter, getting used to being with her again just as she was doing the same for him. 'Are you well, Owen?' she repeated her question. 'I heard you lost the business deal.'

'I did.' He was all flat neutrality, his answer devoid of description.

'What happened?' She wanted details. She wanted him to look at her when he spoke instead of watching the fountain.

'Nothing that matters. The bankers were unwilling to stand by their original sum, so I left their offer on the table.'

'And gave up the fleet? But that was your dream.' She didn't understand. The fleet had been everything for him, the culmination of years of work. This disaster, too, could be laid at her feet.

'I have a different dream now. I will start with one ship and build from there.' He was succinct and stoic, the way he'd been the first time she'd come to Baldock House. All business and no fire. But she knew better now. She knew there was more to him than this.

'I am sorry, Owen. That's my fault, too.' She'd cost him everything with her foolishness. 'I wish I could take it back, I wish it was all a misunderstanding that I could explain away.' But it wasn't. What it was was an undoable action that would exist between them for ever. There was no clearing it up, there was no need to. They were both very clear on what had transpired and why.

'I wish that, too,' was all Owen said.

She grabbed his arm, desperate to touch him, to reach him. He was so far from her, treating her with the same aloofness as he'd treated Lady Stanley. 'Will you look at me? I have something to say to you and I want to see your face.'

He faced her, his expression cool. How she wanted to see him smile again, to see his blue eyes dance. But she would take this small victory. 'I *am* sorry, Owen. Do you believe me?'

'Yes, I believe you are sorry for the smugglers getting caught.'

'For *all* of it, Owen. I am sorry you were implicated. I am sorry the men were caught. I am sorry you lost your business deal because of it. But most of all, I am sorry that you had reason to doubt the sincerity of my feelings for you, which were entirely separate from anything to do with the smuggling arrangements. Owen, I love you.' She could not make it any plainer than that. She clutched at his arm and let everything she felt shine in her eyes. He could not doubt the physical proof of her words now, not with her vulnerability so blatantly on display.

He gently removed her hand from his sleeve. 'I suppose it doesn't matter now. We were never destined to last anyway. That piece was a bit of whimsy on my part. I have only myself to blame for it.' He turned then, his hand dropping to the small of her back as he made to escort her back indoors, a clear sign the interview was over.

'But I am here, Owen,' she protested, taking an unwilling step back towards the ballroom to keep up with him. 'Don't you understand what I am saying?'

He halted and faced her. 'I understand, *signorina*. You want things to be as they were before and then you will leave in May. You are an enchanting creature, but even so, I am in no hurry to have my heart broken again.' How did he manage to look so strong while making himself so vulnerable all at the same time? How could she respond? That it would be different this time? That she would stay? Both would be a lie. She had promises to keep. She *would* leave. She had to.

'But do you forgive me? Do you believe me?' She wanted that much at least and she wasn't too proud to beg for it. His words from that fateful morning still haunted her. *You were reckless with me.* That was the greater sin. He might forgive her for all else, but not that. Owen who was never reckless with people, Owen who had given his life in service to those he loved—his mother, his brother, his people in Seasalter.

For the first time that evening, she saw his gaze soften, but it did not mean victory. 'You can't help it, can you, Josefina? Living out loud, showing every feeling the moment you have them? It's who you are. It's what makes you unique.' His hand skimmed her cheek, an echo of past intimacies. 'As for forgiveness, I've come to terms with what happened. I just don't think I can live with you. I see that now. You're a flame, Josefina. You are meant to consume everything in your path. I can't afford to be consumed and I can't afford to lose you. I lost my mother, I lost my father, I nearly lost Simon. I know what it does to me and I cannot go through that again. I cannot let you consume me and then lose you. I would lose the most important part of myself.'

She held his hand, trapping it against her cheek. 'Do you believe I love you? That I am not like that woman you were speaking with? Artemisia told me who she was.'

'I believe you love many things, Josefina, but you are nothing like her. Do not worry on that score.' He was drifting away from her without taking a single step. His blue eyes were shuttering, becoming polite and aloof. She was losing him. If he wouldn't believe her words, she had to find another way to reach him, to convince him.

'Come to the show and see the portrait.' She held his gaze, willing her stare to root him to the ground, to keep him with her awhile longer. If he could see the portrait, he would know she spoke the truth about her feelings. Even if he would never come back to her, the truth would help him heal. He would know her love had been real even if realised too late.

'Goodnight, *signorina*. I thank you for the stroll.' He left her there, on the pathway. She watched his broad back make its way inside until she lost sight of him. Then she imagined another crack in her heart.

The evening was lost, after that. Owen took his leave of his host and headed out into the night, thankful to escape with his dignity intact. Facing Josefina had been as dreadful and as necessary as he'd imagined it to be. Seeing her at a distance at the opera in that sapphire gown had been a stab to his heart as her beauty swamped him again as if for the first time. It was always like that with her. He'd once thought such a sensation would wear off after a time. But he knew now that wasn't true. She would always swamp his senses.

Perhaps it was best she was leaving. Otherwise, he'd never get over her or past her. She'd always be there in Seasalter and in London. Tonight had proved the large scope of London had not protected him against her. She'd managed to find him anyway, or was it the other way around and he'd found her? It had not taken much investigating to divine Artemisia's plans for launching her. The society columns had been touting the St Heliers' early return to the city since the first of April and speculating that the reasons for it were connected to the Italian protégée Lady St Helier had in tow.

Had he subconsciously wanted to see her? Had he wanted to test his resolve? If so, he'd discovered his resolve wasn't nearly as strong as he'd hoped or needed it to be. She was fetching in her contrition and sapphire. Beautiful and sincere, he had no doubt of that. She was genuinely sorry. She'd said more than that, his conscience prompted, forcing him to acknowledge the rest of her admissions. *I love you.* The words had shaken him. It had taken every ounce of his newfound resolve to brush over them, to remind her they didn't, and couldn't, matter because she was leaving. The only thing that shook him more was the raw pain on her face when he denied her the things she wanted from him. It was for both of their sakes. Did she have any idea how close he'd come to gathering her in his arms, to offering the absolution of a kiss, to exchange her pain for his? Happiness for another month was a tempting offer and he'd nearly taken it. It had been right to walk away. Best for both of them, but especially for him. Only, she'd had the last word anyway and she hadn't let him leave completely.

Come see the portrait. Maybe he would, because misery loved company and he'd been the one to make them both miserable tonight. The only thing stopping him from taking the happiness on offer was himself. What a masterful intrigue she'd set up. If he was miserable, he had only himself to blame. She was offering to wipe the slate clean. Of course, that was definitely in her interest.

She nearly sent you to the hangman.

Apparently his conscience was of two minds where Josefina was concerned. Even if he forgave her, he'd be a fool to forget. Josefina would always be wild, always be reckless. He couldn't change that and in truth he didn't want to.

But can you live with it? He'd nearly died for it. *And now? Are you living now without it? Is this living?*

Maybe the answer didn't matter. Maybe it was all a careful man could have.

Chapter Nineteen

~~~~~~~~~~

They were being careful with her, all of them—
Artemisia, Darius and Addy—handling her
with the same expert skill she applied to packing her canvases. Josefina wrapped the latest
stack of canvases in sailcloth and tucked them
securely into her new supply trunk where it
stood open against the wall of her bedchamber.

It had taken her a couple of days to realise
their strategy of busyness and constant companionship. She was always on the move,
always with them, never alone in the days
leading up to the exhibitions. Mornings were
spent shopping with Addy, gathering supplies
for both of their trips. Addy and Hazard would
leave at the end of May for Florence. She, of
course, would leave far sooner than that. She
could leave next week. *Next week*. Soon. Just

seven more days and she could leave England behind. Just when the weather was starting to get nice, alas.

Josefina began folding clothes she would not wear again before she left. The pile of clothing on the bed brought a wry smile to her. She'd come with three gowns and her brushes, but she was leaving with three trunks full of clothes and paint supplies. Artemisia and Darius had been generous; the town wardrobe would go with her and they'd opened an account for her to purchase paints and canvases and brushes and an exquisite folding travelling easel to take with her.

There was a knock on her door and Artemisia entered. Her eyes swept the room and she sighed. 'Packing is going well, I see. We have maids to help if you need them.'

Josefina shook her head. 'No, I want to pack on my own. It helps me to know where everything is and I can establish an inventory.' It also filled the time, it kept her hands busy and it was the only part of the day when she was on her own, allowed a chance to sift through her thoughts. She knew Artemisia meant well. Perhaps Artemisia even guessed what had happened in the Boscastle garden with Owen and this was her way of easing the pain.

Artemisia drew an envelope from her pocket and handed it over. 'I have your passage. Darius arranged everything.'

Josefina opened the envelope and peeked inside. 'A first-class cabin? That's not necessary.' How would she pay them back for that? It was more than she'd budgeted for. She'd been very clear that third class was fine. 'I can't afford it,' she said bluntly.

Artemisia shook her head. 'It's our gift to you. There's no need to pay us back. There's something else in there, as well.'

Josefina saw it now. 'A second ticket?' For a wild moment she thought it was for Owen, that somehow he'd decided to come along.

'Yes, Darius has found a companion for you, a cousin of his who is a young widow looking for a new start. We think the two of you would suit admirably. He's sent for her. She'll be here at week's end.'

'I'm not to be alone on my adventures either?' Josefina raised an eyebrow. She laughed when Artemisia feigned confusion. 'I know what you've been up to, keeping me busy with shopping in the mornings and outings to the British Museum, the Tower and everywhere a lady ought to go, working on the exhibition in the afternoons and evenings out to grand parties. I haven't had a moment to myself since the opera. I don't think it's been by accident.'

'No, because the last time you were alone, you went into a garden and got your heart broken.' Artemisia strolled about the room, studying the half-packed trunks.

So, Artemisia did know. 'Not on purpose. I went into the garden hoping to apologise, hoping to be forgiven, hoping that there might still be a chance of salvaging my heart.'

Artemisia flung her a rueful look. 'How did that work out?'

'You know how that worked out. It's why you've spoiled me with travelling trunks, supply budgets, first-class tickets and constant company.' Josefina turned her attention back to folding clothes.

'Does it really matter, though? What if he had changed his mind? Would you have stayed or would you have simply hurt him again in a few weeks?' It sounded quite cruel when Artemisia put it that way.

'It's not just that. I need him to know that my feelings for him are real. What we shared was not a ruse.' She gathered up the stack of clothing and strode to a trunk. 'Being someone else's pawn and realising it post facto is an unpleasant feeling, especially when one thinks otherwise and engages otherwise based on those assumptions. I would have honesty between us if nothing else.' Even if nothing could come of it, especially when Owen had been hurt in love before. He deserved more than that.

'You don't have to go,' Artemisia said softly. 'You know you can come back to Seasalter with us, make a life at the school. I need an instructor with Addy leaving. Or, perhaps you could stay in town with my father in Bloomsbury or at Addy's house. It will be empty while they're in Florence. You can recruit for the school, take commissions of your own. Perhaps you and Owen can find your way back from this? It's only been a couple of months, Josefina. These things take time.'

'No. I have plans. I've already stayed longer than I thought I would,' Josefina said firmly. She could not allow herself to be swayed, to be tempted to something that would only bring her pain in the long term.

'Then I shall be deprived of both my "sisters" all at once.' Artemisia gave a rueful smile and Josefina felt her heart twist at her words. She'd found so much more in Seasalter than just a place to shelter for the winter. Artemisia had made her a part of a family, part of a group and a community. Artemisia had treated her as a sister, a comrade in art. She *could* have a life in Seasalter. But it would be a painful one. Owen would be there and it would mean breaking her promise to her father. She wasn't sure how to reconcile those sacrifices with the rewards of staying. It was far easier to pack, to stay busy, to not look around or look ahead, just to put one foot in front of the other until she was on board the ship and London was fading from sight.

'She's leaving in three days. I thought you'd like to know.' St Helier's voice cut through the haze of Owen's thoughts. He lowered the newspaper, the words having faded minutes ago, a half-hour ago, he wasn't sure. How long had he been staring at the same news story? He'd like to blame it on the soporific effect of the quiet atmosphere of the club in the afternoon. The Beefsteak Club would be deserted until four.

St Helier sat down in the chair across from him and signalled for a drink, a sure sign he meant to stay awhile. 'I see you've come to interrupt my peace.' Owen set aside the newspaper and fixed St Helier with a strong look.

'I thought I might find you here.'

'Here' being the Old Lyceum Theatre, the club's home on the Wellington Street.

'Hiding.'

The last was said with no small bit of accusation.

'I am not hiding,' Owen answered. He had, however, been counting on the likes of St Helier to not venture beyond the comforts of St James's. 'I am in my element—one might wonder why you are not in yours?'

St Helier took his drink from the waiter and answered him in all seriousness. 'Because when I see a friend hurting, I cannot sit by and watch them suffer alone.'

He did not pretend to not understand the reference. He steeled himself to blandly say her name, to withstand the onslaught of emotions and images that came with it. 'Josefina will be fine. She'll recover.'

'Not her, you. *You* are the friend to whom I refer. I saw your face when you came in from the garden at Boscastle's and you left shortly afterwards. You haven't been to any parties since. That was a week ago.' He paused and took a swallow. 'I think you're afraid to see her again.'

Owen tossed back the rest of his drink and signalled for another. It was going to be a two-brandy afternoon. 'If I had not been a rich man with a fast mind, I would have hung for her carelessness.' That was an inescapable fact. Whenever he felt weak, whenever he was tempted to forgive her, tempted to see her and let his feelings run their course, he simply had to remember that.

He was not ready for Darius's response. 'Josefina will always be wild. If I may be so bold, I think it's what you love about her, what we all love about her.' Owen had not been expecting that. He'd been expecting minimising, some empty words about how she'd made a mistake, how it had all worked out in the end—easy words to say when it was someone else's bank account on the line, someone else's reputation to be rebuilt. But Darius had not argued with him. Darius had agreed with him and that made the response more difficult.

'Yes, I suppose it is.' He gave a short laugh. 'I remember the first time I saw her, at your wife's welcome-back-from-the-holiday soirée. I danced with her and the moment I touched her I knew what she was—a flame, bright and vibrant, and that she'd burn a man alive.'

Darius gave him a commiserating look. 'You are not the first man to become an Icarus.' He leaned forward. 'I felt that way the night Artemisia burst into my bath and called me to account. I knew what she was and I still could not pull my hand away from the flame. It's not a reason to retreat, man, it's a reason to press on.'

'Easy for you to say—hindsight is on your side and your wife didn't almost kill you.' Owen took his glass from the waiter and let Darius digest *that*.

Darius was not daunted. 'No, but standing up for her did endanger my relationship with my father.' It was a relationship that was still strained, Owen knew. 'It did cost me certain acquaintances within the art community and it did risk my reputation as a critic. I've had to build all that back,' Darius reminded him. 'Artemisia and I have each other and the life we want, the life we are actively seeking. However, it's not a fairy tale. We fight for it every day.' He paused. 'And just when I think we've gained back ground, she goes and does something like this deuced wager with Aldred Gray.'

Owen heard the frustration in his friend's voice and the lesson, too. He'd not thought of their marriage that way before. It did indeed look like a perfect love story on the outside. Darius continued, bringing the lesson full circle. 'I will never change Artemisia. She will be saying outlandish things to the Academy and making outrageous wagers for the rest of her life. I want her to. I don't want to change her. Years from now, when I inherit, she will be the most notorious Countess of Bourne to ever grace the Rutherford family tree. I wouldn't want it or her any other way.'

He didn't want Josefina any other way either. He wasn't looking to change her. He'd told her as much in the garden. But neither could he change himself. It wasn't in him. His people needed his protection, everything he'd built had been for his family, for his people. He could not walk away from that and become a different man. 'Josefina and I, we don't fit well together,' Owen told Darius. 'I think we're often attracted to opposites because they possess skills, talents, values, beliefs that are different than ours. It's an intoxicating novelty and after a bit the novelty wears off. It's not sustainable.'

Darius thought for a moment. 'Are you sure that's all she is to you? An intoxicating novelty?'

'It's all she can be, Darius. I envy her freedom to come and go as she pleases. But that can't be me.' These days, he envied the fact that she'd be able to sail away and leave England behind, leaving memory markers behind that he would have to face every day. His house, the beach, the rowboat, the art school. Everywhere he looked he'd see the echo of her. How would he ever be able to forget? Whereas forgetting would come easy to her. She would be in new places with new people, and eventually with a new lover. She wasn't made to be alone and when that happened she would forget him.

Darius finished his drink and rose. 'I appreciate your time. I'll let you get back to the news and your financial pages. I hope we'll see you at the exhibitions, both of them. Our show opens tomorrow, a day in advance of Somerset House. You can come as our guest. You needn't feel as if you're coming for her if that mitigates any sense of temptation on your part.' It did indeed. What a fine barrister the Viscount would have made, Owen thought. He knew just how to get into a man's head and convince him the action he wanted him to take was the right one. But he would see her, no matter who he came for. He could not be in the same room and not be drawn to her, not seek her out.

He reached for his newspaper, but Darius didn't leave. 'Is there something else?'

'Yes. I've always thought you were a fighter. I think she'd stay if you gave her a reason,' Darius offered baldly. 'Goodness knows, we've tried to give her reasons: a post at the school, taking over Addy's position in town. But she resists. We have nothing she wants, nothing we could offer to offset her leaving, at least. But you do.'

Darius sat back down, levering himself on the edge of his seat. He leaned forward, his voice low as the club began to fill with late afternoon arrivals. 'She came to you and she confessed her feelings. She loves you, Owen. It's up to you. If you want her, a life with her, all you have to do is claim it. Give her a reason to stay.'

Owen grinned at the other man. 'You make it sound so easy.'

'It can be that simple. Once I decided it was, it made all the difference.' Darius rose again. 'We'll see you tomorrow, I hope.'

A gauntlet could not have been thrown down more effectively. Going tomorrow would be a declaration. He fiddled with his glass, holding the tumbler up to the light of the club's long windows. He watched the sunlight dance in the facets of the glass and let his thoughts play through. How could a man love something or someone who wasn't good for him? Was that true? Did he feel Josefina wasn't *good* for him?

She made you feel alive, his conscience prompted. *You were happy, you were free and you didn't even have to leave Seasalter. She challenged you. She awakened you.*

She'd not changed him. She'd accepted him as he was, a lonely, admittedly cold man who rambled around a big house on his own, living vicariously through his brother's happiness. Then she'd breezed into his life, blowing away the cobwebs of the past. He wanted to feel that way again, wanted to feel that way always. She had accepted him at face value. To have her, he needed to return the courtesy. Darius's words echoed. *Josefina will always be wild.* Yes, he thought. And thank God for that. He didn't want her any other way. It was a frightening decision to make. What if he couldn't convince her to stay? What if he'd decided to claim her and it was too late, despite Darius's opinion that she was waiting for him? What if he lost her again? The answer sprang easy and full grown. If she wouldn't come with him, he would go with her. He chuckled to himself. Darius was right. It could be that simple. He rose, his brandy unfinished. He had a lot to do before the exhibition. If he was lucky, tomorrow just might be a new beginning.

Chapter Twenty

The day had finally arrived, the day upon which the last five months had been fixed. In many ways, it was the beginning of the end. Josefina sat ramrod-straight in Darius's town coach, her gaze locked on the passing street scene outside the carriage window, seeing but not truly ingesting the activity. She had too much on her mind. The first of the two exhibitions was today. It was, in fact, already underway. Darius had arranged for her to arrive late. 'A good artist is never on time,' he'd told her with a laugh.

This first show was private, by invitation of the Viscount St Helier only, held at St Helier's exhibition hall on the Strand, a property Darius had rented and then bought after Artemisia's ground-breaking exhibition. It would be followed by a reception and preview at Somerset House for the Royal Academy's official opening tomorrow. The reception was important. Tonight, the artists and their guests would see which works had been awarded prizes. Artemisia's wager with Sir Aldred Gray would be settled. Then Josefina had the official exhibition tomorrow when her portrait of Owen would be on display for all the *ton* to see, hopefully with a blue ribbon beside it. After that, she would be free to go. She let that sink in. *This time tomorrow, she'd be free to go.*

The coach began to slow, joining a queue that wound towards the exhibition hall, but her heart began to race. What a crush Darius had managed to orchestrate. All these coaches to see her work! Not just hers, she reminded herself. In addition to the portrait for the Academy's show, she'd done a series of paintings of Seasalter and the oystermen that would be on display here, but her series would hardly fill the big hall. Darius was acting as an agent for five other independent artists, as well. It would be good to have company, good to not be singled out. But that didn't stop her artist's nerves from surging to the fore as the coach came to a stop and the coachman helped her out. Would Darius's guests like her work? Would Artemisia be proud of her? Would she be glad she'd made the rather significant investment of taking her on? Josefina feared she'd been more trouble than Artemisia had bargained on.

Papa, would you be proud?

She gave a quick glance to the sky as her feet touched the ground. Was it true that the ones we loved looked down on us from above? What did he see when he looked down? His daughter was a featured artist at a London exhibition. She was exhibiting at the Royal Academy and she'd done it on her own merits. She'd not begged favours from his friends or been cosseted in someone's workshop because of her father's name. Surely, he would have celebrated this moment with her. But this was not the dream he'd had and it was not the promise she'd made.

But I am leaving soon, Papa. I'll be off to the Americas. I'll swim in the warm waters of the Caribbean and paint the green-hilled islands that rise out of the sea.

At the entrance to the hall, Josefina drew

a breath and straightened her shoulders. This might not be the promise she'd made, but this was a moment to savour. She'd done good work on her oystermen series. A waiter passed with a tray of champagne flutes, bubbling, fizzing and sweating with their golden liquid. She felt just like that—bubbling with excitement while her palms sweated inside her gloves and her stomach fizzed with nerves. She took a glass for courage and stepped inside.

It was a spectacular space, a wide room that had once been used in Tudor days as a counting house. Now that space was open, a wall of windows interspersed with French doors that led out on to a narrow balcony that ran the length of the building overlooking the Thames below. Perfect light, she thought, for accounting clerks or aspiring artists. She took a sip of the cold champagne, letting it trickle down her throat, as she looked about the crowded hall. She spotted her series immediately at the far end. The five pictures had been hung together to tell their story. Darius and Artemisia were there already and a group was gathered about them. Darius caught sight of her and beckoned her over.

'Here she is, my wife's protégée, Miss Ricci,'

he introduced her. She knew Boscastle and his son, but the others were new to her. One gentleman, a Lord Monteith, was already insisting that he have the painting of St Alphege's.

The place where Owen had learned to read and write. She pushed the thought away. She would not think of him today, she would not let regrets cloud this moment. 'Of course, we have great hopes for her portrait on display at the Royal Academy,' Darius was saying.

After that, Darius and Artemisia circulated her from group to group, introducing her to their guests. There was another glass of champagne in her hands and Artemisia whispered, 'It's going well, you're a natural, my dear. Are you sure you haven't done this before?' Artemisia was teasing, but Josefina gave a bland smile in response. How many events like this had she attended with her father? With his friends? Supporting their exhibitions, chatting up potential patrons and collectors. Perhaps she should have told Artemisia more about her background, but she hadn't and now she was leaving. It hardly seemed worthwhile. It was notable, however, that Owen had kept her secrets, despite what she'd embroiled him in.

He'd not claimed revenge. She was failing in her charge not to think of him, it seemed. No matter how hard she pushed the thoughts away, they came back. He was determined to haunt her. She could practically feel his eyes on her. She froze. Perhaps there was a reason for that. She turned slowly. He was here.

She was surrounded by admirers, by earls and heirs and the *ton*'s glittering assemblage when Owen arrived. Some of his earlier confidence ebbed. Perhaps she would not have time for him. Perhaps she wouldn't even notice he was there, the oysterman among the lords. Perhaps he should wait another day to make his case. *You don't have another day*, his thoughts pointed out. Tomorrow at the Royal Academy would be even more impossible and then it would be too late.

She was stunning to watch and the urge to hide among the crowd, sipping champagne, was tempting. She was dressed in a deep emerald silk that could pass from this reception to the evening reception at Somerset House, a paisley shawl artfully draped through her arms and drifting at her waist, her inky hair piled high in ringlets, showing off the long curve of her neck and the sweep of her jaw. When she laughed, her gold earbobs danced. Every man in the group about her was enthralled. Owen couldn't blame them. He was enthralled at a distance. *She loves me.* His gut tightened at the prospect, with nerves and the excitement such a thought engendered. That such a flame loved him was a heady concept indeed.

Should he approach? Should he steal her away from the group? Owen played a game with himself. If she saw him before the waiter came by with more champagne, he would go to her. If not, he would wait. He was nearly done with his glass when he saw her back stiffen just a fraction, her body become alert, aware. She turned, a question in her eyes. That was his cue.

She met him halfway. He took her elbow and steered her towards the freedom of the French doors and the long, narrow balcony beyond. 'I didn't think you'd come,' she said when they were alone. The balcony was too narrow for strolling, being more for decoration than actual use. But a private conversation could be had while those inside looked on. 'Have you seen the Seasalter series yet?'

'No, I've only seen you,' Owen admitted honestly, letting her see in his gaze that he meant it. 'I came to apologise, Josefina. I conducted myself poorly the last time we met. When a woman tells a man she loves him, she deserves better from him than a cold shoulder.' He would start with the apology and move on from there.

'I understand,' she said, but he didn't want easy absolution. He wanted to explain.

'I was protecting myself. I was hurt and I was afraid I'd be hurt again. As a result, I was unappreciative of the honour your feelings did me. Most of all, though, I was dishonest.' Somehow their hands had found their way to each other. He was gripping them now, encased in their gloves, and they gave him strength to persevere. How had he lasted these months without touching her?

'You are the most honest man I know, Owen Gann.' She gave him a soft smile.

'Not that day I wasn't. When you told me you loved me, I should have said that you made me feel alive, that you'd brought joy back into my life, that I was happy when I was with you, that my life was vibrant again, that it had meaning again. But I was afraid to love you and so I said other things instead.'

She was silent for a long while, her dark eyes suspiciously shiny. Her voice was shaky when she spoke. 'Thank you, Owen. For believing me, for believing that my love for you is real. Thank you for sharing your own heart with me, trusting me with it when perhaps I don't deserve a second chance.' She licked her bottom lip in that little gesture of hers. 'But now, Owen? Are you still afraid to love me?'

'No,' he whispered, just for her, even though there was no one else to hear. He wanted to sweep her in his arms and kiss her. But that was out of the question with two hundred of Darius's guests just beyond the glass. He bent his head to hers, foreheads touching. 'I was wrong to run away from us. I want a life with you. I did not come here today only to apologise, but to propose. I want to marry you, Josefina. Do you want to marry me?'

He heard her make a little gasp. The question had surprised her, shocked her. In a good or bad way? He couldn't tell. 'Owen, it's not that simple.'

'Yes, it is. A friend helped me see that. I was

making it too complicated.' Owen smiled and she smiled in return, but not with her eyes. They were holding something back. Something inside him recoiled in worry. Was she going to refuse? Was she going to hurt him again after all the courage it had taken to get to this point? 'When two people love each other, Josefina,' he said, 'they should be together.'

'Yes, they should. But I don't know how that works for us. I love you, Owen, but I made a promise to my father, right before he died, that I would do what he couldn't. That I would live free, free to travel the world and see the things he could not see, to paint them. That I wouldn't tie myself to patrons, or to be at another man's beck and call, that I would paint for myself. I can't stay.'

The knot in his stomach eased. He'd known she'd say that and he was ready. 'I know. That's why I will go with you.'

She was speechless. Her brow furrowed as she processed the possibility of that. It was a delight to watch her thoughts, her emotions cross her face. 'But how? You can't walk away from the factory, the oystermen, the smugglers—they're all counting on you. Who will watch out for them?'

'I've made arrangements. I've been up half the night writing instructions. O'Malley can manage the factory. Simon can handle the business correspondence and the shipping. I can have my important mail forwarded to ports of call.'

'I can't believe you would do that for me.' She was glassy-eyed with emotion. She smiled and stole a kiss, regardless of who would see. 'You're an incredible man. I think no woman has ever been loved better. Now, come see the Seasalter series and then I hope you don't have any plans, because I'm not letting you out of my sight. We have the Academy reception after this and a very important portrait to unveil.'

We. That sounded wonderful. And if she hadn't given him a direct answer, he had her smile, her dewy eyes, and her arm possessively threaded through his as collateral. There was no mistaking she was a woman in love and all was right with the world at last.

That rightness was furthered as they stood before the series of pictures she'd painted. Seeing the paintings was like watching his life unfold in retrospect. 'I called the series, "An Oysterman's Life,"' she whispered to him. There was St Alphege's on the little hill that overlooked the marsh. The huddle of huts, the weathered two-storey structure of the Crown. The one he liked best was the one of the oystermen pulling their rowboats in from the water. 'I think I see Charlie and Padraig,' he joked.

'You do. I used their faces,' she confessed with a laugh.

He leaned in to study the fifth picture, a landscape that featured the marshes, the pebbly beach and a deliberately fuzzy structure in the distance that managed to look pristine and organised, at odds with its unorganised natural surroundings. 'What is this?' Owen asked, squinting a bit to make it out.

'Don't you recognise your own home? That's Baldock House,' she teased, but only a bit.

'Why is it fuzzy?'

'Because it's the oysterman's dream, isn't it?' She stepped closer to him. He could smell roses on her, sweet and welcoming. 'You aspired to Baldock House, thinking it would mark something, prove something.'

He nodded. 'But it didn't make me happy. I

understood that almost as soon as I bought it. It didn't bring me the joy I thought it would. It didn't bring my mother back.' Baldock House had been a disappointment from the start except for the widow's walk, where he could use the house to do some good. 'I was merely a man living in another's man house.' He studied the painting with fresh eyes. This painting was about one man's journey of self-discovery. 'I can't decide if I like it. It makes me uncomfortable.'

The painting was a potent lesson, not just to himself, who knew the lesson of this painting personally, but it would teach that lesson to any man. Be careful what you wish for. True happiness did not lie in material things. Once attained, the marker moved. It was a warning, as well. A man could spend his life chasing the wrong things.

'It's a beautiful series, Josefina,' he complimented, meaning it. 'You've captured my home, my life, all of it, so perfectly. I might have to buy the whole set.'

She laughed up at him. 'You can't. Lord Montieth has already bought the church.'

'Well, I know the artist. Perhaps we can work

something out.' He gave an exaggerated sigh and they both laughed, drawing stares from those around them. This was how it would be from now on. The two of them, laughing together, happiness welling up inside of him because this woman loved him.

Chapter Twenty-One

It was wrong to mislead him. Guilt tugged at Josefina even as she embraced the rightness of the moment, the rightness of being with Owen, of having him at her side while they made the short journey to Somerset House in the spring twilight, the feel of his hand at her back, ushering her through the reception hall, all of it felt so incredibly right. But it was wrong. It was selfish to claim this man, to take him from all he knew and all those who relied on him. He was going to give it all up for her, to come with her.

That revelation still stunned her. She'd thought her latest confession as to why she couldn't stay would hurt him. Instead, he'd been ready for it. He'd not hesitated. He'd been so sure of himself. *I will go with you.* She envied that about him—his surety, his confidence in knowing what he wanted and what he was doing. Owen never hesitated, never put a foot wrong. Once he was decided on a course of action, he saw it through.

That was why she had to stop him from this course of action. Most of all, she wanted him to decide he couldn't come. She did not want to decide it for him. But she needed him to see that he could not leave, that he would hate himself for it in the end, for leaving his people, leaving his own dreams. She'd shown him the Seasalter series in the hopes that he would start to think not about her, but about what coming with her would cost him. She'd already been the object of his scorn once, she did not want to be the object of it again. She didn't want those blue eyes to look on her with the polite disregard he'd displayed in Boscastle's garden. Owen believed that when two people loved each other they should be together, but when two people loved each other, they also had to put the other first. It made for an imperfect happiness otherwise.

Owen took two glasses of champagne from a waiter as they stepped into the hall. 'Just in case you need some more, besides, it looks good for appearances.' He chuckled. 'I can't remember the last time I've had so much champagne before nine o'clock in the evening and it's only six now.' He smiled. 'Are you nervous?'

'A little,' Josefina admitted. 'I don't want Artemisia to be disappointed. Aldred Gray is such a toad, not winning a prize would be like losing to him directly. My pride is at stake.' She'd tried to tell herself all week that winning didn't matter. It didn't change anything. Winning didn't influence whether she stayed or left. She would go regardless. And yet, she *wanted* to win, for Artemisia, for herself. She didn't need to win first prize, just second or third would do. It would be enough to secure the wager for Artemisia and to prove to herself that she'd been right to leave Venice, to not tie herself to a workshop. She liked to think of it as a little encouragement for the road.

She took a sip of the champagne. 'It's silly to be nervous. It's already been decided. Someone in this room already knows. Being nervous can't change anything.' She favoured Owen with a smile. 'I'm glad you're here with me. It does help.'

Artemisia and Darius joined them. 'Shall we go in? They've opened the main gallery now.' Artemisia was bristling with excitement. It helped as well to know that she was not the only one rippling with anticipation.

Josefina straightened her shoulders. 'Yes, let's get it over with.'

Artemisia laughed. 'That's not quite the attitude we're looking for, my dear. I'd say, "Let's get on with it. I have a feeling I'm going to enjoy this moment all night."'

Inside, the long gallery was already crowded with artists and their personal guests, everyone jostling for position to view this year's work and this year's prizes. Artemisia glanced at the programme in her hand. 'The portraits are at the far end this year.' She shot a look over her shoulder at Owen. 'Are you ready for some fame? Everyone always wants to meet the models who sit for great work.'

Josefina let her own gaze slide in Owen's direction. How would he feel about that? Being an artist's model? This rich, self-sufficient businessman? Would he like the painting? He hadn't seen the work. She was suddenly nervous for a different reason. Would he like the way she'd depicted him? Would he be embarrassed to be the centre of so much attention? But Owen's expression gave nothing away except perhaps that he was pleased to be at her side.

They navigated the length of the hall, Artemisia's arm slipping through hers as they approached the portraits, her voice low at her ear as the two of them stepped apart from their men to see the portraits together. 'Oh, my dear girl, look what you've done.'

It took a moment for everything to register. Josefina found the portrait, her gaze resting on the blue eyes that peered back at her from the canvas, before her gaze moved to the top left corner, where the long, silky rosette was pinned. In blue, to match the painting, had been her overly alert mind's first reaction. Her second reaction was, blue, because she'd won. She'd not only taken a prize, she'd won the category.

'You won.' Artemisia's voice carried the faintest tremor of overwhelmed excitement. 'I can't believe it.' They were surrounded then, by their family and friends: Darius, Addy and Hazard, Boscastle and his son. They hugged her in turn and then she was in Owen's arms, letting the moment make her incautious. She kissed him full on the mouth in her excitement, not caring who saw. What did it matter? This was the man she loved. Why should she not show the world?

'You did it, I am so proud of you,' he whispered at her ear.

'Do you like it?' She looked up into his face, searching for a response, but there was no time. They had to celebrate. They were besieged with well-wishers and congratulations, everyone eager to meet her, to meet Owen, the model, to shake Artemisia's hand and to congratulate Darius. There was more champagne. There were toasts. People wanted to discuss the painting, to talk about her palette of blues, the shading she'd done on the turquoise curtains to hint at shadows, to commend the skill it had taken to depict a meaningful scene beyond the window behind Owen in the portrait. She was swept up in the glamour and the fame of the moment. She'd attended nights like this in Venice, but always for someone else. But tonight it was for her. She was the one in a silk gown, champagne in her hand, the toast of the hour.

* * *

It was some time before the crowd thinned and the reception began to move towards its denouement. Owen had stayed close, but not too close. He'd been happy to let her bask alone in her success. Now that the crowd had dispersed, he was beside her once more. 'Owen Gann, Oyster King of Kent,' he read the caption beneath the portrait out loud. 'That's hardly a scintillating title.'

'But very apt.' Josefina smiled up at him. 'It's who you are, Owen. It's who you're meant to be.'

'You painted me in the office at Baldock House, after all. I thought you were rankly against that.' The office. The desk where they had made love was positioned between him and the window in the background. He still couldn't work at it without thinking of her.

'I was, but I changed my mind.' She cast him a coy glance and he knew she shared his thoughts about the office. She gave a toss of her head, teasing him, 'I needed the window.'

'And I need you.' Owen settled himself behind her, wrapping his arms about her waist and pulling her close, taking advantage of the emerging privacy of the emptying gallery. 'Does this portrait have a story like the Seasalter series?' She felt his breath feather her ear, felt his thumbs gently press into her hips where they rested amid the folds of her skirt. She wanted nothing more than to be alone with him, to make love with him in his big bed and to wake up beside him. Her body was thrumming with the knowledge of those truths.

'Every portrait has a story,' she murmured.

'Tell me this one. Tell me about the man in the picture.'

'You might not like it,' she cautioned.

'Tell me anyway,' Owen said in all seriousness. 'After all, what does Plato say about the unexamined life?'

She gave a soft laugh and leaned against the power of him. 'Well, just remember you asked.'

'Why the office? Why the window?' Owen prompted.

'Kings live in castles and their subjects live beyond the palace walls, free to go about their lives in ways kings can't. I wanted the window to show the separation between you and the world you watch over. You told me once that you lived between worlds, belonging to both and neither. I wanted to depict that, not just for you, but for other businessmen. This is often the dilemma for rich merchants. The *ton* needs their money, but they are reluctant to marry their heirs to merchants' daughters.' The turquoise curtains had been both a sign of luxury and limits, the gilded cage of a king. Freedom lay beyond the window.

'So it's a study in leadership?' Owen asked. 'The price of responsibility?'

'And more. That's just the story of the setting. Then there's the story of the man. This is a self-made king. All around him are the trappings of his kingdom, but he wears no trappings.' She directed him to the hands she'd spent hours painting. 'He wears no signet ring, nothing that announces his position but his own efforts. These are the hands of a worker.'

'Oh, my word, you've captured the little scar on my pinkie, the one I gave myself shucking oysters years ago.' She heard the awe in his voice and it filled her with pleasure that he should appreciate the effort. 'And my tenacity as well, in the grip I have on the back of the chair.' His voice was softer now. She knew he'd noticed the pearls clutched in that grip, the pearls of working men acquired over generations of effort, another nod to tenacity and his origins.

'Yes.' Only the rounded top of the chair was visible at the bottom of the portrait. His hands rested on it, but not merely rested. Gripped. His hands gripped the ornate back of the chair as if they were anchoring him to the life of privilege that surrounded him. By doing so, there was a sharp contrast between the luxurious chair and the rough hands with their scar and pearls.

'Am I a benevolent king?' Owen asked.

'What do you think? Look at the eyes, Owen. Do you see your soul in them?' After the hands, the eyes had been the most difficult for her to do. She'd wanted to convey his vulnerability, his compassion along with his strength and determination. Here was a man who used his power for good, his gaze said. Here was a man who, without hesitation, had spent his personal money to save the smugglers, who had personally rowed out to the oyster beds after a storm to assess the damage because his crew needed him to.

'It's well done, Josefina. I do not know if

I've ever been seen so completely before. It is humbling to be laid so bare.'

She looked about, realising only they remained. Artemisia and Darius, Addy and Hazard were waiting patiently at the other end of the gallery at the door, no doubt to give them privacy. 'I suppose we should go.' Although she would not have minded standing here in his arms all night looking at paintings. She would not have minded if time had chosen that moment to stand still.

'May I call on you in the morning before the exhibition opens tomorrow afternoon? We can settle our arrangements then.' She nodded. Tomorrow would be soon enough to let him down. Let them both have sweet dreams tonight.

'Sir Aldred did not come?' Josefina asked Artemisia as they joined them at the door.

'No, perhaps he knew the results and is waiting to show his face at the official opening tomorrow.' Artemisia gave a nonchalant shrug. 'Oh, well, my gloating will have to wait another day.'

There was a commotion outside in the dark beyond Artemisia's shoulder. A carriage pulled up to the kerb. Josefina squinted, trying to make out the figures getting out, two men. She frowned. 'Or maybe Sir Aldred is just arriving very late.'

Artemisia and the others turned as Sir Aldred Gray approached. The other man hung back in the darkness. 'You've left it rather late,' Darius drawled. 'The reception is over, but my wife is happy to accept your congratulations.'

Sir Aldred hmphed. 'You must excuse my tardiness. I was delayed by business, business concerning our wager, actually.' He speared Artemisia with a piercing look. 'Your protégée won and you think this proves something, that you can teach a measly street artist and a woman to boot with no real training to paint like a master. You think such evidence will enhance the standing of your precious school.' The words were spoken with such hatred and force that Darius took an involuntary step in front of his wife. Josefina felt Owen's grip at her waist tighten. Any charge against Artemisia was a charge against her, as well.

Sir Aldred's cool gaze turned her direction. 'I have someone with me who is eager to meet you, *signorina*. He's travelled all the way from Venice, at my request, and only just arrived.'

Josefina's racing mind froze, a thousand possibilities holding her rooted to the ground when she ought to run.

'What is the meaning of this?' Owen enquired, cold steel in his voice. He, too, had stepped forward in the face of Sir Aldred's vitriol.

The man dissembled. 'Nothing but a chance to reunite old friends who are far from home. *Signorina*, I have someone I'd like you to meet.' He gestured for the man at the coach to come forward. 'Allow me to present Signor Bartolli. I believe you know him.'

'Does she know me?' The big man's chuckle chilled Josefina's blood. This was proof she'd stayed too long in England. Long enough to be found. 'I dare say she knows me—I am her betrothed.'

Chapter Twenty-Two

Owen's first instinct was to protect Josefina. He felt her sway against him, seeking his strength. This man, this Signor Bartolli, frightened her. He drew her to him, keeping her wrapped tight in the shelter of his arm. His second instinct was that this man was a liar. This was the man she'd ran away from, the reason she'd not gone back after her father's funeral, the man who'd propositioned her. He would need very little provocation to plant a punch in the man's face. 'He is not her betrothed.' Owen stared the man down. 'He may know her, but that is a lie.'

Sir Aldred shrugged as if the lie had no bearing on his case. 'That is between them, of course. It's clear, though, that they know one another, which is all that matters to me.' He turned his gaze on Artemisia. 'Did you think

I wouldn't find out what you'd done? That you would be able to pass off Felipe Zanetti's daughter as a street artist you've somehow transformed?'

'I know nothing of the sort!' Artemisia's response was swift.

Addy stepped forward. 'How could we have known that? I picked her at random at the market. You were there. I think you both are mistaken. How could we ever have plotted something like that? To plan to encounter you in the market? To set that wager? There is too much of the spontaneous to it.'

Owen waited for Josefina to come to Artemisia's defence, to affirm Addy's argument, to declare who she was. But Josefina said nothing.

'This is not the woman you are looking for. This is Signorina Ricci. The name doesn't even match,' he pointed out.

'Is that what she told you? And you believed her?' Signor Bartolli sneered. 'Are you her lover? Is that why you defend her so earnestly? Well, you're not the first to be besotted with our *signorina*. Ricci was her mother's name.' He dropped the information with a triumphant smirk. 'I not only know her, but I know her far better than you do, it seems.' He held out a hand. 'Josefina, you've had your little adventure. Now it's time to come home, to Venice, to your father's workshop, to me and all you've left behind. You've given us quite the scare disappearing as you did. We'd given you up until a man came around asking questions.'

'Who might that man have been?' Owen ground out, trying to keep his feet firmly on the ever-shifting ground that was Josefina. There was so much to focus on, so much to distract him from his objective—protect Josefina, first and foremost. All else could be sorted out afterwards. 'Did you send spies?'

'I sent Bow Street. I wanted to know more about the protégée.' Sir Aldred met his gaze with smug victory. 'She's left quite a trail all over the Continent. I wasn't expecting that, but Bow Street didn't fail me.'

'It cost you a lot more to find her than the wager was worth,' Owen noted.

'You don't strike me as a man who would put a limit on the price of his pride, Gann.' Aldred's gaze raked him. 'But I also didn't take you for a man who thought with his cock.

She must be quite…convincing.' He laughed as Owen's fist clenched and unclenched with restraint. 'I don't like to lose.' Sir Aldred's gaze swivelled to Artemisia. 'I especially don't like to lose to a woman who cheats.'

Owen felt Josefina stiffen. She stepped away from the protection of his arm. 'That's enough. *Lady* St Helier didn't know who I was. She never knew. I never told her, I never told any of them. If there's a fraud here, it's me and it's him.' She gestured towards Signor Bartolli. 'I *am* Felipe Zanetti's daughter, but this man is not my betrothed. He would like to be. He propositioned me right before my father's funeral and demanded an answer by the end of the day. He made it clear he would not take no for an answer. So, fearing for my safety and my virtue, I left.' She fixed Sir Aldred with a stare worthy of Medusa. 'Are you pleased now? You've found a woman who did not want to be found and you've brought her face to face with a man who is dangerous to her. Well done. Was winning your wager worth *that*?' She turned towards him and Owen could see what the admissions cost her. Her eyes fought against shiny tears. 'Owen, I am so sorry.' Words failed her then. Something wild and desperate lit her gaze as she turned from him. She pushed past Sir Aldred and headed down the stairs of Somerset House to the street, her emerald skirts fading to black in the night.

Owen moved to go after her, but Darius put a hand on his arm. 'Let her go. This has been a shock to her. She won't go far.' Owen hoped Darius was right. His instincts told him otherwise. He excused himself. His mind was reeling with its own questions and, without Josefina beside him, he was acutely reminded that he wasn't family. Artemisia and Addy and their husbands had their own fallout to sift through. It was not appropriate for him to be part of that. His own carriage pulled up to the kerb and he climbed inside, grateful for the dark. 'Drive until I tell you otherwise. I don't care where,' he instructed. He wasn't going home until he had come to terms with what had happened and what he was going to do about it.

He let the questions come. How was it possible that he'd just claimed happiness a few hours ago and it was being tested yet again so soon? Was this happiness real? He didn't even know her real name and he thought he did. That was the real kicker, wasn't it? *He'd thought he knew.* He thought he knew her. Now a man who styled himself her betrothed had shown up, knowing more about her than Owen did.

He wanted to punch Sir Aldred for spying on her, for digging up a past she'd wanted to bury, yet the lie was all hers. *She had good reason for it; she didn't want to be found.* He tried to rationalise the lie. Even as he did it, he recognised it for the slippery slope it was. How many lies, half-truths or belated discoveries would he have to rationalise throughout a lifetime with her? Was this all? Or was there more?

Does it matter? You love her. She understands you better than anyone. You saw that painting, the way she captured the dilemmas you've faced, the choices you've made to be who you are. What fool throws that kind of understanding away? What kind of fool lets that woman run into the night thinking there's no hope? Love is simple. Don't overcomplicate it.

Love was love. He rapped on the carriage and called up to the driver. 'Lambeth Palace, at once.' Never mind it was after nine in the evening, far too late for a social call. The Archbishop would forgive him once he saw the size of the endowment Owen was going to make him once that special licence was in his pocket. And that was just the start of his evening. Josefina had been full of surprises. It was time for a surprise of his own before she could slip away.

Josefina slipped enough coins in her pocket to pay for a hack to the docks and help with her trunk. She was on the run again. She took a last look around the room. The other two trunks stood open. She couldn't take them for the twin sakes of speed and conscience. She wanted to be gone before Artemisia and Darius came home. She couldn't face them, not after what had happened at Somerset House. Artemisia would be furious, she would hate her now. Josefina had made her look like a fool. Perhaps Artemisia would know how sorry she was when she saw that she'd left the gowns and the trunks. She'd taken only the art supplies and the three gowns she'd come with. Josefina shut the door behind her and headed downstairs, dragging her trunk, thumping on the steps as she went. The staff were abed for the evening. She hoped they wouldn't bother to enquire about the noise.

She breathed easier once she and her trunk were aboard the hack. It was almost a clean getaway. Now she had to hope that her ship would allow her to come aboard early. If not, she would have to find a hotel and then hope no one found her. Only a false name would protect her. It would be a long, anxious two days. How would she face Artemisia and Darius after tonight? All the brilliance of the evening had been stripped away in a single condemning moment.

It wasn't just Artemisia she didn't want to face. It was Bartolli. She needed to hide from him. He would *drag* her back to Venice and he would drag her to the altar, here or there, if he could manage it and he wouldn't be kind about it. And then there was Owen. What must he think of her now? Would he be disgusted? Would he realise what a narrow escape he'd had? He'd been her anchor tonight, his arm about her waist, protecting her despite a mind that must have been reeling with questions and disbelief. And he'd been betrayed for his efforts.

The hack was slowing. Josefina looked out the window as the docks came into view, eerie in the settling fog. Relief warred with sadness. Each necessary step took her further from Owen, but there was no choice. She got out and spoke to the guard on duty, smiling prettily until he went up to speak with the Captain on her behalf. She sat on her trunk, twisted her hands and looked about her as she waited for his return. Sweet heavens, it was taking for ever, and her senses were on high alert. Docks in the dark were not safe places for women.

She slipped a hand into her pocket, taking comfort from the little knife there. She knew how to handle men who couldn't handle themselves, she reminded herself. A knee to the balls would drop even the biggest and her knife could do the rest.

She laughed to herself. She really was getting soft. This was what life had been like up until January. How quickly she'd forgotten what it was like to live on the edge of alertness. It would come back to her.

'Josefina!' A voice cut through the night, a glimmer of blond hair shining in the dark as Owen descended from his coach. She hadn't even heard it and, in the fog, she'd not seen it. She was rusty indeed.

She rose, her pulse racing as he neared. 'What are you doing here? How did you know?'

'Lucky guess. I'm glad I didn't take Darius's advice and wait until tomorrow. You'd have been gone.' Maybe. She didn't bother to correct him. He held her gaze for a long moment, his gaze making her want to melt against him. He was strong and certain. Right now, she was none of those things. 'Actually, it wasn't a guess. I know you, Josefina. I knew exactly what you were going to do.' He reached for her hand, his grip warm around the cold chill of her fingers. He knew and he'd come anyway. Josefina felt some of the fear that had frozen her begin to melt. She shouldn't let it. Fear was a great motivator.

'When you left Somerset House you were frightened. That man upset you.' Owen paused, running his hands down the length of her arms in a warming motion and she thawed a bit more. Thin ice was dangerous. 'You're frozen with fear, Josefina, and you are not thinking straight. We make poor decisions when we're scared. He can't hurt you. He has no papers, no agreements, no claim to you other than his word. You've given no consent and no one has consented on your behalf.'

'He will hunt me down.' Her eyes darted around the foggy docks. Even now, he might be on his way. If Owen had found her, perhaps Bartolli could, too.

'Then let's put you out of his reach, let's stop running.' Owen spoke in reasonable measures, his words slow and sure. 'I have been to Lambeth Palace and I have a special licence in my pocket. We can be wed tomorrow if we like.'

'Tomorrow?' She trembled from the cold, from the events of the evening. 'Isn't that a little precipitous?'

Owen shook his head. 'We've already discussed it. I proposed earlier this afternoon. Love is simple, remember? It's just people who complicate it.' He made it sound so logical, it was hard to remember her defence. Why not marry Owen?

Then she remembered. 'You want to protect me, you don't want to marry me.'

'I love you. If protection comes with the territory, then so be it,' Owen corrected. 'If travel comes with it, so be it, as well. I thought we'd settled this.'

The sailor came down the gangplank. 'Miss, Captain says you can come aboard. Shall I take your trunk?' His gaze split between her and Owen, confused.

'No.'

'Yes.' They spoke simultaneously.

'Wait,' Owen instructed and Josefina bristled.

'It's my trunk.'

'We're not done, Josefina,' he said sternly. 'You love me. I love you. There is no reason we can't marry.'

'But there is! I am a disaster, Owen. I ruin things if I stay long enough. Look what I did to you, to Artemisia. And I wasn't even trying. Now you're getting a special licence and planning a wedding in less than a day, and walking away from all the people who are counting on you. For me. You're giving up *everything* for me.' Her voice trembled as she pleaded. She had to make him see. 'You're too good of a man. I need to save you from me.'

'And who will save *you*, Josefina? Let me. Have you ever thought that, maybe, opposites attract because they're meant to save each other? Balance each other out?' He bent his mouth then, capturing her lips with a kiss full of sweetness and sincerity. 'You brought me back to life, Josefina. Do not underestimate the power of that. When I met you, I envied how free you were, how you could go where you wished and it reminded me of how trapped I was by my own making. Now that I am alive again, I don't want the fire to go out. I will want you always. You, just as you are, are incredible. Don't you see? I don't want you to change. I want your fire, your wildness, you just as you are.'

She looked up at him and wet her lips. 'That's just it. I want you the way you are. You're not a man who leaves those he cares for at the drop of a hat. You are not a precipitous man. It's what *I* envy about *you*, love about you, and now being with me is asking you to act against that.' Cross-purposes was making this impossible. Her heart was breaking.

But Owen was intractable tonight. 'Then we must find another solution, one that satisfies us both. Marry me, spend a year with me in Seasalter, *planning* our voyage to your dreams, planning how I can set aside work to travel with you, and then we'll go however far, for however long it takes for you to keep your promise.' He smiled at her and her resistance began to melt. Maybe she needed to take the leap.

'Miss, are you coming?' The sailor was impatient.

Owen held her gaze. 'The world is your oyster, Josefina. I will serve it on a half-shell to you every day for the rest of your life.'

All she had to do was say yes. Maybe love was simple, after all. She smiled at Owen. 'And I will do my best to be your pearl.' And then she frowned. 'But what about Darius and Artemisia?' Love might be simple, but there was still the exhibition, the mess she'd made of Artemisia's wager.

Owen grinned. 'I've been thinking about that, too, and I have an idea how to salvage that. As for what they'll think of you, let them surprise you before you think the worst.'

Chapter Twenty-Three

They did surprise her, as Owen had surprised her. There was no condemnation, no scolding, no stony glares when Owen carried her trunk back into the town house, only relief, exclamations of joy over her return, hugs and warm drinks in the small parlour set aside for intimate family gatherings.

'This is not insurmountable,' Owen said once everyone had settled to their tea or something stronger. Darius and Hazard nodded, their minds already busy at work. 'This is a discovery. Artemisia can claim credit for having found Zanetti's daughter after a bet with Sir Aldred Gray led to selecting an artist at random from the Covent Garden market.'

'I think that's up to Josefina,' Artemisia put in, causing Josefina to look up from her tea.

'Do you want to be found? This would be a very public announcement. Right now, it is just Sir Aldred's word against ours. We can manage him.'

Josefina shook her head. 'I don't want him managed with a lie.' She would not have these good people do such a thing on her behalf. They had done too much already, most of it unlooked for and undeserved. 'Besides, I am not ashamed to be Felipe Zanetti's daughter. I loved my father. It just became rather inconvenient for…' she groped for the right word '…escaping.'

'Escaping Bartolli?' Artemisia pressed. 'He can be dealt with, as well.'

'Certainly Bartolli, but more than that.' Josefina sighed and furrowed her brow, looking for the words to express it. 'He was the embodiment of all my father wanted me to avoid.' She felt Owen's hand settle over hers, lending validation and support. She did not care that every eye in the room noted it. 'My father was a great landscape artist. He dreamed of sailing the world and painting the great landscapes: the Great Wall of China, the Pyramids, the vast wilderness of America, the green, humpbacked islands of the Caribbean. But he could never go. His wealth, his success, was tied to patrons. He had no freedom to pursue his passion without sacrificing the security of his wealth. I promised I would go for him. It was the last thing he asked of me.' Not just to paint for him, but to live free so that her dreams would not be limited by social strictures.

Addy swiped at her eyes. 'That's a beautiful story, but a hard one, too.' She cast a soft look at her new husband of a few months. 'I used to think that freedom meant being alone, but it doesn't. Freedom can be shared and supported by the people who love you. Your freedom is their freedom. And you are loved here, Josefina. You needn't hide, you needn't choose between your promises, your dreams and the people who love you. I've learned that and Artemisia has learned that.'

Josefina looked around the circle gathered about her and knew it was true. That was the secret that lay beneath every glance these couples exchanged with one another. She'd been blind to it until tonight. It had taken Owen's persistence to allow her to see it for herself. When she met Owen's gaze, his blue eyes twinkled with a teasing *I told you so.* 'Thank you, you've all been so gracious. I am happy to be announced as Felipe Zanetti's daughter, but how will this affect the wager? I don't want Sir Aldred to make things difficult for you.' She wanted to start giving back to these people who had given her so much, who treated her like family.

'We'll let him be part of the victory. I don't think he'll complain much if he can share in the momentary fame,' Darius offered.

'But the school? The wager was supposed to prove that the school provided excellent instruction for women. I'm not sure what's happened proves that.' Simply being who she was would negate the premise of the bet.

Artemisia smiled. 'I think it does other things for the school. After all, if it's good enough for Felipe Zanetti's daughter to paint there incognito and produce a winning portrait for the Academy, it can't be all bad. Families will want their daughters there. I expect enrolment will go sky-high next term.' Josefina didn't miss the veiled invitation. *Stay. Teach.* After the debacle of this evening, she'd not expected that invitation to be extended a second time. Well, maybe she could stay and teach for a while. What had Artemisia said? It's good to have choices even if you don't think you want them? She was starting to see the merits of that.

'What of Signor Bartolli?' Hazard put in. 'We've handled the exhibition and the wager, but those are not the reasons he's here. He expects to go home with a bride.'

Owen's hand squeezed hers as he cleared his throat. 'Josefina and I have taken the liberty of resolving that. We are to be married. I have a special licence, newly minted just this evening and effective as soon as tomorrow morning, although I think we'd prefer to wait and marry in Seasalter.'

'But by wait, we don't mean to wait too long,' Josefina put in. 'Maybe just a week or so, long enough to take care of things here.' Now that she could see the future, a bright, vivid landscape laid out in front of her, she wanted that future to begin now.

There were gasps and exclamations of excitement. People moved from their chairs to congratulate them. 'This calls for champagne.' Darius laughed as he shook Owen's hand. 'Can anyone stomach some more? I'll call for sandwiches, as well.'

'Oh, don't wake the staff,' Josefina protested. No doubt they'd just got settled after the late call for tea. 'We can do it ourselves. Owen is a fabulous cook. We'll raid the larder.'

All six of them trooped down to the kitchen, led by Josefina, Owen in tow, for the most spontaneous engagement party London had quite possibly ever seen. Artemisia lit the lamps while Hazard stirred up the fire, Darius was sent to the wine cellar for champagne and Owen set to work slicing cheese and bread for toasting while Addy rooted through the kitchen for some of Elianora's cream cakes, shipped weekly to the town house during the Season.

Food assembled and cooked, champagne poured, they gathered around the kitchen worktable for toast. 'To love,' Owen said to the room, but his eyes were on her as they had been all night, 'which makes the impossible probable and has the power to turn tragedy to triumph at a moment's notice.' As they drank, Owen whispered at her ear, 'Don't ever forget it.'

* * *

Josefina held on to those words throughout the days that followed: the triple whirlwinds of the exhibition, the prize and *The Times* announcement, penned at dawn by Darius, proclaiming the discovery of Felipe Zanetti's daughter, followed by another announcement posted by the Oyster King of Kent himself, Owen Gann, sharing news of his engagement to Josefina Zanetti. Following that, a first-class ticket leaving immediately from London was delivered to Signor Bartolli's hotel, compliments of Viscount St Helier. Josefina couldn't think of a better use of her ticket. It was an explication of tragedy to triumph in action. What could have ended in disgrace had ended in celebration.

But what she treasured most in those heady, whirlwind days was the quiet time she managed to steal alone with Owen. Today was no exception. 'Where are you taking me?' Josefina asked gamely, settling inside his carriage. It was cloudy outside and she thought it might rain. It wouldn't be a picnic, then.

'To Blackwell,' Owen said cryptically. 'For an early wedding present.'

'Blackwell? Isn't that the docks?' She was determined to prise the secret out of him.

'Yes, and that's all I am going to say for now.' Owen laughed.

'Is it? Care to wager on that?' Josefina moved from her seat, straddling his lap, her skirts riding up on her thighs. 'I have ways of making you talk.' She kissed him on the mouth, her hand dropping low between them and finding him rousing.

'You don't play fair, minx.' Owen groaned, but he offered no real protest, happy to be persuaded if these were her methods. He loved this about her, her spontaneity, her ability to embrace passion openly. *Josefina will always be wild.* Thank goodness for that. A man needed a little wildness in his life. He certainly did. If wildness included lovemaking in a carriage, who was he to complain? There'd been little time for stolen moments since the night she'd decided to marry him. But there would soon be time.

She slipped her hand inside his trousers, having got his fall open, her hand warm about him. 'What's the surprise?' She leaned in for a kiss, her voice soft.

'It's the last piece of business I need to take care of before we can leave for Seasalter.' He chuckled when she made an exaggerated pout.

'You mean to tell me the surprise is business?' She stroked his length, calling him to complete arousal. 'I don't believe that for a moment,' she whispered against his mouth.

'Humour me, Josefina.' He laughed. 'It's not every day a man gets to spoil his bride-to-be.'

Humour him she did, with kisses, caresses and laughter until they pulled into a work yard beneath a sign: The Sutton Ship and Yachting Company.

Owen watched some semblance of comprehension dawn in her eyes as he righted his trousers. There were a hundred questions in her eyes, but she was guessing. He smiled as he handed her down from the carriage and she looked about at boats in varying sizes and states of completion in the yard.

'Your dream?' she asked reverently.

'Your dream and mine. They go together now,' Owen said quietly. 'I want you to meet Richard Sutton, shipbuilder and dream-maker.'

Richard Sutton was waiting for them in his office. A small girl of four or five played on the carpet at his feet with a carved toy ship. 'I hope you don't mind? I like to bring my daughter to work with me.' Sutton greeted Owen with a handshake.

'I don't mind at all.' Owen introduced Josefina, who bent down to speak to the wide-eyed child.

'What's your name?'

'Elise.' The child held up the toy boat for Josefina's inspection. 'I'm going to build yachts when I grow up, the fastest boats on the water.'

'Of course you are. Don't let anyone tell you otherwise.' Josefina handed the boat back to her with a smile. The scene touched something in Owen's heart. His bride was going to make a wonderful mother. *A family of his own.* The thought nearly choked him as he watched Josefina with the little girl. He'd not allowed himself to think beyond the proposal, the wedding. Josefina rose and smiled at him and he let his thoughts run a bit wild. He would have a family with this woman. A large one to fill up Baldock House, sons and daughters to inherit the business, to paint portraits and landscapes.

Richard Sutton cleared his throat. 'Would you like to see the plans?' His eyes were merry and Owen knew every thought he had was plainly written on his face for the whole world to see. He couldn't care less. Let the world see that he was madly, completely in love. Sutton unrolled a long sheet of paper and anchored it with paperweights. 'This is your ship, Mr Gann, and probably the last full-sized ship I'll build,' Sutton said. 'I think everything from here on out will be yachts for me.'

'Ship?' Josefina gasped, turning her dark eyes on him.

'Well, we need something to see the world in and to ship oysters.' Owen smiled, loving the surprise in her eyes. He had another surprise in store. He pointed to a space in the bow. 'Do you know what this is? It's our cabin.'

'It's huge,' Josefina breathed.

'It will be filled with all the modern luxuries one can have aboard a ship: a big bed, a table, chairs, a place for you to paint when you can't paint on deck. Do you see the big window? Perfect for an artist's light. We will live in comfort.'

'I can't believe it—this is your wedding gift?' Josefina was overwhelmed, he could see it in her eyes. 'We're really going to do it.'

'Yes, next year, on our anniversary, we'll sail away, just as I promised.'

'You're planning our anniversary already and we haven't even had the wedding,' Josefina laughed, but it was choked with tears of overwhelmed joy. Suddenly, she was in his arms, her arms thrown about his neck, kissing him hard while Richard Sutton laughed. It was good to be a man in love and he would be a man in love for the rest of his life.

It was good to be a woman in love, something that had taken Josefina a long time to admit to herself. But now that she had, she didn't want to fight it any more. She wanted to give in to it, every day. She stood outside the wooden doors of St Alphege's and drew a deep breath. This was her wedding day and the man she loved waited for her inside, along with her new 'family.' She touched the pearls at her neck. Owen had sent them to the farmhouse this morning with a note that read simply 'back where they belong.' The Gann pearls, collected over the years from various oysters, were a sign of Owen's love and the perseverance that was so typical of her husband-to-be. It had taken years to build this strand.

'Are you ready?' Darius approached quietly. He had volunteered to give her away. Addy and Artemisia were both acting as matrons of honour for her today. Addy had delayed her departure to Florence to come back to Seasalter for the wedding. Simon would stand beside his brother, all of them ready to witness their marriage, while back at the farmhouse his wife was overseeing the wedding breakfast alongside Mrs Harris. There would be cream cakes and ginger biscuits galore.

She nodded, her grip tightening on the spring bouquet of wildflowers in her hands, populated heavily with blue forget-me-nots to complete the old folk superstition that a bride must have something borrowed, something blue, something old and something new on her wedding day. Darius handed her a coin. 'Sixpence for your shoe.' He laughed. 'Can't forget that.' The strains of a violin came from inside the church, the final signal that it was time. Her stomach fluttered with nerves.

Darius took her arm. 'I've never seen Owen so happy. He's a new man thanks to you. He's going to melt, though, when he sees you. You make a beautiful bride.'

It was exactly the right thing to say. Josefina plucked at the skirts of the oyster-coloured silk with its lace and seed pearls—the ideal gown for the Oyster King's wife. It was her 'something new,' a gown that had been stitched at rapid speed and sent down from London just the day before. Artemisia had helped with her hair, putting it up in curls this morning and setting a simple tiara among them—her something borrowed sent down by Darius's mother. 'You're surrounded by family now,' Darius whispered as he opened the door and led her down the aisle.

There was a rustle of clothes as people rose in the pews. Seasalter was a small village and most had come. The girls from the school were there, excited for a day off, the oystermen and Padraig were there with their families. The little church was turned out in spring glory, clutches of wildflowers tied with pastel ribbons decorating the pews and a larger spray of flowers at the altar. A simple, spring wedding, a reminder that spring was a time of renewal, a time when all things were born again, even a reckless woman who'd nearly thrown away the richest happiness of all.

Owen waited for her at the end of the short aisle. His hair gleaming gold, his clothes—a blue morning coat and buff trousers—immaculate, his eyes shining. When he took her hand from Darius, she felt his grip tremble, saw his eyes glisten as they held on tight to each other as the words were said, as vows were spoken and she felt again the power and the intensity of his love.

At last, Owen kissed her, with a whisper in her ear as he took her in his arms for the first time as his wife. 'For ever starts today, my love.'

From this day forward he would be hers and she would be his, bound together with a love that no man would put asunder.

Epilogue

One year later

Josefina stood at the rail, a light breeze toying with her hair as the *My Josefina* made its way down the Thames towards the open ocean. London was already fading from view, the people on the wharf growing smaller, too far away now to see her if she waved. Artemisia and Darius had come to see them off, extracting promises that they would stop in Florence to see Addy and Hazard before going on to Greece and Egypt.

Strong arms came up behind her and drew her close. Her husband. Even after a year, she did not tire of saying that. She was more in love with Owen now than she'd ever been. It was hard to imagine how that could be, but her love for him grew every day.

'You'll miss them,' Owen surmised, dropping a kiss on her cheek. She leaned against him. Leaving was always bittersweet, there was the excitement of going, of setting out on this journey they'd so meticulously planned and yet there was the sadness of leaving behind a life and people they loved, even if only for a temporary time. They *would* be back, in a year or two.

'But I'd miss this more,' she answered honestly. As much as she loved her new life in Seasalter, working with Artemisia at the school, being Owen's wife and turning Baldock House into a home that was theirs, this journey remained important to her. It would bring closure to a chapter of her life. The art she'd create and bring back would be the opening of another. It would be the opening of another chapter for them as well in other ways, too. She laced her hands over Owen's.

'I don't think I wished you happy anniversary yet,' she said. Owen's word had been good—they'd set sail on the very date of their wedding a year ago.

Owen nuzzled her neck. 'There's champagne and a brand-new bed waiting for us to celebrate.'

She turned in his arms. She wanted to see his face when she told him. 'I want to give you your present first and to commend you on the foresight of building such a large cabin. Family-sized, one might say. We're going to need it.'

'We're having a baby?' Owen's face was a delightful mix of shock and joy, and then, as she knew he would, a moment of worry. 'When? We can sail for home whenever you like.'

She laughed up at him. 'Not until December and, no, we're not sailing for home. We've barely begun. Babies are born all over the world all the time.' She hesitated, second-guessing her gift. 'Are you happy?'

'Yes. More happy than you know, happier than words can express. Perhaps this will be a start.' He kissed her then, as London faded and the wind filled the sails. Happiness, peace, love filled her so completely, she thought in that moment she would burst. The world was her oyster, but Owen Gann was her pearl of great price. In loving him, she'd been rewarded a hundredfold and more.

* * * * *

MILLS & BOON

Coming next month

HOW TO WED A COURTESAN
Madeline Martin

'It's later than we had expected, I know, but I have never stopped wanting you as my wife.' He lowered himself to the carpet on one knee before her and lifted his hands in expectation for her to put her fingers to his. 'Marry me, Lottie.'

She shook her head, unable to even work a single word into her throat.

'Please.' He gestured around the room where he kneeled, indicating the crates and wooden pallets stacked throughout the well-appointed study. 'I did this for us. For you.'

She shook her head again, her eyes filling with the tears she'd been so resolved to keep from him.

'Good God.' He pushed up to his feet in a smooth motion. 'You're already married, aren't you?'

'Who would marry me?' she asked bitterly. 'I'm ruined.'

He jerked back as if she had slapped him again. 'Don't say such a terrible thing, Lottie. What we did was…it was beautiful.' Some of the hardness in his eyes softened as he gazed at her with affection. 'It was love.'

That word was almost laughable, love. It sat in her mind like a ghost.

'Perhaps that first time was,' she replied slowly.

Confusion pulled at his brows. 'I don't understand.'

Her heart thundered in her chest like galloping horses over hard packed dirt. She would hurt him with these words, but he had to hear them.

Two letters. In four years.

Yes, that steeled her resolve.

'In order to survive these four years…' She squared her shoulders and met his gaze with all the power of her unguarded emotions, letting him see the hurt and rage and the soul-shaking misery of what she had lost. 'I had to become a courtesan.'

Continue reading
HOW TO WED A COURTESAN
Madeline Martin

Available next month
www.millsandboon.co.uk

COMING SOON!

We really hope you enjoyed reading this book.
If you're looking for more romance, be sure to
head to the shops when new books are
available on

Thursday 24th
June

To see which titles are coming soon, please visit
millsandboon.co.uk/nextmonth

MILLS & BOON

LET'S TALK
Romance

For exclusive extracts, competitions
and special offers, find us online:

- f facebook.com/millsandboon
- 🐦 @MillsandBoon
- 📷 @MillsandBoonUK

Get in touch on 01413 063232

For all the latest titles coming soon, visit
millsandboon.co.uk/nextmonth